The Gospel of Louis:
The Rise and Fall of a Fake, Modern Moses

Daniel Sessions

The Gospel of Louis

For information, or to order additional copies, please contact:

Beacon Publishing Group
P.O. Box 41573 Charleston, S.C. 29423
800.817.8480| beaconpublishinggroup.com

Publisher's catalog available by request.

ISBN-13: 978-1-949472-77-6

ISBN-10: 1-949472-77-9

Published in 2019. New York, NY 10001.

First Edition. Printed in the USA.

Prologue
An Alignment in the Heavens

A table of brilliant, fiery glass held the gaze of the directors as they beheld the future. No magic was at play here—unless it was the magic of having power. A seat at this table meant power to create the future, power to translate will into reality. To the mass of humankind, wielding precious little of such power, this table would seem magical indeed, something from a fairy tale. But directors at tables like this really have stood men upon the moon, really have targeted entire peoples for extinction and hunted them down across many borders, really have disappeared bustling cities with a single bomb. This magic—white, black, or in between—is no fairy tale.

"Sell me on this Louis character," ordered the head of the table, a glowing old fellow orbited by a dozen lesser deities. "What's his edge over the other prospects?"

"Chronic denial of praise can turn a dedicated artist into a nihilist prostitute," replied the consultant at the other end. "It can wind him into a coil until he's trembling for release. It can aggravate a malignant narcissism to volcanic proportions. We can aim this kid's eruption and ride it quite a ways."

"Can he capture and carry forward an audience?" asked the head, clad in a garment easily mistaken for the white coat of a simple and goodly doctor. "Let's have some illustration."

Green was the light gradually given by the radiant table, a reliable forecast of grand rewards at acceptable cost.

A table of thirteen figures dealing out salvation and sacrifice was nothing extraordinary in an era that routinely imposed investment binges and mass layoffs this way. But with eyes to survey and pierce mountain and sea, and with hands to snatch or strike the scorpion nestled in the remotest desert crag, and with brain to wrestle Mother Nature for her recipes: with such endowment can a power deal salvation and sacrifice to entire nations, not to mention to a lad desperate for a destiny.

Chapter 1
Who's Louis?

Louis Koenig pressed onward, already drained after only a few months into his senior year at Silver Spur High School. He was weary of the popularity contests that would graduate into pathetic quests for status at the office and in the suburb. He was bored to tears by the prefabricated identities, the standardized prescriptions for what to pay attention to, what to like or hate, what pitiful threads to cling to in appalling ignorance—in impoverished, starving ignorance of life's multiplex loom of possibilities.

Louis didn't belong here, and this was a deliberate choice. What easy business it was to belong, to adopt an approved identity. Hipster, for instance, seemed to Louis a simple program of cowardice masquerading as bravery, favoring whatever obviously sucks in order to avoid the outraged ridicule reserved for the crime of sincerity. But thousands of miles and years lay beyond the current walls. Louis was keeping himself pure, saving himself for something more than skater, goth, stoner, gamer, jock, preppie … and eventual bee-hood in the hive of some corporation or correctional facility. Selling out to none of these gave Louis freedom to be something special.

Deviators from the beaten path were naturally confusing to the herd, and vaguely threatening. What, after all, did Louis mean by the relentlessly generic clothes in bleak hues of brown, olive, and gray, and the Great Depression haircut, and the proper vocabulary that did without the lazy conveniences of the local dialect? Personal authenticity was something designed and marketed by professionals in Manhattan boardrooms. Louis was incomprehensible, a ghost.

Though perhaps they did comprehend him; perhaps he was visible indeed. Perhaps they understood this noble self-reliance of his for what it truly was: an intentional display of his rejection of them and their shallow, imported identities. Here was someone who didn't rely on the crutches they did. His independence couldn't help but suggest their bondage. He was an outrage. His very presence mocked them.

They tried to bring him into line. Among the guys, any claim to superiority had ultimately to be proven by an act of physical prowess. Since Louis consistently retreated from this challenge, the obvious conclusion was that he made no serious claim after all—he was just some loser, superior only in some unimportant way. The girls applied more sophisticated techniques, mainly avoiding Louis and his baffling disconnection from everything relevant, but occasionally professing their concern about his failure to get a life. They offered to help him recognize the error of his ways, treating him as if he were somehow just blind to the ingredients of success in their world, as if he simply required pointers on acceptable clothes, hair, and music in order to quickly join the living of Silver Spur High in the only real and happy life there could be, relieving him of the clearly meaningless unhappiness he was so unnecessarily inflicting upon himself.

Living his illegitimate life outside and above his particular time and place, transcendent Louis took the best and brightest and otherwise greatest of all humankind as his domain. While the cattle busily fornicated among whatever was merely new and young and normal, Louis communed with the Almighty, with every empire and king, every prophet and mass mover in history. He called forth the dead from their graves to instruct him, to resonate with him, to feed him the sustenance that others got from friends and family and church.

Chapter 2
A Picture of the Artist as a Boy

The biological father of Louis died under circumstances that his son never clearly understood. Louis would learn from relatives that the man had been shackled with a spectrum of mental illness, a hyper-sensitive nervous system, and a consuming interest in philosophy. A toddling Louis was taken by his mother to where the continent divides at the meeting of the Great Plains and the Rocky Mountains, where she found a small apartment with a fine view of the west, with its staggering peaks and majestic sunsets.

When Louis was nine his mother attended a series of Bible seminars, and there she got to know one Edward Miller, a recently divorced fellow nearly fifty years of age with a warm smile and abundant knowledge of the scriptures. Ed had grown wealthy through owning a large stake in a mining company, and he sat on the board of a charitable organization that targeted social problems throughout the globe. He spoke and moved with a confident ease, seemed clean and solid to Ms. Koenig, and they were soon married.

Perched upon the foothills of the Rockies was the estate a younger Ed acquired from a filmmaker who'd used the place as the setting for several of his most notorious movies. Its numerous acres of lawn, shrubbery, and forest rambled across shallow canyons that retained fruitless Spanish silver mines. The house, sprawling behind a patchy veil of ivy and pines, had two stories and two dozen rooms, with a roof of crimson Latin tiles and a stucco face of chalky gold and salmon. Ed and Louis's mother would enjoy the master bedroom upstairs, down the hall from Brandy's room; she was Ed's youngest, two years younger than her new stepbrother Louis, who selected a room downstairs.

Half the lower story had been built against a hill, and this contributed to the darkness and stillness of Louis's domain. This silent bunker had actually been the scene of constant activity until shortly before Louis moved in, as several of Ed's children had through two decades occupied its various rooms. When Louis met them as he got older, they told him of games they used to play with their friends down there. One involved shutting oneself in the bathroom, lights off, and chanting into a large mirror the name of an historical monarch whose reign was famously bloody. Much else had presumably taken place down there through the years, and it seemed to Louis that the walls still held some of the residue, like the ruins of an ancient city.

Ed's sons were pursuing their fortunes in business and law. From what Louis could learn about them, they'd been everything Louis wasn't. They'd been Eagle Scouts by the age of sixteen. They'd faithfully served in a number of church and school positions. And every Saturday they and their father had tended the vast grounds of their estate as partners, happily mowing, tilling, and hacking away with the sun on their backs and the body's own morphine rewarding their work. Of course, Ed could easily have hired gardeners had he any desire to do so.

As for Ed's daughters—well, Louis was quite taken with little apple-cheeked Brandy, but he would find her sisters dull and unremarkable, and would see they bore a grudge against their little sister, who was prettier than they and closer to their father. Brandy's sisters had sided with their mother in her great war with Ed, a lengthy struggle over what rights a wedding ring confers upon a wife, with Mrs. Miller laying claim to a right of complete oversight—to issue advice and consent, subpoenas, and ultimately her veto—on all matters pertaining to any aspect of her husband's existence. The final straw had been a photograph of Ed with a group of colleagues, some of whom were female, which he had carelessly (or perhaps not so carelessly) left in the desk in his den, unhidden. There they were, Ed and his gang, happily drinking and chatting about things Mrs. Miller would never be privy to. She'd long suspected that relevant things were being concealed from her; it had been very difficult for her to tolerate forces operating out there that could affect her but that she was powerless to influence. The photograph had made it clear that she must leave with her older daughters (and a sizeable chunk of Ed's bank account) to a distant corner of the state. Ed then wasted little time in finding Ms. Koenig.

The new wife came as a package deal of course, for here was young Louis to sweeten the bargain, a gifted boy with fine prospects, Ed and the mother agreed; there was no telling what the boy could become through the care and instruction of a strong authority figure.

It soon became painfully obvious that the boy had different ideas on the matter. He simply wasn't willing to take instruction from Ed, to be contained by him, to be molded into the image of this man who'd swooped down upon the little world of Louis to conquer and plunder it.

Actually, the two might easily have become great friends, were they not forced into conflict by the roles they held, the dutiful stepdad having to push and pull another man's child toward things of importance, things the distrustful boy bemoaned as worthless and oppressive. Louis wouldn't call Ed Dad because it didn't feel right. He didn't like church or scouting, because those didn't feel right. And what really didn't feel right was having to work in the yard every Saturday, a labor he performed with more misery and less productivity than a slave. What did feel right was playing video games or throwing firecrackers off the roof to explode all over Ed's vegetable garden.

Before Ed enlisted to tame him, Louis was a free-spirited and disruptive child, full of instinct and energy, always joyfully obsessed with some new interest: perhaps pirates this month, World War II the next. Like many boys, he found it difficult to sit still and dwell upon desk work through extended lengths of time. The training could be quite a hardship for some, forced to stretch here and decay there to become the product envisioned by the board of education. Louis and other young bodies manifested their turmoil through outbursts of noise and violence; these breaches of "citizenship" could no longer be reproved by the stick, but advances in applied chemistry made it possible to attack the problem more profoundly. Young Louis clearly stood out as a prime candidate to become civilized through the new technology. Were he given the choice, he would have jumped at the chance to be able to get through a day of school without his feelings sabotaging his best efforts to be good.

"You mean there's a way for me to *feel* good while I'm *being* good?" the boy would have asked with absolute glee. "I'm all yours, Doc!"

Ms. Koenig, however, refused to let go of sentimental notions concerning the integrity of the human spirit, not wanting the school to damage the natural Louis beyond what was necessary to make him a functioning member of society. Maybe she lacked the historical perspective to realize that no person has ever had the right to possess and develop a mind of their own; perhaps she was unaware of the extent of the damage the school was doing anyway, without medication. At any rate, Louis was left to remain a casualty in the war between the rules and his nature.

Unable to adjust his nature to the rules, young Louis had only one prospect for happiness: adjusting the rules to his nature. It was at the day-care center that he first managed to accomplish this. Nobody was thrilled when his mother first deposited her fat, frowning little urchin into the care of The Child Garden; but it wasn't long after the boy looked the place over that he felt a lot better about life. The facility was run by a couple of older ladies who'd wheel out a tray of snacks several times a day and provide activities for the kids, all of whom were smaller than Louis. It was a matter of days until he was running the place: shoving his way to the prized scooter and leaving the other kids to grapple for the tricycles, stealing snacks over many tearful and vain objections, even forcibly adjudicating the disputes arising among the lesser children. He treated the wardens with the same contempt, bossing them about their duties and making demands for this snack or that activity.

Yes indeed, that was one great summer. Louis kept a vigilant eye out for challenges to his authority, and when one turned up on his radar he confronted it quickly, before it could breathe and build confidence. When some new kid tested him with a bump or a word or a stare, not a minute would pass before Louis had retrieved a wet dishrag knotted at one end, and promptly the offender would be cowering under a rain of smarting blows. The wardens were simply too busy to prevent Louis from running a shadow government. He put down revolt after revolt, each new success coming easier than the previous, each new success reinforcing his capacity to bully shamelessly. Every day of this was a good day, a great day, for Louis; he couldn't help but feel wonderful all the time he was there, and when his mother came to take him home in the evening Louis would go and sleep a deep sleep of no regrets, self-assured that he could maintain his proper place in the world whatever the next day should bring.

As autumn came, Louis envisioned a smooth transfer of his authority from The Child Garden to elementary school third grade. But school was a place with many more children, and many big ones, so Louis wasn't going to just walk in and start swinging at everyone. He would have to work some at building a name for himself, a reputation to precede him.

He quickly raised his flag by drawing a picture for his class.

It was a realistic image, full of truth, almost an archetype: a man and woman taking a shower together. The two faced each other smiling and embracing under the downpour in all their nakedness. About halfway down his body the man sported a cannon and a couple of balls with it, the gun aiming for something like a door at very close range on the woman, whose giant balloon breasts hung sopping and steaming.

The moment it left his pen he knew it was worthy of display. Louis showed the thing around to his classmates, many seemingly amused by it, others distressed. Not only did he show, he told, he told them all about it, mainly sticking to the facts: it's how kids come into the world, it's what moms and dads do together when nobody's looking, it's the reason boys like girls, it's something even kids in the fourth grade are doing.

When his teacher saw this, hot lava must have shot through her spine and popped something in her brain. She seized Louis by a tuft of hair on the back of his head, leading him thereby to the principal's office, where Louis and his drawing were presented to horrified scowls. The teacher, principal, and secretary bunched up the wrinkles on their sagging faces, tingling behind their veil of scorn, tingling at this picture of earthly delights while their scapegoat carried the sin of it.

"There's obviously a problem here. There must be pornography involved," declared the teacher, her suggestively painted lips quivering.

"Mmmmm, yes," agreed the principal.

The teacher went back to her class and the principal proceeded to dial up Louis's mother, who'd been working fifty-hour weeks that had run her immune system into the ground; what she needed now was more stress. Louis couldn't expect much sympathy from her, for Carol Koenig was a Christian, the American kind, automatically crediting authority figures with acting from the same high motives that she herself tried to cultivate. She arrived at the principal's office upset from having to leave work; her son's picture then moved her to tears. There followed an interrogation, led by the principal, with the aim of getting Louis to reveal where he'd seen the pornography that had to be responsible for his picture. Carol was stumped. Louis was flushed and sweaty, wondering whether to tell the truth and say the picture came from inside him—a boy who'd never even seen a pictorial spread in a *National Geographic*—or should he just give them the answer they were so committed to, and say he'd seen some sort of magazine in a dumpster, "where it belonged."

An older Louis would look back and discern why that picture had been so offensive to them. It depicted something that had to exist completely within their terms, completely at their service, otherwise it was something dangerous. In fact, several things in life were like this: wonderful when somebody's, intolerable when somebody else's. Louis's picture made a very important one of these things exist on his own terms—in other words, "an obvious problem."

The principal, after many sidelong glances at the boy's drawing, explained some. "Look son, school should be a place where kids feel safe, and this picture of yours shows something very confusing and upsetting. There's a time and a place for it, for what you've drawn here, okay, but outside that time and place it means trouble. Think of it like fire. It has to be controlled. And fire like this picture, well, it's hard to believe it simply came from a boy's good head. There's lots of garbage out there, magazines that are made to look like fun, but they ruin people's lives. Don't take the bait of those images. Don't fall into their trap. They really do turn people into slaves, okay? You don't want that kind of thing in your head, and we don't want it in our school."

The lad was marched back to class by the principal, whose rare appearance in a classroom proclaimed the gravity of the situation. The teacher set down her romantic novel and commanded Louis to appear front and center before his peers, their eyes sparkling with anticipation, and there he was to "apologize for exposing them to trash." His attempt was interrupted by laughter, his own laughter, when his eyes met with a boy who was himself desperately holding in his giggles.

"Oh fine, Louis, just fine," said the teacher with a labored sigh of resignation. "You can clean bathrooms after school for a week. You'll have all the filth you want, and you can laugh every minute of it. Ooohh, Louis, I hope we won't always have to go through this. Why won't you see that no one is interested in the little pictures you draw, as long as they're so revolting? Can't you see that none of us wants to think about things that make us feel sick and dirty? We're here to learn so we can go out and make the world a better place. Everyone seems to understand this except you."

That had been a hard day for Louis. And cleaning bathrooms was no picnic. The whole experience confirmed his suspicions about the world, that the world wouldn't easily accommodate his inspiration and well-being, that it was pitted against him in a kind of war.

Naturally missing from the persecuted artist's evaluation of this incident was what had truly inspired him to put that image onto paper. He'd drawn it not for the sake of educating and uplifting the other kids, though this was probably its effect on some of them. No, his aim had really been the opposite: to elevate himself on a picture that put others beneath him. He'd calculated that the picture would gain him the admiration of some while serving to intimidate and humiliate the children who weren't prepared to deal with the striking image.

Actually, Louis had been especially eager to see how two of his classmates in particular would deal with it. These were the prettiest girl and the boy she seemed to like most. They were the models Louis used for his picture, and he made sure to include a few details like the boy's freckles and the girl's hairstyle, just enough for a keen audience to identify the couple in the shower. Louis was disappointed when the special targets of his defamation didn't seem too rattled by the picture, and when indeed none of the children seemed to pick up on the clues that should have launched mass derision upon the special targets. The clues were too subtle, and the children too dull, or perhaps everyone was just too taken by the picture's more sensational features.

Stinging through the innards of Louis was a compulsion to have that prettiest girl's interest to himself. There was no blunting it except to obey. One day during recess, he spied her enjoying a stretch on the lawn with the boy she'd been hugging in Louis's shower. Off Louis flew to join them as if carried by wings on his feet and a wind at his back.

He sat with the two for some minutes, casually picking handfuls of grass and making little piles with it. He was looking for some way to put that boy off balance, so he might be made a fool in front of the girl. Louis wanted to reach an understanding with that boy about their power relationship. Louis would show that he possessed the greater ability to use force, thereby establishing his right of way. The boy was a good twenty pounds lighter than Louis, and likely a feeble adversary incapable of much retaliation. Such was the estimation Louis made as he hurled a wad of grass into the boy's face.

The three quickly got to their knees, and Louis watched the boy lean to his side and swing out a foot, which didn't have far to travel to meet Louis's face.

A solid slam on the nose can be quite disorienting, and demoralizing, Louis learned, falling onto his back, bleeding and nauseated. Everything was spinning … a company of spectators appeared out of nowhere … they cheered … the boy packed handful after handful of grass into Louis's mouth … they danced in celebration … the boy kept shoveling it in. All Louis could do was gag and moan, paralyzed and thunderstruck. All the momentum he'd gathered from previous triumph was eradicated here. This boy exploded the world Louis had lived in, exploded the image Louis had had of himself in that world. As the boy and girl departed in the midst of a rejoicing entourage, Louis could feel his Alpha-male chemicals seeping away from him, just as the victor could no doubt feel the upward surge of his own.

Louis tasted grass for days. An understanding had indeed been reached. He could thereafter lift a finger in aggression as easily as he might run underwater. But it was his body that underwent this domestication, his body that resolved itself to retreat. His spirit was still proud. His spirit would contest this subjugation. It would have to be done with guerrilla tactics, indirectly, at safe distance from an enemy who possessed the physical advantage, making it foolhardy for Louis to engage in outright decisive battle.

Chapter 3
Better Happy than Right

Growing up poor, Ed Miller was compelled to seek out wages he could bring into the family to justify his inclusion in it. At the age of eight, he made use of church connections to gain employment on a beet plantation where he was soon producing twice the output of grown men surrounding him.

He happily delivered his significant earnings to his home, a small, cramped, bustling thoroughfare of children and pets, where everything was shared and rationed, including faucet, toilet, and table space. Ed's was a stout and tangible mother who gave ample warmth to her brood. His father was a less present figure, but a figure whose rare presence was heavy enough to leave behind a permanently felt shadow. To provide at least something for his large family was all the man could do, and it cost him far more dignity than it should have. At first, he couldn't catch a break, and in time he couldn't take advantage of one. He spent long hours away from home doing odd jobs for ranchers, delivering milk, hay, and sod as it might be. Ed heard him speak to Mother about what his job really was, what it had always been through all the jobs and all the years. It was being lowest on the totem pole. This meant they didn't pay you for doing something economically useful. They paid you for psychological use. You were for blame. You supported others' feelings of superiority, and the folks who used you the most like this were really the most wretched and inferior types. Father would recount mistake after mistake he made on the job in scrambling to carry out the ridiculous and the impossible with only the barest instructions, being in no position to tell the ranchers that the failure was theirs. He sometimes came home dazed to tears, and as the years passed, he began to seriously consider that he really was to blame and that his level best really wasn't good enough to get beyond a menial job or even hold one.

Chronically humiliated and beside himself in desperation, Father sought to reclaim some stature by asserting rule over his household. If chores or schoolwork hadn't been done, if the children had idled their time away with friends or daydreaming, he'd take off his belt and administer a set of lashes. A hard day for the old man could well result in a hard lashing, especially for the child he'd designated to be lowest on the family totem pole, a boy a few years younger than Ed. Lowest of all and last link in the chain of abuse was the family dog, who, with no concept of justice, took whatever his people needed to inflict. It could be argued that Waggy's behavior toward a few of the neighborhood dogs was his own attempt to reclaim some stature at their expense.

Ed had to bear the weight of Father's program of gaining through Son the things that eluded the old man in his own life. He made sure Ed knew work, study, God, country, and other basic ingredients for success in life. Pressure like this could crush a lad into dust or form him into a diamond. To keep the pressure on, Father convinced Ed to enlist in the United States Army, which turned out to be wisdom indeed. Ed wrapped his brain around doctrine and regulation; he made an intense study of military history, training himself to discern how an opponent's disposition could be used to one's own advantage. Where the driving force of the enemy is greatest, here Ed believed one's own opposing force should be minimized, presenting the enemy an illusion of victory that he'll rush headlong toward, thereby exposing himself. Commit the enemy to a course you are prepared for.

The officers took note of Ed's excellence. So did the grunts, as he seemed to challenge the dependent mode of existence favored by many of them. One grunt in particular, a fat, sloppy, overbearing fellow, was sometimes heard referring to Ed as a "sodomite," which in this context passed for a cutting and clever jab. On the final such occasion, Ed set aside his book and rose up, empowered by Hannibal's staggering victory over the Romans at Cannae. He pranced more than a little gaily with his hand on his hip, and was soon facing his opponent, who was slouching on a footlocker about ten feet away. Ed then posed a question, very theatrically, to the entire company present: "If indeed I am a sodomite, then this fat bastard here should have no trouble waddling over and slapping me straight. And if he can't, what kind of flimsy sodomite does that make *him*?"

This got a few laughs from the gallery, and the bull appeared ready to express his outrage in a manner that refuted the insult directed at his portly immobility—so, predictably, he charged. It was a remarkably simple matter for Ed to grip the beast by its collar and add some to the heaping momentum it had gathered in the direction of a wall. The sound made by face hitting brick was sickening: a singular, unforgettable sound that resolved any questions. Spectacular violence proved to be a very effective problem-solver. Ed didn't make the rules, he just embraced them, made them his friend.

Every Sunday, Ed Miller and Carol Koenig Miller studied the Holy Bible with Louis Koenig and Brandy Miller around their large, wooden, oval dining table after church and supper (Louis being allowed the latter on condition he attended the former). There they'd sit for an hour or so, taking turns reading verses. Louis, it became clear, had some kind of problem with this.

It wasn't that he found the good book boring. He discovered in it more violence, sex, action, and personality than a hundred Rated R movies could supply. The Bible had a downright flair for sex and violence, as when Yahweh commanded Moses to crucify the Israelites who worshiped Baal, inspiring the grandson of Aaron to grab a spear and skewer a couple of fornicating idolaters into a kebab. Yahweh was to Louis an interesting deity, a god of storm and war, a fire within a cloud, an imperfect shepherd, regretful of his creation run amok, regretful of his chosen people run amok, constantly on the verge of annihilating the lot and starting over from scratch, but generally limiting himself to consuming selected offenders with his dangerous holiness, though they sometimes be hundreds or entire populations. Compared to his competition in the savage pantheon of the ancient Near East, Yahweh wasn't really so bad, since his sympathies lay with the vulnerable, whom his laws saved from oppression. His heart seemed to be in the right place, inasmuch as he tried to correct a world where the wicked prosper.

Louis liked the Bible well enough. It was the sound of Ed's voice that Louis had a problem with. Specifically, it was the subtle crackling noise the letter F made with the spittle that collected on Ed's lower lip. Louis couldn't remember exactly when this absurd phenomenon first struck him as something noteworthy. The fact is that it had struck him so, and then it was in his bloodstream. There was simply no escaping it, no purging this thorn from him. Maybe he could hold out and keep a poker face during the first ten of Ed's crackling F's at a Bible reading, but soon enough he would begin to feel some awful worm clenching around his spine, and the sweating started, and his concentration would falter. As Ed's turn to read came for the third or fourth time, Louis was clutching his hair and digging his nails into his scalp and gnarling his slippery, tingling toes.

Often he'd jab a red pencil into his thigh and grind it there, hunched over and swaying back and forth. The Bible really came alive for Louis in this state, the trials heaped on a confused Job, the gnashing teeth of the damned in hellfire.

It got to be that Louis couldn't look at Ed's face or speak more than a few sentences to him. Louis planned his movements about the house so he and Ed had the least possible chance of crossing paths, and when they did happen to run into each other, Louis made himself seem distracted, quickly fetching something from the fridge and disappearing. After a while, Ed stopped asking how things were going.

Louis hated this. It was a hate enflamed by the absurdity of his affliction. He hated Ed, knowing it was wrong to do so. He hated himself, this malformed, worm-hosting self of his. He hated being inexplicably short and rude to Ed, hated wanting to carve the lower lip off his stepdad's face and cast the slippery thing into a consuming fire. He hated God—that ultimate source of all this absurd malformation. Of course he could never let the others know just what was bothering him, so ashamed was he that the cause of his suffering was something so laughably petty.

Other abnormalities came on display for decipherment. When Louis entered his teens, he became hypnotized by a film about the assassination of President Kennedy. He was too young to grasp the complexities of the film's thesis (that the president was killed for refusing to be controlled by his country's military and intelligence directors) but he felt an overwhelming connection to the Lee Harvey Oswald character. Louis recognized the loneliness, the earnest and awkward zeal, the exasperated victimhood. He started acting like the character, dressing like him, letting him do the talking, letting him feel the pain.

His family noticed the change, and having seen the film themselves, they quickly solved the puzzle. They indulged him, humored him, hoping the phase would pass. It didn't. Louis kept watching the movie, kept speaking in the character's voice, leaving Ed and Carol and Brandy little choice but to confront him about his grotesque semi-suicide. Stunned, he pretended ignorance and emphatically denied involvement, claiming they were crazy to come up with such an outlandish accusation. Brandy replied that the evidence was obvious, and freakish. She listed a few of the several points of similarity that had recently emerged between Louis and Lee Harvey, and this sent the boy storming down the stairs to his room. He hid the videocassette, disrobed himself of Lee Harvey Oswald, and considered the affair redacted.

High school meant getting up too early, only to look in the mirror with disgust at pale, chubby flesh with a fresh crop of acne. Louis would put on the cleanser that the TV promised would give him the skin he was entitled to, and as the cleanser sizzled away at his foul skin there in the mirror, he contemplated taking a fork to rake open the pockets of grease and pressure. He dreamed of cutting along the perimeter of his cheeks and chin, then peeling off a swath of skin like fruit leather. Underneath he would find a hundred tiny worms writhing in his raw meat, their gaping mouths tottering to and fro in blind gluttony. Then he'd submerge his giant wound of a face into a bubbling pool of medicine that burned the worms to screaming deaths. That illusion gave some consolation, as did the fact that there were others at school even worse afflicted by this particular thorn.

Silver Spur High School was really just an arena for a dozen little cliques and cabals to constantly scheme for greater prestige and right of way. True, Louis could learn a thing or two about life, especially politics, were he to throw himself into the mix. But he was above that little world of such limited vision, buzzing with the trivia of grades, cars, dating, and college prep. He preferred to take his lessons from history, for here he could encounter the world on his own terms and conditions. Louis could master politics by poring over ancient Rome and Nazi Germany, where the shrewd methods of his schoolfellows had been applied maximally.

By his senior year he'd grown relatively learned in many subjects. In countless cases he could have contributed very meaningfully to the class discussion, but usually he'd just scoff privately at whatever predictable, naïve, knee-jerk offerings his classmates threw up. What a thankless ordeal it was to correct them, to cast pearls before a herd of swine that squealed with resentment when forced to realize the squalor of their sty. There were times, however, when a kid would say something particularly sunny about God or America, with such bright-eyed disdain for the facts, that Louis simply had to wreak proper damage and overturn the tables of their shameless feast. They ate all day, every day. Louis needed to eat, too.

He never ate so well as when he presented to his history class an oral report he entitled: "We won't get fooled again … and again … and again … and again … and again." Its thesis was that Americans have a long and glorious tradition of being duped into the wars they fight. He began with the War with Mexico, explaining how President Polk ordered General Taylor into disputed territory to provoke the skirmish that would be spin-doctored to enflame popular outcry. Next came the War with Spain: "Remember the *Maine*!" shouted Louis. "And remember how our government and our press assured us that our battleship had been sunk by a Spanish mine, even though what really happened was a fire in the ship's powder magazine—an accident, just like the Spanish determined at the time." Scowls were forming across the classroom at this point, but this only stoked his outrage.

"The next war is a most interesting case," he continued. "The British passenger liner *Lusitania* was torpedoed by a German submarine, and nearly twelve hundred civilians—one hundred and twenty-eight of them Americans—met their deaths in the cold ocean near Ireland. This was an outrage to our republic, and it played a primary role in turning American feeling against Germany. The person in charge of protecting ships like the *Lusitania* was one Winston Churchill, head of the British Admiralty, a man very desirous that America should enter the Great War. It just so happens that he knew the German submarine was operating in the same waters that *Lusitania* was in, since the sub had been sinking ships near the passenger liner in preceding days, but he declined to warn her of the danger, and even stripped her of customary escort vessels. Hmmmm, how very strange indeed." The class simmered with automated disbelief in such things. Louis smiled.

"And I'm sure we all remember the incident at Pearl Harbor. Was America reading enough Japanese radio transmission to see the day of infamy coming? Were President Roosevelt and the Prime Minister of Britain—that Churchill guy again—looking for a way to overcome the American people's major unwillingness to yet again launch themselves halfway across the world into someone else's business? Well, I bet we could find out if we were allowed to see the records kept by the U.S. Navy's Pacific facilities in November and December of 1941, or if we were allowed to read the transcripts of the telephone conversations between Roosevelt and Churchill during the same period. But since these documents are still classified—despite decades of public demand to view them—I guess we'll just have to keep calling it a *surprise* attack.

"Does anyone know what sparked Congress to give President Johnson authority to raise hell in Vietnam as he saw fit? Answer: the North Vietnamese possibly, maybe, might have attempted to defend their coastline from an American destroyer that was collecting intelligence to be used by commando teams attacking the coast of North Vietnam. The nerve of those commies, putting their country so close to our ships and bases! They violated the right of their rightful attackers to attack them! Drop your knitting, Mabel, and get my gun.

"All right folks, listen up now, this should really make your blood boil. Are you aware that when Kennedy was president, the Joint Chiefs of Staff proposed carrying out a wave of bombings and shootings and hijackings in U.S. cities, which would be blamed on Cuba and serve as a pretext for U.S. invasion of that country? Yes, I'm afraid so. The highest officers of the United States military planned it, signed their names to it, and sent it to the president, who told them no. He did that a lot … at least until they—"

"You really think we're gunna' believe all this crap, dude?" declared a male listener.

"Um, you're kind a' scary," added a girl. "You should go see a doctor or something."

"Oh … my … God, Louis, you soooo need to get a life," observed another girl.

"I'm trying to help *you* get a life," replied Louis. "This is *your life* I'm talking about here. I don't give a rat's ass if you believe me or not, but my advice to you is put down your little phones that have all your lame-ass, cotton-candy songs and videos and make-believe friends. Maybe crack a book now and again, you know, try to learn something about what you come from and where you're going. Think of me when you find yourself neck-deep in some swamp or sand dune trying to keep your gun clean. Though I don't really see you getting called up to fight the wars your parents start for other people's kids to fight. You'll just keep on sitting pretty, loving the ugly hand that feeds you so well. Damn your blindness. It's a sin."

"All right Mr. Koenig, that'll do," said the teacher. "Fine presentation, minus the preaching."

Quite a picture he forced them to reckon with, these babes here in the very heart of America, their families in deep complicity with its military-industrial complex. They gave him such daggers for forcing that picture on them. For at least a week afterwards Louis felt a reasonable suspicion that physical harm was about to meet him around the next corner. It didn't come. He just didn't matter enough. They left him to life as a ghost.

When Louis read, he liked to have had enough food and sleep so his brain could fire on all cylinders. He usually read for two hours a sitting, twice a day. He approached the first fifteen minutes as a warm-up, letting the blood in his brain get up to speed, and shortly he expected to comprehend and assimilate everything he encountered, in a kind of breathless trance. After two hours he was bubbling with self-satisfaction, considering himself to be in supreme command of whatever subject he'd covered.

Louis became a thought addict. To maintain the buzz that made life worthwhile to him, he simply couldn't leave a thought until he'd explored it to the outer limits of its implications. This deliberation snuffed out his immediate environment and his body, suffocating some of the better angels of his nature, rendering him, for instance, a very poor musician. Now and then he'd fumble around on an electric guitar and amplifier Ed had bought him for Christmas. The strikingly handsome instrument of black and silver, with the vintage amp, conjured the thick and creamy tone needed for playing the Black Sabbath and Led Zeppelin that Louis was fond of—a music of primal, magical force arresting anyone within range of it. Malformed Louis could truly appreciate the music, but he could strain terribly to bring it from himself. Much of it wasn't difficult technically; he saw younger kids down the street play the stuff quite passably after what appeared to be only the most casual practice. Louis was embarrassed to play his guitar in front of anyone, even himself, so akin to some kind of assault did it seem, forcing himself upon a fine instrument and getting it to surrender only the poorest hint of its wonderful capabilities. The kids down the street made love to their instruments. They relaxed, took it slow, felt around in a spirit of discovery without fear of the inevitable mistakes, letting a rhythm emerge and build until it was in the driver's seat, and then they were really feeling the music.

His struggle extended to other arts. Every so often Louis would put some of those precious thoughts of his onto paper, entertaining vague fantasies of writing a book, something to capture his worldview for the benefit of future generations. He had come to view history as mainly a tired plot driven by a vain pursuit of power and glory by an endless train of protagonists refusing to learn from their predecessors, refusing to abandon the same old dream of a thousand-year empire. Every people appearing in the story has considered itself "*The* People," chosen by a deity to subdue and perfect all humankind, and quite deserving of the spoils that always seem to accompany this noble mission. Louis was able, in moments of cheer, to allow that many achievements have in fact been made to the benefit of countless lives. Increasingly, however, he couldn't see the story advancing much beyond tragedy. If God marks the fall of a sparrow, then surely he guides the fate of nations. Yet what a wilderness overrun by weeds was this planet, where nations rot under shabby tyrants and perish in furnaces for idiot Baals. Millions are ground into mulch and mud to move lines on a map. Tens of millions slowly disintegrate and vanish in silent famine. Shot, gassed, incinerated, sliced, blasted away—all of it with such impunity, such routine. In sum, it appeared an outrageously careless picture of cosmic meaninglessness, exhausted, skeletal, sickly pale, riddled with gaping black holes that suck the light and life away. Could there possibly be a God paying any attention? What a strange God it would have to be. What sort of creator puts a little sweetness in a world, just a taste of it, then sends life on a mad chase that brings forth massive evil? Nature obeys what it should protest. The grass should refuse to grow; the birds must withhold their music.

History is a mindless repetition of tragedy—but of course Louis realized he wasn't the first to have noticed this. Was it really worth setting this fabulous insight down upon paper one more time? Shame on him who writes more than he reads, went the old saying, and Louis bore no such shame. His was the shame of writing nothing, despite having read so much—or indeed, because of having read so much. This boy of seventeen was acquainted with a fair sample of what humankind had ever thought or done. And this acquaintance served less to inspire his literary imagination than to crush it. Louis considered many premises for exploration on paper, but all were extinguished by his inevitable awareness of the premise having already come forward by some pen or other, as well as the counter premise. Every possible school of thought on anything had already been articulated, with every philosophy having its equally well-reasoned opposite. Every hero's quest, every downfall from pride had been told of by some earlier bard. So, time and again, Louis would close his notebook of aborted dreams and swallow another lump of frustrated artistic zeal. What a hackneyed story the world was, cursed the dejected suitor. From the depths of this paralysis and despair, Louis looked out on an increasingly attractive Plan B.

Plan B had occurred to Louis one rainy morning as he pressed his way unsteadily through the thick and nauseating human soup in the halls of Silver Spur High School. His body a cache of nervous energy, his limbs stiff, his feminine hands cold and clammy, Louis tried to seem casual, tried to walk upright with eyes forward. But like dogs they could smell his weakness, the misalignment between his willful spirit and its unwieldy physical utensil. Then it came to him. Yes, that could do it. He'd make a painting, one that would surely gain him artistic fame. He'd paint an image bold and real, sealed with the ultimate token of authenticity. After school he purchased the two-by-three-foot, blank canvas that would catch the splash created at the peak of his inspiration.

There would be at least some difficulty in painting this picture, Louis realized. The canvas must lie low in his room and in the back of his mind until he was ready for it. There Plan B had stayed. In the meantime, Plan A was to get by on a feeling that his study of history was nevertheless meaningful and could lead to something valuable. He continued to consume the experience of humankind and let this work its effect on him. He nursed his little ember with a hope that it might someday soon set him ablaze with inspiration for something that would render Plan B unnecessary.

Chapter 4
What the Doctor Delivered

Ed reclined in his cushiony leather chair in his serene office at the Institute for the Progress of Human Wellness. He stretched his back and massaged his skull, looking out through a large tinted window onto lush autumn leaves glowing against smartly trimmed emerald grass.

Dr. Crowley flew in from Back East this morning. The doctor had already communicated with Ed at some length about something that had been in the works for some time: a project upon which the doctor fixed all his hope for immortality in the field of behavioral science. Ed had been brought on board Project AQUARIUS as the owner of a dossier featuring a respectable inventory of Black Ops—mainly PsyOps, the earliest of which Ed carried out in his twenties. Also listed were Ed's two decades of Institute employment, his master's degree in sociology, his accumulation of private wealth, and other personal assets that might prove useful.

Dr. Crowley whistled and hummed as his shoes tapped the Institute's polished, marble corridors. He stopped at Ed's door and knocked the motif of Beethoven's Fifth Symphony. Ed invited him in, and the doctor entered, with his bald, perfectly rounded head, commanding nose and intense, dark eyes somehow suggesting his acquaintance with powers mysterious and fantastic.

Ed rose with a hearty smile and gave the doctor a firm handshake, eyeing the black and gold briefcase the doctor carried. Crowley placed it on Ed's desk and took a seat beside a massive, detailed globe, which he spun a little and studied as Ed returned to his chair and contemplated the briefcase before him, sighing a bit and looking to the doctor for reassurance.

"It's a big deal, I know," offered the doctor, still fixed on the globe. "But if this works out, we'll both have a portrait in the hall of fame."

Ed took in a deep breath, grinned, and shook his head. "The implications … could be quite grand."

"They could indeed," assured Dr. Crowley with deep gravity. "I'm pleased you realize the significance of what you're being entrusted with."

Ed nodded solemnly.

"Delusions of grandeur surely exist," observed the doctor. "The pathological failure to think realistically about oneself and one's situation surely exists. But there is also failure of willpower, failure to persevere, failure to properly manage and execute, and ultimately failure to guide a perfectly fine delusion into grand reality."

Ed gave the doctor another nod of acknowledgment, knowing delusion to be the sound basis of some of the grandest, most powerful realities.

"Well," said the doctor, "there you have it. And take heart, Ed, it isn't all that unprecedented really. It's not like we haven't seen this type of thing before."

Chapter 5
An Invitation to the Game

"Oh come on, everyone's gunna' be there," said Brandy's fellow sophomore Haley, an incredibly exotic, almost unreal presence sparkling before Louis, little glints of blue and purple riding the black waves of her hair as it caught the evening sunlight and autumn breeze, her enormous dark eyes unbearably insinuating, melting him under their gaze.

"Why do you guys want me to go so badly?" he asked, reclining in a lawn chair, book in hand.

"Because it's dumb that you sit around and read all day about stuff that happened a thousand years ago while your life passes you by. You don't go to any dances, you don't have a girlfriend, you don't belong to any clubs or teams, and you never go to see our awesome football team play," said Haley.

"He doesn't have a job either," Brandy chimed in, gathering her sandy blonde hair, lovely in its own way, into a sensible pony tail.

"Nor a car," added Louis.

"What would you use a car for?" asked Haley.

"Not much," said Louis, rubbing his eyes. "Certainly not for all that high school stuff, which really is just stuff, stuffing for people to fill up their empty lives. It sure keeps 'em busy. They grow up looking up to older kids who do the high school stuff, and very early in life the assumption forms that it's important and worthwhile. Am I losing you guys?" asked Louis, feeling some trouble in shifting to meet the girls where he thought they were at.

"We get it," said Haley. "We're not stupid."

"I know," said Louis. "I like talkin' with you guys." For a few seconds of uncomfortable silence, Louis considered the possibility that in some alternate universe the three of them could be doing something other than talking.

"Look," continued Louis, "I know the football games are fun and all, but nobody's gunna' care a year or a month from now what happens at the game Friday night. And it's the same with girlfriends. I just don't think it's worth all the trouble. It's like when you make a deal with the Devil, you get into it because there's this thing you sorely need which is presented all nice and shiny, and that's all you see. You don't see what it's gunna' cost you. That's true with lots of things, and in the case of a girlfriend, that's where a guy gets the one thing he really wants in exchange for a huge price, which is his time, money, and freedom, and his own opinion about things."

"The one thing a guy really wants?" Haley asked pointedly.

"*You* know what I'm talkin' about," said Louis, with a hopelessly pathetic grin. "But uh, all I'm saying is that a lot of what's supposed to be fun turns out to be a trap. Of course, you guys have considered the traps in life?"

"The football game is a trap? Riiiiight," said Brandy.

"Oh sure," replied Louis. "You see, everyone at the game automatically lets themselves get worked into a frenzy cheering for their team, even though it's just inevitable that at game's end half the people will be pissed off to the point of crying and fighting like little kids. They've invested themselves that much. And what gets me the most is how artificial the connection is between fans and their team, a team they're *accidentally* cheering for, because if they'd grown up a few miles down the street they'd be cheering and bawling just as hard for the other guys. You give your total allegiance to a set of colors. You bind yourself to a mascot so completely that you'd kill someone over it, over a goat in a sequined vest. Don't you think that's stupid?"

"You're gunna' think yourself into a wheelchair, dude," said Brandy. "It's a mountain goat, by the way, which is kind of a noble animal. And it's a trippy vest."

"Fair enough," he said. "But look you guys, it's the same with graduation. I don't really give a damn about it. It only means on to college for another four to six years of bull crap, just to earn the privilege of going on to give thirty years of my life to some damned bloodsucking corporation. Oh, it's all so rewarding to get your degrees and promotions so you can have your house, your boat, and whatever the hell else, but do you really think these people are happy?

"I mean, look at Ed. You'd think he's really happy being such a success in life," said Louis, surveying Ed's vast property. "But I'm not so sure. Lots of times he'll get home from work with this haunted expression on his face, like he's guilty of God only knows what, and he'll just make a dash for his liquor cabinet and go straight to bed."

"His job is stressful since it's so important, and he's not allowed to talk to family or friends about it, so that makes it harder," Brandy said indignantly.

"Ed has friends?" Louis said a bit under his breath.

"You have friends?" Brandy retorted.

"Yeah, Louis has friends, they've just been dead for hundreds of years," Haley noted accurately. "Louis, what *are* you gunna' do after you graduate?"

"Well, I'm hoping," said Louis with an air of sincerity, "I'm hoping an asteroid will hit or the president will push the button before I have to deal with all that."

Such a sorry character the girls looked down upon there, lying back with his book, in all his lofty wisdom just a vulnerable boy afraid of the world.

Sure, the girls enjoyed him as the misfit, the friend-starved loner always available at their request, a captive audience to their feminine charms. They enjoyed sensing his eyes give high appraisal to their tanned and fit young bodies, enjoyed being idealized by his romantic longing that raged from years of deprivation. The girls loved that this intellectual master of the universe could so quickly be brought to his knees by the mere proximity of their flesh.

But when he spoke of looking forward to an asteroid, thus revealing the full extent of his desperate inadequacy, something in the girls properly recoiled from Louis and kept him at a safe distance. What was the point of getting too close to someone like him? The girls had the occasional chat with Louis, but that's all they'd ever do with him. They'd save their hearts and bodies for a real man, someone who faced the world on its own terms rather than retreating into a shabby little dream-world of his own, someone who could meet the demands of a fistfight, a girlfriend, a career, a normal future.

"Oh, just come to the friggin' game with us," said Haley with growing impatience.

Louis moaned. He felt their heavy, disapproving stares on him, as though he was their stubborn little brother refusing to accept their mature wisdom, clearly hurting himself in persisting against the current—but hurting the girls too, since a rejection of their values and norms had to cause the girls at least some amount of shame and insecurity, even if the rejection came from an obvious loser. Yes, he was quite certain that this invitation to the game was merely their attempt to ease him into an acceptance of their ways, a selfish act on their part as much as a favor to him. But, at the very least, he'd been invited, after all. It was something to be invited to go somewhere.

"Okay, all right, I'll go to the game with you," he heard himself say. "Just ah, bear in mind though, what I've been saying. See if it applies."

At this Haley smiled wide, and she gave Louis a slug across his shoulder, precious contact that made all this game foolishness seem nearly worthwhile to him. Brandy and her friend withdrew toward the house, and Louis returned to his book on great battles, though he couldn't help but snatch a glimpse of Haley's meaty quadriceps springing to definition as she pranced up the steps to the porch. "Too difficult," thought Louis, shaking his head. "Too easy," Haley seemed to say back, swinging the door shut behind her.

A crisp October evening found Louis sitting on the porch waiting for Brandy and the gang to take him to the football game. The moon glowed brightly against a clear and darkening sky. Louis gazed out into space and traced the flickering stars just beginning to peep through.

What a fool he'd been to get suckered into this. What had gotten into him, thinking this could do him any good at all? Is this really what his life had been sorely missing, a mass rally to shut down the higher brain functions, a plunge into the warm quicksand of collective hypnosis?

He sat stewing like this, until a shiny black SUV glided up the long driveway. Haley was behind the wheel and very much in her element as she blared the horn at Louis, pulling him firmly into the here and now. Louis wasn't surprised to see Brandy riding shotgun; however, he was a bit stunned to behold the several other girls, probably too young to drive, who were riding along, too.

Despite his poor attitude, Louis had prepared for the occasion. He was wearing the most stylish stuff he had: gray corduroy pants and a long-sleeved maroon shirt. To remove tonight's possibility of uncomfortable silence, he'd stayed more than two seconds on the celebrity gossip channels on TV, and he'd even rehearsed some lines from movies that Brandy and gang would be familiar with—new releases, since nothing cool had come into existence before the girls had. He planned to ask Haley about the health of her father's medical practice, and about the health of her dog, who she jogged with every other day.

It never came to any of that. The moment Louis stepped aboard, the several girls paid him hellos and a few thrilling glances, but then picked up their multiple streams of discourse right where they'd left off. Louis could have been a random car emerging from a speck in the distance, gaining their notice as he closed in on them, only to pass by in anticlimax and return to nonexistence. He settled in behind Brandy, then traded stares with Haley in the rearview mirror. The girls were all more or less gorgeous, and they even smelled sublimely attractive. Louis had long been aware that beautiful girls often traveled in packs, so it didn't strike him as odd that so much beauty was concentrated into this one chariot tonight. That Louis was there, too, a withered corpse among blooming flowers—this felt very odd indeed.

He could have been a little quicker fastening his seatbelt in a vehicle packed with talkative young ladies and driven by one of the same, but Haley drove masterfully. Her braking and turning were fluid and easy, while her hands commanded the steering wheel not stiffly at ten and two but nimbly at seven and five. She'd been taking driver's education, but her sense of the road couldn't have come from any manual. Louis felt her power surge through his very bones as she gunned the accelerator. His head swam under her spell; he felt wrapped in a blanket he could live in forever.

The stadium lights poured into a huge bubble of energy that swelled against the night. On catching his first view of the celestial thing as he cruised down the mountain to it,

Louis was feeling as receptive as putty. Oh—a chorus of angels could well sing it—oh that he could somehow hang onto this feeling for more than a few minutes! The warmth began to forsake him as soon as he set eyes on the hundreds of anthropoids cramming into the circus. As the girls led Louis under the rumbling bleachers, something inside him became roused to climb out of its Haley-induced stupor. Something harder and colder than putty was standing up and recognizing the roar of the crowd and the thunder of stomping feet for what it all should be: celebration of the arrival of Louis. If only the night was his, if only the crowd was all his. If only these people weren't so worthless, they'd realize who Louis was, the things he could do for them. But no, they were here to see guys smash each other and girls exhibit themselves in tiny skirts. It was a celebration of sex and violence, just the right amount for self-satisfied Christians to get excited and still feel they'd be going to heaven.

The magic of the game experience was undeniable, Louis discovered. The lush green of the field against the red and silver and the black and gold of the warriors was by itself irresistibly captivating to him. Add to it the drama unfolding from the clash of all the factors of training and natural ability, strategy and luck—in spite of himself Louis was spinning, awash in a tsunami of feelings crashing through his fortress of philosophy. Here before Louis lay a splendid world, and how very disheartening it was for him to see it, this world living independently of him, so unconcerned with him, so heedless of his counsel, yet getting on so marvelously.

"Hey buddy, how's it goin'?" asked the familiar voice with an elbow to his arm.

"Oh, Haley, hey … it's … I like the …" said Louis, drowned out by the crowd. "It's really powerful and inspiring, really exciting," he managed to say, doing his best to maintain a controlled and civilized facade.

"Told ya!" said Haley, grinning.

The guys in red and silver were the ones Louis was supposed to cheer for, and this he did, however robotically, while continuing to feel bombarded by frightening emanations from insurgent regions of his psyche.

At halftime Brandy and Haley left Louis and joined some other friends sitting nearer the field. "It's cool with you, right?" they said. "Oh sure, no problem, have fun," he said.

The stands emptied some as kids went to relieve themselves or find other friends or fire up a doobie in the parking lot. Louis sat alone amidst a few other anonymous teens. For several minutes he studied an older couple who seemed happy enough just to be out with each other in the quickening night air. He struggled to assess the game experience so far, distracted by horns sounding and banners waving as the marching band took the field.

He soon spied Brandy and Haley mixing with a group of guys. In dismay Louis watched the girls' flirtatious body language, their lithe figures swaying to and fro, their doe-eyed faces beaming. Haley appeared fixed upon one fellow in particular, whose bulging neck looked good enough to eat. The two talked and laughed, rarely breaking eye contact, and finally the guy pulled Haley up against him and they embraced, their bodies henceforth glued together, rocking in unison. Brandy, meanwhile, had found her own beau and was sitting at his side, enjoying his wiry arm around her back and his stout paw upon her hip. Louis tried to look away but simply couldn't.

Kids trickled back to the bleachers, and Louis observed these ridiculous people with their freshly wiped bottoms, all looking so happy, so at peace with themselves and their little world. They'd enjoy the remainder of their inconsequential game here, grunting, flagrantly mindless of any larger realities. Well, the world was turning, the world was always turning and moving through space, and this whole thing, everything here and now was doomed to be a shadow of a whisper, buried and forgotten.

The second half started, and Louis was shaking. The game, the crowd and the starry night all blurred together now into one slushy matrix. He wanted a bomb to go off. He would gladly push the button on his own vest of dynamite. The cheerleaders jumped, jiggled and squealed, and the mob's feet rumbled the bleachers and pounded his tailbone, rattling the nerves along his feeble spine and up into his brain, the mass idiotic enthusiasm mounting to the scream of a jet engine, collapsing and shriveling him.

"Hey Bro, you okay?" came a voice.

"Oh, Brand, yeah … I've just got a bitch of a headache for some reason," squeaked Louis, wiping the sweat through his hair and forcing a smile. It came to him that melting into a puddle in front of all these devils simply would not do. He could hold his mess of a self together until he got away from them. Their hell would come surely enough. Let them drink their fill of foolishness and ripen.

On the drive home Louis sensed that Brandy and Haley were riding a lusty, almost drunken thrill from the victory of their team. It was just the three of them. The younger girls had been pried away by other friends' promises of midnight revels that Haley now proceeded to describe for Louis with physiological detail, dazzling him until he was quaking with envy.

"Damn it all," said Louis with a half-chuckle. "Lurking behind masks of wholesome innocence … such advanced devotees of the cult of Venus, like their parents in the cult of Mars. Wow, though. Those girls are only like fifteen, right?"

"Yeah, fifteen going on twenty-two," said Haley. "Those masks of theirs are gunna' fly way the hell off tonight. When the clock strikes twelve, the uh … sacraments are taken, and the uh … rites are performed. The wildest depravities you've ever seen." At this, Louis's ailing will to live broke through his choking nausea and laughed out loud in affirmation.

"Oh my, that's just fine," he said. "Imagine the parents finding out and shipping their princesses off to one of those maximum hardship wilderness camps. Probably a matter of time before someone secretly films one of these parties and puts it on the internet; kind of a shame how it's getting so hard to keep a good cult secret nowadays. But listen Haley, that's such quality reporting, I have to conclude that you've, uh, been on scene, you know, saw it all firsthand."

"Aw, I'm just a nice kid who fell in with the wrong crowd," said Haley, like a fast-talkin' dame in a film noir. "Just remember, you ain't heard none of this from me."

Brandy was going to stay the weekend at Haley's. They invited Louis to come spend more time with them tonight, with hints that a certain kind of girl might be called to join them, so a certain boy might be made a man by morning. He declined, citing his headache. A part of Louis recognized the opportunity he was missing here, but a larger part of him counseled against fighting this battle from a position of weakness tonight.

"All righty then, ladies," said Louis, stepping out onto the driveway, away from the black magic of Haley and her SUV. "I'm going to raid Ed's liquor stash and find something strong for this headache." And the girls were off.

Louis walked into a dark house, switched on a small yellow lamp, and fetched some pills for his head. He peeled off his sweat-soaked shirt and used it to wipe the film of glistening grease from his volcanic face-flesh, then he balled up the putrid garment and tossed it down the staircase. It was rare that he went topless, but everyone was gone for the weekend and it was a rare mood he felt, wandering into the living room and spreading himself on a couch, listening to the cavernous silence, his consciousness the drifting smoke of his own ashes. Louis had died some tonight, and the dying proceeded as he lay there limp and wasted and defective, a heap of smoldering rubble—curiously untroubled, though, as he ascended lightly into sleep, alone in the dark.

Chapter 6
An Invitation to the Big Game

Louis awoke to a whole day to himself, master of a grand estate. He got up, downed a few more headache pills, made some toast and eggs, then sat at the table. He ate in the stark quiet, looking out on colliding earth crust, the skyward-smashed knuckles scraped by bracing air that rolled through canyons to the excitement of moist snouts.

After a while, he rose from the table and descended the stairs, and, for no reason he knew of, he ambled about the empty rooms, running his fingers across the walls and furniture, observing the bookshelves, paintings, and wallpaper. He stopped in the bathroom with the large mirror and tried to stare down the dismal figure he saw there, locking eyes with it for minutes, peering deep into its soul.

"Worthless … crippled … rotten child of hell. You there, in hell, come out," Louis commanded quite audibly, touching a pardoning finger to the glass.

On a normal Saturday Louis would start reading around noon, but today he needed more than the usual fix. He went upstairs and tried the door to the master bedroom with hopes that alcohol or other goodies awaited him within; but no dice, it was locked. Louis leaned against the wall near Brandy's room and seriously considered trying on some of her underwear, having read that a fair percentage of guys find such a practice rewarding. He imagined himself frolicking about the house in nothing but Brandy's skimpiest unmentionables, and Ed coming through the front door to behold a scene belonging in a shady and secluded grove. He could see large men in white escorting him to his future as a lab mouse. A walk in the yard might be a better idea.

He strolled by the vegetable garden, its cornstalks faded and bowing, its rambling pumpkins aflame on rich, black soil. A deer path led him through a congregation of trees, their pastel leaves glimmering with sun and rustling in mild mountain breeze. He sat on a bench by a clear pond and watched the birds and fish abiding.

Wandering some more, he eventually made his way down an incline of bluish pines to a canyon that led up to a clearing where Ed built a storage barn during the Carter administration. To a younger Louis the barn seemed mysterious and spooky, though he did manage to sneak inside it once to search for anything fun or edible. The weathered, brown structure now appeared from behind its shroud of forest, and he went around to the back door and located the plastic rock that Ed's daughters had long ago identified to Louis as containing a key. Against some friction he got the bolt to clear the doorframe, and he pushed open the door, releasing a gush of cold and dank air. The Miller children's motorized toys sat idle under dust and cobwebs. A spoon rested in a bowl on the counter of a small kitchen. A half roll of tissue paper dangled beside a toilet. A sense of activity, of vigorous life taking place hereabouts, washed over Louis. Present reality seemed illusory in comparison, a stark emptiness.

A tall, wooden cabinet stood grimly in a corner. From a cup stationed atop it Louis plucked a key, and he unlocked it, easing the door open on creaking hinges. And there it was, just as he remembered it, sturdy and smooth, black and pitiless, looking down on Louis with scrutiny and contempt. He gripped the thing and brought it down to him. He hefted it and studied it. Then he grabbed a box of ammunition and walked out into the warm daylight.

To conduct a trial of the weapon he searched about the woods for some quiet little cove, and found one sheltered within a hundred glowing hues on broad leaves. He slid a cartridge into its chamber—and he blasted a wad of metal balls into a rotting stump, blowing a hail of chunks and splinters across the forest floor, the heaving echoes of it wholly jarring the stillness of the canyon.

Naturally Louis had considered taking a gun into Silver Spur High School on some unsuspecting afternoon. He could never really imagine himself holding up under the pressure of such a thing, though. His heart was surely cold enough to *wish* a bloody cataclysm on all those people; he would surely be elated to *read* in the newspaper that such a thing occurred. Their confusion and tears would surely delight him at a comfortable distance. He had enough sense to realize what a different thing it would be to personally annihilate a cringing, pleading victim, and stand the horrible intensity of it.

In desperate hours his thoughts had, therefore, regrouped around a proposition more in line with his capabilities.

He often reflected upon that winter morning when he and the other students at Silver Spur Middle School were informed over the intercom that the kid who'd been missing for several days had finally turned up. A couple of boys had found him in the mountains, actually not far from the Miller estate. Rumor and hearsay would fill in the picture: the body was difficult to notice under its blanket of snow, the boys stumbled over it, brushed it off a bit, saw that much of the head was gone, and that a magnum revolver lay at hand in a frozen pool of darkened blood. The scene took on iconic proportions in Louis's imagining: a humble altar on a mountaintop beneath a silent gray sky, icy clouds swirling by over a free-flowing spring of hotly vivid red, the sacrament spilling down a slope of soft white and gradually freezing into black. He looked that kid up in the yearbook and learned he had a younger sister at the middle school, a pretty girl with arms covered in angular symbols she'd carved into herself. Louis tried to figure out a good way to approach her on the subject of her brother. He wanted to tell her that he admired her brother for his act of revolutionary protest against the conditions of an inhumane world. He wanted to assure her that even though her brother must have felt totally alone up there on the mountain and felt that his struggle was unrecognized and insurmountable, Louis would carry her brother's flame and would never forget her brother's battle with the world and his bold indictment of it.

That's certainly what Louis had wanted to tell her. He never did, of course. There might be some chance that she'd react poorly, even wildly, to his advance, and any kids who overheard it would instantly be bouncing off the walls and throwing their feces at him.

Louis gave the sunlit leaves another good look. He pumped out the spent cartridge, took up a fresh one, grasped it sentimentally, and slid it on in. Back to the house he trod, with no fear.

By the time the sun began to fade beyond the upheaving horizon, Louis was speaking in tongues. He'd been hopping and dancing for a good while, running up and down the stairs, hooting and grunting, flowing with the current of some buried program. The words came out English at first, mainly vile obscenities, and this disintegrated into strings of random syllables, nonsense thrown together by electrical storm, until it sounded as though he was in fact speaking a bizarre but quite coherent language.

By nightfall, Louis was exhausted and dripping. Ecstatic to his fingertips, he seized his weapon, took it downstairs to his room, and retrieved from his closet a blank canvas that had something scrawled with black marker in the bottom right corner: *Louis Koenig, Plan B*. He placed the canvas vertically against the barren wall atop the wooden head of his bed, adjusting the canvas to receive the greatest possible distribution of paint.

Laying himself onto the bed, and resting his head on a couple of pillows, he floated, staring up at the dim yellow glow of the ceiling. He hoped it would be Ed who found him down there, partly because he wanted to spare Mom and Brandy the sight of him, but also because he believed Ed was the one most likely to preserve the canvas in recognition of its artistic value.

Holding the shotgun firmly with both hands, he placed it upon himself, and settled the muzzle into the spongy tissue where his neck became his chin.

"This is it then," Louis declared aloud with a smile.

"Not joking. Last call," he said, giving Him or It or Them a chance to realize he was serious.

"You have been weighed in the balance and are found wan-ting," he declared to the emptiness.

"I judge your creation pi-ti-ful, flawed, co-rrupt," said Louis, grandstanding before the invisible accused.

"Anything to say in your defense?" he asked, waiting half a minute for an answer.

"Forever silent? Fine. I have contended with the Almighty and shall now instruct him," Louis proclaimed.

He stared at the ceiling in contemplation of the task that now lay directly before him. The real weight of the task was starting to make itself known. What must it have taken for that kid on the mountain to pull the trigger and blast himself into the great beyond? Was it a flash of impulse, or steady determination? As the ceiling itself closed in on Louis, his major instinct was to shrink from the task, to lay the gun aside and continue slouching along with Plan A. Even the odd mood he'd been enjoying for much of today wasn't sufficiently powerful to override his fear of Plan B, that colossal monument to dejection for all humankind. But could he really go back to Plan A and get by on its vague hopes? Was it not better to force a solution right here? Louis tried throwing himself back at the advancing ceiling, looking straight into it, like he might convince himself, very suddenly perhaps, that Plan B was his proper path. If only Plan A could somehow pay off. The pressure of his dilemma was becoming intolerable, and now, having issued such brave indictments, he nearly offered up a simple plea for help. He breathed slowly and very intentionally.

"Halt, Louis. Feel your power. Feel the power you have to make a choice."

The voice came from the hallway, or maybe from the house itself, from the vibrating timbers in the walls, a somber voice, thick and heavily distorted as though it passed through an overheated amplifier. Louis slowly brought his gaze down from the ceiling. Standing in the doorway was a luminous man, seeming to hold his position against some sort of wind.

The fellow had eyes rather like mirrors. The lines and curves of his nose and lips were symmetrical and pleasant. His hair looked very much like Louis's own, on a good hair day. He was wearing a respectable dark suit over a crisp white shirt, with a profoundly red tie fastened in place by a small circular pin that sparkled gold. His silvery skin seemed vibrant with subtle motions, like a sea of sunlit waves viewed from high above, or a brilliant firework show behind smoky glass; indeed, on closer examination the skin appeared composed of many colors, which together produced the general effect of silver. There in the doorway stood this composite man, who, taken all at a glance, looked as solid and sound as a silver dollar.

"Pull that trigger and flee this world of evils you know, for another of evils you don't."

Louis was frozen. He lay still, shut his eyes, and felt his heart pounding in his head. He held to the shotgun and tried to breathe. Time passed. He opened his eyes.

The man was there, waiting patiently with one wrist under the steady grip of a ruling hand.

"You judge all creation like a lost little bee who cannot find flowers or hive, and so begins to wonder if there ever was anything sweet in the world."

"Oh?" uttered Louis.

"Lost little bee, do you realize what you're throwing away with a little pressure on that trigger?"

"I think so," said Louis, thawing a little. "I'm giving up the world and all its empty promises."

"Empty promises … such as?" asked the figure blocking the doorway.

"Such as the promise of happiness, or *any* promise of the good life in this world, through wealth … power … fame … love … freedom, it's all empty. Because … it's extremely difficult to really get hold of any of these in the first place, since they're so hoarded and monopolized. But even if you do get hold of some of the good stuff, the effect wears off and you've got to go chasing after more. Fulfillment is an illusion, bait in a trap. All glory is fleeting."

Now a little orange flared into the figure's eyes. He released his wrist and put an open hand to his mouth, seeming to cough.

"Fleeting, sure. I wonder if you actually know this, or did you merely read it in one of your books? Wouldn't you like to *really know* the good stuff? Or are you simply resolved on deleting the possibilities of Louis Koenig?" asked the figure.

"Possibilities?" Louis prodded.

"There is honey to be had out there: those things you dismissed as trifles, those things you dismissed on faith. Yours is the power to have them all if you'd care to apply yourself. You still have a destiny here, and I represent a providence that wishes to see you fulfill it."

"And what is my destiny here?"

"To have what you so desperately want, to attain all that you have been denied. You will lead others to their destiny; you will fill their emptiness with what they are seeking. This calling has always prompted you."

"I … lead others?"

"Is it really so difficult to believe?" asked the figure.

Louis put aside the shotgun. The figure smiled, the fire kindling in his eyes again.

"Why would anyone follow me?" inquired Louis.

"Because you'll offer them what they've been looking for all their lives: Escape. Be bold enough to simply tell them that this escape is possible, and you've already won half the battle, more than half, regardless of what gateway you propose in particular. The desire people have for some complete answer to be out there ready and waiting for them—this is the rich soil in which you'll sow and reap."

"But what sort of answer, what escape can I offer them?" asked Louis, now sitting upright.

"Why not go with the old standby? Rest assured, you cannot go broke selling the story that the end of the corrupt world is at hand … some special people are launching the golden age … and *you* have been selected! Right this way, just *follow me*."

"Old standby indeed," mused Louis. "How many times has that one been tried?"

"More times than I can count. Take it from me, though, it works. Of course *you* would never fall for such a hackneyed premise … but there are just sooo many people out there who'll think you are the only person ever to offer it. Come on Louis, you know what idiots people are, how short their historical memory is. They're out there right now, privately begging for something to come and sweep them off their feet.

"Look at their lives without the solution you can give them," continued the figure. "Look how they seek their answer in whatever ridiculous gimmick that pops onto the TV screen with a toll-free number. At the very least, you can give these people the opportunity of trying *your* gimmick, your particular coloring of the old standby."

"My particular coloring?" Louis probed.

"I'm quite sure we'll come up with something if we put our heads together," the figure assured. "We'll tailor a product to fit a demographic neglected by the market."

"Hmmm," mumbled Louis.

"Not convinced?" asked the figure. "That's perfectly understandable. You're not accustomed to seeing your designs come to fruit. Take young ladies, for instance. I see a stout lad reaching his prime, who somehow manages to drown instead of swimming in that sea of beauties out there," he said, pointing a shining finger in the direction of Silver Spur High School.

Louis frowned and nodded.

"Are they really such wild and terrifying creatures, such impregnable fortresses? I'm afraid the whole world has become one hateful riddle to you. Your study has made you weak, when it should have made you strong. You've learned plenty enough to be able to criticize and distrust everything. You therefore aspire to nothing and do nothing."

Again, Louis frowned and nodded.

"What you should have learned from history and all your books is that the world is subdued by a simple formula. It's not half as perplexing as you've conceived it."

Louis searched his mental cabinets for a file he thought was there.

"What you must understand is that the psyche of the masses is not receptive to anything that is halfhearted and weak," declared the figure, waving a smoldering finger at Louis.

"Weak like me, I suppose?"

"Like your indecision, your pessimism, your timid resignation. People long for a force that remedies their own weak and anxious nature. They crave certainty. They crave a commander whose certainty tolerates no competing doctrines."

"Then this commander has to be a pretty good liar," observed Louis.

"He has to be good at articulating the lie that people need to hear, and good at demonstrating his complete belief in its truth. He must confirm that their deepest wishes are proper and within reach. They don't want the truth as much as they want someone who boldly proclaims what they'd like to be true but are uncertain of by themselves."

Louis snarled at his classmates for their hatred of the truth and their blind commitment to what they'd like to be true.

"They are desperately weak," continued the figure, "and so they are susceptible to that which is whole-hearted and strong. They need the big lie more than the small truth, and the bigger the lie, the better. Not only is bigger more inspiring, but the bigger a lie is, the less likely will people suspect it. People readily suspect the small lie, since they themselves lie in small matters all the time. They waver in attempting a big lie, however, under the fear that commonly accompanies such audacity. It is their experience that a grand claim can hardly be made without the solid foundation of truth, they being too halfhearted to establish a grand claim on other foundations.

"So, the effective lie must be big. It must also be simple, free of the pesky complications that so depressingly clutter reality. And it needs to burn, with an overblown sensationalism that anyone can appreciate, like the circus.

Last, and certainly not least, it must be repeated. Over and over and over again. The most ludicrous fiction disproved a hundred times will still ring true in ears that hear it with the chimes of the clock."

As Louis sat there on his bed and tried to digest all this, the spectral being accommodated, his ten thousand lights pulsating as if to add some final flare to the proposal. Louis tilted his head, much as a dog whose interest has been piqued, and he noticed the figure's suit shifting from black to a deep blue, then to a deep purple, then to black again, while the tie remained the same rich hue of red. To stare too deeply into the fellow didn't agree with Louis—nor does the first-time homeowner too seriously inspect the bricks and wood.

"Well, there you have it, the keys to the kingdom," concluded the figure. "Run with me and the sky is the limit. Put your little canvas away and let's really paint something."

Worn down by years of famine and defeat, humiliated, desperately needing to believe in himself and the possibility of better times, Louis Koenig fell easy prey to the promises of this strange messenger. "All right," said Louis at last. "Sold."

"Excellent," said the specter, beaming with triumph, eyes fully ablaze. "Let's get to work. Congratulations on your rebirth."

Chapter 7
Finding His Voice

From the moment Louis struck his deal with his visitor, things were better. The vital quality of what it was to be alive was replenished, and life felt fresh and inviting to him. Even the acne cleared up measurably. He couldn't help but thank God for the miraculous therapy he was experiencing—though not in so many words did he offer thanks, and not to an old shepherd in the sky. Rather, his whole being constantly volunteered a feeling of thanks, and Louis seconded that feeling in contemplating what source was owed the thanks, what source had revealed itself as God to him.

Almost every day Louis had a session with the specter. Frequently it occurred upon Louis's return from school, when he'd go downstairs and find the specter in the den.

For several weeks the specter's entire program was for Louis to learn about living in a body. One lesson involved Louis holding his breath. "Hold it until you can't," the figure said, and Louis held his breath until his pulse pounded in his head, and when he finally let go the specter told him to feel the blood and oxygen pumping all through his body as he breathed.

Another lesson involved Louis keeping his hands under hot running water. "Hold them until you can't," the figure said, and Louis kept his hands beneath the gush until they were bright pink and throbbing. When he finally pulled away, the specter told him to feel the poisonous tension of the school day boiling off. Louis learned to stretch, awakening tissues that had slumbered for years, his cartilage crackling in sudden animation. He learned to notice his body telling him of parts that were tired and parts that still wanted in on the action.

There were at first some small moments of weakness in which Louis questioned the usefulness of all this, but the specter was there to assure him of its importance. The figure explained that most people knew these things about their body instinctually. It was unfortunate that Louis had somehow missed out on such knowledge or had unlearned it if he ever had known it. The important thing was that Louis Koenig might still run a fine race if he'd just start with essentials, and by small steps build up to speed. "Tall oaks from little acorns," said the specter.

One afternoon, after a day of walking the halls of Silver Spur High with a fluid, steady gait and an easy posture, Louis hurried downstairs and found the specter by the computer Ed kept in the den.

"Put your hands under the hot water, and uh, put a hot cloth on your face and neck, then come sit down," the figure instructed. Louis did so with pleasure.

"Well," said the figure, pressing his hands together and pursing his lips, then grinning slightly. "Let's write your book."

Bubbling with the joy of a gambler on a roll, Louis turned the computer on and brought up a blank screen. The specter began his dictation.

"Every era has its share of crisis and upheaval, and of people who think theirs must be the final era. In Joshua Goldberg's time, these people happen to be correct. His is the final age of the world as we've always known it. His is the first age of the world as we've always wanted it. His is the generation chosen to experience the return of the son of God, the gathering of the righteous, and the fiery cleansing of the Earth.

"Joshua is a child of lowly birth. Against a raging wind he must kindle his flame, and how searing the flame he must carry! For his is the flame that reveals the hidden and reduces the greatest into the least. His light makes plain the craft of the banker, the robber with a public relations department. His eye penetrates the smoke screen of the priest, the lunatic whose delusions are published in gold and leather. Who but the priests and bankers of the world will rage against the man who comes to give God and wealth? Who but the generals will rage against the prince of peace?"

Louis finished typing, raised a skeptical eyebrow, and examined the specter. "The Second Coming of Christ in the form of a guy named Joshua?" said Louis, awaiting reassurance.

"Have no doubt. This story is sacred to you. Joshua's message to his people is your message to your people," said the specter. Louis let this sink in.

"Okay," said Louis. "And the message is?"

"The old standby, of course: Prepare yourselves, for the kingdom of God is at hand."

Just then the front door slammed upstairs and the sound of feminine voices lightened the atmosphere. The specter vanished, leaving Louis to look over his half-page embryo. Soon Brandy and Haley were descending the stairs, Pepsis in hand.

"What's up Bro?" said Brandy.

"Hey ladies," said Louis, swinging his chair toward them. There it was, that smell, warm and healthy and joyous, like sunshine on the smooth skin of a merry toddler. Patience, Louis, climb the ladder.

Haley glanced at what Louis had typed. "Fiery cleansing of the Earth?" she asked with pretended horror. "What class is that for?"

"Oh, ah …" Louis stopped himself. He was about to give the halfhearted and weak answer that he was just doing this for school, English class perhaps. Yet even with only two paragraphs to its name so far, he already felt rampant confidence in the work he had undertaken. So, he looked Haley straight in those eyes of hers that safe-kept a hundred mysteries and promised a thousand pleasures.

"Actually, it isn't homework. It's a *book* I'm writing. It's about … well … a sort of messiah, who turns things right-side up."

The girls' faces lit up with amusement and interest. "Let me see," said Brandy, approaching the computer screen.

"Ah-ah-ah," Louis cautioned with a wagging finger, his typing out of sight with a click. "All in good time. In fact, you'll both be the first to receive a free, signed copy once it's published. But until then, I'm afraid I can't let you compromise the integrity of the artistic vision."

He was aware of how ridiculous he sounded just then, but this didn't sting him as much as it would have a month ago. As the girls retired to Brandy's room upstairs, Louis knew the specter was proud of how this test had been handled. Louis was sure he'd proven himself worthy of further instruction.

Chapter 8
Product Development

Unto us a child is born, and the government shall be upon his shoulder.

No star appears for the birth of this child. No trumpets herald his arrival. No wise men gather to pay him homage. Into a land of robbers, he comes obscure as a thicf in the night.

Between a convenience store and a carwash sits a manger where animals sleep, called Mission of Saving Jesus. A slanted cross flashes neon red onto the discarded refuse inhabiting the street. Inside, somebody sets down a backpack by the front desk and slips off into the night like a ghost.

"Oh Jeez, not again," an elderly black janitor eventually says, seeing the purple bag rustle. "Look like we got another one here. I ain't see who drop it off this time, neither."

The janitor stands his mop to the wall beside a tramp passed out in urine, and with a work-worn hand he hefts the bag onto a mess of employment applications and church pamphlets. A great puff of his cigar smoke ascends like incense, he glances at a nurse, and the prize is revealed.

The infant yawns, stretches his little limbs, squints his gray eyes, and returns to slumber.

There is nothing instantly pleasing about this child, nothing to make someone love him on sight, this wandering boy so difficult to corral, always so far away from the other children, so far behind them.

When he does speak it is to the adults. The little pilgrim from another world can't understand the strange land around him. He hides in the bushes when a jet passes overhead, since he saw on TV that jets drop fire onto people. No, say the adults, jets drop fire onto *bad* people. He calls the police about a store that sells drugs. No, say the adults, the pharmacy sells *good* drugs.

The learned doctors hear of his concern that something is hiding inside him, or maybe outside him. It could even be hiding from him in plain sight. The doctors ask him what the thing is, but all they get are half-answers about what the thing is *like*. The hiding thing is like unto a key, or a window, or a plow. Life just isn't okay for the poor fellow until he finds it. Oh, but why such struggle, little lamb? Why no rest for you within your well-kept fold? Mild delusional schizophrenia, obsessive compulsive disorder, a touch of autism—a quaint mixture in this one, a rather interesting case. Our watch must be kept on him, the doctors counsel, and our medicines must be applied.

With eyes open to the darkness of the world, and with a heart to carry it, how deep is the darkness to him! He takes evil so personally.

The supervisors have never seen such a unique failure to meet the demands of life. Joshua insists that every box of fries have two dashes of salt and every soda have one scoop of ice, even during the noon rush. He actually feels some sort of pain when people bring back their burgers because they don't resemble the picture above the register. The supervisors try to help him see that it's just business. It's about doing what you can get away with. It's about advertising something as the total solution to profound needs, and then delivering something a little less. It's about using the cheapest possible inputs, which includes working fast, so fast that life becomes a worthless approximation of itself.

To put Joshua in a white collar behind a desk proves even more catastrophic. Here he lasts as long as it takes for him to get hold of some accounting records, which to him indicate the necessity of giving raises to all the cooks, who "do so much and get so little," he explains to the owners as they help him off the property.

Joshua begins to suspect that this world will beat him if he doesn't join it. He wonders whether to continue his journey here. Death seems a welcome solution, but a terrifying mystery.

The young man without a penny or a friend or a calling is approached by a couple of solid young men with all the answers.

They assure him he is army material. Joshua can do a pushup or two, does well enough on their tests, isn't a serious felon or a drug addict or an obvious homosexual, and he needs money, health care, education, and direction. Maybe here he can give others a chance, he hopes, give people a real chance to teach him something about being normal and happy.

"But what will I be doing?" Joshua asks before he signs the papers.

The men point to the posters hanging around their office. "Defending freedom and democracy, of course. You know, protecting the American way."

Constantly bearing in mind the noble cause he is serving, Joshua carries his weapon with little discomfort, and actually some finesse. The sergeants appreciate his dutiful conduct, and the other recruits in all their types warm to his willingness to learn about their lives.

The time arrives for Joshua to ship out. He is needed east of the Mediterranean, where he will "assist in stabilizing crucial allies in America's fight against ……ism." He will "augment the security of a facility detaining perpetrators of insurgent activities that undermine the region's moderate governments." It will be Joshua's "duty and privilege to uphold America's longstanding commitment to the stability of our partners in a region vital to American interests."

And, once again, Joshua proves to be a stunning failure at life, displaying, at best, a disconnection from reality bordering on mental illness, and at worst, a contempt for authority bordering on treason.

"Why, private, why would you do something so insane?!" wails the sergeant, his face sweaty, red, and trembling with horror. "Are these people friends of yours? Are they guests at a desert resort, and you're their room service? If you really like serving Arabs, we can drop you off down the road and you can wait tables at an actual resort, and serve the Arabs that are on our side, the really big tippers. But in here, you will accept the realities of war, the hard realities. In here you are dealing with The Enemy. You will not serve them beyond the prescribed amount. An extra roll, even a moldy-ass roll that's hard as a rock … or an extra sip of stale, warm water … or half an aspirin for the guy who keeps slamming his head into the wall: private, that is dereliction of duty, and a subversion of our mission here."

"Sir," says the private, "I can't shake the notion that there could easily be falsely accused young men rounded up and thrown in here. It could be me behind those bars. And if they did strike us, I think we can make them less of an enemy by treating them more like the friend we want them to be, sir."

The sergeant's chiseled head convulses. "I can't believe I just heard that. From a *soldier*! Aren't you embarrassed? Aren't you ashamed? It's like you're a child. Where … where do you come from? I'm from a place called Earth, private, a God-forsaken place where there are certain established ways to achieve a purpose, and a soldier is the first to accept this reality. Our purpose is achieved by keeping the screws on these bastards screwed down good n' tight. The ones we got in here don't wanna' be our friends, okay? They're killers, real savages. The fact is they don't care how good we are to them, how much we build out here in this wasteland, how much progress we bring. We're just this corrupting, polluting force that offends their backward God, and they're being faithful to their God if they blow us up every chance they get and drive us out."

No less than a major is called in, taken away from far more important matters, to instruct Private J. Goldberg that he is doing a great disservice to his country by making life less difficult for the inmates. The strange young man has to understand that "the prison environment is carefully structured to maximize deterrence and intelligence. The harder it is to be a prisoner in here, the more fear we put out there of being an insurgent, and the more our prisoners surrender actionable intelligence in exchange for relief. It's simply necessary that they go without comforts until they give us what we need for our mission. We can't let 'em take anything for granted. Clothing, sleep, sitting, silence, light: it all has to be earned. No more trays of tea."

The major couldn't help shaking his head at having to spell things out like that.

They still let Joshua carry a gun, but his main duty now is to clean things, to wash and scrub whatever he is told to.

What Joshua looks forward to is his leave, when he goes into the towns and feels the ancient pulse of the life there. He walks the dirt streets, listening to the jabber of humble storekeepers, the rhythm of artisans hewing stone and wood, the joyful hoots of beautiful children at play. He sits down at an open-air cafe and tries to order tea in Arabic, and he sips a few cups as the sweet light of evening falls across the rolling hills.

The comforting pulse subsides when he reflects on the many in these little towns who are cast into his prison, young men dragged out of bed and hauled away in the back of a truck, hooded and shackled alongside twenty or thirty others to be dumped at Joshua's feet and interrogated about the latest flare-up of the insurrection that has simmered here for decade upon decade.

Joshua reads what he can about the history of this place, and he even learns what he can from the inmates. "What brings you here?" he asks.

"Prison is the natural place for the just in an unjust society. We want a society that supports a well-being much broader and deeper than the current rulers allow. And so, not content to be dogs, we fight for it."

"But aren't there elections here?"

"Yes, but these are easily rigged. Favored parties dominate the media, wield the police, and count the votes. Reform here is impossible without violence."

Joshua asks if they've considered the example of Gandhi, who led his nation to self-determination without resorting to arms. The inmates answer yes, they actually have looked into that, but discovered that non-violent resistance only works if there are people with influence out there who witness your protest, see what brutal treatment you're getting, and sympathize enough to act forcefully on your behalf. Some causes achieve victory this way, but other causes have image problems and can turn the other cheek and go down as slaughtered lambs without creating much concern or even notice. It's difficult to get blind eyes to see you, and cold hearts to feel you. But bullets have a way of getting people's attention.

"Yes," answers Joshua, "but may God will that the attention is not simply more bullets."

As he hears their stories and he continues to research, something dawns on Joshua. He is here to protect American interests, and he cannot serve both God and interests.

American interests mean what Rome's and Britain's and Russia's meant. In each province of the empire, partner with and protect local elites who share your predatory interest against the local population. Prop up a royal family who will rule the place with an iron fist. Call this iron fist moderate.

The days creep by and Joshua's rifle gets heavier. The darkest, honeyed tea can't soothe his sore throat. He looks and feels like the truest prisoner of all. Faces turn away from him as he carries the punishment for the healing he tried to bring, that ridiculous magical-thinking nonsense.

Things get especially heavy for Pvt. J. Goldberg one night during mopping detail.

"The crazy Jew is hereby granted clearance for the cellar. Now move your dumb ass and don't be talkin' to nobody down there."

The cellar doors slide open, and Pvt. Goldberg descends an acrid corridor into the rusty, dripping bowels of the prison, down in a network of tunnels several thousand years old, as ancient as the bronze-clawed kings of the river valleys who ruled when lions roamed about and the land was full of gardens. Here below several layers, a deep evil unveils. The clanging of the prison's organs won't cover the sound of it, the crying and groaning through the walls, through the centuries. There is awful dying down here. People are slowly being devoured all around him. This is what Joshua has been standing upon. It's what the whole world stands upon. He is immersed in terror. Someone who has taken air for granted is hanging by his feet, with a dirty rag wrapped around his face; now a man pours a stream of water onto the rag, chanting, "Render unto Caesar." The nightmare that is possible will surely become real. Who's to stop it?

Singing to Joshua is the voice of hell, the unrestrained demons who use all that is possible. "Without God, all is allowed that is possible! Oh, how free we are, free to be the very gods of the Earth! If God existed, how could we be so free?! Oh, praise this heavenly hell that is Godless Earth!"

To those with ears to hear, the groaning of the prisoners and the singing of the gods grow to a maddening worldwide chorus.

Are the prisoners without help? Can they truly be forsaken, dying on their cross alone, apart from God? Oh Universe, let there be God! Oh God, be God to your creation! Be! Do not leave us alone to eat and be eaten! Be help against the evil demanded by this world! Be!

Chapter 9
The Temptation of the Homeless

At school Louis remained a ghost, but no longer an angry one. Content to bide his time in purgatory while anticipating a glorious exaltation, he was constantly studying drafts of the specter's dictation, making alterations and coming up with passages to fill in the gaps.

His schoolmates bothered him a good deal less. They were still the same simpletons with the same predictable idiocies, but Louis now felt more amused by them than outraged. The girls skittered past, buzzing about everything surface-deep, self-satisfied in the beauty of their bodies and futures, ignoring Louis as usual. The guys ape-grunted their viewpoints without fear of correction, explaining to the class that good ol' Coach told them there's no substitute for victory, meaning the United States could clear up a lot of its problems by nuking the places that are too evil to thank us for being the only world power in history to constantly use its power for the benefit of other peoples. We go out there and slay the monsters that threaten freedom and democracy, because that's why God created America. Sure, now and again we may destroy a village or a city or a country, but always in order to save it from a monster.

No venom now flooded Louis. He didn't molest the girls with his covetous eyes. He didn't erupt and spew that every world power in history has considered itself on a divine mission to slay monsters and benefit other peoples, destroying villages in order to save them. The Nazis were saving Europe from Communism. Louis took a deep breath and rebuked the surrounding foolishness with his pen and manuscript, striking back and setting the record straight, his future brightening with every additional page.

He kept up the exercises the specter gave him. One involved kneeling and bending forward, arms reaching out to the ground with chin tucked against chest. Besides limbering him up, it heightened his sense of spiritual awareness by boosting the blood flow to his temporal lobes. After holding the position for about twenty seconds, Louis would bring his head and torso upright to feel the presence wash over and align him.

One still and snowy afternoon, as Louis was performing just such an exercise, the specter suddenly arrived with information about a certain mountain that stands east of the Mediterranean.

It rises from the earth like a bronze helmet half-buried by the sands of time, marking the resting place of some soldier fallen long ago. Just now its crest catches the golden light of the setting sun while its vast flank withdraws under a veil of shadow. On its peak is the form of a man. Yes, there sits Joshua, bathed in the creamy glow.

There he sits upon thousands who lie stacked in the earth, slain in fierce battle, battle atop battle on this spot in age after age, graveyard atop graveyard. Lowly shepherds pass by quietly, fearing to disturb the ancient and troubled souls here. Likewise do these souls in the mountain give place to Joshua, the most ancient and troubled soul.

He won't go back to the prison. As the sun creeps beneath the horizon, Joshua declares aloud, "God, I sit here until you rise from your hiding place and justify the world to me."

Slowly it grows darker into night. Joshua sits alone, saying, "Account for it, God. How can I straighten what was forged crooked?"

Night is bitter, stinging cold, laying ice on the desert.

The day arrives with Joshua still sprawled against a stone, facing west, and thirsting.

Hours drudge by in the baking heat.

Then comes a voice unto him, saying, "Leave this peak of desolation and go find water in the village below, where God hath placed it for thee." But Joshua turns it back, saying, "Get thee hence, Satan, for if I leave this mountain without seeing God, I shall thirst forevermore." And the Devil leaves him for a time.

The sun sets again, bulbous, crimson, and ripe.

Night falls with its frost and darkness.

Then comes unto Joshua a man holding a lantern, and the pleasant light of it grows to fill the mountain top. Behind the man there marches an endless, shimmering train of followers. The man commands this legion to fall upon the ground in reverence before Joshua. Now bright as lightning, the man hails Joshua, saying, "Truly thou art a mystic and a philosopher, perceiving holy things that other men know not. Nevertheless, art thou not still a man, born of flesh and ordained to serve it? How great a curse, therefore, to hunger and thirst for righteousness! Can he be filled whose inheritance is an orchard of fine fruit, which he is every day in the midst of, crying out in hunger for cakes to fall from heaven? And how great a curse to seek the deliverance of this Earth unto the meek! For should the humble of this Earth finally gain it, goodbye in that very hour to their humility. Therefore go now, remove thyself from this barren table, thou art excused from it. Get thee down to thy proper place. Satisfy thyself in all the flesh permits; for God is the author thereof, and art thou greater than he?"

But Joshua rebukes the man holding a lantern, saying: "Shall a man cast into prison embrace it as his home? Nay, for his heart recalleth freedom and his mind studyeth escape. Get thee hence, Satan. Thy light blindeth." At this the Devil curses, and he departs with his wretched entourage, their light dissolving into pale mist.

Awaking to bites and stings of creatures eager to devour dying flesh, Joshua burns beneath a swirling mad sun, his eyes and throat in flames, the breeze and clouds seared off from the sky.

"If God is great," he utters, "if God hath great power, and great knowledge, and great goodness, then surely my cry is heard, and surely it will be answered." So, Joshua waits in great faith and aching.

After many hours in the furnace he is too weak to continue. His organs are cooking in thirst, pained at the effort of staggering onward to total depletion. He can barely inch toward his rifle, preparing to leave the world on this mountain.

Then there comes upon him, with a gust of wind, an old saying in this ancient land: "If you take a step toward God, God will take two steps toward you. But, make it your full step."

He must make his step to the full. He leans back on his rock to watch the sun creep to the sea a third and final time, offering God a final chance at the rescue Joshua must have. "Oh, Creator of my soul, I know not how to live," he whispers, watching and waiting for an answer.

As the sun budges downward, it grows purple and fat like a heart in its death throes.

The waves settle into silence on the darkening sea.

All becomes still.

A star shatters into a shower of glistening sparks. Now another star shatters, and suddenly many stars are bursting into spark showers, blue smoke twisting across the heavens as the celestial fires plummet to the sea, water crimson and simmering.

The ground below Joshua shudders. The stone behind him wavers against his disabled body. The pull of the Earth threatens to swallow his sinking matter.

A lesion tears open in the swollen sun, and through it emerges a maggot, fanged and clawed, scaly and blood-slimed, squirming out, sprouting wings, and growing into a dragon. Towering up from the head of the thing is a great golden crown, and the face of the thing is a mouth, a gorging monstrosity of blades jutting in rows from raw gums, scoured by a perversely willful tongue. Following this dragon are lions, eagles, bulls, serpents, and other beasts, each follower wearing a crown of silver above a gaping mouth. The sky fills with the terrible glory of blooded fangs, dripping horns, talons splattered with torn flesh, leeching tongues raging out from shrieking throats, and a throbbing sun behind a fuming, scarlet sea.

Pressed down into the mountain, Joshua struggles to breathe.

And Joshua beholds the globe of blue and white overshadowed by the hand of God, whose outstretched finger blasts the great cities with a fire that consumes their idols and abominations and all their cunning craftsmanship. And Joshua hears the globe heaving sighs and singing praises as its corrupt flesh is seared away at long last.

Now Joshua beholds over all the Earth but a single place the fires do not touch: a rain-clouded forest garden having a fair city at the center of it, a city without rot to be burned away, without high places to be abased or low places to be exalted. And Joshua hears a harmony sounding from the city.

But how is it that a city is found in purity, having no need of fire to cleanse it of defilements?

Wondering greatly at the mystery, Joshua then beholds the manner of the city's coming upon the Earth. It is born of a rough tent in the wilderness. Above it, the shining presence of God rests as a shield, guarding the heir that shall inherit the Earth from the dragon and his beasts, who fly roundabout in a frenzy, vomiting black rivers of poison at the city from their great mouths, sorely vexed at the holiness that subverts their reign. And thus they battle against the light of the city until the day of fire, when the crowns of the dragon and his beasts slip from their brows and tumble to the ground. The crowns are melted down by the people of the city, and the gold and silver are poured upon a temple that stands in their midst. Headlong, the dragon plunges into the darkness of the oceans, his servants close behind, to stew and scrape along cold floors of deep canyons for a thousand years, drinking the full bitterness of every cup of injustice they had sent forth upon the Earth in the days of their power.

Having witnessed these things roll out before him, Joshua is enveloped by infinity on all sides, the endlessness of divisibility and the boundlessness of increase, time and space without limit—or else limited, reaching some beginning, some end, some nothing at the edge of everything. A dreamless sleep overtakes him.

He awakes in the morning to the sound of sheep. They wander through the bushes, grazing in serenity. Joshua notices his thirst has somehow been eased. He feels he is drawing on fresh energy. The sea lies placid beneath a clear sapphire sky as he sits against his rock in the cool breeze, rubbing his head in recollection of the branding his consciousness received.

From behind him comes a voice, soft and elderly. "Long ago, on this very mountain, did El survey his kingdom to see if all was well with it. But seeing many poor in the land, and debtors, and fugitives, and many in bondage, and many without kin, El did witness their oppression, and did hearken unto their cries. El did lead his son Yahweh onto this mountain and did bless him here, that he should go unto the people and be mercy and help to them. And Yahweh went forth with great power to lift up the desperate." Joshua turns to see a sturdy old shepherd in a coarse robe covering sun-kissed skin. The man strokes his salt-and-pepper beard.

Joshua greets the man in Arabic and asks if he is the one who gave Joshua water.

The man smiles. "As you gave unto the least of my brethren."

Joshua nods in understanding.

"I am weary of wandering," the shepherd says. "Many years have I lived in a tent, finding no place to call home, no place where I might settle and plant a good thing and see it grow to give fruit. And so, I pass everything by, except a wanderer in need."

"The life of wandering is hard," says Joshua.

"But rightfully ours, who find no home in the prison," says the shepherd, looking out across a vast desert. "Where is the kingdom of God to be found upon the Earth? Shall its mother be forever lost in the wilderness?"

Joshua nods in great understanding. "Here is a man after my own heart," he says.

"The spirit of God is upon *you*," announces the man, putting forth a sure hand in the direction of Joshua. "God has anointed you, Yeshu'a, to bring good news to the oppressed, to bind up the brokenhearted, to proclaim liberty to the captives, to provide a home for the wanderer, and to foretell of the Earth's renewal."

Joshua stares humbly into the dirt, then out onto the sunlit sea.

"There is a light in you, Son of God, and it must come forth into the world, or it will burn you up. Your candle was not lit that it should be placed under a bushel. Has your sojourn in this land awakened nothing in you?"

"Many feel themselves to be the Son of God," Joshua replies. "Emperors and generals do. Vagrants and vagabonds do."

"Yes, Alexander felt it, Christ felt it. And I say unto you truthfully, neither of these could have accomplished what he did, without this feeling."

Joshua wonders deeply at this.

"I do," Joshua affirms, "I do feel the Creator has anointed me, even as you say. But what good news shall I bring to the oppressed in a world where the strong must eat the weak, where this has always been the way of nature, a way whose justice is beyond my understanding?"

"God is about to do a new thing, and former things will be forgotten," declares the shepherd, simple and bold as the sunrise. "A path will be cleared in the wilderness for the kingdom of God that is at hand. Arise, Yeshu'a. Shine. For your light has come, and the glory of God has risen upon you. Do not fear the reproach of others, do not be dismayed when they revile you. Though thick darkness covers the people of the Earth, the glory of God will appear over you, and nations will come to your light, to the brightness of your dawn."

The old man turns away now to guide the sheep down the mountain, and Joshua watches the shepherd and his flock fade into a ribbon of sunlight on the sea.

Three days later, Joshua is sleeping in the hold of a tanker advancing gently across the Mediterranean, bound for Babylon of the west, Rome beyond the Atlantic, republic turned empire, military machine, economic vampire.

Chapter 10
Honeymoon and Second Thoughts

Ed made no objection to Louis spending hour upon hour down in the den, sealed off from prying eyes, taking over the computer and a vast store of encyclopedias, turning the place into his own personal office. Ed rather encouraged Louis with the occasional comment to sail full speed ahead with whatever wind it was that he'd apparently caught hold of. A miraculous easing of tension ensued between them, not least because Ed's crackling lip-spittle, while still present, somehow ceased being significant enough to drive thorns into Louis.

Once in a while Brandy and Haley would catch Louis taking a breather from his hardy efforts and they'd ply him to reveal some of what he'd written. The only concession he ever offered was two free signed copies of the book upon publication. The girls seemed offended that their valuable input was not sought after by a boy who'd seen too little of life and people to be able to write anything meaningful for the public. They informed him that he had become "totally lame" and "so gay" since he started fancying himself an author. If his thing had to be published for the girls to get to read it, they might as well forget about it altogether.

Fortunately, Louis understood the language of the American teen, which was loaded with goodies like "totally lame" and "so gay," all of which translated to "of no use to me" or "confusing to me." What Brandy and Haley really alleged, therefore, was that he was frustratingly difficult to use or figure out, and this, of course, was just fine with Louis. Their beauty-reinforced offensives had come to mean much less to him since he had fallen in love with his book. His engagement to it put him in a comfortable position to shrug off all sorts of pressures that would previously have moved him.

As graduation approached, Louis had amassed nearly a hundred pages of typed manuscript. He made no plans for college.

During the final week of school Louis looked bemusedly on the bright faces of the kids of Silver Spur High, and he wondered what the future held in store for them. When would the cold truth of all he had told them finally shatter the lie they loved so stubbornly? They were so in love with themselves, so in love with the concept of their own well-deserved wellness. How Louis would delight in seeing their faces when it all fell down on them, as he knew it surely must.

Yes, they hear the lie they want to hear, but who can blame the creature for acting according to its nature? A smiling Louis generously allowed the creatures their nature as he walked in their midst, their glowing eyes set upon their Holy City, upon the lie so essential to their comfort and health.

Louis skipped the graduation ceremonies. He made a brief appearance to collect his yearbook, and without looking back he slipped through the repulsive throng as it clamored to puff up pages of gilded memories with generically sentimental notes that fabricated a community, a self-importance, and a worthwhile set of years. When his diploma arrived in the mail some weeks later, he viewed it for several seconds, sighed, shook his head at it a little, then cast it among some papers in a drawer. Perhaps they had at least taught him how to read and write; it hadn't been a total loss.

Leafing through his yearbook, and looking himself up in its index, he found that he appeared on two pages. The first featured an unimpressive photograph of him, weary and hostile, placed alphabetically among photos of the rest of the graduating class. But the other page, he was astonished to discover, identified him as the winner of a "Most likely to" category. Huh! This was something.

Most likely to drive a hearse. Fantastic.

As for Brandy and Haley, he wasn't surprised to find it required bits of space from more than a dozen pages to give the two their due homage. Haley won the sophomore categories of "Best legs" and "Most likely to be a movie star." Outstanding. He felt honored to know her. Brandy's appearances were less flamboyant (debate team, newspaper staff), she being the lower-key member of the axis on which turned a significant part of life at Silver Spur High. For a moment Louis waxed warm and soft about the special partnership of these girls: Haley in point position, working the spotlight and public relations with her style and ease, while Brandy keeps back a few paces to handle a broader surveillance, catching comments, reading body language, making note of possible enemies. By senior year they'll be unstoppable, Louis reckoned, if only they can avoid stealing each other's boyfriends and turning on one another.

Summer proceeded with Brandy and Haley picnicking and sunbathing in a variety of splendidly isolated settings across the Miller estate, while Louis kept unfolding his tale at a pace as strenuous as he could manage. It demanded perseverance and discipline, but Louis wouldn't quite call it labor—for at the end of the day, regardless of the economic value of what he'd produced, the work process itself had been valuable to him. The pouring out of himself into the paper (as otherwise into the stone or wood or soil) in the service of his own angels gave him gladness not measurable in dollars. He found himself able to carry on at length without the immediate presence of the specter, the entity's residence being somewhere near enough to reliably respond should a troubled Louis require.

The shortlist of titles for the book included *A Thief in the Night of American Slumber* and *The Greatest Story Ever Told, Part II*. Louis was rather fond of the latter, but the title decided on was *Jesus Needs a New Earth*.

They gave their testament what they considered to be a sufficient editing, the specter pushing Louis out of several ruts of unprofitable checking and rechecking. It was bliss to witness a clean hard copy glide out from the printer, heightened senses reveling in the dark, sweet-smelling ink on the sheaf of warm papers, with the specter clasping his hands together and glowing in satisfied approval.

Naturally, Louis was keen to take whatever route would ensure the book's speediest and widest publication, but at this critical juncture he discovered his guide to be of disturbingly little service. The man of worldly success waxed oddly stiff when probed about where to send the book, seeming to be on the verge of saying something, then halting as if he himself had need of consulting some higher authority. As Louis awaited, the specter apparently grew defensive, assuring Louis that "I do know a thing or two about publishing." The fumbling and discomfort soon had Louis rubbing his eyes and temples, and even striking his head, at which point the figure blurted out, "I do know what's to be done. I'm leaving for a while." Before Louis had opportunity to object or inquire further, the figure raised a solemn hand and stepped out into the hallway.

Louis understood this to be some sort of test in which he must prove himself capable of advocating for this stack of papers, come what may in scrapes and bruises. In looking on the internet at publishers, he learned they were reluctant to read manuscripts sent directly from the general public, preferring instead to get them from agencies that sifted the uncut jewels out of the constant torrent of word rubbish gushing forth day after day. Passing through an agent and an editor, a manuscript became polished and publishable, which is to say it underwent a forcible conforming to a set of rules that make a book easily consumable.

The most important of these rules seemed to be that the consumer of literature needs narrators who are easily identified and identified with. A narrator must be a character in the story who tells only what comes from her own mind, heart, eyes, and tongue—her own point of view expressed in her own voice, which the reader must be able to readily recognize. Challenging the reader with ambiguous or rapidly shifting voices and points of view is disorienting and disengaging. Expressing something in a voice and point of view that is outside a story character is incomprehensible (though typical for novelists until the psychological realism of Henry James).

Naturally, Louis bristled at the prospect of marring his stack of papers with the overhaul required to comply with these demands. The more he read on the internet about agents, editors, and workshops, the more he pictured an endless series of complications designed to makeover a young author's book and dreams into something far less extravagant, to effectively sterilize anything too offensive to the public's proper outlook. Any self-respecting agent or editor having any desire to be seen as a necessary figure would just have to show a mere lad at least a hundred necessary alterations, never mind the quality of what they were dealing with. They had to keep new literature within a set of conventions they were highly familiar with, thereby keeping a place for themselves as the most capable judges of the current craft. Thus, Monet's paintings, "mere impressions" unfamiliar to the experts, didn't qualify to be exhibited as "proper art."

Mom and Ed and even Brandy congratulated Louis on his stack of papers. They wished him success at finding a publisher, while not seeming to hold their breath too much about it. Oh, they were sure he'd written an interesting story; they said they couldn't wait to read it. Clearly their main sentiment was that Louis had impressed them with his dedication in trying to see this thing through, as they hadn't quite forgotten the times a younger Louis had ridden a spurt of creative enthusiasm only to abort his song, book, or screenplay at the first occurrence of frustration and self-doubt.

Setting aside his unreformed manuscript for the moment, he got to work on his query letter, or single-page summary of his novel, which was required of Louis to get his foot in the door of any agency. The first paragraph of the letter pitched the story as powerfully and concisely as possible: "A good-natured orphan learns the hard way that he can't be good in a bad world, as he fails in business and the military by being a true Christian. He discovers his special mission must be to show that the will for goodness has the power to transform the world, and with his band of disciples he turns a jungle into a garden."

Of the several reputable agencies that received Louis's query letter, two replied with an interest in receiving his entire manuscript. This was enough bobber jiggling to reinforce his optimism. With these sent off (in Monet condition), he passed the days in bittersweet anticipation, frequently doing the specter's exercises around the yard in the sunshine while looking down onto the hubbub of town life spread across the valley below. He also read a good deal of news magazines and played the occasional videogame. Brandy grew more tanned, fit, and blonde. Ed spent time tending his crops and mowing his lawn. Mom visited relatives Back East. Louis checked his email daily, walked down to the metal mailbox many a time, and picked up the phone faster than usual.

The days turned to weeks and the waiting turned to stewing. Were they just now getting around to looking at his manuscript? Perhaps they'd done so already, and others could now read its slime-pasted pages in a dumpster somewhere in New York City.

It was puzzling. If Shakespeare himself came back to write a novel, and he submitted it for publication under the name Skippy Watson, what would the rejection letters say? What gnats they'd obsess about, and what elephants they'd miss entirely!

Louis could just see some girl fresh out of college sitting in her own little office, which she deserved because of the gilded piece of cardboard her Daddy bought with eight installments to Western State University. She scrunched up her pretty face, shook her head and giggled in dismay as she tried to make it through the first ten pages of Louis's manuscript. She was getting bored with it, and would much prefer delving into her celebrity magazine. But no, she had a job to do after all, so she thought back to college, to all she'd learned there in the few dozen hours she'd spent not puking off a balcony. She took out her bright red power pen and explained to the author why this story wasn't working for her.

"This character needs more background info," instructs her generic penmanship. "What's this character's motivation? Why should I care about him?"

Several pages further into the manuscript, the author is informed that it's also possible for a character to have "too much background info," something which "really slows the pace, knocks the momentum from the plot." So, she's got me coming and going, fumed Mr. Koenig. If only I'd written about a bright, attractive, urban, female professional trying to juggle the glamorous demands of the boardroom and the cocktail party and the shoe store and the search for Mr. Right.

Or perhaps his work had the honor of being rejected by a more sophisticated guardian of the status quo.

Louis could see this one even more clearly, more frighteningly. She was wearing the same stylish glasses as the younger had on, but this elder made them seem much less a toy or a stage prop, and no longer a shield but a weapon. His instinct with this female was not to hit, but to run. There she sat securely in a forest of literature and periodical journals that overflowed the bowed shelves on award-decked walls. Nestled comfortably within her lavish watchtower, sipping gourmet coffee, she seemed to inhale the manuscript, merely to whiff it, before moving on to the next in her stack of applications for entrance into the holy order.

Were she asked to explain her rejection, and were she suddenly overtaken by honesty, she might say that she disliked Mr. Koenig's novel because it struck her as merely a diatribe against a world she understood and identified with, a world that had been good to her. But since such a narrowly personal basis for judgment would be most unbecoming of a professional agent and editor and critic, she would certainly prefer to depict her antipathy as rising from the book's purely literary failings.

And therefore, "The author's rendering of the holy city that Joshua and his followers construct displays all the realism of a cartoon. No attention is given to the details of human relations within this millennial commune. Instead, we're just expected to take the author's word for it that the citizens simply tune in to some kind of magic light that makes problems go away, as though the wave of a wand can overrule the entire problem-plagued history of such utopian schemes."

And further, "Despite the author's attempt to build suspense as we await the unleashing of God's wrath upon the planet, this climax can only arrive stillborn after we've been constantly assured that the holy city will be spared. When finally the nukes start flying and the wicked world is cremated, the reader isn't affected by it, as all the characters we could care about are sealed off somehow in cartoon city, carefree and unaffected."

Wrong, wrong, Mr. Koenig boiled. You've got your degrees in literature, lots and lots of gilded cardboard, but aren't you really just a businessperson? What do Joyce and Proust and Kafka really mean to someone whose polished mahogany desk comes from keeping the market well-stocked with hamburgers and hotdogs such as the bright, attractive, urban, female professional trying to juggle the glamorous demands of the boardroom, the cocktail party, the shoe store, and the search for Mr. Right? Though I guess I can't blame you for falling back on an old standby.

Just consider, Madam, that the author renders only a silhouette of life in the holy city so as to convey a sense of its possibilities—a life so fresh and new that it can't be thoroughly described to the reader, indeed *mustn't* be, since the reader is drawn more into a myth that carries room to be filled by the investment of her own imagination. And the reader *is* affected by the fiery cataclysm that overtakes the Earth, for she can feel with the commune dwellers the miracle of being able to write a new era of human experience upon a fully clean slate. I fear that the high learning of my esteemed judge is employed by her low motives.

As long as Louis could call upon the balms of stretching and breathing clear air under warm sunlight, he could allow his poisonous rage to pass from him, and he might half-acknowledge that his bespectacled persecutors were not so different from himself. But should his limbs prove sluggish and the sky collect clouds and haze, his rage was quick to assert its prerogative, leading his thoughts to scenarios in which he and his book fell victim to prejudice and misunderstanding.

The period of suspenseful silence was broken by the arrival of rejection letters. One advised that his story's concept of the Second Coming was basically not Biblically sound, and thus unlikely to appeal to a Christian readership, the main people interested in the genre in which he was writing. The other letter, meanwhile, lamented his story's heavy reliance on Bible references, which hold little interest for a general audience.

One of the letters went on, explaining that a story must be interesting without requiring too much thought, since many readers are not so much intellectual as intellectualist, reading to adopt the appearance of a thinker. Jane and John Reader can bear only so much philosophy, and even less preaching, before they flee to the nearest television. Louis was surprised that they thought he had need of this revelation. Few had a lower estimation of the public than he did, and he'd been sure to make his story sensational, simplified and emotionally satisfying. If this agency found his story too heavy, they could only prefer a bedtime fairytale, which, of course, they'd be certain to criticize as too fluffy for a public of thoughtful readers.

Anything you write will be skewered on one horn or the other, so just sit there and tremble at the perils of moving in any direction, or else fling yourself devil-may-care into any project at all, the stupider the better. Maybe write the untold story of the animals' mutiny on Noah's Ark, since it must've been pretty crowded and smelly in there, and the animals must've resented the drowning of their families.

Taken aback by these scrapes and bruises, Louis wondered whether he should give the manuscript a thorough rereading, if only to confirm to himself that he did indeed have a right to call those who rejected it idiots.

He carefully analyzed how each passage affected him. He tried to put himself into the mindset of an average reader and consider how each passage might affect them. Is that part really so interesting (or boring), or is it just the mood I happen to be in as I read it? Do I like this part because it's good, or just because I'm the one who wrote it? What was I thinking when I wrote that passage? What purpose could I have thought it serves? How is it essential to Joshua's story?

Does this branch grow from the tree, or just dangle lifelessly from it by the flimsiest strip of tape? What branches are yet wanted on the tree, their absence stunting its development, denying the tree its greatest potential? Has my "inspiration" really been so masterful a guide?

Louis began to feel very uneasy, as though he could be sobering out of a pipe dream he'd been enjoying for the better part of a year. He felt the debilitation of doubt again. He thought he'd left that behind him.

But he'd thrown himself into this book so justified, for he'd never felt the muse so strongly. Often the choicest words and phrases had popped into view so fluidly and inevitably that the book seemed to be blooming on its own power. Louis had channeled a raging current from a divine source, and he'd paid for it with headaches and sore eyes. There'd been times when he felt the process to be rather a sort of mining and vomiting—mining the depths of himself and drawing forth the goods in an extended (and taxing) vomiting.

The basic fact of the situation was that Louis needed to start getting some of the things he longed for, and soon. He had no desire to just keep on breathing through the next fifty or sixty years, eaten like a vegetable by those higher up the food chain. He peered into the distance and all he could see was an endless line of bleaker and darker days, the light steadily sucked from him so others could live more brightly.

Perhaps he might try college? Louis had nothing against learning. He had something against striving for a gilded piece of cardboard that mainly serves as proof of your ability to show up somewhere on a regular basis and assimilate the information and perform the tasks considered important by some titled figure.

As for a career, although plenty of people appeared willing enough to prostitute the most productive years of their life away to the highest bidder in exchange for the toys and trappings so revered among the great herd, to Louis this seemed an unfathomable transaction.

It would all, quite simply, not be worth the trouble. Louis would rather take the easy way out with some form of Plan B. Most would call this cowardly. The term he preferred was "sensible." If most weren't capable of understanding his choice, the price was ultimately theirs to pay. For if the past is any guide, life and the future are poor investments.

At the very least, he had tried. By writing his book he'd given life and the world a chance, and he was beginning to feel that such a small crown of laurels could be enough for him to rest on.

Left to his own devices in this crisis of faith, Louis might well have thrown in the towel; but the specter was still in his corner. He reappeared one rainy afternoon to a Louis who had almost fully reverted to his old skepticism as he struggled to repair what had come to seem a ridiculously flawed manuscript. With refreshing force and authority, the presence rebuked Louis for his loss of belief. Was it not obvious that Louis and this book were meant for each other, each being the other's clearest avenue to fulfillment? The book gave Louis a stake in life, a hill claimed and held in self-defense against life's predators and blowhards aplenty, who coax and carry off the insecure prey. Louis would do well to realize that the mainstream gatekeepers' rejection of the book was nothing too extraordinary, and certainly well short of disastrous, for a book that was never intended to appeal much to the establishment and its audiences. In fact, Louis should verily rejoice that worldly power had manifested an interest in suppressing the book. No finer clue was needed that the book hit the mark.

Quaffing a celebratory Pepsi on ice, Louis was encouraged to keep steady and optimistic in his search for interest in supporting the book. He recovered a feeling of destiny, a sense that fate had decreed a proper instrument for Louis and the book to reach their audience.

Chapter 11
When in America, Do as the Romans Did

Ed had been watching Louis struggle and figured he should step in.

"Say listen, Louis, ah, I don't mean to interfere or anything, but … my firm, the Institute, does have some dealings in publishing. Now this is not to say that you can't get your book published on your own, you know … I'm really sure you've done a great job with it. What I'm saying is that, if you want, I could give your manuscript to a few of these places we do business with."

That was fine with Louis. He gave Ed three copies, with gratitude.

And that's how *Jesus Needs a New Earth* became a book. One hundred and sixty-seven pages of manuscript went to the press pristine, wholly bypassing the customary stage of disfigurement at the hands of some lordly editor. Merely a signature and a handshake were required of Mr. Koenig— and the acceptance of a check for twenty-five thousand dollars. Five thousand copies were printed.

It was magical: which is to say, reality somehow rolled out a red carpet where it usually rolled out a train of obstacles. Strangely absent were the delays and the floundering he had come to expect in pursuit of anything. Louis had thought he was supposed to be learning how to carry things forward on his own, but now springing into full view for him was what seemed to be his true lesson, one he had become willing to accept: the way forward lay in partnering with power, even becoming its dependent. For some reason reality was on very good terms with Ed's people.

A slice of the public actually got something out of the Joshua story. Some were so overcome by it that they simply had to meet this Louis Koenig and tell him how Joshua and the holy city scratched their itch. To welcome such visitation the address of the Miller estate had been printed on the back cover, along with a message: *Camp Earth Enlightenment Center* provides a place to learn and live with all things necessary for knowledge and life. Seminars and study groups hosted by Brother Koenig personally. Meals served. Transportation provided. Bring a friend for a free signed copy of this Newest Testament. All welcome. God speed you, for time is short.

People trickled into the Miller estate, three or four in a week, and were treated to a tour of the lovely premises. Brother Koenig had remarkably little trouble answering their questions. He fully accepted the Joshua story as his Golden Ticket, and instincts lit up all through him to protect and advance it. A sense of smell, as it were, rapidly developed to enable him to sniff out his visitors for what it was they hoped to hear him say:

"Well, Karen, during much of the writing I was truly caught up in a vision. The past and future were opened before my mind's eye, and I just wrote what I saw.

"Actually, I agree with you: I do sound like all those others when I say, 'The end is near.' The world is tired, and plenty of people feel something's coming. But listen, Bernie, they can't do much about it, 'cause they don't know the signs they should be looking for, and they don't know how to prepare for what's coming. It's not enough just to feel 'The end is near.' You've gotta' get ready for it and take part in the glorious opportunities opened up by it. We all know the house is gunna' burn down, right? Only here we also know where the open window is, we know how to get to that window, and we know what awaits those who escape through it.

"Oh, I'm simply your brother following Christ; why he's chosen me to preach of the manner of his return and help call his believers to watchfulness and preparation—well, your guess is as good as mine. I'm no different from you.

"The chosen, they themselves know who they are. They hear a voice. And it's been getting louder. Hasn't it? Rejected by the world, because they're not of the world. The world accepts its own, while the Lord chooses what the world has rejected, and these become the foundation stones of his kingdom that comes to Earth. The time has arrived for those who hear the voice, who hear the world's rejection and the Lord's invitation. Accept it. Act on it.

"Who is Joshua? Where is he now? I'm convinced he's near. I can't wait to see him standing among us. But he's the one in charge, and we'll see him when he's ready. He'll see us when we're ready. Of course, for a time he's been finding himself. And I admit, just like you, I look for him everywhere, really, in the papers, on TV, and in everyone I meet. My sense is that he'll first become known to his special followers, to the very watchful. We'll see him, maybe right here, but it won't be long now.

"Look, that's all right, Leah, we've all got our weaknesses. Everyone here is struggling with something, but we're all one big family, so we help each other out.

"No problem at all, brother, you could come here dressed in a potato sack, it just tells me your heart isn't set on appearances. But if your *soul* is worn and ragged, well that's important, it's something worth setting your heart on. I mean, a man whose clothing is his major lack is better off than most. You're quite welcome to have what you need from our surplus clothing over here."

Ed arranged for the Institute to distribute copies of the book to homeless shelters, jails and prisons, health clinics, welfare offices, agencies serving veterans and the unemployed, libraries, colleges, even a few churches. Ads were placed in periodicals. When enough folks had become interested, Brother Koenig started giving a seminar and leading a study group every Tuesday and Friday evening. These were haphazard, improvised affairs at first. Brother Koenig would set up two dozen chairs in the living room or out in the yard. Coffee and cakes and copies of the book would be passed around. A selection from the book would be read aloud by Brother Koenig. He'd offer some commentary about how it related to the Bible, to history or the news. He'd receive any questions and comments from the others, address these, then call upon some to select passages especially meaningful to them which they would read aloud before the group.

No such evening was ever complete without a general airing of grievances against the God that failed, the America that had let these people down. Brother Koenig endeared himself to his visitors by supporting their vaguely articulated indictments with concrete data. They sat in awe of his command of history and international relations, a reverent hush overspreading them as his pace quickened, his volume increased, his arms swung, and his forefinger wagged. Brother Koenig could channel a frightful amount of energy in one of his rants, provided nobody interrupted him to challenge the accuracy of his statements.

Such a challenger, a young man roughly the same age and size as Brother Koenig himself, began showing up at the meetings, and it quickly became apparent that he was intent on halting the spiritual growth of the other participants.

One evening Brother Koenig was itemizing the evils of the British Empire, which, like the American Empire that would succeed it, was widely promoted as benevolent despite certain facts. The facts on Britain included funding the Royal Navy by forcing the Chinese at gunpoint to purchase British opium from India, fueling the Royal Navy by exploiting Iran as Britain's own personal oil well, and enriching British manufacturers by turning India, China, Egypt, Turkey, and Iran into Britain's own personal market, forcing these nations at gunpoint to deny their native industries the protections found necessary in the development of every industrial power. Brother Koenig explained that international corporations continue to rely on force, free-trade agreements, and IMF and World Bank loan conditions, to deprive developing nations of the power to protect indigenous companies, workers, resources and ecosystems.

"But didn't the Royal Navy clear the pirates out of the world's shipping lanes?" the challenger piped up. "Didn't the British build railroads and telegraph lines through the wilderness, connecting villages in need to villages with extra? What about the roads the Persians built across the lands they subdued, and the common language that Alexander provided his realm, and the roads and harbors and aqueducts the Romans built throughout their empire? Isn't it true that lots of trade and peace occurred in areas subject to imperial power?" The challenger very genially asked the group if they remembered the scene in Monty Python's *The Life of Brian* where the Jewish rebels angrily ask "What have the Romans ever done for us?" One rebel then mentions the roads, and another the aqueduct, and another the safety of the streets at night, and so on until they all agree that Judea was actually a lousy place until the Romans showed up.

The group sat aghast, awaiting a rebuttal from Brother Koenig, which, upon recovering himself, he proved able to deliver, pointing out that decent infrastructure served the occupying military as much as the occupied populace, while the peace provided was peace on the emperor's terms. For instance, the Jews were allowed to worship at their temple, but not without pollution from imperial idolatry, such as men exercising nude in the Greco-Roman way. It must have been hollow peace indeed, since the empires were constantly having to suppress revolt, crucifying hundreds of thousands, including a certain King of the Jews.

Another evening found Brother Koenig lecturing on the dangers of capitalist globalization, especially its crippling of the American worker by placing him in competition with easily exploitable developing-world labor. The freedom of private investment capital to cross all borders and buy up whatever it wants, including public property like water, and be protected against laws that injure profits, like environmental and labor regulations, has the effect of making the rich vastly richer and more powerful. We've got a worldwide superclass: One percent of the world's population with almost as much net worth as everyone else put together. God must have created the world for one percent of his children. We never stop hearing that the capitalist is the only goose that can lay the golden egg, and therefore we must cater to him in every possible way.

The group was enjoying a good bask in the validity of Brother Koenig's points until the challenger stated, loud and clear as a bell, "Capitalist investment does increase the capitalist's share of the world economic pie. *It also enlarges the whole pie.* Labor gets a decreased share of a bigger pie, but that share actually amounts to *more* pie than labor was getting before the capitalist investment. Wealth inequality does increase, and that can lead to dangers, but we mustn't forget that all parties gain wealth from the investment, including many millions of former peasants in China, India, Indonesia, and Brazil, who've been lifted out of poverty into a middle class that has money to spare even after the bills are paid. These people who leave the subsistence farm for the productive capitalist factory are the people who've been getting the most *meaningful* gains in wealth."

A deflated Brother Koenig stuttered somewhat in his reply, conceding that maybe in some places the peasants do have the miraculous opportunity of slaving in a noisy, filthy death-trap of a factory for three crumbs a day instead of the two crumbs they'd been getting on the farm. The capitalist places his frying pan in the midst of the flames of poverty, and thinks himself an angel for giving the peasant the opportunity to jump from the flames to the pan. And the capitalist has made sure he is the only way out of the flames, having destroyed through his media and military all the alternative instruments for wealth creation, any other geese that might lay the golden egg. The assembly-line humanoid gets his three crumbs for letting Western companies integrate him and his country into the global pyramid. It's an offer you can't refuse when you're just above starving and every crumb matters.

Opposition to Brother Koenig threw him off his rhythm and sowed doubt and confusion in the faithful. He hated being pulled down from a state of fluid inspiration where everything manifested as simple and certain. Of course, Brother Koenig knew very well from long years as Louis that simplicity and certainty were frequently illusions. There usually existed more than one defensible way to look at any issue of importance, making truth a dull, gray thing, lifeless and uninspiring, unable to push or pull the intellectually honest in any direction. What was needed for an active life, and for leading others to action, was the simple certainty of black and white. The specter instructed him that an effective leader doesn't admit the existence of gray. He doesn't admit he could be even partially wrong. He doesn't admit his opponent could be even partially right. He doesn't waver from being always light and his opponent always darkness.

He doesn't make a statement that's limited in any way. Brother Koenig failed to meet this standard, his challenger frequently maneuvering him into gray areas full of complications. The fellow was relentless in sapping the vitality from Brother Koenig's message and proved impervious to the hard stares and cold shoulders of the others, who craved sermons as black and white as Brother Koenig could serve. When Brother Koenig began fearing confrontations with his equal and opposite force, to the point he suffered a series of nightmares on the subject, he resolved to act decisively. He privately took the guy aside after a study group one night, and in a quite serious tone Brother Koenig threatened that harm might very well find the unwanted intruder if he ever showed up at the Enlightenment Center again. The guy calmly responded that he was simply providing balance to the discussions so those attending could get a fuller picture of the truth. Brother Koenig replied that any picture these people would get was going to come from himself. He had accepted this responsibility, and if he led the people astray then that was his to answer for. The guy was silent for a moment, no doubt contemplating his options for further resistance to Brother Koenig's authority. Hands began to appear in the moonlight, several sets of large hands slowly approaching the scene. The guy departed down the long driveway.

In the wake of this purge Brother Koenig restructured his interaction with the people so that similar challengers had less opportunity. He had a small stage built for himself on a prominent heap of earth a short distance from the house, something to elevate him and set him apart from the people while he taught them. This height and distance served to discourage the impulse to question Brother Koenig as one would a common person, and it reinforced hopes that this was in fact a man apart, someone who didn't share in regular human failings.

Brother Koenig began wearing long and smooth pullover robes he purchased online, yellow, green, and blue. When not attending to visitors he'd be studying for his next sermon or practicing guitar so he could provide his own musical accompaniment. He'd bring his amplifier on stage and punctuate his words with electric power:

"And Joshua's people were filled with God's grace, with his energy and his peace, given the fullest measure they could hold. And thus, they were spirited through the labors of the day—

Chord: A Major (Full distortion)
Chord: D Major (Clean)

—yeah, all right. Thy kingdom come.

"If the son of God returns—not from a cloud, but up from the mean streets of the empire …

"Could he possibly fail to recognize establishment hypocrisy now, though he saw it so clearly in Palestine a few thousand years ago? Back then he spoke against the wealthy and powerful who the world had made comfortable and satisfied, who had little use for a kingdom of God on Earth. He spoke against the hypocrites, the trumpeters of their own godliness, the whitewashed tombs full of skeletons. And now in our modern world, just who and what would be the likely target of our Lord's righteous anger?

"A prophet saw a great eagle rise from the north and spread its wings, casting a shadow over all the Earth, carrying war in one foot and some kind of peace in the other. And many called it good, but woe unto those who call evil good and good evil, who put darkness for light and bitter for sweet.

"So nice and easy to call it good if you're nestled in its bosom, oblivious in the eye of the hurricane, busy with mutual funds and SUVs, waving the stars and stripes at parades, going to church on Sundays with God on your side, with a Jesus who's tall, white, blue-eyed, CEO of his own successful business, proud owner of a Ford truck. How comfortable to have your own personal Jesus this way. It would be tough to have the real Jesus walk among you and say disturbing things that cause you to nail him up one way or another in half the time it took the Romans and the priests of Jerusalem to do it.

"But what would Jesus have against America? Doesn't the red, white, and blue mean justice, freedom, and equality, everything that Jesus wanted?

"In 1953 the United States helped the British overthrow the democratically elected government of Iran. In 1954 the U.S. overthrew the democratically elected government of Guatemala. In 1973 the U.S. overthrew the democratically elected government of Chile. The CIA, the Pentagon, and the State Department employed propaganda and disinformation, economic boycott and sabotage, mercenary armies and aerial bombardment, bribery of officers, politicians, and crowds, bribery of unions to go on strike and of government workers to make mistakes, the training and equipping of military and police forces, funding of political parties, a whole quiver of media assets to print and broadcast CIA-approved and even CIA-fabricated material. In the words of CIA Director Colby, Chile was a prototype or 'lab experiment' to test how American money could be applied to discredit and bring down a government.

"What did these overthrown legitimate governments have in common? They implemented popular policies that threatened the interests of American corporations. Iran took control of its oil away from the British corporation later called British Petroleum, which through four decades had pumped Iranian oil while keeping nearly ninety percent of the proceeds. It had been agreed during World War II by President Roosevelt and British Ambassador Halifax that Iranian oil would be pumped by the British, Saudi oil by America, and Iraqi and Kuwaiti oil by both Britain and

America. Thus, American Standard Oil firms were anxious to see that the Iranian seizure of corporate oilfields was nipped in the bud before it could spread to nearby countries by force of good example. Guatemala took control of some uncultivated land owned by the United Fruit Company and gave it to peasants. United Fruit owned the vast majority of land suitable for banana cultivation and kept ninety-five percent of it uncultivated to keep up the price of bananas. Chile removed long-standing corporate control from lucrative economic sectors like copper mining. Firms in Chile such as Chase Manhattan Bank, ITT, and Pepsi ran to the White House and got President Nixon to order the economy sabotaged and the government overthrown. He explained that Chile's defiant path could not be allowed to project an image of being successful or safe. The CIA's own assessment was that Marxist Chile didn't threaten United States security, it threatened that Marxism might be made to appear attractive.

"The eagle doesn't like it when people try to go their own way with their valuable resources. If they're successful then people everywhere will want to try the same thing, the domino effect, leading to a world where the most sacred freedom is extinguished—the freedom to own and rule as gods. For this freedom to be preserved, people must be made terrified of rising up against the gods. Offenders must be turned into useful demonstrations.

"The CIA, Pentagon, and State Department installed and supported new governments in Iran, Guatemala, and Chile. What did these regimes have in common? They were fascist—that is, controlled by generals and policemen on behalf of capitalist oligarchy. They bought lots of weapons from American firms, put lots of money in American banks, let American banks and oil companies come over and make money without democratic interference. These regimes watched carefully for any signs that their people might again be straying down the devilish path that leads to ending the sacred freedom of the gods. A red flag would be someone with a Bible out in the villages teaching that the primary concern must be to address the needs of the poor and the sick directly, in opposition to the primary concern of enabling the wealthy to make as much money as possible, with something trickling down to the poor if they assist. Someone with a Bible teaching that Yahweh's and Christ's primary concern is not the thriving of giants, but the liberation of the lowly— well, the teacher would be seized in the dark of night by a group of men armed with American weapons and training, who deliver the captive to his crucifixion. And likely some of his disciples would be rounded up to have their toes cut off in front of their families and neighbors. Such wonder-working terror, courtesy of the God-blessed USA. Really makes you proud to be an American when your taxes go to death squads that kill Christ in the name of Christ, when your government makes you complicit in nailing entire nations to a cross, and all to preserve the dominant position of our chief priests, our aristocracy of money.

"The list goes on. You've got the U.S. government overthrowing democratically elected governments in Congo '60, Ecuador '61, Dominican Republic '63, Brazil '64, British Guyana '64, Bolivia '64, Ghana '66, Greece '67, Jamaica '80, Fiji '87, Nicaragua '90, Bulgaria '90, Haiti '91, Albania '91. And if we review the history of the U.S. government preventing democracy from coming to power at all in a nation for many decades, the list of victims is simply too long to recite, simply too astonishing. For the first three decades of the twentieth century the U.S. Marine Corps occupied Central America and the Caribbean as the plantation police for U.S. corporations, propping up local noble families and National Guards to collaborate. This was openly referred to as a racket by the Marines' own highly decorated General S. D. Butler, who declined to participate in a plan by a group of reputable U.S. corporations that he lead a force to overthrow democratically elected President Franklin Roosevelt. All throughout the developing world the U.S. has been funding, arming, training, and protecting police states, crushing movements of the poor and oppressed, in virtually every country in Latin America, the Middle East, and South Asia at one time or other since the Second World War, and many cases before. Those who don't see this clear pattern prefer not to see it. Pick a country at random and do some research on it. Did somebody say Indonesia? Vietnam? Philippines? El Salvador? Argentina? Chad? Egypt? Jordan?

"You know, the Roman legions marched with the eagle on their banners, and it's very fitting that America does this as well.

"Around the time of Christ, Spartacus and his band of slaves revolted, as did Jesus's own nation and many others under Roman rule, only to meet the worst fate Rome could devise. And now Spartacus returns to free the slaves again. There he is, a prime minister or president leading his little nation out of bondage. What fate awaits Spartacus in our own age?

"Look in the Bible, in *Revelation*. The Dragon crouches as he waits to devour the heavenly woman's child the moment it's born. How many times since World War II has some leader tried to deliver his poor country into independence, only to despair as the child is strangled in its crib? There have been so many promising children: Mossadegh's Iran, Arbenz's Guatemala, Lumumba's Congo, Allende's Chile, Aristide's Haiti. So many untimely, unnatural deaths. As it was with the Romans, so it remains: no revolt within the empire shall be allowed to live. If there is ever to be one that succeeds, if the child is ever to live, to have a place on this Earth, God must take special measures.

"It must be acknowledged, in all fairness, that the eagle hasn't been the only beast in the forest. The eagle of America inherited much of its domain from the lion of Britain, its tired paws blood-caked from centuries of securing markets and resources for some of the world's first mega-corporations. And of course, there's been a certain bear prowling its neck of the woods. If I have mentioned the eagle's infamous murders in Iran '53, Guatemala '54, and Chile '73, I should also mention the bear's notorious murders in Hungary '56, Czechoslovakia '68, and Poland '81.

"We read in the gospels how Satan came to tempt Jesus, offering to give him rule over all earthly kingdoms. Isn't it interesting that Satan could give this? Is there something basically satanic in the power of earthly kingdoms, something arrogant and abusive in concentrated power wherever it exists on Earth, even in the National Security Council or the corporate boardroom? Why is it so difficult for the so-called Christians of this country to be suspicious of an American power complex that's the mightiest entity the world has ever seen? When did proud loyalty to colossal earthly power become something Christian and righteous? When did righteousness become refusal to apologize for anything done by our country's earthly power, refusal to recognize the board stuck in our own eye while we eagerly hack away at the splinter we see in the eye of neighbor after neighbor?

"Brothers and sisters, a highly renowned scholar of the Roman world named Toynbee could see by the Kennedy years that America had become just what Rome had been, the leader of a worldwide anti-revolutionary movement in defense of vested interests, consistently supporting the rich against the poor in all places under her power. Rome helped the Sadducees control the Jewish temple and kill irritating preachers of new kingdoms. America helps the Saudis control a quarter of the world's oil supply and kill those who preach that the oil should be controlled democratically to finance economic development for all Arabs. It's a system of mutually-supporting oligarchies: military and economic interests from the imperial center partnering with noblemen and police in the provinces to stabilize conditions favorable to themselves at the expense of the mass of people who are allowed no real power to alter conditions. The oligarchs of Rome portrayed the maintenance of the empire as an ever-vigilant war on barbarism, certainly not a war on independence and reform. This cover story was easily pitched to a Roman populace that was very patriotic, culturally rather unsophisticated, and preoccupied with materialism, entertainment, and celebrity, if any of this sounds familiar. The citizen was glad to believe that the empire was about promoting civilization, which justified his bread from Egypt, his gladiators from Gaul, his circus animals from Sudan, his gold, silver, and slaves from Spain. So were the publican, banker, and contractor justified in extracting taxes, interest, and natural resources from the provinces. The soldier was justified in burning villages by the hundreds in counter-insurgency campaigns against terrorist extremists like the Jewish zealots, and smashing the revolts of the lower orders exploited by the local aristocrats who sold their nation out to Rome.

"The Empire is fundamentally about war on Not Empire. The task for the oligarch is to enlist mass opposition to Not Empire, and this he does by trumpeting something scary about it—not what actually scares *him* about it, mind you, but something that everyone can be afraid of, like barbarism, or totalitarianism, or drugs, or terror. No lie is shameful if it furthers the cause, and no amount of blood is too much. Like Stalin said, 'One death is a tragedy, a million is a statistic.' Or as Cain put it, 'Why should I care?' See, the oligarch believes that God is obviously dead, that he can get away with anything, that he's entitled to do whatever his exceptional power allows, and in sum, that he's one of the real gods of this world. He lives in a kind of moral twilight zone beyond good and evil, a place difficult for you and I to imagine.

"Amen."

Once Brother Koenig got going like this he simply couldn't tolerate chatter or bathroom breaks or distracting movements of any kind. These requirements of his fell most heavily upon the few children at the revivals, towed along by parents who were trying to revive what they weren't allowing the children to have in the first place.

On one occasion a small girl started crying because she found Brother Koenig to be "loud and awful." He stopped his sermon and ordered her mother to "silence her," to "take her behind some trees and spank her silent." Fortunately, the girl soon ceased crying with a few kind words from her brother (the biological kind), who explained that the man on the stage was an actor just playing a role, like a clown at the circus. See, he said, the guy's even dressed like a clown.

Next sermon Brother Koenig was all smiles and candy to the children, getting down on all fours to roughhouse with them, capering around with them on the swings and teeter-totter in the sandbox.

Chapter 12
Wise General Fights from Position of Strength

Brother Koenig's audience swelled modestly into a range of overlapping types.

There were black folks, and up in these parts this was something of a novelty.

There were hippies, young and old, peculiarly infatuated with things grand, and perhaps inclined to discover too much grand in things commonplace.

There were veterans of U.S. war in Southeast Asia or the Middle East. Some had ailments they attributed to these toxic battlefields. They frequently discussed their personal research into the herbicide dumped by the U.S. Air Force across South Vietnam, poisoning the life in that jungle, withering it right away or giving it cancer and hideous deformities over time. Also discussed were the radioactive munitions used by the U.S. in the Gulf War alongside the bombing of chemical weapons facilities and nuclear reactors, sowing the sand with organ failure and genetic mutation. The veterans lamented the utter devastation they'd seen heaped upon civilians and all their basic infrastructure of water, power, and sewer, with bombers coercing a population toward some political objective in a process that's not terrorism if done by jet. Some told of startlingly naked, outright atrocities they hoped would someday enter the light of public scrutiny.

There were college students, frequently in their sixth or seventh year of working on a bachelor's degree in history or literature or film, interesting people who lacked the childish materialism and tunnel-narrow focus required for success in corporate employment.

Most numerous were casualties of U.S. war on disreputable drugs. In and out and in and out of correctional, rehab, and mental health institutions, these were persons whose drug use, delusions, and violence stood outside the range prescribed for them by doctor, pastor, and general, making them unpersons in the eyes of respectable society. Several were drifters who appeared to be marching to the mysterious beat of a drum heard only by themselves. It wasn't always clear if these individuals actually understood what Brother Koenig and the others were talking about (maybe they understood only too well), but they were fellowshipped nonetheless. They were certainly well enough connected to reality to help themselves to the food given out after Brother Koenig was finished enlightening everyone from his stage.

It came to be that a dozen or more of the regular visitors wouldn't leave the Enlightenment Center much at all, camping out in various parts of the property with tents and sleeping bags they had brought with them or got from Brother Koenig. He instructed that camping must be done out of sight of the perimeter fence, along which the neighbors liked to power-walk in designer exercise outfits while keeping a sharp eye out for anything that might contaminate or smudge a community of sparkling people and properties. Brother Koenig approached Ed with a bold proposition: that the storage barn Ed had personally built during the Carter administration should be emptied of its motorized toys and converted into a facility for those in need of a toilet, a shower, a shave, or a bed. Brother Koenig added that he would be willing to contribute his own funds to the worthy project. Ed smiled at this, gave a few words to the Institute, and the renovation was fast accomplished. The barn became a place to chew the fat, and a robed Brother Koenig was known to appear there bearing a case of beer with a reminder to the regulars that right-of-way at the barn must be accorded to new visitors. He might also mention that campsites free of scattered garbage were a very welcome sight, and that barn toilets must always be regarded as superior to a shady set of bushes.

Those who had become fixtures at the Enlightenment Center did require some tending. Brother Koenig, Ed, and personnel from the Institute were kept on their toes monitoring the sprawling grounds of the Miller estate, seeing to it that campfires stayed in their pits, that quarrels didn't escalate into blows, that the ill were attended to, that meals were served on time, that vans were dispatched for those in need of transport. This caretaking could tax Brother Koenig's pleasant demeanor, since he'd much rather spend his time in other ways, such as designing the Enlightenment Center's website. Its homepage featured a large golden sun rising up from behind a range of jagged blue mountains, slowly illuminating a set of foreground icons, one of which linked to the full text of his book in black characters on pastel green background, another of which linked to his blog, a running commentary on all things of interest to the Joshua enthusiast. Brother Koenig did accept the caretaking as a necessary part of his calling, however, and felt it all completely worthwhile when he overheard his guests using the barn phone to invite friends to "Come over and hear this dude play electric guitar while he tells stories about Jesus. But it's Jesus arguing with bankers and politicians. There's food and beer."

Come over they did, and quite a picture they made shuffling in and out of the Miller estate, deep within the uppermost echelon of white suburbia. Ed was notified by the police when neighbors called to report being disturbed by the goings on, the typical complaint moving in the vein of, "Officer, what do you mean they have a right to be there? A religion? What kind? *Christians?* Now that just can't be true. You should *see* these people! They all look like criminals, just a bunch of very trashy people. I'm sorry but there's no other way to put it. A lot of them look like devil worshipers. I'm very active in the church, and I know Christians when I see them. Listen, aren't they breaking some sort of zoning regulation? Don't they need some kind of permit? You know, there are young girls in this neighborhood, okay?" To which the officer had always to deliver a standard reply, "No need to worry. It's taken care of. All forms have been filed properly, all hearings have been attended, all instructions of county and state officials have properly been acted on. The Camp Earth Enlightenment Center has the law on its side. Please report any further concerns. Good day, Ma'am." More than one caller claimed to have friends in high places, places to which the caller would surely resort, places far higher than that occupied by the mere officer, who had to restrain his amusement at these self-styled pillars of Silver Spur, allowing them their deluded self-importance and their cluelessness as to the actual height of the places occupied by friends of the Enlightenment Center.

As Brandy's living space was more and more diminished by her stepbrother's admirers, she objected to her father, only to be told that "Louis has earned the right to his little fan club here, and it's something the firm has taken an interest in." Brandy would have to be patient with them. These people were here to improve themselves, and she should remind herself of this if it became difficult to side-step them and dodge their leering eyes. But her reputation had suffered, she protested. None of her friends came over anymore. She tired of the constant questions at school about what was really going on up there at her place, about who her stepbrother really thought he was. The mocking was wearing her down. This wasn't how she'd pictured her final years at Silver Spur High. She couldn't wait to go on to college, out of state preferably, where she could make a fresh start.

Well, Ed was sorry about all that, he said, but he'd always told her that the charity work he was involved with might someday demand certain sacrifices. Yes, Brandy replied, but she'd never thought the sacrifices would all have to be on her end. Nobody else, least of all Louis, really seemed to be suffering under the new arrangements. She only hoped this whole thing didn't somehow blow up in their faces.

So she rarely spoke to her father anymore, unless it was to get something from him. She almost never spoke to Louis, and certainly never addressed him as Brother Koenig. "A prophet is never esteemed in his own village," he figured. Instead, she reserved a particular look for him which he got on the few occasions she encountered him, the sour face a lady gives a child upon catching him playing with matches. Louis could feel an impulse to take Brandy aside and tell her she was right to see through him, but Brother Koenig knew his calling didn't permit this.

As Brandy's world was cooling, Brother Koenig's was warming nicely. His special position offered him special advantages in the pursuit of life's goodies, and he began selecting from his congregation those upon whom these advantages were best applied.

Alicia was seventeen, a taller girl with a Mediterranean face. Her limbs were slender, graceful, and strong, her chest and hips just large enough to identify her as female. She had come to the Enlightenment Center a few times with an older gentleman in a wheelchair, her uncle, crippled in Vietnam, Brother Koenig quickly learned. This man was very much the cliché of the damaged, embittered vet as seen in the movies. That such people actually existed, and in numbers, seemed to amaze the neighbors, who appeared greatly offended when a missing limb or shaken brain disturbed their pleasant view with undeniable evidence that their wars have a cost.

Less excited than her uncle by the topics that so animated the guests of Brother Koenig, Alicia was frequently resorting to her phone when not wheeling and fetching as Uncle required. Brother Koenig first broke the ice with her by helping to maneuver Uncle across a bit of thick lawn as the fellow voiced his approval of parts of the book where "The Army was just like that—that's the Army I knew" and "Jesus is just like that—that's the Jesus I know."

One Friday evening in summer, Brother Koenig came down from his stage after an hour-long musical sermon. He joined his people at the freshly filled buffet tables, dishing himself up a generous portion of gumbo and pouring himself a tall glass of beer. He then sat on the edge of his stage, dining and chatting. Gradually the sky darkened and visitors departed. Brother Koenig noticed that Uncle was being wheeled away into the woods by a few of the guys who had tents staked there. In a flash, Brother Koenig was advancing upon Alicia, brandishing two bottles of beer and offering a "backstage pass" to the Enlightenment Center's "VIP sites." She consented, her grin ripening her glowing features.

Brother Koenig handed her a beer and led her into the dusky forest with a question about where she was in life. She said she recently dropped out of high school. He said he could hardly condemn a decision that he himself had very nearly made. Locking eyes with him as she sipped her beer, she said she was working at a restaurant down in the valley. He turned on a lantern and they continued walking. Alicia commented on the spaciousness of the estate, and Brother Koenig mentioned the Spanish silver that legend held to be buried in the area. She inquired, apparently jokingly, whether he'd ever stumbled across any of it, and he replied, apparently seriously, that he had indeed recently come upon a great store of treasure, one every bit as valuable as all the silver lying beneath the grounds of the estate. Alicia then delighted Brother Koenig by finding some worth in silently considering his statement's possible meanings.

"You're good," she concluded.

He then set down the lantern, stepped forward with an air of reverence and ceremony, and asked if he could love her. Alicia choked up some beer, trying to hold back her laughter, and Brother Koenig giggled some himself to put her at ease, but promptly repeated his grave request, saying straightforwardly that he truly desired her, he was overflowing with love for her and had to know if she would let him love her.

"Oohh … I see," said Alicia, in dissonant tones of perplexed amusement. She looked on Brother Koenig, and he knew she must be sizing him up: him, the Enlightenment Center, and everything he might have to offer.

"I've got things to share, things to show you," he said.

"But what about Uncle?" she said.

"Just leave him to me," said Brother Koenig. "He can sleep here with his buddies. We can give him a tent of his own if he likes."

She announced her verdict by putting her hands on Brother Koenig and kissing him for a good while.

A deer path led to a tent that was lit inside with torches. Here Alicia helped herself to the beer in a cooler that was buried under a stack of coats and blankets. Meanwhile, Brother Koenig went to inform Uncle of the situation.

Uncle George was exchanging stories with other veterans by campfire. Brother Koenig hailed the group merrily and asked if he might have a brief word with George, while the others should feel free to "commandeer a few" from the barn refrigerator. The fellows dispersed agreeably enough, leaving their friend to Brother Koenig, who commenced to testify that George was obviously well liked here and fit right in just as Brother Koenig suspected he

would, since his spirit was as great as any Brother Koenig
had yet come across. George's niece was special too, Brother
Koenig affirmed. "Actually, I've just been talking with her,"
he said, "and now I need to tell you, George, how much love
I have for her. She wants to sleep here tonight, with me, and
she wants you to be okay with it, and I do too."

Before George could marshal himself to respond,
Brother Koenig declared the man and his niece to be "shining
stars," and testified with a clenched fist that they were in on
the ground floor of something that was about to "take off and
show forth signs and wonders." Brother Koenig explained
that it was really an honorable love which he desired to share
with Alicia, even if the world could view it as somehow
wrong. Perhaps George himself had misgivings about it, and
this was all right with Brother Koenig, for he understood how
George could feel that way. It might be difficult at first for
George to recognize the beauty and uprightness of Brother
Koenig's union with Alicia, since "the world has taught us to
be unable to recognize true love and its proper expression,"
counseled Brother Koenig. "The world's *Evil Mind-Control*
is what we are trying to purge from ourselves here at the
camp."

The folks at the Enlightenment Center accepted the
concept of Evil Mind-Control before they ever knew about
Brother Koenig and his book. Everyone agreed that there was
a force exerting a massive influence upon them against their
interests. Many called it simply "the world," while others
called it "Satan," or "human nature." To several it was "the
CIA." The college kids in the congregation called it "false
consciousness" and "dominant discourse" and "the narrative
from power." It was widely associated with American
corporate and political culture, the emotionally manipulative
marketing and public-relations apparatus that sells $3000
watches, $30,000 weddings, and $300,000,000,000 wars.

Only Brother Koenig recognized what a great blessing was this Evil Mind-Control. For here was an enemy to be united against, a slogan to anchor and standardize his people's worldview, and above all a stigma, a label with a definition sufficiently vague to allow Brother Koenig a broad range of plausibility in affixing it to just about anything that got in his way.

Uncle George was thus left to a night of reflection, his outlook on "love" apparently in need of thorough remodeling.

An empty bottle of beer played with firelight as it stood on a table beside Alicia, who reclined in a chair facing the door of the tent, her legs crossed beneath an open copy of Brother Koenig's book. Her lover now swung open the door flap.

"Everything went okay?" she asked.

"Fine," he replied. "Uncle George is fine with sleeping here tonight, and he's fine with … you and I being together."

Alicia asked for another beer, but Brother Koenig asked if he could interest her in some wine, and she happily accepted. He strode to a corner of the tent where there sat a large wooden thing that looked very much like a pirate's treasure chest. Brother Koenig produced a key from under his robe and opened the shimmering chest, drawing from it a handsome bottle of red wine, a corkscrew, and two glasses.

"Mmmm," sounded Alicia with flickering eyes. "You got any other treasures in there?"

"Come and see," said Brother Koenig.

Alicia abandoned his book for his magic box. She kneeled before it, pupils bulging as she beheld the cornucopia at her fingertips.

"I myself only rarely partake," observed Brother Koenig. "This here, for instance," he said, pinching a bit of the item in question and inspecting it up close, "this loosens me up for practicing the guitar, helps me to really work the strings and feel their energy through my body, and the music becomes more tangible and significant for me. On the other hand, reading becomes difficult. Your focus expands at the price of its sharpness."

"Sure," she replied. "Math gets harder, art gets easier."

"Yes. I think it stimulates the right brain at the expense of the left," said Brother Koenig, "stimulates intuition and mysticism at the expense of analysis and science. Benefits and drawbacks, like anything from the doctor or the supermarket, so why make a federal case out of it? Well, the doctor and the drug companies want you doing *their* drugs, not yours. And a war on folk intoxicants is a great excuse to crack down on target populations, to legitimize constant surveillance and raiding and jailing of politically dangerous communities. Nixon the alcoholic pill-popper declared war on drugs in response to six straight years of hippies rioting on campuses and blacks rioting in big cities. Just like sherry and brandy drinking WASP Republicans aimed Prohibition at beer and whiskey drinking Catholic immigrants, who tended to be working class, anti-war Democrats. Police are addicted to what brings funding to the department. They just can't get enough asset forfeiture, grants from the DEA, military gear from the Pentagon, the meth-like rush of playing soldier against civilians, kicking in doors and shooting anything that moves, treating every anonymous tip as an opportunity to become Marines invading Panama."

"Yeah, totally," said Alicia, "You've really got it. The drugs that are actually killing people are prescription painkillers. The danger of pot and acid and mushrooms is they break you out of being a robot, break you open to possibilities beyond the world of Leave It to Beaver."

"Exactly!" said Brother Koenig, rejoicing at the well-toned mind on this waitress.

Alicia handed him a glass pipe, into which he fitted a substantial nugget of controversial material. He presented her the loaded instrument, which she put to her lovely lips and ignited, inhaling deeply until she was wildly heaving a cloud of blue smoke into the tent's mellow, golden atmosphere. A richer, creamier gold increasingly cradled them in new significance as the young man took his turn at the pipe.

"Wow … this is good … good stuff," commented the young lady, after what may have been many minutes of warm silence.

"I believe it comes from India … that is, the strain goes back to India, though it's grown here in Colorado," observed the young man. "Hey look, let's have some of this fine wine."

Brother Koenig expertly removed the cork and poured out the smooth ruby liquid that was soon lubricating throats and thoughts. Alicia wondered aloud how Brother Koenig had gotten the contents of the chest. He replied that this was "sort of classified information," but he could tell her that he had been "selected to be administrator of marvelous powers," and he was to "bestow blessings upon searching spirits, and trustworthy." Alicia surprised Brother Koenig, again pleasing him, by the particular drug she now pointed to, one which had long since fallen from the profound popularity it once enjoyed. She explained that she had always wanted to try it. Brother Koenig retrieved what he determined to be a suitable dosage for each of them, and together they launched to inner space.

The two sat for a moment, sipping wine, letting molecules reach their neural ports. They talked sparsely, mesmerized by the flames and shadows that danced across the forms and faces of one another. Brother Koenig eventually suggested they should have music. He arose, locked the treasure chest, and took Alicia by the hand for a stroll through the woods.

After some time on a winding moonlit path, they arrived at an especially cozy clearing circumscribed by several giant slabs of gleaming stone. Within these pillars Brother Koenig had stationed a tent, in which he'd placed some mattresses with sheets and pillows, a CD player, four speakers, water, paper towels, sanitizer, lotion, bug spray, and a variety of snacks and liquors. Just inside the tent lay a fire pit and a formidable stack of wood Brother Koenig had collected personally.

Noticing that Alicia was sensibly scanning the bedding, Brother Koenig issued her a lantern with a challenge that she find even a single bug, or anything at all offensive. She looked for a minute, and said she wasn't seeing bugs, but a bird's view of streets and fields, walls and palaces. "Now see this," said Brother Koenig, switching on the exhilarating first song on Led Zeppelin's *Houses of the Holy* at a moderate volume. "Ooooh," she said, "oohh my God."

The guitar reached her as a revelation, she said, in words not quite adequate to the bolts of color Brother Koenig knew to be ripping across the heavens of the ancient polis she was viewing, fiery suns bursting and ghostly moons beaming onto a honeycomb of rooftops, rain of rawest red and plushest purple drizzling down upon a patchwork of fruited plains where tiny farmers paused their plowing to gaze up at the majesty of mind-mixed paints applied afresh by every surge of sound. As the young woman did thus awaken to her visions and prophecies, Brother Koenig kindled a little fire while staring boldly into his own amazing flux of imagery: a soup of highly luminous horned centipedes squirming against a glass barrier, with an occasional human face appearing in their midst, staring out at Brother Koenig through the invisible wall of the awful prison. It was getting easier for him to reconcile with the fact that ugliness had always kept a solid hold in him, very near his core and his genius. He'd had to harbor more than his fair share of ugliness, but he could now look forward to a future of being able to share the ugliness with many others, this ugliness that had always demanded recognition.

As Alicia looked upon the fire, Brother Koenig fully disrobed to display a not unattractive physique, which improved in tone before her very eyes as he executed a series of stretches and yoga maneuvers, contorting into whatever position his tension and energy led him to, provoked considerably by Alicia's strategic touching. When Brother Koenig paused for a rest, she took her shirt off. He sat captivated as she proceeded to remove clothing until she wore only socks. Soon she was attempting the exercises Brother Koenig had done, and he set his hands to kneading the smooth dough and fine meat of her slopes and bends. She fell upon him and they vigorously embraced, handling each other roughly and without reservation, slippery and raw-scented, pumped up and blooming with hot blood coursing, flooding them with surging waves of desire that exploded where flesh met flesh.

There might be rolling and wrestling, even leading to scrapes and bruises and howls into the night sky, while other times it was a slow burn, a simmering held in check by cuddling and contemplation; because the girls were all a delightful novelty to Brother Koenig, he was very gentlemanly to them and receptive to all their feelings and appetites, finding each girl to be a unique assortment of spiritual and sensual qualities worth exploring and experiencing, much like he would appreciate artifacts in a museum or pictures at an exhibition.

Despite this large element of romantic intimacy in Brother Koenig's relations with the girls, he increasingly aimed to promote a sense of formality, to sow in the girls an implicit conception that they'd been selected from on high to administer a sacred rite in which they were privileged to enjoy very close proximity to an especially valuable individual, a modern Moses in training, with very important work to do, and thus it was best that the girls perform the sacred rite with a professionalism that discarded the tiresome play and power struggles of an equal relationship. He tried to maintain before the girls the same posture he generally kept before the congregation, that of a holy instrument constantly in the grips of an obscure process of inspiration, ever channeling the Spirit to bring forth insight and guidance. To play this role well he couldn't be called Louis or Mr. Koenig, it had to be Brother Koenig or Brother K, a proper title for an official position. It was necessary that he be seen as Brother Koenig the prophet rather than Louis the human. His well-being depended on it, as did that of his entire congregation. No physician can heal those who know him.

Jealousies and other discontents among his lovers and followers would of course crop up from time to time, and Brother Koenig tried to soothe these by giving the needy individual a seemingly spontaneous moment of deep eye-contact or a comment concerning a characteristic she fortunately possessed. His broadest strategy was to keep everyone aware of the many benefits, present and future, of being on good terms with him.

Chapter 13
The Gospel of Louis

It was eight p.m. The temperature was eighty-two degrees outside. Upwards of forty people sprawled out on the lawn, some with picnic blankets.

Snap. Click. Hum of amp. Scrape of plastic pick against metal strings. Silence.

Brother Koenig's tone was subdued as he began, "Never was sturdier or sharper sword thrust against harder armor, not Jonah in Nineveh, Daniel in Babylon, nor Paul in Rome, but Joshua, standing at the foot of a hill of stairs that led to lofty and gilded chambers behind whited columns crowned with a great dome. It was Joshua, standing at the iron gates of the emperor's whited house with its shining columns and lush gardens. He preached of his revelation on the holy mountain, of the ripeness of the beast, and the harshness of its fall—

Chord: E Major, oozing with distortion.

"He called out to the bloated, finely clothed power-brokers, to the buyers and sellers and brokers of We the People's power. He called out to the money-masters scurrying in mad intoxication, in blind avarice for a greater share of the plunder of the world. Joshua pleaded unto them, saying, Come ye out from under your spell, for the kingdom of God is at hand. Behold yourselves. Acknowledge the shame of you. For I was like unto you all, a prisoner, beholding not the wickedness I served. And when at last I beheld it, I was ashamed, and desired death, knowing no way to escape the beast that ruleth over all the Earth. But the way of escape is open, and there is life outside the prison.

"Now hear me, ye servants of the beast! declared Joshua. Hear a voice that is not money! Hear your invitation unto the feast wherein all shall eat, and none shall be eaten. Will your trafficking and merchandising keep you from attending the feast? The despised shall attend it. Blessed are those who reject the beast and its world, and blessed are those it hath rejected. Where is judgment not perverted by money? Where is the heart that is not committed to properties and honors? Who among you eateth not the flesh of the weak, and is not drunk on the blood of the poor? Ye strive little for justice, but greatly to maintain your dinner party, and to sit in its golden seats. Oh merchants and politicians, how surely your prison keepeth you. How hard it is to leave your exalted seats. Yet verily even a harder thing shall afflict you when the beast is fallen. For they who prosper most under the beast are they who shall weep most when it is fallen, when their riches become a millstone upon their backs.

"And woe, declared Joshua, woe also unto you poor who in blindness serve the beast, seeing no other god to serve upon the Earth. For though ye are crushed and devoured by it, the beast yet seemeth unto you a goodly father, a wise shepherd who beateth his sheep only that he might more surely deliver them into the greenest pastures. Ye have set your heart with the beast, and though it hath made you poor, ye think yourself great to be under its greatness, and ye aspire to become greater under it and to sit in its high seats. But it is a hard thing for the poor to enter the kingdom of God if their heart is that of the rich.

"Oh the red-gold shine that filleth your eyes! cried Joshua. Oh the jingle of flattery and congratulation that ringeth in your ears!

"But the multitude scorned Joshua. Some cast money at his feet, and did laugh, saying, The jester hath surely earned his wages. And others placed money in his hands, and did advise him to obtain a shave, a suit, and a job, that he might become prosperous like they.

"The next day Joshua returned with a voice of thunder, saying, Fire! Death! Behold the fire on the horizon, rolling forth to spoil your festival! Behold the costs that ye exclude from your balance sheets! Seeing restricteth your business. Truth is obscenity to those built upon deception. Hear now the obscenities of a man crazy from seeing. The fires ye feed will rage hotter and wider until you too are consumed by them—

Flurry of crisp notes in C Minor, piercing with distortion.

"Fire shall lay waste these whitewashed temples, thundered Joshua, wherein ye do commit blasphemies, taking upon you the name of God while ye oppress, yea, while ye grind the poor and crush the foreigner and are deaf to the cries of the little ones ye have made orphans. Oh merchants, engines of suction, ye who make merchandise of men! Ye join houses to your house and add fields to your field until there is room for none but you, and ye alone enjoy the land. Ye have eaten up the vineyard. Ye prefer a man in his weakness. The charity ye do him is a token. Ye will deal with him in his weakness, saying, Here is a loaf of bread that thou mayest live, but thy life shall be to labor in our fields and reap many bushels for us. Ye strong ones do therefore collect your mountain of grain, but with great pride and flattery, believing that soil and man require your excellence to yield a piece of fruit. And when ye hear the murmuring of the weak, ye rebuke them, and ask, What is amiss in the land? Do not the owners give bread unto the poor? Do not the owners render a greater part unto Caesar than do the poor? Do not the owners carry the nation and very world upon their backs?

"Thus, announced Joshua, do ye mighty ones keep fat on the mountain of grain, rebuking the hungry and asking of them, Is not the evil ye complain of very good? Is not the bitterness ye taste very sweet? Legions of false prophets do ye hoarders pay to tell this tale with all their cunning, to whitewash your loot chambers. But hear ye the word of the Lord on this matter. Repent, and relieve ye the burdens of the oppressed, before your wickedness is turned upon you and ye are made to drink from the bitter cup ye have served out.

"Oh politicians, wailed Joshua, ye professional hypocrites, ye lackeys to Mammon! Unto what are ye best likened?

"Ye are like a woman who selleth herself in the house of her lawful husband; and though she often praiseth him in the streets, her heart is laden with contempt for him—a simple man who seeth not, or else careth not, that what was pledged to him goeth to others, and that his house is a den of sin; but great fear dwelleth in her heart for the day he putteth his house in order.

"Ye are like a king who declareth unto his people from a fortified tower, Trust that I preserve you from great evil in all I do: I cut out your eyes that no evil be seen, and your tongues that no evil be spoken among you, and I cut off your feet that no evil place be reached, and thus I preserve you from the greatest evils.

"Ye are like a giant who rejoiceth at his strength among dwarves, taking their cities by fire and sword, and binding down the captives; and when the dwarves strike him with their pebbles, much lamentation is heard from the giant, who crieth loudly, Why doth such injustice afflict the righteous?

"And Joshua perceived that the hearts and minds of this city were walled with an expert masonry. He declared in a terrible voice, Behold your beautiful temples while ye may, for suddenly they are charred bones in smoking ashes!

Passages in E Major, G Minor, B Major, distortion and scraping suggestive of collapsing metal.

"Then came unto Joshua those bearing authority and wielding force under the beast. They said unto him, Why speakest thou these hard sayings against the priests of our temples, who do only that business given them by God and the people? Knowest thou not that they labor diligently to serve even thee, the least worthy of their care? Why then wouldst thou see our temples in ruins? If thou wouldst see these destroyed, what manner of temple wouldst thou raise up?

"And they took Joshua and jailed him, and his jailers came unto him, saying, We desire that thou impartest unto us of thy knowledge concerning the destruction thou hast prophesied. Tell us who shall bring this ruination to happen, and how they shall do it, and when. And Joshua answered them, saying, A landowner feared that his property would be overtaken by thieves, so he gave a sword unto his servant to protect the gates. This was the sword that cut the landowner's throat as he slept. Which is the hammer that destroyeth the temple? Even the same that was forged to build it up.

"But Joshua's jailers pressed him, saying, Thou hast not answered us, and we shall force from thee an answer. And Joshua replied, I have given you your answer, and ye shall force none other from me, though ye have all the tools of your devilish craft, for the Spirit is upon me. Then his jailers leaped to strike him, but in touching him they flew back as from a shock. Then stood they trembling, and even the hardest soul among them dared not lay hands upon the Son of God. And they left him for a time.

"Then came the learned doctors unto Joshua, and he inquired of them concerning his confinement. And they answered him, When thou art no longer ill, then shalt thou go forth into the world. Then asked Joshua of them, But what is the illness ye find in me? And the doctors answered, Behold thyself, thou unclean thing. When didst thou last wash thyself? Where is thy dwelling place, and what labors performest thou for thy bread? Art thou some beast from the forest? Thou didst place thyself among the prosperous and proclaim thy fantasies unto them, and because they did not receive thee thou didst threaten great violence on them. Because thy nation would not follow thee thou didst threaten it with destruction. Denyest thou any of this? How then denyest thou thine illness? We would help thee to abide well among thy fellows, that thou no longer makest a shameful disturbance. Knowest thou not that the people feel sorry for thee, saying among themselves, whence cometh this madman, this fellow who perverteth and stirreth up the nation, who in his confusion would lead us down dark and crooked paths? And whence cometh his belief that *he* is fit to help *us*—for are not ours the paths that are straight, and the faces that are bright?

"Now Joshua said unto these doctors, Consider ye a great cauldron of water, and a host of crabs therein, which live in calm, perceiving nothing beyond this their only habitation, perceiving not that a flame is kindled beneath them, for this is a subtle flame which causeth no alarm among the crabs, and inspireth no exodus from the cauldron. Rather the flame doth lull the crabs into a warm stupor, and causeth them to abide in place even as it doth proceed to cook them. But behold that into the kitchen wandereth a crab fresh from the wide and cool sea. When this one is placed in the cauldron, verily I say unto you, he feeleth a sting, and flaileth himself about with great tumult. And when the others ask why he disturbeth their comfort, will he not reveal unto them the prison in which they abide, and the place of freedom outside it? Will he not provoke his numb fellows to an awareness of their awful situation, and declare that destruction awaiteth those who will not awake? Therefore, I ask of you again: Where is the illness of this prophet? And where is the health of the dead?

"And these doctors answered, Nay, but thou art surely ill, even a classic case of the illness, for thou seest some great and fiery cauldron which imprisoneth the people and causeth them to be destroyed, whereas we see no such thing in our nation. And thou considerest thyself a prophet, who alone seeth the truth and giveth it unto the people, whereas it is plain to us that this calling cometh not of God, but rather from disorder in the brain. Yea, the illness doth surely possess thee, making thee to see illness in all but thyself. Therefore, by denying thine illness, and by finding illness in all around thee, thou dost only confirm thine illness to us. But our desire is that thou wouldst see it in thyself, that thou wouldst help us to cast it out from thee, that thou mayest then be set free to abide well among thy fellows.

"Then Joshua answered them, Oh ye clever ones, who with marvelous cunning have dug a pit before the feet of the prophets, lest they should go forth and change the hearts of the people. Should anyone move from his place, ye have your pit before him, and ye cry out, Look here, this one is fallen! For in moving he did fall. And ye say, We will stand him upright, but we must have a fee. And so ye take him, and stand him upon the spot where ye would have him. But with me ye shall not so do.

"But the doctors smiled in their peace, and said unto Joshua, Oh thou of little faith. We are able to set aright even thee, and thou shalt stand in health, agreeing with us in all matters, forsaking all illusion. Thou shalt not any longer find revelation in a god that is strange, nor shalt thou call wicked a nation we know to be righteous, nor shalt thou imagine forces ruling from places unseen, nor shalt thou turn the prosperous from their path by prophesying destruction, nor shalt thou stir up the poor. Thou shalt have health, and all things shall at last be simple and easy for thee. Thou shalt be like unto those thou inwardly enviest. Yea, we know that thou hatest the prosperous for their success, and thou hast sought to discover great wickedness in them, that thy hatred be justified. But despair not, our little one. We shall make of thy sword a necktie, and thou shalt go forth and prosper in the real world.

"And Joshua, perceiving their pride and satisfaction, said unto them, And so ye would remove from me a sword of justice, that I might wield instead a sword of oppression, and ye therefore gain an accomplice in your crimes to stand with you when ye suffer the judgment of the meek. For a judgment awaiteth all ye who cover the eyes of the people and strangle the breath of the prophets. And even as ye sit here this day handing down judgment, know also that a day cometh when those ye have oppressed shall sit over you, and that which ye have had shall be taken from you, and in that day shall ye be made to burn with desire for a breath which shall not be allowed you.

"Then replied the doctors, Tragic that we, whose first rule is to do no harm, should be harmed by those we labor to help. Thou blind man, hate not the seeing who would lead thee forward. An awful storm rageth in thee. Thou shalt begin thy walk into the sunshine.

"But God caused an angel to descend upon the prison at night, and the jailers were caught unawares, bound under a deep sleep while the doors to the captives were loosed open. Now as Joshua rose to leave, he beheld many about the place who did not do likewise, and he perceived they were sound in limb but lame and broken in spirit. And Joshua asked of them, How can ye lie in bed, seeing that the doors to your flight have been opened?

"And one answered him, What, these doors? They have several times come open for us. Shall we flee this prison for that prison called the world? And to where shall those flee who carry their prison wherever they go, being themselves their own prison? If thou knowest an end to the prison, then flee to it. But no place under the moon is without its evil. God hath affixed to us a quantity of evil that cannot be diminished, for the evil is ever being transferred, as water here pressed down must elsewhere come up. Life is perverse, a snake mad with hunger, devouring its own tail.

"And Joshua went unto the man and stood at the foot of his bed, and said unto him, Thou hast well said. I perceive that thou hast looked the world over and through, and hast found only a corpse. Thou hast seen the Devil's kingdom, wherein a man gaineth for himself a house and a wife and a goodly supper, and sleepeth satisfied, but surely he waketh to hunger again, and desireth now a castle and a mistress and a great feast. And how doth he eat, except he killeth that which he standeth above? Yea, the world liveth upon its own corpse, and prosperous and well-honored have been those who could so live. But now I declare that blessed are those who cannot so live. Blessed now are those who know the world and do therefore pass it by. Blessed now are those for whom the world is not a home but a bridge. So I ask of thee, wouldst thou have a home beyond the bridge? For were there verily an end to the prison, wouldst thou flee unto it in fact, or even then remain in thy bed?

"Then answered the man, I would flee unto it of a surety. And Joshua said unto him, Rise up then, and take thy flight with me. And the man arose, and many others did likewise, and followed Joshua into the midst of the capital city.

"And they did encamp upon a field. But little rest took they, having lain fallow through many seasons, and being now eager to bring forth fruit.

"In the daytime they placed themselves before the prosperous. At the foot of the gleaming towers and at the gates of the sumptuous feasts wherein much wickedness was devised, Joshua and his band did preach repentance unto the greatest under the beast, saying, Come ye away from your crooked path and make with us the straight path on which the kingdom of God arriveth. Blessed are they who refuse to be deceived, though they carry a heavy heart. Cursed are they whose heart findeth comfort in delusion. Let not your hearts be gladdened by myth. Crave not flattery for yourselves and your empire. And Joshua did suffer with his disciples the stings of beating, spraying, electricity, and jailing, but very few were the well-stationed whose conscience was stung, and the great ones under the beast continued to work darkness under a cloak of bright colors, believing their works to be shielded in the security of these colors.

"In the nighttime the band went among the lowly, the crushed, and the cast away, calling them forth from their wasting places to claim their inheritance in the kingdom of God. And Joshua declared unto them, The beast's is not a righteous kingdom, *and neither is it the only kingdom.* Therefore blessed are they who have reserved their heart for the kingdom of God. Yea, lift up your hearts, for I bring you good news indeed. There is a kingdom reserved for you, a kingdom in which ye are no longer devoured, and in which ye need devour none to be filled.

"Among these lowly ones were many whose poverty was not hidden. And Joshua said unto them, Blessed are they whose lack is manifest, for they are one step from the kingdom of God. Cursed are they whose lack goeth hidden, for unto them must first come a fall before they step into the kingdom.

"Now a certain man had made for himself a cigarette, and the leaves therein were green, and he was about to partake of it. Then Joshua asked of this man, What is it that thou takest into thyself?

"And the man was not offended, and answered, It carrieth me away from mine oppression. And the man offered it unto Joshua, who took it in hand and got a sense of it. Many were astonished at this. Then said Joshua unto all who had gathered, It causeth a dream, yea, it carrieth me off to a quiet forest. Sleep lifteth the burden from a man, and delivereth him from the evils round about. Being asleep, he seeth not the evils, but neither is the sleeper able to see the kingdom of God when it riseth round about and standeth before his very face. Woe unto him, for his greater deliverance passeth him by. Awake, therefore, out of any dream that keepeth you from seeing the kingdom. Discover that the fullness of the kingdom is sufficient for you, truly so full that dreams are desired no more. Likewise spake Joshua unto those who lived upon the bottle.

"So Joshua and his disciples did for a season preach warnings and good tidings unto all the inhabitants of the capital city. Nevertheless, few and elect were those who could step outside the Evil Mind-Control. For so great was the allure of the beast, and so wide was the power of its name and image, that even the steel-shaking words of Joshua could reach the sleepwalkers only as the boasting of a drunkard or the vanities spouted by a child at play. Spellbound the pride-swollen sank deeper into the swamp, singing, Who is like unto the beast? Who is able to make war against it?

Interlude comprised of riffs from Iron Maiden and Megadeth, suggestive of a monstrosity hurtling unstoppably toward devastation.

"But Joshua and his disciples continued in faith. And Joshua spake prophecies concerning the coming of the kingdom, likening it unto a rock slide mounting from the stir of a pebble. Said he, I see a stirring near the cradle of humankind, a place doubly, triply, ten-times afflicted by evil.

Only the very power of God can redeem it. A land of sun and green, it is called the heart of darkness.

"There sitteth a man beneath a covering of trees: a man of war who liveth in exile. One morning he ariseth very suddenly, the hand of power now upon him. He taketh up his rifle, and with faithful brothers in arms he goeth forth to claim the throne of his own land.

"They march through misted forests, and many join them along the way, seeing the hand of power that is upon the warriors. The man of war leadeth the column in a jeep, his breast bare in faith against danger. Their trust is not in the arm of flesh, for neither did the Hebrews rely upon swords when they carried the ark in their midst.

"And they reach the borders of their promised land, where arrayed against them is a great and fearsome host of men and machines of war.

"Spears fall through the clouds, and the machines of the enemy burst open, vomit fire, and are consumed. The warriors of the enemy in their ranks and files wither to the ground as grass pressed by wind.

"The man of war and his company enter their holy land, rejoicing. And in passing through the slain of the enemy, all marvel at the manner of slaying. For many of the slain do appear unharmed, save bleeding from their mouths, noses, ears, and eyes.

"The column marcheth onward to the seat of rule in the land, and many thousands do join along the way, the youth round about dropping their playing sticks to take up guns in the column. And many marvelous things do appear on the march. Angels ride across the heavens with showering sparks. The night sky is as day for the unceasing lightning. The clouds above the column glow as coals in a fire, many colors manifesting. Mountains and trees speak out in loud voices like elders counseling the young. In these wonders do the people see favor for their ascent.

"Hearing of these things, the king's guards abandon their stations and the king fleeth the seat of rule. Then cometh the column unto the palace, and at the head of a great multitude the man of war departeth from his gun, and he taketh up the crown in the midst of flowers and song.

"And as dawn calleth out from darkness, the new king doth raise his voice unto the nations, proclaiming that those who have thirsted for righteousness do now have a home and patron in the land of Uganda, for God's own hand hath redeemed the land for their sake.

"These signs Joshua revealed unto the inhabitants of great Babylon, that seeing these things come to pass might soften idolatrous people who were greatly hardened against him.

"Short was the time until the prophecy was fulfilled. And many who had heard it foretold were astonished at the news of it, and felt a shock through their minds and hearts, and now could they hearken to a question, and truly consider it, and discern the hardness of their ways.

"And many did sell their spacious houses, and their polished chariots, and all their shares in the profit hoards, and they did place the money at the feet of Joshua to do with as he saw fit. And Joshua distributed unto his disciples according to their needs, that all had sufficient, and any disciple having two coats or pieces of meat did verily rejoice in giving unto those who had none, for such was the Spirit that rested upon all the disciples.

"And the rule they followed among themselves was this: From each according to his ability, to each according to his need. And they followed this not because they had read of Marx or Lenin or Mao, but because they had read of Christ in the New Testament.

"Amen."

Chapter 14
The Story He's Sticking to

A warmer sun was beginning to bring trickles out of deep mountain snow. The Enlightenment Center expected to see raging creeks in a few months. In the meantime, Brother Koenig made the evening news.

A lot of people had recently found cause to be interested in him, and this included reporters, a few of whom Brother Koenig invited to the Enlightenment Center, showing them around while answering questions. The award-winning Dianne Apollonia from local public television made Brother Koenig the subject of her *Sunday Profile*:

THE PROPHET NEXT DOOR

"Three years ago, Louis Koenig, then a senior at Silver Spur High School, began writing a book. Nine months later, it was finished, and he called his novel *Jesus Needs a New Earth*. It was published to little fanfare, and to date has sold just two thousand copies, though sales have picked up recently, for reasons I'll shortly explain. The hero of Mr. Koenig's novel is Joshua Goldberg, an American orphan who enlists in the U.S. Army and is stationed somewhere in the Arabic-speaking world, where he soon grows disaffected by what he perceives to be the injustices of American policy there. He sinks into depression, goes AWOL, and is on the brink of suicide when he experiences a revelation, that he is the second incarnation, the Second Coming, of Jesus Christ.

"Joshua returns to America and preaches of the coming apocalypse that will cleanse the Earth of evil, and he gathers a following who will join him in building a holy city that will survive this cleansing. Joshua and his followers eventually go on to build their city in the African nation of Uganda, but they don't leave America until the fulfillment of a prophecy that Joshua gives concerning the rise to power of a Ugandan man of war, who Joshua says will emerge from exile to win a spectacular battle and take over his country in a display of dazzling supernatural phenomena.

"In all, Mr. Koenig's novel may strike readers as a vivid exploration of an intriguing fictional premise. But recent news out of Africa has many people wondering whether there might be more behind this book than just a lively teenage imagination.

(Footage of black militiamen celebrating in streets of Kampala; new president addressing crowds from balcony)

"On New Year's Day, Robert Hubele rode into Uganda's capital at the head of the People's Army of Salvation, a mostly Ugandan militia that spent much of the last decade deep in the jungle of northern Congo hiding from Uganda's regular army. Hubele's militia had been just one of the many irregular armies staking a small claim in lawless central Africa, until last December, when Hubele led this meager force to a stunning victory in a fierce battle against the Ugandan regular army, clearing the way for the People's Army of Salvation to swell in numbers and gain control of the vast majority of Ugandan territory.

(Aerial footage of battlefield devastation)

"Hubele himself is a controversial figure. For several years he held the rank of colonel in the Ugandan regular army, before being forced into exile in the Congo with a number of his subordinates for their role in an attempted coup against the civilian government of Uganda, which accused American intelligence agencies of supporting the plot. Human rights groups allege that during his ensuing stay in the Congo Hubele forcibly conscripted child soldiers and directed massacres in villages aligned with rival militias.

(Photo of smiling Hubele wearing combat fatigues and red beret, standing among young militiamen with machetes)

"But how was it accomplished, this man's swift transformation from fugitive to president?

"Most observers point to the extraordinary battle in December in which Hubele's militia inflicted thousands of casualties upon the Ugandan regular army, destroying dozens of tanks, even downing a number of fighter-bombers and attack helicopters. They accomplished all this with apparently only a basic arsenal of machine guns and rocket-propelled grenades. For the government of Uganda, it was a crushing blow to materiel and a mortal wound to morale, spurring thousands of soldiers to defect to Hubele's ranks.

"The battle was no doubt pivotal to Hubele's seizure of power, but several of his followers describe something even more extraordinary and mysterious at work in their conquest of Uganda."

(Footage of young militiaman on street in Kampala, speaking in Swahili)

Voice of translator: "I was eating supper when my brother ran to me and shouted for me to get up, and I ran with him to see the People's Army of Salvation coming through the hills to my village, and the sky lit up with colors and lights and I saw angels flying and I heard them singing. My brother told me that God had sent this to us, and we joined the march that very evening."

"Others tell of comet storms and luminescent rain. Spirits are seen emerging from the earth, from mountains and rivers. Entire landscapes come alive, seeming to breathe, beat with a pulse, even speak words of encouragement. Such colorful testimony of the conquest of the People's Army of Salvation is in abundance, painting a picture of a spontaneous uprising riding to triumph on a wave of psychedelic and spiritual transformation.

"The question is how Louis Koenig's novel could apparently have predicted all this.

"Skeptics contend that any competent student of central Africa could easily have made the same prediction. Information about Hubele has long been publicly available. Also, in the years before the publication of Mr. Koenig's book, several reports from Uganda described the weakness of the government there as it struggled largely ineffectively against an outbreak of militia banditry that was sapping the country's agriculture and tourism. And, when the highly animated nature of African religious sensibility is added to the mix, you've got your prophecy.

"But this explanation fails to satisfy at the Camp Earth Enlightenment Center, a large estate on which Mr. Koenig lives and teaches. I spoke with several people there who consider this young man to be nothing less than a prophet."

(Footage of Enlightenment Center, Brother Koenig walking and talking among followers in large heated tents)

Elderly black woman: "I been lookin' all my life. I spent … (sobbing) … thousands a' dollars buyin' anointed handkerchiefs, holy oils an' soaps, all kind a' books an' tapes, jus' lookin' around forever. And now, finally … this is it. I feel it—I *know* it. All of us do."

Dianne: "Is Mr. Koenig a prophet?"

Elderly black woman: "Yes, oh yes. I read the book and now it's happening, in Africa, praise God, in Africa! Jus' like the book says it would. Praise God I'm part of it."

Graying hippie man: "I'm not really about religion … (chuckling) … but I do think Brother K is onto somethin' here."

Dianne: "Brother K—that's what you call Mr. Koenig?"

Graying hippie man: "Right, yeah, he says we can call 'im that. Uh, but like I said, you know, he tells it just like it is, I mean, how American society is full a' hypocrisy and everyone's brainwashed and thinkin' they're Christians and all, when really they're just about as far from it as possible, you know?"

Dianne: "How are they not Christian?"

Graying hippie man: "Well, it's like … didn't Jesus say that when someone hits us we should offer our other cheek, instead a' hittin' back? Seems to me the so-called Christians in America are the first ones to wanna' go to war, even against countries that haven't hit us. Huge military budgets and reservin' the right to bomb and invade is real important to 'em.

"And they don't seem to care about the poor and the sick and the hungry who don't go to the church for help, you know? The so-called Christians are the first ones to wanna' cut food stamps and Medicaid and anything the government can do to help. If there's a depression and lots a' people need work, but they can't get any 'cause there's no investment from the capitalists, and the government could borrow idle money from the capitalists and put it to use in production and employment, well, the so-called Christians are right beside the millionaires screamin' how it's better to actually starve in capitalism than to possibly starve in socialism. Better to have capitalist bombs actually destroy you than to have the capitalists' opponent possibly destroy you. Bein' a Christian has nuthin' to do with the Sermon on the Mount, it just means you put up a picture a' Jesus in yer' house where everyone can see it, and you go to church on Sunday all dressed up, while the rest a' the week you just run after money and step on yer' fellow man to get to the top."

Young man: "Is he a prophet? I don't know *what* he really is … (glancing over shoulder) … hey, I'm just sayin' I don't know how he gets the knowledge … (glancing over other shoulder) … okay then, he's a prophet. I just, what I mean is he's very young but he's somehow gotten such a wide view of the world and how it all fits together. He helps me see the reason for things in the world, the reason why things have gone so badly all over the world all through time. This helps me see how things don't have to be the way they've always been, and a new horizon opens up."

Dianne: "What reason for the world's sorry state does Brother Koenig put his finger on?"

Young man: "Well … it seems like it's built into the world, like you have to accept it to get by in life, no matter how good a person you are. It's like it makes sinners of us all. And it might be so powerful that the only way we can expect to overcome it is through God, by God raising his hand and taking special measures."

Graying hippie woman: "It's avarice. Brother K uses the term avarice when he talks about the wickedness of the world. It means a kind of greed or hunger that can't be filled, but in trying to be filled it will devour everything."

"I got Mr. Koenig to myself for a few minutes, and he gave me the grand explanation."

Brother K: "Sure, Dianne, it's fine if you want to call me a prophet, or apostle, or witness of Christ, or just brother. I do consider my book to be a prophecy and a witness of Christ."

Dianne: "Explain that."

Brother K: "The Joshua of my book is a portrayal of what Jesus Christ will be like when he comes to Earth for the second time. As I wrote the book, I was experiencing some very rare and precious things; I might actually say I was taken up in a vision, caught up in a continuous vision of the Second Coming of Christ, where he would come from, what he would feel and act like, how the current world would treat him, what his conflicts would be, how he would gradually come to know himself and bring forth the Christ in himself. Joshua rings true as the picture of the Christ we should be looking for, and what just happened in Africa confirms this."

Dianne: "Let me see if I understand here. The Joshua of your book makes a prophecy that's now apparently been fulfilled, and you're saying that everything else about him that you've portrayed—"

Brother K: "Will also be fulfilled. Yes, I believe that this person has actually been out there for some time now, out in the world, doing the things I've recorded in my testament of him."

Dianne: "So Christ is already here on Earth for the second time, and engaged in the very ministry ... the very events you've somehow seen and recorded?"

Brother K: "Yes. He's working to gather his elect in various ways, and much of this work is low key, like a thief in the night, you know, not something that shows up on the radar of a distracted world, at least not at first. But this news from Africa is great news, because it means that big things are really starting to happen in preparation for the storm that's coming."

Dianne: "And Uganda is the place, that's where we should soon see Joshua building up his holy city?"

Brother K: "Yes. And the place has several advantages. It's a beautiful country of cloud forests and wildlife and fertile soil, plus it's got mountains that can shelter you from a blast, or ah, whatever should occur. Churchill called it the jewel of Africa when it was part of the British Empire. The British actually offered it to the Jews as a national home. If Moses had just followed the Nile instead of crossing the Red Sea ..."

Dianne: "But where is Jesus now? Where might someone look for him? Your book has him preaching in Washington D.C., then New York City—"

Brother K: "Wouldn't he be the interview of all time, Dianne? Actually, I don't claim to know just where he might be at a given time, nor do I claim to know just what he looks like, or even that he's necessarily going under the name Joshua. But it is my feeling that he'll spend a good deal of time in America, because this nation holds a powerful place in the picture of the end times given to us by prophets of old. I'm excited, Dianne. The cleansing of the Earth is *very* close now, and the kingdom of God is sinking its roots into the Earth as we speak."

Dianne: "Now, forgive me, but let me ask your response to a common criticism of your book. As a recent column in *The Mountain Survey and Prospect* puts it, your conception of the Second Coming of Christ is, quote, ludicrous on its face and cannot be taken seriously by any Bible-reading Christian. The column lists several passages in the Bible that seem to contradict the notion that Christ's return will be a secretive, low-key affair. Isn't he supposed to return triumphantly in the clouds?"

Brother K: "I am indeed aware that there's been some persecution, and I am aware of those scriptures which some have interpreted to cast some kind of doubt on the message of my book. Some people are committed to certain ideas. They sit full-time in a think tank trying to come up with ways to support these ideas, even if it's to show that one plus one equals three. Yes, there will be a point in time when Christ will descend from the clouds in glory, in a very grand and obvious event, just as the Bible says, but this will occur as the culmination of all the lower-key groundwork being done right now by Joshua Christ in his ministry, and by us here at the Camp Earth Enlightenment Center, not to mention Africa."

Dianne: "Do you find support anywhere in the Bible for your view of the Second Coming?"

Brother K: "Jesus says he'll come as a thief in the night. Is the presence of a thief instantly known to a slumbering household? Doesn't he arrive and go about his work in obscurity, known only to the awake? That's plain enough, but lots of folks just won't stand for it, even when they see prophecies fulfilled."

Dianne: "Let's talk about the Camp Earth Enlightenment Center. Tell me what goes on here, how this fits in with the bigger picture."

Brother K: "This is the place I live and teach, and anyone is welcome here who has heard and accepted the call to prepare for the kingdom which is at hand."

Dianne: "What kind of preparation is involved?"

Brother K: "Learning to live as a member of a Christian community, which is the way all people on Earth will live after its cleansing. We help each other. Nobody here is without the means of production. We each have this community to draw upon to enable us to produce, and the community is paid back and then some by those it helps. We grew quite a bit of corn and beans out here last season. We also help each other break out of the world's sick ways of perceiving things, so we can uncover and bring forth the bright human potential that the world has kept buried."

Dianne: "What are some of these sick ways of perceiving?"

Brother K: "Well, all right, let's take the perception of freedom. Here we are in the free world, so look no further for freedom. It's all right here, free enterprise, the free market, free elections, freedom of the press, freedom of religion, and so on. The land of the free is the place to dedicate your mind, body, even soul, to whoever will take it, for as long as they'll take it, for as little as they can possibly give you for it. And when you're suddenly no longer wanted and you've lost the privilege of being useful, you're free to search for anyone who might grant you even just the privilege of being used, free to grovel at the feet of those who have pretty much all the power in your relationship, since you have no union, no money in the bank, and there's millions of others just like you, isolated and desperate in what's referred to as labor market flexibility. You're free to elect the corporate-sponsored blue guy or the corporate-sponsored red guy, and maybe even a green guy who you won't really know because he isn't allowed at the corporate-sponsored debates. You're free to print and read in the press and to hear and see on the airwaves whatever six huge media conglomerates and their corporate advertisers allow. You're free to worship your own version of God, as long as the altered state of consciousness is reached by reciting prayer formulas and singing and going without food. But if the pathway is a plant or a mushroom, as it has been for thousands of years across the globe, then God has suddenly become an intolerable danger to society, and you're free to have your possessions seized, free to rot in a concrete box where you're free to be raped and slashed by people whose crimes actually involve victims. You're free to speak, unless it interrupts what the grown-ups want to say, especially at their corporate-sponsored national carnivals, eh, conventions, where you have the right to remain silent and sit in a concrete box and rub your burning eyes, so that blue guys and red guys are free to deliver the important message of freedom forward values together goodness fireworks, and corporations are free to exercise the VIP backstage access they paid for. And if you're disgusted with this circus, and you simply assemble some citizens to petition the government for redress of grievances, to protest some harmful policy, you may very well enjoy the freedom to be spied upon and have your communications monitored, the freedom to have government agents planted in your assembly to misdirect, sabotage, and discredit it. Since the commies and the terrorists will try to use America's freedoms against her, the authorities must protect America from the Constitution. We have the FBI's Counter-Intelligence Program and the CIA's Operation CHAOS protecting America from the First Amendment during the Southeast Asian Wars, the Central American Wars, and the Civil Rights Movement, trying to blackmail Martin Luther King and teaming up with police to kill Black Panthers in order to prevent the rise of an authentic black messiah, in the FBI's own words. In a national-security state directed by corporations, the Bill of Rights exists mainly as a pleasant symbol of what we like to think we're about. To a commander-in-chief at war—and we're always at war— liberties undermine national unity and fighting spirit, and due process undermines efficiency. See Lincoln and Wilson for the fine excuse war provides to suppress political speech. We the people can cling to the comforting fantasy that our authorities share our enemies and interests—or we can acknowledge the obvious reality that our authorities share corporate interests, and their enemy is us. An aware and active public is the great threat to those who enjoy more than a fair share of benefits."

Dianne: "Your description here … I can't help but think of Orwell's *1984*, the future he envisioned, the masses being told their slavery is really freedom. This is the kind of world you see around us?"

Brother K: "Yes, I'd have to say it is. If that seems foolish, then ask yourself how well you can judge how free you are if you've always carried the assumption that your society is the very definition of freedom. Most Americans simply won't question the article of faith that 'I'm proud to be an American, where at least I know I'm free,' as if whatever happens, however corrupt and degraded their situation becomes, they should just be proud and know they're free. I remember being forced to sing that song in elementary school, to take in the poisonous idea that freedom in America is simply automatic. This delusion of freedom helps you look past some pretty hard facts, such as, you're not in control of your government, you're not in control of your daily work, you're driven to sell what is precious so you can buy what is worthless, and all your conceptions of what it means to be free, healthy, human, and righteous are tailor-fitted to the drive to maximize profit, making you essentially a well-crafted tool."

Dianne: "Some people might wonder whether you, or Joshua, offer a viable alternative. Hasn't your program been tried several times already, the many socialist experiments that have failed, whether the scale was a small utopian community or a large Marxist state?"

Brother K: "Right, and so they must all have failed because of some defect inherent to the project, like expecting too much from human nature, expecting people to commit their best efforts to a community instead of to themselves. That certainly is a widely favored explanation, but there's another that emerges pretty clearly from the historical record. These experimental societies haven't usually been allowed much of a chance to get on their feet, let alone succeed, because their success threatened those who were quite satisfied with existing society. Take Latin America, where centuries of capitalism have given maybe five percent of the people two thirds of the assets, abominable wealth concentration that hasn't changed much from the time of the conquistadores. About forty percent of the people are in poverty or hovering just above it. The land has plenty of minerals, plenty of good soil, plenty of natural resources to give everyone a comfortable living, and yet masses are living almost like animals, while a few are living like princes in walled palaces because they've got some blood-stained scroll that solemnly affirms their control of the resources. Maybe if the very means of life weren't the private possession of this little clique of gods, there could be the wherewithal to feed the hungry, clothe the naked, and nurse the sick. So maybe you do what Guatemala did in 1954, Cuba in 1960, Chile in 1971, and Nicaragua in 1979."

Dianne: "You seize the means of production on behalf of the people."

Brother K: "You do just that. Perhaps you even compensate the capitalists for their properties, at the value they themselves declared on their tax forms. But very shortly, as the new arrangement is just beginning to make improvement in the masses' standard of living, someone has put mines in your harbor. Someone is blowing up the schools and health clinics you're building. Someone is contaminating your crops and your motor oil. Someone is paying your unions to go on strike. Someone is suggesting to your generals that they'd be much happier running a dictatorship for corporations. You can't buy parts for your tractors and buses anymore. A steady rash of inflammatory articles appears in the local paper, explaining that the experiment in Christian socialism is part of Moscow's plan to take over the world. And if the Russians aren't scary, there's the Chinese and the Iranians. Demonstrations are held in the public square by a group calling itself Citizens for Immediate Action, demanding the overthrow of your program of enslavement. The experiment in Christian socialism begins to fail, visibly and memorably.

"Pressure and breakdown are what Christian socialism comes to mean to observers near and far. Call it conspiracy, fine, but call it history. In Europe as the New Testament was translated into the tongues of the common people, Christian socialist communities sprouted up, and I'll point to one that didn't fail—if you'll point to one that wasn't besieged and crippled by the surrounding lords and bishops, who recognized what a threat real Christianity was to their wars and wealth and dominance. Our current lords and bishops carry on a very established tradition."

Dianne: "Interesting. Quite a lot to chew there before swallowing, you know, it's not the familiar explanation for socialist failure. So, if you've got pressure from forces who want your experiment to fail, and I'd also say pressure from weaknesses inherent within any socialist system, even one free of the sabotage you've described, how can you believe that your experiment will succeed?"

Brother K: "My belief is that God has a special interest in overseeing this final, greatest experiment, and ensuring that it goes his way."

Chapter 15
Meet the New Boss

Davy was nine when he came to Camp Earth, Uganda. He made the journey over the ocean with a lady and man who adopted him a few months before the flight. Lots of other folks from America came on that airplane too. Now he's almost twelve, and the camp has become his whole world.

They've got Davy on cotton field three. They have three fields of cotton for you to work on and two orchards of coffee. They also have two big warehouses: one where the cotton is ginned and stored, and the other where the coffee is worked down to beans and stored. They keep you working at one thing for months so you get good at it, but after you've got good at it you want to try something else. Maybe they'll let you. Maybe they won't. They probably will make you work at something else if you're talking too much with the others around you.

It's all hard work. You can count on that, and they keep you at it almost all of the day no matter where they put you. But of everything, it's the cotton fields that Davy hates most. There you have to pick and pick and pick the cotton with your fingers shredded and your knuckles swollen and your back straining for an ocean of time under the weight of the sun. You also dig out weeds with a hoe, which is more exciting than picking, and if you're older you get to chop up dead cotton plants with a machete and till them under with a tractor, which are the best cotton jobs you can get. Over in the coffee orchards you have some shade from the banana trees while you're picking the coffee cherries, which are smooth. Davy hasn't worked very much in the warehouses yet, where you work the roller gins that clean the cotton, and you clean the coffee cherries and dry them in the sun and take off their husks, which seems like fun if you've been picking cotton for months and months.

The workday is done when they broadcast the horns from the speakers they have at several places across the camp. It's getting harder for Davy to find good moods to push him forward. Even after the horns sound and the worst is over, it's still hard to be happy, since in a short time he has to be out in the field again. Sleeping, eating, and drinking are what he looks forward to, what pulls him forward. He dreams a lot of flying way up above the jungle and looking down on trees that are like waves in a green sea, and nothing stops him from going whatever direction he wants, the wide world is open to him, full of living, colorful things growing up from valleys and climbing up mountainsides. But then it always happens that he gets heavier, the Earth pulls against his flying, and then he's marching in sand and rocks, marching against a stinging wind in an empty desert.

After the evening horns, Davy puts the sack and hoe away in the cotton warehouse, then he follows the others to the sheds near the center of the camp. These are made mostly of sheet metal. He steps into a room he shares with about thirty others, and he lies down on his mat for a few minutes before supper is served. There is delicious rest now for everything that aches: his back, his hands, his eyes, his feet, really his whole being. But suddenly the sweetness is jolted away by the singing of some older ladies, damn 'em, and Davy wraps his pillow across his ears to keep it out. It rubs him wrong how they broadcast their happiness onto everyone. Davy would love to howl like some jungle animal whenever he felt the need, like these singers. But of course, that would seem weird and out of control, and the camp would be ashamed of it. Oh, to be some animal out there in the forest, blessed by nature with what you need to survive and be happy, even all by yourself. Now Davy is suddenly jolted again by some guy who just yanks the pillow out of Davy's hands and stands over Davy with a sour stare of punishment. The boy trembles with powerless outrage at this guy who must be the husband of one of these ladies whose howling has a right to invade everyone's head. Finally, the pillow comes back to Davy, and rather than risk putting it over his ears again, he just sits there and takes in a sickening dose of the noise. He waits until everyone leaves the shed for supper, and then, broken down and drained, he cries very hard into his pillow.

Supper is always a really good stew of chicken, pork, fish, rice, corn, beans, and potatoes, at least some combination of these. Some of this food is raised here in camp, and maybe in the future Davy will get to tend the pigs and chickens. There's plenty of coffee to drink, and tea, and there's cool water they get from the well behind the temple. The camp members eat together sitting side by side on long wooden benches at long wooden tables. A prayer is broadcasted as the eating starts, so just when you're digging in to the thick warm stew, you listen to the thick warm voice of a man say something like:

"Thank you, thank you, mighty provider. We eat, in fact, we eat. We do not starve, as we could. Thank you, thank you, praise, praise. We eat now of thy providence. It is very good. We eat in great awareness of this good.

"The world starves, yet *we* do not go hungry. Oh praise. The world is confused, yet *we* understand. Oh thank you for thy providence here, where we are filled, where we know.

"The world is lost in darkness, yet *we* have found light. Indeed, we are the very chosen! We have been chosen to eat and to know. It is given us here to eat and to know.

"The world burns in a fire of discontent. It burns and falls with the dragon. But *here* we are saved from burning. We do not burn, blessed fact. How can we not give thanks and praise for this good? We give thanks. We give praise."

During the prayer Davy's mind is on the meats and vegetables he's enjoying, and it's easy to feel good about the prayer and to be thankful for good things you have.

They also broadcast the prayer during breaks from work when the members cool down with water, and the nice voice will pray about being thirsty and drinking, and being weary and resting, and being grateful for the blessed fact of having clean water.

After supper Davy's head feels heavy and tired, but now it's time to talk about the book. Everyone has their own copy of Brother K's book, and you have to study it with everyone after supper. Some people study it even during free time, which is an hour you get every day to do something besides working and studying with everyone. Though an important member once told Davy not to call this hour free time, because all the time here is free time. We're free here all of the time. Reading things other than the book and the Bible isn't allowed, but there are members who have weird books and magazines hidden out in the jungle. Davy once heard Brother K admit that books, magazines, newspapers, and internet can have some truth, and even movies and TV might have bits of truth, but then Brother K got really serious and said it's definitely not okay to dare the Evil Mind-Control by trying to find truth in worldly materials, because it's like trying to snatch a piece of chicken from a crocodile's mouth. He said the world is always going crazy for something new and silly that gives people a childish thrill and distracts them from their sad situation, and they forget that anything ever existed before the new amazing thing, which is really just one more thing to add to the giant pile of crap that fills people's lives out there. The commercials turn you into a little kid who's always crying for another toy. This is bad enough, but much more dangerous is the stuff the world writes and says about the camp. This is very concentrated Evil Mind-Control, and it needs only a minute with you to erase all the progress you've made here in camp, and suddenly you find everything is twice as hard for you. Anyway, most members seem to use their free time like Davy does, not to read but to sleep. Even if we could read whatever we wanted, we still wouldn't have the time or energy to do it (though Davy's pretty sure he would find the time and energy to read all he could about this camp).

Before Davy came to camp, you could choose who you would study the book and the Bible with after supper. But they say these study groups became dens of sin where people helped each other come up with weird ways of thinking. One person would find something in the book that made her say the camp should be a certain way, such as there should be votes taken about what to grow and what to build, and other people in that group would say they read it the same, and pretty soon they had their own little church going. The camp was breaking down into a bunch of little churches, and only Joshua's true church could ever hold the camp together, so Joshua told Brother K to give every study group an adviser who is specially trained to see Joshua's way. The advisers notice the Evil Mind-Control when it creeps into discussions of the book and the Bible. Lots of members aren't good at seeing the Evil Mind-Control and they don't realize when their discussion becomes a sewer pipe for the world to send its pollution into the camp. You can study the book and the Bible without an adviser if you're alone, but even this is dangerous. When he's alone with the powerful words and acts and feelings of Joshua and Jesus, a strange force rises up in Davy that makes him feel angry at the camp instead of grateful. The Evil Mind-Control is strong and smart enough that it can even come through the book and the Bible, unless an adviser is there to help you read it the right way. When Davy reads by himself, Joshua and Jesus are like a real person who lots of the time is weak and unhappy, who lots of the time is mad at the authorities and doesn't follow the rules, and who says the kingdom of God is for the weak people who get stepped on by the strong people who are good at playing by the rules of the kingdom of the world.

Study group after supper is about finding places in the book and the Bible where Joshua and Jesus are more the way Brother K and the advisers like him. The study group they have Davy in has ten other kids around his age. The adviser over the group is a large, older woman who has made herself totally clean of the Evil Mind-Control, and the kids are supposed to learn from her example. She's always happy, which shows us that her way is the right way. To Davy she looks like a doll or a puppet, with her face always the same, eyes that are wide open and bright and blank, and a smile that looks like it's sewn into place. Her soft voice sort of swings like a gold pocket-watch. She makes the book into a comic book. She turns Joshua into a superhero with super powers so he's not even a person anymore. She's always calling him savior and king and reminding us that God revealed himself to Joshua on the holy mountain so that Joshua doesn't struggle or doubt anymore, and he establishes Camp Earth and it's the end of history. It seems kind of dumb to Davy that God would show up on a mountain and admit that the world has been ruled by the Devil all these years but God's gunna' make up for it all by cleaning off the world so there can finally be goodness.

The lady is always reminding us that Camp Earth is the place where God begins the new holy way as the world finishes getting ripe for destruction. She sometimes makes it seem like the kingdom of God is something that will arrive in the future, and the camp is like a landing strip for it. Other times she talks about the kingdom of God being already spread out upon the camp, and those who can't see it need clearer eyes, since eyes in the world are trained to be blind to the truly valuable things.

It just doesn't do any good to ask the lady questions, like, "If Camp Earth is God's answer to Joshua's struggle in the world, what could God's answer be to Davy's struggle in Camp Earth? If the kingdom of God is already spread out upon the camp, wouldn't it be powerful enough to be noticed, like the light of the sun? Why doesn't Joshua just visit the camp for a day to show himself to the members?" The lady already has the answers ready for any questions at all, answers about Joshua having very good reasons for having the camp the way it is, even if it's different from the holy city in the book.

She tells us we should ask ourselves, "What would Joshua do?" As long as we know the correct answer: Obey. Obey the leaders of Camp Earth, who stand in for Joshua until he finally arrives in camp.

Davy has more than a gut feeling that Joshua would do something else. Davy is very proud when he gets the lady to admit there are lots of parts in the book and the Bible where Joshua and Jesus disobey authorities who are supposed to have God on their side. But then the lady explains that the authorities here in camp really do have God on their side, not like the corrupt leaders of the world, who should very well be disobeyed by Jesus and Joshua and all of us. Our leaders in camp can only do as Joshua tells them. There are times when Joshua himself stands in person before our leaders to instruct them. If Joshua were one of the kids here in camp he would be the most obedient of all, and the hardest worker. She says Davy should quit trying to discover cracks in something crafted by God, quit spinning his wheels in the mud when he could be moving up the mountain. He needs to remember that we have the truth here in camp, we don't need debates to know what Joshua would have us do. The right way has simply been given to us as a blessing so we don't have to search around in darkness like the world does.

The lady says she understands why we might want to doubt and disobey. We all grew up in the world and most of us still carry some of it with us. It hides inside us and comes up in the form of doubts that destroy our faith. That's how we recognize the Evil Mind-Control. Anytime we have a thought or feeling that makes us feel bad about the camp, we know right then that we're dealing with Evil Mind-Control, and we should say to it, "I know what you're trying to do, I won't let you make me a slave, get away from me." The lady says we get stronger and freer as we fight the Evil Mind-Control like this.

Davy wonders if he'll ever get even close to having the strength and freedom the lady seems to have. Lots of others in camp seem to have it. What's Davy's problem?

He's on the right track, they say, if he realizes the problem is with *him*. That's really the first step to any improvement for him. He has to stop blaming this or that around him, the cotton picking and the study group and the singing, and he needs to take responsibility for himself and his Evil Mind-Control. It's obvious that plenty of people are happy here in Camp Earth, and it should be obvious that it's plenty possible to be happy here himself. It must be that he needs to invest himself more into Camp Earth, they say. He needs to work with more spirit at the cotton, he needs to study the book more deeply, he needs to pray right. He has to really tell God how much he wants to know for himself whether the work he's part of here in Camp Earth is the work of the Lord in the end time. He can expect God to testify of the camp's great mission by a powerful feeling that will flow through Davy's heart. And if he doesn't get this feeling right away, he should look inside himself for what's keeping him from getting it. Maybe he's been doing something he knows he shouldn't, so he's gotta' stop that. Probably he's holding onto thoughts and feelings from the Evil Mind-Control, so he's gotta' get rid of those.

Davy says his heart might be deaf. What happens to Davy if he just can't get it? "Come on now," they say, "you mean to tell us you've never felt God here? God testifies by a warm feeling, a wonderful sense that you're part of a grand purpose, that you're part of the people and the trees and the stars around you, that you're part of the magic of being alive in a very special place and time. Just look at the temple, son, look for a minute at the temple at night with its beautiful lights. Or just ponder the wonders of the book for a while and think on the triumph of Joshua. Or just lose yourself in the music of Brother K. Or look out onto this big family you've got all around you here. You'll feel something tell you that God's right here. It's a feeling you just can't get out there in the world."

"Don't they have lights and music and good feelings *out there*?" Davy is about to ask, before some voice in him shrieks, "What a question from a member of this camp! As if there's no difference between the camp and the world! What must be done about this boy?"

Davy needs to feel good about Camp Earth. Oh, how he wishes nature provided more to him, made the right way natural to him. What comes easy to him is wrong. And the right only comes by forcing, by constant battling. This seems upside down to Davy. Why was he formed so faulty, the opposite of what he should be? The war on Evil Mind-Control can seem like a war on Davy, a war on his strongest feelings.

Maybe he just hasn't battled hard enough yet, and he's only getting what he deserves. He knows that other members have struggled like him before they've come around to seeing the light. They've told their story lots of times in front of everyone, and he believes them. Davy imagines that enough prayer will finally snap something loose, and a river of sweet cooling medicine will gush all over the hot and tired parts of his brain. It's actually Davy's deepest hope that some kind of grace will pour into him like this and transform him forever.

Unbeknownst to the lad was that a sizeable number of camp members at this time were very much like Davy: creatures neither wild nor domesticated, living each day with only as much strength as they could muster in their quiet desperation, semi-alert for some opening through which the scheme of things might be altered to their benefit.

Chapter 16
Complications During Delivery

We have to get up at dawn, when the damned light makes us see. Bad morning to you, hell sun.

Breakfast is served after people have had about ten minutes to get themselves going. At least one thing Davy likes about this place is the food. Breakfast is porridge of wheat and oats with pieces of egg, plus there's bananas and pineapple and coffee. The coffee comes from the camp's own beans, which get roasted after they leave the camp, then some of it comes back for the members to drink. Pretty much all the camp members have a big drink of it in the morning, Davy especially, because it helps you feel strong for what has to be done. The coffee might be the best thing in Camp Earth as far as Davy is concerned. Now he bites into a banana and lets his porridge cool, while his tired eyes follow the swirling ghosts escaping his bowl into the wet air. He tries to focus on the powerful effect of his sugared coffee and tries to block out the slurping and smacking pig noises of the other eaters. Thank goodness the prayer is loud enough to block some of this out. Davy gets into his porridge and coffee while thinking about thankfulness, but before long the horns are broadcast. Groaning and stumbling, Davy marches out to labor again. The sun will get higher and hotter. The air will get hotter, heavier, and thicker until it's soup. Thank goodness there will be breaks for water. Thank God for the well by the temple, for the cool sweet clean water that advisers take out to overheated members. These water breaks have probably been the highest points in Davy's life, and he has really felt his heart sing thanks with the broadcast of the drinking prayer.

The camp by this time took in about twenty-four hundred acres and nearly one thousand people. Its layout resembled a baseball field. Home plate was the temple, where Brother K lived. Standing on somewhat higher ground than the rest of the camp, just nestled between two toes at the feet of mist-shrouded mountains, this was a pyramid of four sides, built mainly of wood, some taken from the surrounding jungle. It had three tiers, each fifteen feet high, the sides of the base tier being one hundred and five feet in length, the middle tier ninety feet, the top tier seventy-five feet, these lengths being at the floor of a tier, with the sides tapering inward so that a tier's floor had more area than its roof, which itself had more area than the floor of the tier above. A grand steeple rose up through the center of the structure, emerging into sky from the roof of the top tier and climbing heavenward by the month, aiming, it was commonly believed, to reach the apex of a triangle at more than one hundred and five feet from the temple foundation, a point just beyond the roof of an imaginary seventh or "golden" tier. Construction on the bottom-heavy ziggurat had proceeded more or less steadily for nearly a decade now. The members had given the temple countless hours of sawing and hammering in addition to their labors in the fields, and in return it gave them at the very least a unifying purpose, along with a tangible and constantly visible reminder of their investment and accomplishment in this community. They were encouraged to view this temple as the final great hope for humankind. And thus, while in the rigors of investing their fullest labors, members would lift their eyes up from their toil and look upon their beautiful building, investing their fullest hopes. Many expected the completed temple to act as a sort of conduit for divine energy to descend upon the congregation and empower them to live as ideal models of the new and holy way. In front of the temple lay the stage on which Brother K performed, made of fifteen-foot wood planks projecting horizontally from the temple foundation, with supporting earth that abruptly dropped nine feet where these planks' forward edge met the upward edge of planks projecting vertically from the ground below. Access between the temple and stage was achieved through two eminent sliding doors set in the center of the front of the base tier. Metal gates ran along both flanks of the stage and turned to follow symmetrical diagonal paths terminating in the mountains behind, sealing off the temple and its grounds from the rest of the camp.

What's inside the temple? When's Joshua gunna' get here? Questions so fundamental, obvious, and honest could only be heard from the mouths of babes, as the adults seemed to have wrestled to their own conclusions on these matters and now steered clear of them as they would sleeping elephants. When a child became too insistent on these questions, the other children could demonstrate maturity by reciting an official response. "Inside the temple is where Brother K talks to God. Don't you know that?"

"Talks *with* God," an adviser on scene might clarify, likely adding that Brother K chose the temple spot through divine guidance, and everyone is grateful to be part of building it up.

"But what are they taking into there all the time? Why can't *we* go inside?"

The other children could demonstrate commitment to the camp by converging on the boy to help him get a clue. "Wow, that's really selfish to think the temple belongs to *you*. You must not have much faith if you've just gotta' see what's going on in the temple. Do you really think Brother K and the watchers aren't looking out for you? Who do you think gets you the food and water and safety you have every day? You're so ungrateful, you don't deserve to be in camp at all, no way do you deserve going inside the temple. You'd be happy if you didn't make things so hard for yourself. Stop trying to drag us down to you."

As the child internalized the shaming, the heat of it softened him for an adviser's sculpting. "Someday soon, we will *all* certainly enjoy everything the temple has to offer, if our faith and our labors make us worthy. But for now there is still preparation and building to be done. We'd like you to be a part of it, son. What's inside the temple is tools, tools to help us be God's people, to help the kingdom of God fill us, and then fill the world."

With temple at home plate, at about the pitcher's mound lay the tables where eating was done, and study groups assembled. Between the tables and the temple was a large clearing of low grass that served as a courtyard where games and exercises were held and where members sprawled out for Brother K's performances. Between the tables and second base stood the nineteen large rectangular sheds that sheltered the members' sleeping quarters. At about third base stood the "bean barn" where coffee was processed and stored, adjacent to the coffee orchards of left field. At about first base stood the "ginning house" where cotton was processed and stored, adjacent to the cotton patches of right-center field. Between these areas of major activity, belts of wild green growth rambled unevenly.

Camp Earth was surrounded by no fence, just scores of miles of fairly thick, frankly frightening African jungle. Occasionally a desperate member would slip away, but he'd be back soon enough. Gorillas and chimpanzees were sometimes heard in the distance, an eruption of hooting and screaming suddenly blasting out from some mountainside, stirring up a wave of commentary from birds and humans:

"Big man must a' caught his bro's messin' 'round with his ho's." An old and haggard lion once wandered into the coffee bushes, it being quite rare for a lion to roam so far from the grassland. Perhaps he was out of his wits for having been toppled from his pride by a younger and stronger male, or maybe he was just senile from his obvious age. At any rate he did succeed in thrashing to death the camp dog, a German shepherd whose bark wrote a check his bite couldn't cash. The cat tried to carry his unusual prize back into the forest but was scared off empty-mouthed by an adviser's pistol. Brother K considered himself somewhat favored by this dog, who in reality offered the same affection to anyone regarding him enough to stroke his gold and ebony fur. Brother K lauded the dog's single-minded service and sacrifice and insisted on personally burying him within temple grounds.

The dog was born and trained in Germany, then flown to Colorado where he would sniff out and patrol the Enlightenment Center for several months before hopping his final plane, arriving in Camp Earth, Uganda, when the temple was just a square outline in the ground and the few hundred pioneer members here were dwelling in tents. One of these pioneers was a man named Bill, who would years later take under his wing a young addition to the camp named Davy. Bill could see that Davy was disoriented, and that the boy's adoptive parents were like many of the parents here, faithful members who meant their children to be offerings, tokens of their parents' devotion to the camp. Bill kept the new lad in sight, and every so often he gave Davy a bit of wisdom about camp life, like the best way to treat a blister, or where it was that the mosquitoes lived, and it was always done like Bill was just stopping for a moment while on his way to something else. It didn't take long for the boy to catch on that the game was to keep his "parents" and the advisers in the dark about the not officially approved relationship.

There was a place in the forest beyond the coffee trees where Bill would go to relax during free time, a shady and quiet cranny of ferns that was shielded by mossy boulders and the hulking trunks of warped, vine-strangled trees. Bill showed the place to Davy, who began using it for naps, and when the two happened to meet in this special spot they talked about camp life. They even studied the scriptures, which was breaking the law of no studying together without an adviser. Bill said this law was good in spirit, it was here to prevent error, but he had to agree with Davy that there just weren't enough advisers to tag along with every two members who had Jesus on the mind and a Bible nearby. The boy got Bill to confirm that in the camp's early years the members were trusted to help each other figure out scriptures and were trusted to keep their own guard up against the Evil Mind-Control. Bill also said that too many members just weren't up to it and they easily fell into abusing the scriptures.

Brother K and the advisers had good reason for saying Evil Mind-Control will thrive where members interpret scriptures without guidance, not to mention off in a secluded area. Bill and Davy talked and studied together in their little place like some frontier family out at their own cabin in their own canyon, too far from civilization for too many generations. The man was overpowered by a huge impulse to let his guard down and say what he felt like saying, not pausing at all to think about whether he was just giving voice to the Evil Mind-Control. A lot of what the man said could really trouble him after the fact, and the things that troubled the man most to say were what the boy most wanted to hear. This boy was an explorer who simply couldn't trust the official map. He just had to get Bill a talkin' about all the stuff the boy couldn't hear from the other members, whose talk all seemed like it came from a single page they'd all memorized, the boy complained. It was hard for the man to not give in.

Davy got Bill to talk about what the camp was like in the beginning … and how it had changed into something different.

"In the beginning, things were … more innocent, I guess," Bill said. "There was more … possibility … than you might sense now. When *you* got to the camp, Davy, I bet you probably couldn't feel a big difference from what you'd just left. I mean, I bet you did feel things were different as far as the weather and the jungle and all, but when us old timers first got here from the U.S., we were just in a new world of … well, it was more than just the weather. We felt like we could make this camp into whatever we wanted. Everyone felt this way, and you'd really shoot out of bed in the morning to clear the fields and work on the temple. I'm tellin' ya' Davy, even Brother K helped out with the work back then, did most everything with us, worked and ate and slept just how the rest of us did. Really. Saw 'im do it and loved 'im for it."

Davy shook his head at this, saying he couldn't picture Brother K picking cotton with him, getting his shiny colorful gowns all soiled up. Bill laughed, but assured Davy that for a while Brother K had in fact been "more like one of us than he seems to be now, now that things are … more complicated." Davy wanted to know just how things had become complicated.

"Well," Bill said with a deep sigh, "I guess that's the question, Davy. I mean, lookin' back on it now, I see it as bein' kind a' bound to become complicated, but startin' out it didn't seem complicated at all, or even that it ever could be. Stuff just happened a little at a time. And there was never really a time when I thought things had become too complicated for me to feel good about the camp anymore. I still have those wonderful feelings about the camp that I had in the beginning, son, I really do. But …

"One of these complications was that Brother K spent less and less time with the members after the first level of the temple was built. He just started livin' in the temple, and some of us kind of asked, you know, So Brother K is livin' in the temple now? And the watchers said, Yeah, he is, since the first level is ready for the work he needs to start doin' in there. And we said, Fine, sure. But he just came out less and less, and now …"

"He pokes out once a week, to sing and guitar at us," said Davy.

"Well, uh, okay," said Bill, "but he does keep busy enough, ah, givin' himself to study and prayer so the camp can keep the Lord's guidance. Maybe we don't see his work or understand it like we did before, but he's in there at it day after day, just like us out here."

"Didn't Brother K take some girls into the temple with him?" inquired Davy.

"Uhh, yes, Davy, Brother K did invite a few … special young ladies to join him in the temple," Bill admitted with a blank expression. "I guess you've probably heard the rumors we've all heard at one time or other, and I'll just say that the Evil Mind-Control would have us view Brother K's situation in the worst possible light. Yes, Brother K does live with some young ladies, but I've known him for years and I've seen how much love he has to give. It's really a special situation, and it serves Joshua's purposes. I guess it's true that some a' the girls' families complained a little at giving 'em up, and lots a' members couldn't see how it served Joshua. The watchers had to remind us that the kingdom of God can only be dwelled in by those who are refined through faith, and obedience, and sacrifice. What Brother K requires of us will forge us into the substance of the kingdom. What we perceive to be trials are really opportunities to prove our worthiness to receive the gifts God holds in store, and those of us unable to obey will lose our stake in the kingdom."

"Oh," said Davy, squinting some, as if straining to picture his stake in the kingdom. "What else is different from how it was in the beginning?" he badgered Bill.

"What else? Right. Well, startin' out I thought we'd all kind a' be workin' our own schedules, you know. Maybe some of us would want to work evenings growin' corn and some of us would prefer to work mornings growin' beans, or something. But Brother K and the watchers had it all worked out for us already. They'd done their calculations, and they told us the camp would be best off growin' x amount a' cotton and y amount a' coffee, and we should each work as long as there was light so we can bring in the funds to build up the temple as soon as possible, the temple bein' the key to the kingdom. And most of us said that'd be okay. We just agreed we were happy to be workin' to build up our camp. And besides, Brother K was right there hackin' away and sweatin' with the best of us, bringin' those first harvests.

"So a few years go by, and we'd gotten some pretty good harvests behind us, and the second level of the temple was just beginnin' to go up, and Brother K'd been livin' in the first level for a little while, uh, with a few girls. So around that time is when some a' the members started complainin' some about things like their clothes and their rooms and their free time. They started askin' for things for themselves, even though this would take funds away from buildin' up the temple. The problem was they stopped lookin' at the temple as bein' a blessing. The Evil Mind-Control was workin' on 'em to see the temple as somethin' that took from the members without givin' much in return. Cotton and coffee was goin' out by the truckload, but most a' what came into camp was put away into the temple before members could see, and this made some members yell that the congregation had as much right as the watchers to keep track a' what was goin' out and comin' in. Members were yellin' this right up at Brother K on stage.

"The watchers warned about the Evil Mind-Control bein' a strong influence on us even as the camp makes progress. They told us that all income from cotton and coffee is used for the benefit of Camp Earth, and that a good portion a' the income has to be reserved for buildin' up the temple and gettin' the watchers their equipment. But we can all expect to have more time to relax, comfortable beds, even houses to ourselves, and we can also expect to make the camp self-sufficient, which means bringin' a variety a' new crops into cultivation along with new jobs and crafts. We can all look forward to this, but for now the camp is in a very important stage of growth that requires sacrifice … sacrifices that'll make the blessings of the kingdom that much sweeter to us."

"So, we're still in that stage of growth and sacrifice?" asked Davy.

"We are," said Bill. "And Davy, I believe that you and I will both see the rewards. I feel like it's gunna' be soon, I really do. Things'll be better, son, and you'll get to know those wonderful feelings I told you about, and you'll shoot right out a' bed in the morning."

Davy nodded, giving Bill an if-you-say-so glance. "So those members that were complaining … did a lot of them go into the box?" asked the boy.

"Uh, some of 'em did keep on havin' problems with the Evil Mind-Control, and yeah, they ended up in the box, and a lot of 'em are better off for it. Ya' see, some of 'em were really tearin' down other members' faith. Heck, even I was startin' to lose faith a little. There was this song I couldn't get out a' my head—you probably don't know it, Davy, but it's about how the new boss is the same as the old boss. I tried hard to block it out. Some a' the members were pullin' out their Bibles and shoutin' out verses that they said

showed Brother K was wrong about the Second Coming a'
the Lord. Things were gettin' way out a' hand."

"Like what verses were they?" Davy pried.

Bill sighed, put his hands to his face, rubbed his short
beard some, then pulled a pocket Bible from his pants. "Okay
son. Twenty-fourth chapter of Matthew. You've got Jesus
himself talkin' about his coming at the end times." Bill gave
Davy the Bible and pointed to verses twenty-three through
twenty-seven, which the boy read in a soft, low voice:

*Then if any man shall say unto you, Lo, here is Christ,
or there; believe it not. For there shall arise false Christs,
and false prophets, and shall shew great signs and wonders;
insomuch that, if it were possible, they shall deceive the very
elect. Behold, I have told you before. Wherefore if they shall
say unto you, Behold, he is in the desert; go not forth:
behold, he is in the secret chambers; believe it not. For as the
lightning cometh out of the east, and shineth even unto the
west; so shall also the coming of the Son of man be.*

A powerful energy surged up and down Bill's spine,
and as he tried to figure out its origin and whether it was
good or bad, he noticed the boy's face had become
transfigured. The atmosphere tingled with reverberations as if
a gavel had come down with a crack. Davy was rocking back
and forth, soaking in the words of Jesus. What a terribly
dangerous thing this was that Bill had done so foolishly.

"Now look, Davy, you've gotta' remember there's a
definite way the Evil Mind-Control would have us look at
those verses, and that way is to see Joshua as some kind a'
false Christ and Brother K as some kind a' false prophet,
okay, and to expect Christ's coming to be some kind a'
fireworks show that's not the sort a' thing Joshua has been so
far. But actually, Joshua doesn't contradict these verses when
you keep in mind that his coming is really a *process*, and the
final phase is what'll be obvious to everyone. He'll come
here to his holy city, bringin' with 'im all a' the chosen that

he's been gatherin' up out there, and he'll reign over us in such goodness and glory that we'll shine bright as lightning across a world that's in darkness.

"And, you know, there's people in camp who believe, uh, that at the very least Brother K has given us all a book that shows how Christ would live if he was livin' on Earth in our time, and I mean, it's sort a' like Jesus comin' back if people are inspired to take a fresh look at 'im and take his teachings seriously in our time, like Joshua does in the book."

The two sat in silence. Davy looked hurt and confused, and Bill felt ashamed of seeming slippery to this boy. Bill felt justified, though, in trying to steer the boy from heresy.

"Look son, I don't mean to tell you what to think, I really just wanna' help you steer clear a' dangers and stay out a' the deep end. You know you can talk to me about whatever you want, and I'll be glad to hear you out. But you also know there's lots a' folks in camp who have a hard time listenin' to anything that sounds even a little like Evil Mind-Control, and if you were to go about camp readin' aloud from Matthew twenty-four they'd panic like a bunch a' horses at a snake in the grass, and there'd be stompin' and screamin', and eyes bulgin' and nostrils flarin', and even though you'd be sayin' the very words a' Jesus, they'd be hearin' a hiss and a rattle. I don't know if you ever had to try an' calm down a spooked horse, son, but it's almost impossible when his heart is pumpin' four times faster than usual 'cause his mind is fixed on snakes. And that's kind a' the state we were in when the box started gettin' used on these snakes that were bitin' into everyone's faith."

The box was a metal coffin kept in a pit at the edge of the jungle. A member would go inside to work on purging the Evil Mind-Control. They'd lie down in there, usually unwillingly (to be expected, since they were after all under the influence of Evil Mind-Control) and stay for hours (rarely days) in a condition of freedom from distractions, free to concentrate on making themselves free of the Evil Mind-Control. It involved a lot of sweat and very little movement. To focus a member's thoughts on gratitude, and to remind of the debt owed a community by any of its members, the box had a cluster of holes through which water could find the struggler's lips, the refreshment being administered with words of encouragement, or derision, depending on who was pouring the jug. Ideally part of a member died in the coffin and a fresh creature emerged, free to see the good things that were on his plate, and not see the good things that weren't.

The box arrived as part of an official campaign for humility. Because a portion of the membership was needed to assist in implementing the campaign, the office of adviser was created. Emboldened by their promotion, advisers oversaw sessions in which members felt the relief of divulging their misdeeds and revealing what Evil Mind-Control they'd been holding onto. A confession that seemed wanting would be supplemented by the helpful observations of other members. Opportunity was given for prideful members to stand naked before the congregation and gain detailed notification of their physical imperfections. A headstrong youngster would receive an invitation to a boxing match where he'd square off against an adviser twice his size in front of all the other kids, who encouraged their peer into continuing the contest until the will to fight was extinguished. Several members found their turmoil focused and released by a few good lashes.

It must be recalled that prior to the campaign for humility, many members had become very casual, lighthearted, and arrogant toward serious things like the dangers of Evil Mind-Control and the need for camp authority. These members had been living day after day as though no real harm could come of dabbling with worldly media, engaging in off-hand speculation about key scriptures in the company of uninformed minds, or brushing off the direction of camp leaders as the mere opinion of mere men. The campaign for humility provided a renewed appreciation of the distressingly real consequences of flirting with Evil Mind-Control.

Davy told Bill that the box didn't seem like something Joshua would approve. The boy began scanning the book for passages that supported his charge, and he was soon clenching his fist and pulling his hair. Of course, Bill knew there were several passages in the book and the Bible suggesting Joshua and Jesus would sooner allow evil than inflict violence to resist it, and Bill knew there were several other passages suggesting Joshua and Jesus could indeed resort to whip and hellfire. This Christ was lamb and lion, sage and child. As Davy struggled to establish Joshua as someone who wouldn't shut people into a hot and dark cage, Bill felt it was time to give this boy a straight and honest answer.

"Son, I've read the parts you're lookin' for there, and I've gotta' say it's hard to imagine Joshua usin' the box on folks. When the box came into camp, it was another of those complications."

"But the advisers say the camp is governed in all ways according to Joshua's will," noted Davy.

"They do say that," replied Bill. "And I think they say it for good reason. Now look, I do believe Joshua is behind this camp. But, that bein' said, I'll also say that I don't believe Joshua is behind each and every thing that's done here. The advisers can make mistakes, the watchers too, and even Brother K can. The reason they say Joshua is behind everything here is they feel real strongly that they've gotta' keep this camp together, keep it movin' forward; the members have all gotta' believe that Joshua himself is behind every policy, otherwise things can spin apart, and everyone'll be the worse for it. Lots a' history's great codes of law were established by tellin' the people that a god was behind it. Really important peoples like the Romans and Spartans and Babylonians, the Egyptians too, and the Israelites. Think of all they accomplished, what they gave to humankind, because they had that solid foundation.

"I think the camp actually is governed by Joshua's will, but he allows us room to carry it out. Like he'll tell Brother K that the camp is to be of one heart and one mind, and then Brother K tries to make this happen. So there's gunna' be complications that might not fit with the picture you or I have, or even the picture the book has, of just how Joshua's camp should be, you see? There've been things done here that maybe should a' been done differently … but uh, maybe somehow even things like the box can serve the Lord's purposes. I've seen the box work wonders on some folks, like it presses and sweats the Evil Mind-Control right out of 'em. I'll tell ya' Davy, it's a fact that this camp has grown in wealth and numbers, and it's a fact that we've stayed together through some rough times. So … I don't know."

Chapter 17
What Were You Thinking?

Davy had known Bill a couple of years when he got the man to explain just why he had joined the Camp Earth Enlightenment Center back in the U.S. The two had nearly a full hour of free time in their special spot for Bill to justify choosing something Davy hadn't.

"Well son, you see, ah … I grew up in the Midwest, okay, lots of farms and churches and folks who read the Bible. Now as a younger fella' like yourself, I went to school, went to church, played some football like we do here. I guess I was pretty good at football, not especially good at school though. I didn't pick up on things as fast as you seem to, Davy. All things considered, I don't remember too much about growin' up that made me real upset.

"Then America's war on Southeast Asia was really gettin' heavy; you've heard of Vietnam, it's east of here," said Bill, pointing, "across thousands a' miles of Indian Ocean. The war made a real ugly place of it, what maybe could a' been a beautiful place. It's a lot like camp, a lot like central Africa. So I was called up by the U.S. government to go there with a lot of other American boys, and I don't know that even one of us knew what that war was really about, but it seemed to me that most of us thought we were servin' our country, you know?

"Now, I loved the Army. I mean, I really did. I think when you're part a' somethin', when you're part of an organization that's a force for good and improvement in the world, or at least is supposed to be, you just feel good about things. For whatever reason, in the Army I just felt totally alive and fully human, you know, like everything inside me that was supposed to be firing was really firin' to the max. And I was a good soldier, Davy. I got all kinds a' scars and plenty a' medals to go with 'em.

"So, I was there in Vietnam about a year, and I wanted to stay as long as I could. My commanders said I should stay, and I would have. But … one afternoon … kind of out a' the blue, something happened. I was havin' some food at a little outdoor cafe, and uh, I noticed that not far from me there's this guy in an orange robe who's sittin' down in the street, and it looks like he's prayin'. There's some commotion in the crowd that's gatherin' around 'im, while at the same time there's an eerie sort a' stillness. And he sets himself on fire, Davy. Must a' been gasoline on 'im, 'cause he was covered in flames. He didn't scream, he just sat there and burned to death, right in front a' me.

"Well, why did he do it? How could he do it? Okay, I thought, this must be one of those monks in that part of the world who meditate all day long until they can't feel their body anymore, or something. But you know what, son? There was a fella' that did that in America, the very same thing, burned himself to death just outside the building where the war was bein' directed. It turns out he did it for the very same reason as this other guy. They wanted to show us what was happening, what we were doin'.

"We were burnin' that whole place up. Thousands and thousands a' farmers, folks not too different from the ones I grew up with, were bein' swallowed by our flames. The U.S. Air Force flew so high up in the clouds that the people below couldn't see or hear what was comin', so when the firebombs hit the villages it was like the Earth just suddenly split open and hell itself came ragin' up. It took me a while to realize it, but these were actual people we were burnin' up, which isn't a very easy thing to realize. It takes special help to realize it, the kind of help that these fellas who burned themselves were tryin' to give.

"When you see folks as actual people, you can see how they could want things like dignity and independence for their country, something fairer than what they'd been forced to take all through history, first by the Chinese, then by the French, then the Japanese, then the French again, and finally the Americans. The Vietnamese were supposed to have an election, and about eighty percent of 'em were gunna' choose this guy who was a lot like George Washington. And Davy, if you recall from school how the British king felt about George Washington of the American colonies, I think that's near enough how the U.S. government felt about the George Washington of the colony of Vietnam. The U.S. government just wouldn't allow an election they knew was gunna' remove their power there, so they said to hell with democracy and they set up a regime so phony and ugly that any actual Vietnamese person was of course gunna' do what he could to get rid of it.

"The U.S. government sent the Air Force, Marines, Navy, and us Army boys to protect that regime, that phony regime that lasted about twenty years in one form or another. The CIA was sent there too—yep, the same guys Brother K talks about bein' all over the world—and they played a huge role in helpin' the gang the U.S. had put in power there, trainin' 'em in the best ways to keep farmers from givin' support to their George Washington. The CIA called it Operation PHOENIX. It meant goin' into villages in the dark of night to kill or capture whoever the CIA had a fancy to. The same thing has happened in lots of other countries. The CIA makes a list of thousands of actual people who support a

George Washington, and the list goes to the army and police of a phony regime that hunts the people down and does the worst things imaginable to 'em. And who cares if thousands a' bystanders are caught up too, you know, who's countin'?

"But you know, Davy, I didn't realize any of this or even think to find out about it until that man on fire woke me up. What he did … I just can't communicate how strange and powerful it was, the way he offered himself as a sacrifice for others, for thousands a' farmers, as well as for thousands a' guys like me who had eyes that didn't see.

"All the time I spent there fightin' I felt so alive, but I was so asleep. I mean, I couldn't help seein' that we were bombin' the place back to the Stone Age, but I thought we were doin' it for good reason and were actually helpin' the people there. Any evils we did was okay because we werc doin' it to stop the ultimate evil, and that was the Communists. I'm sure you've heard about 'em. And honestly, Davy, the Communists were very real and very oppressive, and they wanted to dominate the world and control people's lives. No lie. And it was the Communists who were givin' weapons to the Vietnamese George Washington, who was also a Communist. So I thought if we were fightin' the Vietnamese George Washington then we were savin' Vietnam and the world from the evil a' Communism.

"Most a' the Vietnamese people didn't see things the way us Army boys did. To them, *we* were the ultimate evil, and it was the Communists that were helpin' to save them from *us*. America was behavin' like France and Japan and China had, as just the latest foreign power tryin' to keep Vietnam how we wanted it. When the Vietnamese thought about oppression, what had to come to mind was their own long experience under these foreign powers that used Vietnam and took its treasures, while Communism promised to be a system that let common folks and the entire country enjoy the treasures. Communism really did involve huge problems though, I mean massive evils, when it was tried in places like Russia and China. But most a' the Vietnamese people saw it as somethin' that could do better than what the French and the Americans were offerin'. At the very least it meant weapons from Russia and China to help Vietnam break free a' the French and the Americans.

"You look confused, son. Well, the whole thing is still confusin' lots a' folks to this day, the honest folks anyway.

"After that guy burned himself in front a' me, I went and did some prayin' and thought about what we were doin' there and tried to read more about it. I went to my commanders and I asked 'em, 'How come if we're really helpin' these people here, so many of 'em just keep fightin' against us?' And without stoppin' to think about it my commanders said, 'The Communists put 'em up to it, the International Communist Conspiracy. What we're doin' here is the Lord's work, and it doesn't matter what we've gotta' do, even if we've gotta' kill 'em all, we'll be savin' 'em and the rest a' the world too from somethin' worse.'

"That was the story, and my commanders were stickin' to it, and they wouldn't understand why one a' their best soldiers would start seein' things a different way. I told 'em I just didn't feel right about soldierin' anymore, at least not for the mission we'd been given there. So they just kept on burnin' up farmers and I went home.

"So, I got back to the U.S., and right away things looked different to me, 'cause I really started payin' attention to the things that I'd felt so good about goin' off to fight for. Like goin' to church on Sunday. Well, it was the same old church that it was a year before, but now I really wondered about what the pastor was sayin' at the pulpit and the hymns we were singin'. A lot a' the words were about Jesus, but the whole idea seemed to be that everyone should just feel blessed to have the way of life that God approves. Folks would come up to me, nice folks I'd known for years, and they'd tell me how great it was that I'd gone and defended freedom. And I'd say, 'Thanks, but it's a real confusin' war and I'm not sure what sort a' freedom it is that we have in mind for the people over there, destroyin' all they have so the Reds can't use it.' The church folks made faces and noises and said, 'Oh come on now, don't let the hippies make ya' forget about yer' country.' And I'd say, 'Well, we can't let America forget to practice its ideals.' And they'd say, 'Yeah, we're glad ya' fought for freedom.'

"I kept goin' to church and talkin' to whoever'd listen, but it looked more and more to me like they were just playin' a game, and anyone was welcome to play with 'em so long as you played by the rules, one of which was that God, Jesus, and the Founding Fathers are always a hundred percent happy with American power, no matter what the military and the corporations ever actually do. So, a good American is someone who never apologizes for American actions, like America is God. And when Jesus says take the wood out of your own eye, he means everyone except America. This game ain't about worshipin' Christ, it's about worshipin' somethin' easier, an earthly power that really does seem almighty and godlike, much like ancient Rome must a' seemed.

"I'd sit there in church and stare up at this huge wooden cross we had behind the pulpit, and to me it symbolized the unjust suffering a' the oppressed, but to the folks around me it seemed to mean some sort a' guarantee they were automatically on the Lord's side and they should just pat each other on the back for how right with God they were. This pretty well scraped me raw, and I'd start sweatin' and feelin' a fire burn inside me as they sat there smilin' and singin' away. I'd see a fire reach up out a' the floor, and their singin' turned to screamin' as they were blackened and devoured by flames, until they were skeletons sittin' on piles a' glowin' ashes. I'd actually smell burnin' flesh.

"I guess maybe I became a little too disappointed with these folks and this church I'd grown up with and had respected quite a bit. They were caught in a rut a' pride and blindness that's real easy to get stuck in, even if yer' a good person. Heck, I myself had been in the same rut right beside 'em, and had gone off to kill Vietnamese without thinkin' twice about it. So I guess when I saw those church folks in flames I was angry at myself too for havin' been such an upstanding member a' their self-love society.

"But they didn't want to hear, didn't want to see. And I didn't want to play their game, so I cut out church entirely. Still got into the Bible though, from time to time, and started pickin' up on the dark side it has. The Bible can be real depressing, Davy, it's not all this bright message a' salvation. Lots of it is sorrow about how life is unfair, you know, how it's hard to understand why God lets the way of the wicked prosper.

"I started losin' touch with old friends. I also started drinkin' … ah, alcohol, Davy, it's ah, supposed to make you feel better … and I guess it kind a' does, for a bit, but in all it's bad for you if ya' drink too much, which I did. How's it bad? Well, okay, you start drinkin' when yer' feelin' down, which I was. Then it lifts you up and makes you feel real strong and warm and satisfied. But what it's actually doin' is slowin' ya' down, shuttin' yer' mind and body down even though you feel good. And you drink more to stay feelin' good, but soon enough that feelin' just disappears like a ghost, and yer' left feelin' sick and down, lower than when you started.

"So yeah, I drank, and I got pretty fat too. Some mornings I just couldn't get up from bed, couldn't do any work, couldn't see the point in doin' anything. That's actually the hardest feelin' I ever had, like I was comin' apart, like I wasn't meant to live anymore, I was so weak and broken down. I remembered how strong and alive I'd felt in the Army, how good it had felt to have a foundation, somethin' to pull me together. It's frightening to live without a foundation, without answers to the big questions, lost in a dark forest. Your thoughts and feelings have to have somethin' to rally around or you just sort of dissolve. The light had just about gone out on me, Davy, and I kind a' got to wishin' the light would go out on everyone else, too. I mean, sometimes I'd sit there in the dark and just wish the whole thing would stop. I could see the whole Earth in flames, spinnin' off into the nothing of outer space. I nearly turned a gun on myself. I've had buddies who've actually done it, and I've spent lots a' time thinkin' about 'em.

"So, as I said, I was also gettin' into the Bible a bit, especially the Revelation about the end times, which is filled with all kinds a' strange images a' war and devastation, just like my own head was. But the image in the Revelation that really stuck with me was one that sort a' steered me away from goin' out like those buddies a' mine, and it got me feelin' there was still some possibility in life. Matter of fact, Davy, we've heard Brother K talk about this very image from time to time. It's the heavenly woman in the pains of tryin' to give birth to the kingdom of God on Earth, which is extra painful with a dragon beside her that's standin' by to devour the child. The birth happens, but God takes the child off to heaven. I tend to think that's an accurate picture a' what seems to happen to anything too good in the world. It's gone before it can really get its legs, you know? That part a' the image isn't so encouraging.

"The kingdom was on Earth for a while, though, and you can read in the Bible about what it was like, how the early Christians were somehow able to really live the words a' Jesus, to love the people nature says you're supposed to take advantage of. But just like the Revelation says, the kingdom didn't stay long, God took it to heaven. Maybe the dragon was too powerful. But here's what happens next. The Revelation says the heavenly woman flees into the wilderness, to a place prepared by God, where the dragon can't get to her, even though he tries. The way I read it, the heavenly woman is lyin' low until the time is right for her to deliver the kingdom of God on Earth again. That struck me as somethin' that made stickin' around on Earth worthwhile, to maybe have a chance to have some part in the delivery.

"A feelin' a' fresh air and light came into me, and I guess you could say I started to seek that heavenly woman out. Or at least I felt it wasn't hopeless to keep an eye out for her.

"I didn't know just where to look for that woman though, and truth be told, I wasn't lookin' much at all sometimes, when I'd feel like I was just fine where I was, workin' days at the meat plant, goin' bowlin' and fishin' with buddies on the weekends, or maybe to a movie with a girlfriend.

"I would also feel a real need to move, to do somethin' I wasn't doin'. I don't know if you ever felt this way, Davy, but out there in the world it can be like no matter what you're doin' or where you are, there's always this feelin' that you're lost, that you're missin' somethin' you're supposed to have. So you're always on the lookout for things that might be able to fill you. Some folks get married. Some buy a car or a boat or a big house. Some join the military. Some join a church.

"I looked into some churches, and some churches came lookin' into me, too, but the way I found out about the camp was … I guess sort a' by accident. I was waitin' to see the doctor one day, and this was at a place where soldiers like me could see the doc for free, but only if you'd been shot or had gotten wounded in certain other ways, which I always thought was really wrong, since lots a' soldiers got wounded from the war in lots a' ways the U.S. government just didn't want to recognize, so as to save money and to make their wars appear less harmful. When your country is real glad to send you off to fight for it, then just as glad to wash its hands of you when you come home all broke up … it doesn't feel much like *your* country. Anyway, there I was, and I guess someone must a' brought in his whole family, 'cause now I was sittin' there with a bunch a' little kids who were just hootin' and jumpin' around, and there was a whole table full a' books an' magazines you could look at while you were waitin' there, and these kids were takin' 'em and throwin' 'em at each other and runnin' left and right, just scatterin' stuff everywhere. It was real funny to see, until they got to hittin' each other pretty hard with these books, doin' some real violence and gettin' bawlin' mad about it. Then a lady came by, and the moment they saw her they started pointin' at each other and cryin' real hard, like they knew they'd done wrong but just couldn't help it. The lady told 'em there'd be no ice cream, and this pushed 'em right over the edge, and a whole team a' nurses had to help collect these kids and get 'em to another room. So, after this tornado had passed, I gathered up all these beat up books an' things the kids had strewn everywhere, and I just glanced at the covers a' some of 'em, and one struck me a little. Jesus Needs a New Earth—and I thought, Yeah, he really does, since the old one seems dead-set against him. But what a weird title.

"Now uh, I happened to take that book home. Okay Davy, I stole it, but it seemed such a strange book that I didn't think I would find it anywhere else, and anyway, I would really give it as much of a good read as anyone else. I gave it a chance, and wouldn't ya' know it, here was *my* story writ large. Whoever wrote this book understood where I was at. There was definitely this feelin' I had about it, like Joshua was that woman in pain tryin' to give birth to somethin' good in this world. It made me feel that there were people who wanted to help deliver the kingdom like I did."

Bill pressed his rugged fingers along his stubbly jaw and gazed with resignation across a darkening forest of awakening monsters. He had more to tell the boy as they sat there in the thick, low cry of the jungle, but the man felt that the boy would do better without the full story, which contained certain truths that were simply not helpful under the circumstances which he and the boy both faced here in Camp Earth. So the man didn't finish his story. He didn't reveal that he'd sought out the Enlightenment Center against his better judgment, didn't reveal that he just hadn't been able to fight a feeling his body and soul demanded he feel, didn't reveal that a heart desperate for something can easily be taken by a counterfeit.

"Do you wish you hadn't come to Camp Earth?" Davy pushed.

Bill hesitated.

"Have you ever thought of leaving?" the lad risked further.

"Yeah, son. Lots of us have wanted to leave at one time or other. But when the advisers say we're surrounded here by a sea of wild jungle, beyond which there's disease and famine and war, they're pretty much tellin' the truth. We're just gunna' have to take this day by day, like Jesus said, takin' on each day without carryin' the load of future days. We'll give what we've got to and we'll make it to better times. It's hard. But things have a way of correcting if you keep your head up and try to be of good cheer. Just think, Davy, how you probably never expected to have a friend like me and a special spot to talk things over, but here we are. And thank goodness you've got yer' coffee to help you out at least twice a day, like you always say. And Davy, if ever you feel yer' sinkin' down too low, you can call on the Lord for help. Call on the one who sank the lowest. Call on your creator for the strength that was created in you. Do it, especially when yer' havin' a hard time believin' in such a thing as God. You'll feel that the weight you have to carry is a weight that others have carried, too. You'll feel there's a power given you so you can carry, like you have an ally against what life can load onto you. This help is God, basically, God for all living things. You have God with you because you're his child, so to speak. You're part of his creation, you're legitimate, and you're never doomed or alone."

It was a few weeks after this dangerously powerful session that Bill and Davy were arrested.

There the man and boy were, at it again in their sanctuary, when suddenly a pair of advisers appeared out of nowhere and stormed right in, breaking up the conversation in mid-sentence. Advisers didn't normally stroll in the jungle, and Bill felt pretty sure that some member must have tipped these guys off about what had been going on here. Davy and Bill were no longer in control here, the advisers were, so the pleasant little place was now all about fear and shame and anger. This was now a crime scene, where scriptures about false prophets had been dug up and analyzed, where complications and disillusionment had been alleged in detail, all before the tender mind of a boy, all (crucially) without any of the authoritative advisory clarification the camp was due.

"Kind of a strange place to be. Just the two of ya' talkin'? Huh? Just relaxin' and talkin' about life. Okay, nuthin' wrong with that necessarily. But looks like you got yer' books with ya', and also a Bible? Okay. Any magazines or newspapers? Electronic devices? None? Okay. Remind me what's yer' name? Bill Magnusson, okay. And how 'bout you, son? Davy Schmidt, all right. We'll just look around here for a minute. You sit right there Bill, and Davy why don't you sit on this rock over here? Thanks.

"Okay, looks like y'all do just have them two books and a Bible on ya', and we appreciate ya' didn't try an' hide 'em from us. But you know we can't just leave it at that, okay, when we all know you been doin' a little more than just relaxin' out here. You both know better than to try an' interpret scriptures together without guidance. It's real easy to get all the wrong ideas when you look at the scriptures the wrong way. You gotta' realize the Evil Mind-Control is stronger than you. It doesn't matter how smart you are, okay? Yer' just fillin' yerselves with dangers, dangers that yer' bringin' into camp with ya'. What happens is Joshua's message a' peace and humility gets lost, and you get to thinkin' his message is about rebellion. It's happened time and time again, goin' way back, okay? Bill, think about the example yer' settin' for Davy. What both y'all need to start thinkin' is, 'How's what I do gunna' affect others?' Y'all need to start carin' enough about yerselves and others that you'll keep the pollution out."

Davy kept quiet and sat still while Bill walked a tightrope. On the one hand the man had to demonstrate submission to the advisers, had to make them feel respected, not only for the weapons they carried, but also for their valuable advice that brought moral clarity to sheep who'd lost the path. On the other hand, he had to avoid sinking into groveling that could reduce him in the eyes of the advisers and the boy and himself. Bill gave short answers that were as truthful as they could be without being suicidal, and he did it with childlike reverence. Yes, he and the boy had found the same place to relax, and sometimes had the scriptures on hand, and a few times got to talkin' about 'em. Yes, Bill knew it was wrong, knew he would a' done better not to do it, but he kind a' slipped into doin' it, just tryin' to help the boy understand parts a' the book and the Bible that were a bit difficult, so as to strengthen Davy's faith.

Bill's calm answering impresses Davy very much. This man is fit for the task. He's so in control of himself, like he's chatting with friends. Davy controls nothing, least of all himself. He's right now battling himself to just be able to breathe and keep his hands from shaking, so that maybe he can tell the advisers how much Bill has helped him. But the boy can't. There's no breath in him, his dry and squeaky throat will fail him if he tries to talk, and he'll only end up crying. It doesn't matter anyway, because the advisers don't really care what good actually comes from Bill and Davy studying and talking in their special spot.

The advisers stepped back and conferred about the correctional measures to be employed. The informant must have caught Bill and Davy at their mildest, because the advisers decided that the offenders were merely to be put "On Notice." This meant Bill and Davy should consider their full range of conduct to be the legitimate object of the advisers' extra scrutiny for the next little while. It meant purification in the box could be counted on were the man or boy again found inviting the Evil Mind-Control. It meant Bill must move his mattress to the shed farthest from where Davy's was, and the two could have no further contact with each other unless unavoidable in the course of their camp duties. If Davy needed help with scriptures or anything else, he was to ask the adviser in charge of his study group, who'd been placed over Davy by wisdom and foresight. And Bill should also call on the adviser of his own study group with whatever concern he might have, and should bear in mind that a number of faithful members were open to arrangements leading to the right kind of relationship: man and wife, committed to checking the Evil Mind-Control in each other, enjoying the respect of the congregation and the blessing of Brother K.

Chapter 18
What a Guy Wants

Brother K peeled himself from the back of his concubine, his skin sticky for going many days without washing. Brother K preferred that he and the girls carry a rich odor, and that they trim themselves in the manner he designated. The consort beside him now stretched, and with a minimum of fuss she rose from the broad low bed and strode off to the medicine cabinet, leaving Brother K to his sacred contemplation.

His relations with these chosen females had lost much of the romantic pageantry he volunteered in the flower of his youth, the novelty having faded over the years into a stable regimen in which Brother K simply made use of the girls, when and how he might desire, and then gave himself over to other interests until he again felt desire for their company. He figured he never *really* hurt the girls, even though all could appreciate that should he ever want to, the power dynamics in the relationship would permit it. For the girls would gladly hold up under a bit of rough treatment if it meant keeping their position in Brother K's harem, inside the temple, away from the hard and heavy onslaught of the fields and the study groups. Indeed, their station was an honor jealously guarded, and the girls were constantly intriguing against each other to secure a greater share of Brother K's attention.

Of major concern to the girls, it seemed to Brother K, was that he might become so infatuated with one of their number that he'd lose all desire for the remainder of the harem and dismiss them, perhaps at the insistence of this queen herself. Therefore, even as each girl felt compelled to engage in tireless self-promotion in order to gain or at least retain favor with Brother K, the girls were also a community ever on the lookout for any imbalance that might arise among them. So as soon as Brother K was perceived to take a special liking to one of them, a newcomer perhaps, as soon as she became the recipient of his sweet glances or invitations to table or bed more than she was due (the greatest offense being consecutive beddings, which deprived some other girl of her turn with Brother K, for as a rule he tried to maintain a regular circuit), well then most of the harem banded together to cut the princess down to size.

In the last little while it was one Sarah who, through no fault of her own, had become the chief apple of Brother K's eye. She was barely thirteen, and much to the dismay of the harem, had no obvious physical shortcomings that could compromise her standing as a concubine. If she did have something slightly amiss with her body, it might well serve as an opening into which the other girls could drive a wedge to separate her from Brother K. The girls had learned that the best way to accomplish this was not merely to suggest the flaw to Brother K in hopes of implanting in him some revulsion toward it, though this was often attempted. More effective was implanting in the girl herself some awareness of the imperfection with an inflated sense of its significance so as to damage her own estimation of her attractiveness. The usual effect was that a girl Brother K had found highly satisfactory even with her big this or small those or odd-shaped that, became unattractive to him very quickly when she stopped believing in herself and no longer conducted herself with enthusiasm.

But Sarah couldn't easily be attacked this way. She was actually getting prettier and closer to sheer perfection as time went on, so the harem had better find *some* way to act against her, and sooner rather than later. She had to have some weakness, maybe some odd habit, just anything really, that they could fix on and get her to fix on, so Brother will come to his senses and realize Sarah's just a simple child who doesn't deserve the attention that's poured onto her. It was sickening how he ministered to her for hours and hours, taught her music and art and all the rest from all those books of his, laughing together like brother and sister. The sounds they made together rubbed salt into the wound, kind of a *scraping* that spreads through you, until you're sweaty and dizzy and crying, aching in all your organs, worst of all when he took Sarah to bed, their squeals ringing shamelessly through the whole temple, piercing through all armor. And when the squealing died away there was no peace, because your undying worm remained in you to squirm at each and every sigh and hum and coo of contentment between prince and princess. What secrets was he now telling her about the camp? The harem would have poisoned her, but knew that Brother would suspect them and have them punished in some hellish way. The harem had really always known she would arrive, this one, and now that she was here, maybe the best they could do would be to push down their vomit and try gaining favor with her, so maybe she could get Brother to keep for them some kind of place in the temple. The things they had done for him weren't enough, the slimiest, boot-licking things. They could still wake up tomorrow and have a hoe thrown at them for a new life in the fields.

Tonight the camp should get a memorable show. Brother K had been retooling a few songs from the era of young people trying to start the world over again, real classics that should stoke the fires in waning hearts. The coffee trees, many of which were in place here before

Brother K arrived and were only now mature, were reaching peak production, and the members had to have spirit for the upcoming harvest. Of course, a good harvest meant bonuses for advisers, and this was fine with Brother K, who sensibly desired that these eyes, ears, tongues, and fists of his got something for themselves from the camp arrangement.

It was now his ninth year in Africa. During his fourth and fifth years the wave of murmuring swept through the camp, revealing to him the need to commission members out of the camp mass to be advisers. The majority of the membership had participated to some extent in the murmuring, increasingly bewildered that a grand and apparently private palace should be built upon their sparse physical comforts, and that the realities of camp life in general should veer so markedly away from the democratic socialism of the book. Against discontents as obviously reasonable as these, Brother K preferred not to have to reason, and he simply pulled an almighty trump card, calling the camp together in special assembly and announcing that Joshua desires certain members to occupy positions in which they'll offer special guidance and protection to the camp. Joshua had seen the strife in his camp and desired that his congregation put their fallible reasoning aside in acceptance of whatever camp conditions that he in his higher wisdom has seen fit to establish. An indescribable thrill coursed through Brother K when a large part of the congregation (hundreds of real people) appeared to actually accept this "Declaration of Joshua" as a workable solution to the camp's unrest. Naturally some puzzlement was voiced concerning the extent of Joshua's involvement in the adviser-selection process, inasmuch as many kind and helpful members were passed over while office was given to a considerable number of prideful and self-interested ones.

Basically, two types of member had gotten promoted to adviser status. The first type had shown genuine fervor for camp ideals and mythology, without showing much concern that camp realities measure up. Totally in love with the book and Joshua, they simply couldn't think of themselves as being part of anything other than the golden city of their story. Merely to state a matter of fact, most were white women. They were given charge of running the study groups. Brother K perceived that they derived a vital psychological satisfaction from the certainty of orthodoxy. Questions, doubts, criticism, debate—all it meant to them was insecurity, which made them nervous and irritable and very protective of Brother K and his doctrine. They cherished unity and stability, and therefore cherished the strong authority of the temple, which settled conflicts and set standards. They could be counted on to strive to keep the ideas of the members, especially the younger ones, within the acceptable range. And for all their diligent labor they never asked the temple for special rewards and privileges. It was good enough for them that their labors supported the ideology that gave them a constant stream of joy, and they were content to live right alongside the common members as examples of what it meant to be enlightened.

The other type of adviser required extra perks to be content, simple tangible goodies that reliably produced the elementary pleasures that gave their lives purpose. These people had shown little authentic emotion, except perhaps disdain, in relation to supposed camp ideals. What concerned them were facts on the ground, all the grubby little particulars forming the solid terrain called daily life, a cold, hard terrain that nevertheless offered some fine sensations to someone adept at snatching them with a cold, hard heart. They were men of various ages and colors. They had shown a mechanical and perfunctory air in their approach to labor and study, doing only as much work and knowing only as much doctrine as necessary to pass as a member and receive the benefits of membership. They understood how things are gotten away with, and they could hardly fail to be wise to the rather glaring scheme that was being gotten away with all around them. While others mourned the injustice of the scheme, these men mourned not occupying a seat at the top of it. Cabins were quickly thrown up for them on a low hill by the ginning house and on another small hill on the other side of camp by the bean barn, so that twenty-four of these advisers could be accommodated at each site. Brother K ordered new pants for them, sturdy but light weight, arranging that the advisers at the coffee site received gray pants, while those at the cotton site received tan. Brother K then issued each site an allotment of weapons: semi-automatic rifles, pistols, Tasers, and night sticks. But he did this only after each site swore an oath in their own torch-lit ceremony, an oath declaring that these special members accepted responsibility with Brother K to do what was required to ensure that the camp would be presented to Joshua in a state of order, unity and purity. Despite the chuckles emerging here and there from a few men unable to suppress their irreverence as effectively as their fellows, Brother K delivered oath and weapons with utter solemnity and the appearance of complete sincerity, as though every man present was convinced of the serious reality of Joshua's expectations of them. Brother K's magnificent performance sent a clear and powerful message to these men, his toughest of crowds: Laugh at all this hokum and you'll only be laughing at the basis of the better life you're being offered. Idiots, you'll only be mocking your own grander role in the fantastic play called Camp Earth. Take it or leave it, but really, for your own sake, take it.

Brother K always dealt with each site by itself, telling certain of the tan advisers to be wary of certain of the grays, telling certain of the gray advisers his suspicions regarding certain of the tans; presenting the tans with a case of whiskey and tobacco, presenting the grays with yet another of the temple girls whose services Brother K no longer desired. His aim was that each site would fancy him a generous chieftain worth serving and would fancy itself his most beloved pillar of support, a status proudly to maintain, while each would have to recognize that it mustn't turn its arms on Brother K since he could summon help from the other site. The desired effect was that each site would dutifully monitor its half of the camp and keep a jealous eye on its rival, thereby aborting any revolutionary notions that might stir in any quarter of the camp.

And if the tans and grays ever managed to get along and conspire about taking the camp, or if the common members somehow got organized for action and somehow overcame the tans and grays, there remained the deterring prospect that Brother K and the watchers reserved in the temple some weapon of last resort. Brother K dropped hints around some of the more able advisers, cryptic comments about "grand and godly powers" being nursed up in the temple for release at the appropriate hour.

The king lay there inside his spacious palace, the conscious possessor of much that he could possibly want from the world. His taste for material goods had never become *too* extravagant. He did own a dozen robes of exquisite color and fabric, five luscious guitars, a thorough set of exercise equipment, a super-sized multimedia entertainment console, and a decent library. He ate lobster, crab, tenderloin, drank plenty of fresh coffee, and shared with his harem a love of red wine. Anything he wanted was trucked overland to him following a less-costly preliminary journey by boat or plane, or else it was air-dropped right into camp. And he had stacks of catalogs from which his girls could order almost anything they wanted.

He and the watchers had always considered it perfectly legitimate to claim a portion of camp income to allow themselves a reasonably comfortable lifestyle. It was a justified expense to reward the talent and initiative they brought to the camp, and to compensate the planning and supervision they contributed here every day. Comfortable conditions also provided Brother K and the watchers the undisturbed state of mind necessary for the effective execution of the camp's preeminent duties.

The general membership had asked to be given a more comfortable lifestyle of greater material goods and leisure, an understandable, predictable request, and one that demonstrated their basic ignorance of camp needs. Expenses must be kept low, and productivity high, in order to ensure a competitive product and to maximize funds for further investment into the camp. The members' proposition was essentially that the camp take on needless expenses that could damage or even destroy the viability of the whole camp enterprise. Fortunately for everyone, cooler heads prevailed.

It had occurred to Brother K that, were he and the watchers to live the simple and modest life of a common member, the expense of maintaining the temple lifestyle could be transferred to improving the comforts of the congregation with no damage to camp finances. But Brother K and the watchers truly enjoyed their temple lifestyle—and camp finances could very well suffer if the common lifestyle was the greatest incentive that propelled the finest efforts here. More leisure among the congregation would simply result in their abuse of it, with unguided reflection altering healthy perspectives until the camp was awash in disturbed outlooks, much as a garden gives itself to weeds in the gardener's absence. Minds not engaged in twelve hours of supervised labor and study per day will easily become the Devil's workshop.

Besides, Brother K and the watchers didn't owe the members. It was the members who owed. It was the skill and gumption of Brother K and the watchers that put this whole thing together. Although, well … the Institute, being a charitable organization, was subsidized by tax exemption, so here was some help. In addition, Brother K had become aware that a great deal of the technology and expertise in the temple had sprung from government funds and labs, the Pentagon being an especially fruitful sire and generous patron, so here was some help (the same socialist help long enjoyed by American corporations having anything to do with electronics, aviation, computers, the internet, satellites, automated production, pharmaceuticals …). There was also, quite obviously helpful, the labor of the members. But even so, Brother K and the watchers were the rugged individuals whose contribution to Camp Earth was uniquely crucial. They were the arch supporting this camp, and Brother K liked to think of himself as the keystone of this arch, upon which the members depended, and without which these dependents could only be scraping by, living in a car or under a bridge back in the States, or as prey to the ravages of war in some brutalized zone of destitution somewhere in giant Africa. There was simply no question that Brother K and the watchers put an enormous amount of time and effort into Camp Earth, which gave a thousand forsaken people a livelihood, a physical and psychological livelihood. It was unquestionable that the temple authorities provided for the homeless and hungry and sick, and for lost souls who weren't able to find motivation and purpose and boundaries on their own.

If Brother K lived like a king it was because he deserved to. He'd worked his way up from a pauper, from that hideous life as Louis Koenig, and now that he had something comfortable between himself and that gutter, he was justified in doing what he could to keep it.

He supposed this conservatism had to be among the most ancient instincts. Anyone achieving possession of something beneficial is compelled to keep hold of it, no debate occurring, only the purest recognition of one's reliance on the possession for happiness. Then proceed the contrivances to convince others of one's *right* to the possession, a classic pursuit through the ages, comprising many a learned book in noble homes and many a windy sermon from revered pulpits. Brother K mused a bit more on these and other platitudes, then joined Sarah for a film and a few sets of quadriceps presses.

Chapter 19
A Little Child Shall Lead Them

The Friday evening horns called Camp Earth to supper, after which, mercifully, there would be no study groups—for tonight would be the Brother K Experience.

The members nearest the stage at Brother K's performances had been with the camp since its early days back in America. So much of their heart and identity was bound up with the camp that to them, Brother K could, by definition, do no wrong. Etched into them brain and bone were several passages from his book and guitar compositions. Some of these folks were couples married to one another by Brother K himself. Some safe-kept and occasionally studied personal documents of blessing and counsel that Brother K had written in his own hand specifically for them. They looked forward to the Brother K Experience all week, and when their Friday zenith arrived they were good and ready to let loose with wild dancing and chanting and singing, so that by the end of the performance they'd be floating in a state of ecstatic exhaustion, from which they could glide into restful sleep and arise refreshed for another week.

Sprawled out in a broad swath behind the dancing maniacs was the great bulk of the congregation, many appearing to derive at least mild amusement from Brother K's performances, reclining in their weary hundreds to forget themselves in a rainbow wash of sound and light. A few who still had energy left after a week of labor and study, mainly children, could be seen jumping, jigging, and imitating the grandiose mannerisms of Brother K, squinting their eyes and pursing their lips and thrusting their imaginary guitars forward with manly force. Some of these youngsters had come here from America with their convert parents or guardians, while others were native Africans transferred from refugee camps in which the Institute had delivered aid. In fact, about a third of the entire congregation were black African refugees of all ages who the Institute had selected for Camp Earth after screening them for disease. These folks had generally received the camp as though it was nothing other than God's own instrument for healing and redeeming their shattered lives. Many of them could speak Swahili in addition to English, though the use of Swahili was frowned upon in Camp Earth, because the whites tended to wonder just what it was the blacks were talking about, and a lot of whites shared an assumption that the language of God and Joshua was English, or more properly the King James English that Joshua speaks through much of the book; of course, these same whites easily pardoned themselves for saying *y'all* instead of the holier *ye*.

It was understood that the rear of the assembly was reserved for the members having special difficulty resisting the influence of the Evil Mind-Control, and these sat under the care of the tans and grays, who held a position at the very back by the tables. The troubled members showed a very dismissive attitude toward the Brother K Experience. It was their custom to slouch forward with their elbows on their knees and their fingers in their ears and their eyes tightly shut, seemingly falling asleep, or else they chatted loudly among themselves, and even talked at the good members in front of them, drawing attention away from Brother K and inhibiting the spiritual replenishment he offered. As much as the tans and grays preferred merely lounging about the tables while sucking down their booze and cigars, it was their duty to step forward and correct the deviant members. A knock from a nightstick usually did the trick, but electricity was also frequently employed. Sometimes the music, heat, smoke, and the hot sauce combined to make the tans and grays quarrel among themselves, their champions clubbing and shocking and testing each other in ritualized displays of jungle prowess. But mostly the tans and grays kept to their separate factions and directed their violence at members in need of it.

In all, the violence was rare, and the great mass of members showed little concern about it, never having experienced it firsthand, and being too caught up with the stage show to care much about what was going on behind their backs. Besides, there was really nothing wrong with it; the tans and the grays had been given authority to protect the camp with force, and force was necessary to restrain and reform the troublemakers.

As dark fell upon the jungle, torches everywhere came to life, and stage lights cast blue, silver, and white upon the temple. Huge speakers on the temple flanks began to crackle and hum out to the camp. A little prologue of metallic scrapes and swooshes threw the living forest into a yelping frenzy, the animals vainly protesting the rude disturbance they knew to be imminent. A stout, bald gray occupied a set of drums in a low-lit area of stage about twenty feet to the side of center and very near the temple face. The man tapped a half-muted cymbal crisply and steadily as the mouth of the sanctuary began to spread open, slowly gaping to a width of two feet, revealing only a black veil. There it hung across the miserly opening, undisturbed, until a figure now suddenly slipped out through it, wrapped in flowing fiery orange and wielding an instrument as black and full of mystique as that veil, or as the abundant wig cascading to the figure's shoulders. Yes, it was Brother K, stepping forward upon the stage, his guitar and a collar microphone both connected wirelessly to an effects processor. As the lights shifted to a heavy red, he spoke in a thick, grave voice:

"And the dragon manifested itself unto Joshua, saying:

'Who art thou that wouldst contend against me? Knowest thou not the greatness of my works?

'Have I not been with man since the beginning, breathing life into his wandering outcast soul, his only guide since God closed Eden?

'Am I not the river that waters his silent desert?

'Hast thou not beheld the pharaohs, the empires, even all the glories of man? Did not all spring beside the banks of me?

'Hast thou not beheld that God leaveth man alone, leaving men to be gods unto themselves? Is not man hereby given unto me, unto the service of my great glory? I rejoice!

'Behold the rulers of the Earth, ruling by sword and coin. Am I not glorified in them? Millions are the hearts grinded into dirt, that one of these gods might add an inch to his stature.

'Behold that God moveth not from his secret place, and saveth not the millions. Will he stir for thee, worm that creepeth blind upon a world God hath given to me?

'Thou art given unto me. I am the God of this world, and there is none other beside me.

'Therefore, heed my commandments. Thou shalt gain for thyself all that thine advantage alloweth. Thou shalt prosper according to thine advantage, according to thy strength, according to thy cunning. Thou shalt place thy trust in the arm of flesh.

'Rebel not any longer against me, son of dirt, for I am the very wisdom and salvation thou seekest. I have written my law upon the heart of man, and every child understandeth me. All who prosper in this world do keep my commandments.'"

Now Brother K got to working on the guitar with a lengthy series of chunky, barking passages ascending in tone, building a tower ever higher into the heavens, until a needling outcry of furiously hammered high notes signaled that the celestial abode of God may at last have been pierced. And then an abrupt silence, a stark stillness and suspense awaiting the divine reaction. When the jungle had recovered some composure, the stage lights made the temple blossom into gold, and Brother K spoke in a warm, soft voice:

"And Joshua answered the dragon with prophecy:
"When the spring sun rises
to greet water's maiden above,
then spring will spring indeed
and Earth will bathe in love."

The front rows broke into a frolic as Brother K and his drummer unleashed a golden oldy that filled the camp with the sound of a new age. In a black female voice of silk and butter, Brother K sang about the dawning of a thousand years of harmony and revelation, and a lot of members were moved to tears. The summer of '67 was still fresh in them. No one could ever convince them that what they'd felt that glorious summer wasn't *real* love. They'd since lived long and full lives, and still knew the love of that summer to be the realest love they'd ever felt. A God of power and goodness should make that love available on tap, and it would overpower the avarice made available on tap by the almighty dragon god, actual lord of this world. Loose the spigot then, that we may know thee, hidden God! Give us a magical plant, abundant in supply. Strip it of side effects. Let us soar for a summer … a thousand years … but let us not slide back into the mire! Why must it be the Devil's brew that never runs dry? Shouldn't God be worthy of the name?

As Brother K played, sweating heavily and contorting himself into a variety of flamboyant poses, a scuffle ensued just up against the stage. A black boy had somehow managed to get his fingers onto the platform's edge, and he was pulling himself up.

Squirming through the grasp of outraged members trying to stop him, and kicking a few for their efforts, the lad forced himself up onto the stage. Brother K wasn't expecting such insolence, so he merely stood flabbergasted as the child darted past him and disappeared through the veil between the temple doors.

To allow this one obvious gap in temple security on performance nights had been a custom favored by the watchers as a sign of trust and openness, while favored by Brother K as an avenue of escape should the membership ever attempt to gain the stage and lay hands on him. The little opening must always have seemed to some in the crowd to be an implied offer, a tempting one that nobody dared accept until this boy just now. For a few seconds Brother K stared blankly at his audience, then at the drummer, then set his guitar against the temple and slipped inside in hot pursuit, holding up his gown so as not to trip.

When the boy was later asked to account for himself, he explained that all this waiting for paradise had taken a toll on him, the prolonged suspense making him restless and plagued by doubt, finally reaching a point where he simply "had to get into the temple to see what was real," hoping new strength would flow into him from the new awareness he would achieve.

Just inside, he lost his footing on a couple of stairs and stumbled downward, crash landing onto soft, blue carpet. He got up instantly, then stood for a moment in the midst of a lobby. Directly confronting him was a pair of horrific guardians stationed in front of a dark wall. Dimly lit in cold silver from below, the two figures, a masculine canine and a feminine feline, kneeled with human legs and held forth up-turned paws as if to support something or present an offering.

The child darted left and ran down a hallway adorned with goldenly spot-lit, finely-framed paintings featuring mighty storms with massive clouds illuminated by lightning and the fire of armies in pitched battle. He made a hard right with the hall and continued forward into cool pleasant air that was very different from the hot heavy air outside. A scene now opened to his right: here was a long cavern filled with a blue glow from a row of television screens perched above tables stacked with wheezing computer drives and electronics consoles—a vast array of dials and meters and blinking red and green lights, with a snake-pit of wiring behind. Lining an opposite wall were long shelves heaping with boxes, folders, and papers, below which stood a row of metal cabinets of contents indeterminate. Seated at a computer was a man whose shiny face caught the shifting colors.

The lad proceeded down the hall, then paused for another large room that opened on his right. Here was another weakly lit setting, this one a coppery glaze. Keeping a vigil from high on a wall were shadow-casting skulls, fantastic animal skulls glaring down fiercely in a long row above a broad, black, flat television screen and a pair of brass lamps. Given center place in this lineup were jungle primates. Filling out the sides were grazers with terrific horns. Toward the ends of the row were big cats with magnificent teeth. The very ends were occupied by a grassland-scavenging biped's most formidable competitors: leopard and hyena. There were also tables and chairs, counters laden with cookware, cartons and containers climbing to the ceiling, a sink, a stove, a refrigerator, a microwave oven. While the skulls and lamps did produce some arresting effects, the boy would explain that "there just had to be something better than this in the temple," so he turned to the hallway and kept going.

At the end of the woody corridor of golden pictures and sweet woody smells, a lamp's rosy radiance revealed a staircase. The child shot toward it, passing the remaining sights of the first tier. Just before setting foot on the stairs, however, he noticed a figure standing in a darkish corridor that led down a long stretch on the boy's right. The man looked up from his clipboard, laid eyes on the child from perhaps fifteen feet away, and, making no attempt to seize the lad, simply raised a hand. Just what this signaled, whether halt or hello or something else, the boy later said he had little idea, and could only brush this aside and press onward. The man then dropped his hand to a device into which he communicated a few phrases, while the boy bounded up the stairs two and three at a time.

A spacious chamber unfolded before the lad's view, and here at last was something enough to stay his feet for more than a few seconds. Decked about the walls and ceiling were strings of soft lights of all colors, and within this spectacular artificial galaxy a large rectangular window looked out on the ancient light of true stars winking above moon-soaked mountain peaks. Heaped all across a floor of soft, green carpet were clothes and magazines and toys, a hoard of toys of all kinds: internet phones, laptop computers, digital cameras, CDs, speakers, exercise machines, a massive TV, a pool table, a roulette table, paints and clays, canvases and sculptures … all things the boy would love to try out, things he could easily be allowed to try out during free time, he later complained.

Deep in the back of this scene stood a disorderly table of bottles and dishes, beside a great bed perhaps seven times the area and forty times the volume of the child's meager mat. Pillows the size of pigs shimmied to the rhythm of someone who was up to something on that vast bed.

It was a girl, and the black boy could see plenty of her fair skin as she strove to stabilize her young frame in an extreme position which threw a range of her taut muscles into stark detail. Suddenly, an older girl appeared through an open doorway in the distant wall that faced the boy, and following her was yet another girl, this one of darker skin (though certainly not as dark as the boy). This pair of older girls wearing very little strode with plates of food to sit down at the table near the bed, where, munching and laughing, they addressed the young girl engaged in focused effort on the bed. "You're doing it wrong," they told her.

The boy later confessed that he couldn't figure out what the girl on the bed was trying to do, let alone whether she was doing it wrong.

The girl on the bed lost form, collapsed into the pillows, and coughed. "No, you guys, I was feelin' it where Brother says you're supposed to," the glistening beauty asserted.

"We just wanna' help you though," the older girls said in close harmony.

The boy now threw himself into the discussion. "Hey!" he barked.

The eaters dropped their food and the bed nymph sat up. Six bewildered eyes fixed onto this lad, this bold, bizarre, terrifying image of midnight skin seeping sweat and blood. There followed a moment of paralyzed indecision in which the girls may have assessed whether the thing before them truly consisted of matter occupying physical space. A girl at the table then screamed, perhaps signifying her affirmative conclusion. What now overcame the boy, he would later state, was an intense desire to issue violence upon these girls who to him represented his oppressors. He therefore began searching for a suitable weapon, but finding none at hand and hearing footsteps coming up the stairs behind him, the boy presently recovered his desire to behold the secrets of the temple, and he thrust himself past the girls in a mighty explosion of goblets, ashtrays, and half-eaten meals.

He emerged into a much smaller room lit tenderly by a tall, flower-shaped lamp standing in a corner. A mattress with pink sheets lay on the floor, across from a television set. The carpet was scarcely visible for all the magazines and dishes and clothing strewn about. The walls were plastered with pictures of women, a kaleidoscope of painted faces and young, slender bodies in costly apparel, making the place a shrine to some concept of female beauty. The boy now aimed himself at another open doorway and entered a room much the same as the previous, with a flower lamp, a television set, a mattress (though with lavender sheets), and glossy fashion clutter across the walls and floor.

A blue light was leaking from under a shut door, and through this the child found yet another of these apartments, except that the lamp was off, the television was on, the air was filled with a smelly smoke, and the mattress was occupied by two men and a girl. The trio squinted hard at the intruder, and then merely objected that their smoke was being allowed to escape. The boy turned and obligingly shut the door he had come through, and the threesome returned to their embrace. The boy was left to try the knob on yet another door, and through it he slipped out into another hallway of spot-lit paintings, politely closing the door behind him.

Toward one end of the hall a pair of green lamps illuminated what looked like an open closet, around which several boxes had been stacked. The opposite end of the hall led onto a staircase lit in a subdued yellow, and it was toward this that the youngster now moved, ignoring several doors and pictures, pausing only briefly at one large painting.

It was so packed with crisis it seemed to convulse. Brilliant hues burst out everywhere from black abyss, making the setting appear at first glance to be deep in outer space or deep inside the Earth. Great buildings of cold sapphire glass towered in the background, their glowing windows casting a sparkling, silver light into the night past dark human silhouettes peering down onto the pandemonium. Grotesquely deformed humanoids crept from simmering lesions in the foreground wasteland, the monsters lurching out to spew their bulging, sour innards upon a mass of vaguely bug-like people, who seemed thus pushed—and forth went this parade of freaks, this clot of living refuse, surging malignantly into an avenue of fine houses, bringing brown and yellow twirls of stink as well as medieval pitchforks, frontier six-shooters, and AK-47's, scrambling over gates that no longer held off the unpeople from the real people. Property here ceased to be private, almost every bit of space featuring some gruesome violation. At a splendid villa a gang of dirty peasants heaved chests of shimmering coins out a third story window, and on the ground a squad of unshaven derelicts clawed through one another in their rush to seize the spilled treasure. Meanwhile, a neighboring household fared no better under the wild rabble that frantically pillaged every opulent chamber, with a fat man in a bloodied nightgown teetering on the roof of his palace, prodded by knives and crooked faces to leap down into the waiting arms of yet more tormentors.

The movement of the mob riot was upward, toward the glass towers. At the foot of one stood a semicircle of coarse folk gazing up at the imposingly phallic structure, hurling stones at finely dressed figures hanging wretchedly from nooses cast out windows, with some sufferers even nailed abominably onto window frames.

Several strong diagonals directed the viewer of this hell-scape to a certain spot high up in its musty atmosphere where, nearly obscured behind clouds of infernal smoke, something hovered in surveillance of the terror and jubilation. It was a lidless eye, with a blood-red iris, a pair of eagle's wings sweeping out from the whites, and bolts of neon blue lightning striking down from the pupil to blast assemblies of malcontents all across the scene.

The boy ascended the golden stairs to the top tier of the temple.

Meeting him was a quiet cavern without carpet or decoration, just tools and materials strewn about numerous benches. It had the dark, still gloom of an attic, except for something further in. There was white light creeping around a wall of boxes, along with the faint sound of cheerful whistling. Stepping toward the slivers of gleaming light, the boy passed spools of cable, bundles of wire, stacks of metal beams and sheets, piles of bolts and screws, welding torches, drills and hammers, shears and pliers.

Beyond the wall of boxes sat an old man. Enthroning him was a richly upholstered chair swirling with wine red, purple, and indigo. A computer faced him from the junction of two long tables welded together into an L, and within this right angle sat the man in his goodly white robe (which many found reassuring), expertly tinkering with the intricate wiring of a contraption trapped firmly between his legs. Among his books and papers there rested a bust of himself, and a clock with a brass pendulum swinging and ticking between two silver columns under a golden dome. The wall nearest him featured several schematics and diagrams, the most prominent being a sort of pillar comprised of a series of colors, beside a map of the topography of two hemispheres of terrain, with each color on the pillar marking certain areas on the map.

And dominating this brilliant scene so nicely shielded by the wall of boxes, there was something like "a tree of metal," as the boy would tell it, rising straight up through the very center of the tier. Beside the giant apparatus stood a tall ladder and a chest of tools.

This? How could this be the grand payoff for all the striving? In disbelief the lad looked around to make sure he wasn't missing anything, and the harmless old man pretended not to notice as the boy went searching through closets. Eventually, the glowing fellow stopped whistling, set his device onto his desk, swiveled his chair around, and confronted the child face to face.

"Aahaaah, my boy," the old man said with a smile. "Come to steal fire from the gods, eh? I guess you're nearly ready for it then, and more or less on schedule."

Chapter 20
Why Did the Boy Run Amok?

The boy had seen more of the inside than any adviser had ever been treated to. Yet he exuded disappointment at not having seen anything he understood to be worthy of the temple. The boy claimed that he himself could organize a better temple, and in less time. Asked by the watchers what he'd be satisfied to see in the temple, the boy replied, "Joshua would be there, and he'd answer questions." Asked by the watchers what made him think he could recognize Joshua, the boy replied, "Joshua would recognize me." Smiles flashed all round at this audacity toward the gods, at this naive presumption to hurry the gods forward in their providence, and it took the watchers a minute to recover a stern enough tone to announce that Joshua had in fact been in the temple at the very same time as the lad, who didn't have the eyes to see this.

After his interrogation there was some concern in the temple about what should be done with him. Brother K couldn't help feeling sympathy and admiration for him, even to the point of wondering whether the lad should be given some position in the temple. The watchers agreed with Brother K that the boy could very well be taken onto the payroll as a useful asset, were there not the unfortunate necessity of making this offender appear before the congregation as punished and discredited. This boy Len represented radical defiance of the order the temple had established through many years of diligent efforts. His rebellion simply could not be allowed to project an image of success or safety, especially in front of a congregation that largely shared the boy's discontents and temptations.

And so, a few days after the incident, with supper consumed and dusk having fallen, the speakers broadcast a special invitation from Brother K for all to gather before the temple. The people assembled to see a dazed black boy sitting stiffly on a tall stool at center stage, facing his audience with his half-shut eyes fixed on the spot where he'd shot past Brother K.

The tans and grays having taken positions at the sides and rear of the mass, the temple doors now slid open in their slow, dramatic way, and out through the holy veil there stepped an adviser.

He was a man slight in build, with a gaunt face bespeaking long years of intense hunger. Without his sunglasses and combat boots he could appear frail and somewhat ridiculous as an authority figure, so he wore them, and often walked about swinging a stick. He was one of the tans but enjoyed a special status, since Brother K was perceptive enough to recognize this man's talent for mass communication. Brother K had learned that this man harbored a keen interest in history and art, and although the man was fond of reminding the congregation of his background of unskilled toils at subsistence wages, he had actually been for most of his working life a kind of journalist, whose employers had nicely compensated his skilled pursuit of the right research to tell the right story that supported the right conclusions—a fine situation snatched from him at the snap of fingers, his employers suddenly accusing him of "professional misconduct," they having discovered overnight a commitment to pious and high-minded ideals of journalistic integrity. No matter that their business depended on utter lack

of such integrity, telling only that side of the story that
benefitted their paymasters. As the profession itself was
misconduct, the accusations thus amounted to saying that he
should be ashamed of doing his job so well. He didn't know
whether to laugh or cry through the ensuing years when the
only place for him in his profession was on its blacklist. He
was eventually informed, after a great deal of scrounging and
festering, that this catastrophe wrapped in absurdity was
meant to punish what had actually been a very real and grave
offense of his at an office luncheon, where he had let alcohol
lead him into foolishly factual comments about the religion
favored by certain important people who happened to be
within earshot, people who had endowed his place of
employment with considerable moneys.

The dejected man, in need of a forum where his skills
could enjoy a fresh start, came to the Enlightenment Center
with Brother K's book in hand, and soon he was interpreting
the book and expounding the mysteries of the kingdom for
anyone who cared to listen, in effect presiding over his own
study group. Of course this alarmed Brother K, who'd
already been counseled by the specter about such people:
"While the healthy, common folk instinctively close their
ranks to form a community of the people, intellectuals run
this way and that, and cannot be used as elements composing
a community." So, the man could only be a destabilizing
force within the community, and furthermore, since his
abilities appeared to match Brother K's own, the man stood
as a prime candidate to usurp the prophet's role and
authority. Brother K considered inventing some pretense to
expel him but decided instead to pluck him out from the
membership, bring him close and employ his talents to both
their satisfaction. Brother K felt this man could be used, since
the fellow seemed to crave influence and recognition (which
might be affordable) rather than truth (which wasn't). And
so, Brother K made very good use of this man and even

considered him a friend, while never ceasing to fear and suspect him; indeed, Brother K noted which tans seemed envious of their special fellow and ordered each of them to spy on the man and report his activities and contacts.

But there the man stood on a stage in the middle of Africa, washed pure in blue and white light, commander of a captive audience of a thousand, with a black child seated a few paces to his right. Secure in his tight leather boots, the man removed his sunglasses and placed them in a pocket of his loose, tan pants. He fastened a wireless microphone to his relaxed, long-sleeved white shirt, and now the booming speakers saturated the camp with his sage and earnest voice:

"Good evening, brothers and sisters. You look bright, you look really good. Well, I'm glad to report some clarity about this trouble that struck a few nights back. I know we've all been really puzzled with what happened. All of us have known Lenny awhile, and it mostly seemed like he was doing well, not carrying too much Evil Mind-Control. Now that he's had a good talk with some of us there's a good understanding about what he did, and he's become able to see what a wrong and sorry thing it was.

"Len said he'd been feeling unhappy. But rather than examine himself for Evil Mind-Control, which should always be step number one, he turned the blame outward: he came to believe others were doing him wrong and keeping happiness from him. It became easy to believe that he simply deserved to take whatever he wanted, with stealing being something only others did to him. So he stole the temple. This was both sinful and foolish. The temple would have given him a generous portion in due time, if only he hadn't lost faith in the process of growth and preparation that's necessary for the temple to bless in abundance. Think of the investment Len spoiled. A hard-earned share in the kingdom of God on Earth had been in store.

"Len said that breaking into the temple was something he saw as a solution for him—a simple, easy solution to a deep problem. And when we heard him say that, we said, Whoa Len, that's just classic Evil Mind-Control there, come on now. The Evil Mind-Control steered him into a false solution, a false shortcut, even after all this time that Len has been working alongside us for a real solution. But that's the power of it. We have to remember that the Evil Mind-Control works by getting us to think and act in ways that oppress us, lulling us, cooking us and making dinner of us, but without us knowing it, without us feeling any sting. In fact, it cooks us in ways that we find attractive and pleasant, until we're mush in the cook's belly."

The man took something from his back pocket, which he then held up to the crowd. He spent a few seconds leafing through the thing's worn and soiled pages, shaking his head with a sour expression that conveyed a genuinely pained disapproval. Len shot an occasional glance at the congregation, which glowed in the swaying light of evening torches.

"Here's something we've been warned about. It's a magazine, just filthy. Len says he found it in some bushes by the ginning house. None of us should be surprised that it's dripping with Evil Mind-Control. Len admits that he looked through it and took it into his mind and heart, which means he endangered all of us with it. Now of course we'll cast it into the flames, but before we do, Brother K wants me to help you confront it and understand how it got Len to do that terrible thing he's so sorry for."

The man scoured through some pages, stopped on one in particular and struck it with the back of his hand.

"Here we go. We'll start with this. This is what love is, according to the Evil Mind-Control: love is a shiny rock. If you get this love-in-a-package then you're all set with love. You don't have to get love any other way anymore. It's all taken care of from now on. It even says right here that 'A diamond is forever.' The shiny rock proves that a woman is loved and that she's worth something, and the bigger the rock, the more the love and the worth. By the way, if we read carefully here, it says that a respectable love-package will cost at least a few thousand dollars. Think of the waste this calls for, the good use such money could be put to instead. Think also of the saps out there who don't have money to burn on sparkly nonsense but who are convinced that loving a woman means being able to afford it, meaning a life of corporate prostitution. And totally ignored is where the diamond came from, who had to fish it out of some riverbed at gunpoint right here in Africa. If you saw, actually some of you here maybe really have seen it and lived it, but if you saw how the diamond got from the earth to your finger, love is the last thing that comes to mind."

The man leafed through more pages. "And here, this is what beauty is according to the Evil Mind-Control: beauty comes from a plastic tube. It's something skin-deep, something you put onto your face, that's all. Now you're someone worth caring about. It's that simple. It's that convenient. They provide so many choices of color and shade, you feel like it's actually *you* who's choosing how to be beautiful. How fortunate that they alert us to ugliness, otherwise it might go unnoticed. Apparently, ugliness is woman as nature makes her. They give us their picture here of such a woman, sitting alone at a mirror, hair pulled back sensibly, face without any paints or surgeries, but frowning. Meanwhile, the picture below shows a woman out on the town with friends, her eyes smeared black and blue, her lips blood-red and swollen like an inviting female organ, and her hair all done-up in some artificial way just like her girlfriends. The condition of ugliness is diagnosed, and the medication is prescribed for it. My goodness … page after page of skin and hair … really perverted obsession.

"We've also got good parenting here, according to the Evil Mind-Control. Good parenting is a talking doll. It also dances and plays peek-a-boo. Fine, looks fun for the kids. But then we read, 'Get them the gift that every kid has gotta' have this Christmas and show them how much they mean to you.' Oh, now I see. The talking doll measures the love, like a diamond for the kids, as easy as pinning a medal. I've just gotta' do whatever it takes to get that talking dolly for them, or else the other mommies and daddies love their kids more than I love mine. So the Evil Mind-Control has turned Christmas into a contest for the talking dolly, and now you're honking and pushing and cursing in celebration of the birth of our Lord. If mom and dad do succeed in getting the talking dolly no matter what the cost, then congratulations to them as much as to their kid, because little Ashlyn or Skyler will show their prize all over the neighborhood, and all the parents will see who the really good parents are.

"There's plenty more in here. It's just crazy. *Sales*! Maybe the whole world is burning up and falling down around you, but you can't be bothered about it because there are *sales* that can't be missed, and new trends every week. You've gotta' keep up, gotta' keep an eye on what the neighbors are getting, because imagine the shame you'll feel if they see that you don't have a hot tub yet, or a swimming pool, or tiles in the walkway, or whatever vehicle that's the trend. And heaven forbid you have a wedding in last year's color of fabric. These are the treasures that are supposed to make life worth living out there in the world of the Evil Mind-Control, and there really is something attractive about it all, this concept that salvation comes through these graspable goodies that have only to be manufactured and held up for worship. But never forget that these are oppressive gods that demand sacrifices for the salvation they offer. Every new magazine is just the newest gods demanding the next round of sacrifices, more payments with interest, more prostitution to corporate johns. Damn it Len! It's enough to make you crazy.

"But the Evil Mind-Control's got crazy covered, too. We've taken in page after slick page, and we're feeling a little unsettled for some reason, so how neat that here at the last of it we get three pages full of something they call Val … pro … set, which is a nice green pill they've come up with to cure what ails us, something they're calling *generalized anxiety disorder*. But how do we know we really have this illness, this disorder? Well, they give us a very official quiz here, so let's imagine we're someone out there in the world and we'll just answer these questions to see if we're ill and need their pill. Says here, 'Are you unable to stop worrying? Do you feel restless? Are you tense and irritable? Do you have trouble sleeping? Do you feel frustrated or threatened by something that cannot be identified?' And then it says, 'Well, you deserve to feel normal again.' Ha! Oh my. As if it isn't normal to feel ill in a sick society, to feel anxiety in a society driven by marketable fads and market bubbles, a society that refuses to consider basic needs like healthcare and employment as even remotely important as compared to being able to make a killing in the stock market. Isn't anxiety the perfectly sane response to an environment of such rampant insecurity, in a cauldron where people are just so much flesh to be devoured? Apparently not, because we've just been assured that our anxiety is a disorder. That's right, *we* have the disorder. So, let's buy this Valproset and the problem is solved, though not entirely solved, since it also says way over here in really small letters that taking their pill may give us problems eating, pooping, sleeping, or thinking. But so what. The important thing is that we stop worrying. We sit back for a ride that's accelerating toward a ditch. It won't matter to us that our driver is a bunch of rich frat boys who can't get their kicks if there are road signs to obey. It won't matter to us that these sociopaths have got their good old Uncle Sam tearing out the road signs and pouring in more gas. It won't matter to us that the drunken joyride ends with a cushioned landing for the driver, who walks off with a shrug while the rest of us fare as we may in the burning wreck left behind. Getting eaten should be very worrisome indeed. But the pill will have us sitting nice and still, no disorderly anxieties, no feeling the warning stings in a cauldron that no longer seems to be there. So let's be real clear about what crazy is according to the Evil Mind-Control: crazy is feeling unhappy with life out there in the beautiful world of the Evil Mind-Control, feeling opposed to it. And health is feeling at peace with it and going along with it. The whole thing is genius, it really is. You've got the powers-that-be out there selling us a solution to the very problems they've caused, and it's a solution that implies no guilt and requires no change on their part."

The man shook his head, then flung the magazine across the stage in violent disgust. He caught his breath for a moment as he wiped his brow and glared over at a stoic Len. Then the man gestured to someone in the front row who promptly tossed up a copy of Brother K's book.

"You see, the Evil Mind-Control is all about illusion. It doesn't deal in real solutions, it deals in shortcuts. It creates illusions for us to buy, and we really do pay. Let's remember Joshua's confrontation with the profit jobbers and interest mongers in the plaza of high finance. So, let's all turn if we can to page, uh, ninety-seven here in our books, where we've got Joshua confronting the illusion that market value represents actual worth:

"Then Joshua commanded the servants of the money lords: 'Go no further on your path and be not blind to where it leadeth. Here is a sign placed in your path, warning you, Beware the yeast of the Pharisees! Ye proclaim that yours is the way of freedom, righteousness, and abundance. Ye declare that your great wealth is justified, since all day long ye are busy in the market sowing and reaping. I saw you from a distance and was hopeful, for your diligence giveth appearances of much fruit being grown. I come near and discover you barren. In all your clamoring, what thing of worth do ye bring forth?! Plain to see is the wealth ye accumulate. Mysterious is the wealth ye produce.

'And now ye shall surely say: If we have taken much from the market, we must have given as much.

'But now I ask: Is the world so just? Woe unto your fortunes if the market were as just as ye describe it. Were there such a market, would ye not quickly pervert it to your favor? What profit-place will greed and power ever leave to justice? The world suffereth the strong to do as they will, and the weak to do as they must. Therefore, great are the spoils accumulated from the weak. Acknowledge that ye strong ones need pay but little to lay hands upon what ye are able to sell for much, cheating the weak of the wealth they produce, and the ignorant of the wealth they spend, and sponging this wealth unto yourselves as what ye have earned. Ye prey upon your brother, circling high above him and striking down upon him in his weakness and ignorance. The world is your father, and ye are firstborn son and apprentice to it, studying advantage, securing every advantage unto yourselves, advantage securing advantage. And so the prey is yours, but think not that ye have created wealth. Ye pay crumbs for a biscuit, and sow yeast therein that ye may sell it as a cake, beguiling the market into imagining a vain thing. Behold the market, how it riseth up on the yeast ye sow in it, how it increaseth daily in hollow cakes! See how it groweth into a great vanity which the whole world doth praise and worship! For truthfully, I tell you, not since the days of Babel was such an idol upon the Earth, seducing men to such reverence, such dancing, and such violence. Man hath crafted through the ages many towers to reach the heavens, but especially vain is your tower, whose bricks are mixed with sawdust, and whose craftsmanship is concealment of infirmity.

'Hear that which ye already know in some buried part of you. A storm cometh, a rain that shall fiercely wash away the corruptions and vanities ye have sown in your market. Many of you who now revile me shall be swept away. Your cakes will surely shrivel, and then shall ye reap from the market but crumbs. Cursed is your barren trafficking. Its worthlessness shall be made plain. Be not amazed when the axe findeth the fruitless tree.'

"And of course," continued the man, book now shut, "Joshua's great wisdom only provokes laughter and allegations of insanity, since these are folks at the height of their power and pleasure, in no mood to be told by some lowlife that they're under the control of a dangerous illusion that they themselves are helping to create. The music in the air that lulls them into their sleepwalking has played as long as anyone can remember, constant and pervasive, seeming as natural as the music made by the motions of the heavenly spheres. The tune goes something like this," said the man, shifting to the smooth syrupy voice of mid-twentieth century advertising: "Things of high market value are of high worth. People of high market value are of high worth, and they create lots of real wealth for others. Wealth ends up in the hands of the people who create it, and therefore wealthy folks are the ones creating lots of real wealth, and poor folks are the ones who aren't. Whatever the market demands or allows is right. Happiness is a commodity. Fulfillment is consumption. Living is selling yourself in the market in order to shop for your fulfillment. A market based on deception and blind emotion is a rational market. A market where profits belong as much as possible to private investors, and costs belong as much as possible to the government and public, is a free market. This market is the only possible society." The man hummed a few notes for a pleasant jingle.

"Joshua has very little effect on the vampire bankers and vulture capitalists because he's up against a chorus of richly endowed think tanks and broadcasters, a legion of clever arguments and pretty faces singing that thievery is actually charity, that gluttony is just and necessary, that idolatry is actually good character, hard work, and success.

"But thank God," cried the man, "that the Lord Joshua established Camp Earth. We have here a sanctuary from the world, from its futility, from its poisonous illusions and false gods and empty solutions. We have the Lord's minister here to strengthen us and serve us while Joshua completes his work in the world and we complete ours here. We live and work together for something extraordinary: the divine purpose of bringing real happiness into the world. This requires that we keep a single and pure consciousness, which is impossible when any one of us invites the Evil Mind-Control here, whether by faithless whispering and criticizing, or laziness, or in Lenny's case, fooling around with truly pornographic magazines that glorify the counterfeit kingdom of the Evil Mind-Control. Come on, Len! We've got a real solution here."

A gasp rose from the crowd. The adviser wheeled about, and saw that Len was on his feet. The boy thrust a flat, rigid hand of indictment at the temple, and poured himself out in a desperate, squeaky holler. "Ain't nothin' in there! Y'all so stupid! Ain't nothin' in there except a bunch a' toys an' *magazines*!"

Whatever the truth of the proclamation, its persuasive power was much diminished by the derelict image of its advocate. The combined response was a groan, mostly hostile, but with sorrow enough to indicate that the boy had struck through into flesh. A few seconds of theatrical scoffing ensued as level heads everywhere wagged in condemnation, with other heads wagging in something more like dismay, or tilting in wonder and computation. Members chuckled nervously and shifted their glances away from those who slapped and pounded themselves about the head and chest, and those who shouted their agreement with the boy.

"Ooohh Len," wailed the tan, clearly aching for the boy's welfare. "How does that make any sense? Would we leave the world and journey all the way out here to build something special, just to fill it with the trash that made us leave the world in the first place? We'll hear what you say, but it's pretty obvious where your message is coming from." A portion of the crowd, probably still smarting over Len having broken through their defense of the stage, helped the others to understand. Len was grimly silent, closing and opening his teary eyes in deliberate ritual.

"All right Len," said the tan, "You don't need to say more anyway, because you hit the nail right on the head. You just gave us the very essence of the Evil Mind-Control's message: that there's nothing to the temple and the camp after all, and all our devotion has been toward some nutty scheme. As if we haven't heard that from the world a hundred times already, Len. Of course by definition ours is a nutty scheme, since it opposes the correct scheme the Evil Mind-Control is imposing everywhere, a scheme so legitimate that human progress inevitably imposes it—or else the Pentagon, CIA, and IMF shove it down people's throats, by dictatorship and death squad if need be, but preferably by secret agreement among gentlemen, otherwise known as a free-trade pact. If you really want to try your luck out there, you're free to leave the camp at any time. In fact, we'd like you to leave. Because the Evil Mind-Control has power, and it's hard enough to remain faithful to the mission of Camp Earth without you giving strength to the adversary. This commotion about you in the last few days has been really disturbing, and it'll take some work to set ourselves right. It'll be easier on all of us here if you just get out and take your Evil Mind-Control with you."

They gave the boy a bag with some food and water in it and cast him off at the head of the muddy road that snaked through forty miles of bush to connect the camp to a village with an airstrip and a decent harbor. They told him he could never return, no matter how bad life gets out there. Guided by a thin glaze of moonlight, Len disappeared into the night.

The well-placed of Camp Earth couldn't stand so fundamental an offense as Len's. Hungry, as indeed many members were, he reached for what had obviously been sustaining a fortunate few these many years, dangling rather brazenly up there above Len each day of his toil, very near to his heart and mind, and always kept just beyond his hand and mouth. In front of a great mass of want, he simply took what was wanted. If a mere boy could do it …

To the faithful of Camp Earth, Len was essentially the annoyingly sober voice at their cocktail gathering who very rudely called attention to the realities the party was meant to distract from. He refreshed memories that the camp system could be challenged; indeed, he demonstrated it was susceptible to blows that could be dealt by even a single common member of sufficient motivation and vigilance. His stunning violation of the divine sanctuary proceeded practically unopposed by any of the relevant powers until too late. Not least disturbing was the absence of any lightning to strike him down the moment he threw himself into the holy veil. All this implied a terribly commonplace and worldly relationship between temple and congregation, something any faithful member could only find disgusting and not worth recognizing. Perhaps in the boy there was something of the sore loser spoiling the fun he wasn't having, reminding everyone that their beloved pursuit was just a game, a plastic and cardboard game at that.

Chapter 21
Maximizing Output per Unit of Input

Who knew we had such greatness among us? He was right there beside us, so low and hard to recognize. Like Jesus says in the Bible and Joshua says in the book: the last among you shall be first. Len pretty much was last among us. Not even Davy gave him a second look. Now everyone has to think about Len every day, especially Davy.

What an awesome thing it was to smack the entire camp to attention. Len came out of nowhere, jumped onto the table, took a huge bite of the thanksgiving turkey with his dirty dog mouth, then took his beating with no repentance.

Davy wishes he had gotten to know Len even a little. He remembers seeing Len a few tables away in a study group for kids who have trouble reading the book because they hadn't gone to school like Davy did. Just a talk with Len at supper, or just watching how Len went about his day, could have revealed something. The courage of Len … where could it come from?

Shockwaves blasted outward from Len's breakthrough at the veil, waking Davy like an actual smack, sending the most life-giving thrill all through him. He thanks God that he experienced it, that he was looking at the stage right when Len climbed up the crazies in the front like they were stairs and sprang himself onto the stage like a black cat. How he headed straight for that veil, with Brother K just standing there like some clown doing stupid tricks for the kids on the lawn. All at once the entire temple popped out toward Davy in the crowd, and for the first time he noticed it was a building of wood and metal, not really so different from a shed. Everything in camp and the jungle came down to Davy's level, and he could see that it all shared in the same reality with Davy. He was part of it. He was fit for all of it. This was a feeling so rare and sweet for Davy, such a taste of life and power. Oh, thank God for it, thank God for Len.

They say this coffee harvest might take three weeks. Davy is assigned to picking, which is what he expected. He's glad to be getting away from the cotton fields. What surprises him is that he's *excited* about the coffee. He feels something good toward the trees loaded with smooth, red cherries that hold ripe coffee beans. He wonders how much of these beans the camp will harvest, and what the watchers just might do with the income. Davy could even chew beans right there on the job, so he'll be able to harvest better.

The pickers are put into teams, and Davy's is a cluster of people he has no special reason to like. The temple says the teams should pick enough baskets that the average is six baskets for each member each day, and if a team doesn't pick enough baskets, then the slow members will have to be "specially motivated" by the team to do better. Davy expects himself to get at least six baskets each day, so they'll see he's a worthy member, and he won't have to get special motivations.

Six baskets. By Davy's reckoning a worthy member is someone who produces at least as much as he takes from the camp. He knows that for now the members have to produce more than they take, so the difference can go toward building the temple, which is supposed to benefit the members, especially when it's finally finished. Brother K and the advisers say that everyone in camp will get back what they put into it, but how the camp could be automatically fair like that is too mysterious for Davy to solve. It seems perfectly possible to Davy that some people in camp get more than they contribute, others managing to get by with less. There are a few tans and grays in particular who don't contribute much except funny sayings. There are members who get to dodge and coast along because they know advisers real well. It seems pretty obvious that the advisers and the watchers get lots of benefits, but Davy has to admit he doesn't know enough about their contributions to say they give too little. It's much easier to understand, and to see, what the average members give to the camp.

The pickers are crammed together in the orchards way closer than Davy and common sense would suggest. When Davy does suggest to a gray that it feels too cramped to be very productive, the gray tells Davy that it may seem that way, but in reality, it's better to be close by teammates because they'll keep up Davy's pace and intensity.

Getting knocked and shoved by slimy members climbing over each other does keep up Davy's intensity. Damn these people, though. Insects burrowing under his skin, crawling through his blood vessels. Here the dumbdumbs go again, howling up at the sky for favors, telling someone up there to give them presents. This isn't Davy's song. Shrinking God into a nice little package for themselves, and so happy about it! Why should they get to be happy for it? The more Davy thinks about it the less he can breathe, and the more he wants to claw himself. Davy's not happy, but at least he's right.

God seems a lot bigger than Davy, and very far from him, as Davy is on the ground floor of the noise and heat and pressure of God's creation. No matter how hard Davy or anybody is working, the advisers just keep yelling, "Come on now, let's pick here!" Great advising! We keep forgetting every ten seconds what we're doing here, wearing these baskets in front of these trees that are bending with fruit. And how could we figure out where the fruit is, if the advisers weren't here to stroll along behind us and wave their sticks at the trees? Not just wave their sticks but point them, too, sometimes directly at the coffee! The camp can't waste its tans and grays on actual picking, these magicians who wiggle their wands just so and coffee somehow jumps straight from the trees into baskets!

Sweat is streaming down from the pressure, heavy, hot, and thick all around. The advisers too are under the press of this harvest, grays yelling at tans to "bug off and keep out of the way," tans yelling at grays to "get your sorry act together and stay awake at the helm," and grays yelling at grays to "stow the bottle and at least pretend to care." All this pressure must be coming from the temple, where Brother K and the watchers must be under the least pressure of everyone, Davy figures. The pressure gets heavier as it moves down from the top. The top presses down onto the middle, and the middle presses down onto the bottom, and the ones on the bottom have to carry the weight of everyone above them.

What's Len doing to make it out there? Maybe he'll find a village he can stay with. They say the little bastard as good as poisoned the camp, and the harvest is sweating the sickness out of us.

All the standing and reaching and lugging build up to a pounding soreness, and Davy wants nothing more than to take off his basket and lie down right where he is and cover his ears and let his body swim in the feelings of relief. But he has to keep on working, and work has to keep on hurting. Are there better ways to harvest the coffee, or does Davy have to hate it? What a relief the water breaks are, the juice, and the lunch with coffee. Without these … well, Davy just thanks God for them.

At night he wraps his head tight with pillows. He thinks about Bill, the only friend he ever had here. They took him away for talking about Joshua. Even straight from the book, Joshua is a knife they have to use carefully, so it only cuts what they want to cut. They're very nervous because they know Joshua can also cut what people like Len want to cut. How amazing that this whole camp stands on Joshua, the very thing that should actually take it down!

Oh Joshua! Oh Jesus! Oh God! Where are you really? What is Davy really doing here? He's all by himself in the wilderness of Africa. Where can he find strength? Davy can't stop himself from crying into the pillows he presses against his skull.

There was once a new thing under the stars, down here in East Africa. Here was a creature whose growing brain arrived at a question mark, an empty space above the world he'd been crawling. Alone beneath an infinite stillness, how heavy felt his heart that night as he cried out the world's first prayer, stretching and straining toward God, God who now, for the first time to any creature, ceased to be automatic, ceased to be easy, ceased to be simply the providence of instinct. Creation had been blessed to not have to ask about God. But this new creature, stranded so radically in the vast ocean of silence he had discovered, did have to ask, and needed to hear something.

Davy presses into his head and his eyes, and he prays. He is able just now to call upon God—someone or something somewhere—who this camp has made sour and ridiculous to him.

He focuses in on what power could have caused him to come into existence on this planet. Help me, your child, to find strength to live. It must be that I'm supposed to have enough strength to live. Davy in his weakness wonders with huge awe how Len could have found the strength, the superhuman power, to do what he did. Not a hundred Davys put together could storm the temple like Len. There is power to live. There is lion strength out there. Where is it for Davy? He would settle for just being able to get by.

The singing, the shouting, the aching, the hollowing, it's all gaining in force, day by day, hour by hour. Davy could be dying.

He's only filled a single basket. Of all the places and times he could be in, he happens to be here and now, almost out of power to keep his head above water. Doom and panic flash and burn to his core. There's no way out. He might as well hit someone and go to the box. In a box is where he is already, and it's getting to feel like the other box might be a nice change. It could really be best for Davy if something strange and powerful was to come along and shake him, to shift him around inside, to trigger a reflex in him.

If something could trick Davy into believing … believing that the coffee he picks … isn't for the temple … but that it's all for a temple that's Davy's own.

The pyramids of Egypt, Bill once said, weren't really built by slaves, but by workers who believed they were serving a god who made their river flow and their crops grow.

A gust of wind swirls up around Davy, touching him through his sweat, confirming that things will be better now that he's picking coffee cherries in his own orchard, working at his own trees. The new reality attracts his concentration so much that the aching and hating can hardly break through it. The others are singing hard to whatever God they come up with, and it doesn't sting Davy anymore. The singing is funny, maybe even sad. It's fine that they have it.

How fast I can pick, red ones and purple and pink, so smooth and solid to the fingers. Davy strips off the pulp from a few cherries and starts some of the bean-chewing he'd been planning and putting off; they taste very satisfying.

By evening horns, Davy has filled seven baskets full to the brim. The advisers nod and smile at him about his coffee, and say, "That's a worthy member." Davy's team seems happy they're getting an extra basket from him, though some of them secretly hate him for making them look unworthy, he suspects. Their baskets aren't full. Their cherries aren't ripe, with lots of yellows and even greens mixed in. Everyone sees how ripe and beautiful Davy's cherries are, how they glow like rubies in the setting sun. He memorizes this fruit of his as he pours it into the carts that go to the bean barn, where members like Bill pour out the carts into water to wash the cherries. Then they rake the cherries in the sun to dry them. Then they take the hulls off the beans, and load the beans into sacks, which get loaded into trucks that go off down the long road to a warehouse in the town.

Davy eats his supper silent and proud and savors the power he feels added to him with every swallow of his holy coffee. The coffee gives soothing and peace, and it recharges him for study group, which he pretends to pay attention to while he skips around in the Bible and the book to learn things on his own.

A bubble forms around Davy as his hands glide through branches and seal thousands of ruby cherries with his sweaty, bloody fingerprints. The realities of the harvest do not get past the shield. The members stumble and complain, but Davy does not. He isn't just getting by, he is excelling.

The wise man builds his house upon rock, not sand. The truth sets you free, not a lie. Yes, these are the words of Jesus, Davy has to admit, and he feels the slice of their sharp edge. He begins to feel again the stinging, the branches scraping the skin off throbbing fingers, the barking and singing nearer and harder. Oh, Jesus, the truth is terrible. The truth isn't worth the pain. The lie makes something beautiful out of something awful. Davy is managing to stand—even if on a trapdoor, he is standing. If it gives way someday, then he'll probably hang; but right now, without his lie, he'll hang for sure. He cannot stand upon the truth. Davy must work in his own fantastic orchard.

It is evening, and many excellent days are behind him. Every coffee cherry he has picked has added to him, instead of taken away. It's also been nice to have the others amazed at him, at his secret strength, at how the pressure has built him up while so many have just been crumpled by it.

"There can't be any standin' around, waitin' the day out! That's cheatin' the camp!" says the gray who's the team leader, slobbering out the sides of his mouthful of crooked teeth. Members are mixing rest into their picking, because they're "out of gas," they say.

"A good will is fuel enough," says the gray.

"The spirit is willing, the flesh is weak," says a member.

"Well, the camp provides us fuel for the flesh and the spirit, okay, and we owe it to the camp to pick as much as we can every minute there's still light! There's no reason for anyone to not get six baskets. I'll go get some torches and we can work through suppertime if that's what it takes."

Actually, there are several good reasons to not get six. And it's impossible the shark mouth doesn't know this. How about, we're just plain tired? Of course we're tired, doing this day after day. What about, the nearest cherries have been picked? Of course the rest of them can't be picked as fast. Do we have to pretend the problem is really members cheating the camp? Yes, we do. We all have to nod in agreement at the shark as he stalks back and forth behind us and suddenly chomps down on us with helpful accusations.

"Come on, let's pick 'em! Up there, right in there, see?" says shark man, waving his wand at a cluster of yellow cherries. "There's still good pickin' for us! You too son, keep goin' strong." Davy's body tightens and begins to rush with something hot and not very pleasant as the stick hovers by his ear. "Okay, see how yer' missin' all these right in front of ya'?" The stick is vibrating with urgency at big branches of cherries that are way more green than red.

"Yer' a real good picker, and I know you can see that coffee I'm pointin' at … so let's keep after it," says the shark. "Don't be like some a' these others cheatin' the camp."

Totally right is how Davy has been doing this coffee thing. The reddest fruits make the best coffee. What a waste to throw yellow and green ones into the mix. It's been important to Davy that the coffee coming from his orchard is ripe and full of worth. But now the temple will make him ruin it.

The temple knows things that Davy doesn't. Maybe they need a certain amount of funds, which means filling a certain number of baskets, even with unripe beans. Instead of producing real worth, maybe it's best to try and cheat the marketplace, to build this camp on shortcuts, just like the world would. Maybe the temple is so close to Joshua that he lets it do the opposite of what he says in the book. Davy has noticed that in the Bible God commands the Israelites to not murder, but then commands them to kill women and children in the invasion of the holy land.

The team is scrambling and stepping onto each other, clawing at pale fruits.

"Those really aren't ripe yet, they'll ruin the coffee," Davy instructs the shark. A sickness floods Davy's chest and stomach.

The man standing over Davy looks quickly left and right, wipes the oozing foam at the sides of his giant mouth, and brings his jaws down toward Davy's throat.

"We've all gotta' do this thing like we're told, for it to work out. There's been councils with Joshua, okay, councils about how this camp is gunna' run the right course. So, when word comes down to keep on pickin' coffee, even the cherries that have some green on em', then that's what you an' I have gotta' do. There's lots a' different coffees, see, and plenty a' folks can only afford lower quality, and the temple has them in mind at this point. It's great how ya' take pride in yer' work son, but don't be too proud to take an order."

All Davy's momentum drains through his legs into the ground, and he's back where he was at his lowest point of dying in this hell harvest. His head swells with ringing and dizziness. Every day will be another grinding test, another marathon, endless. His cheeks flame up. His knees are melting. Hot tears roll down his raw, red face. He's picking whatever the shark points to. All is lost. Just little Davy against the world.

Something has to help hold him up.

Something sounds to him like the echoes of voices, a long train of voices down the hallway of time, father talking to son.

"Let it go, son. You'll stand on other ground."

Davy's sight now rises above himself, and his viewpoint is high above the forest. He looks down onto winding rivers and scattered villages, black folks out in fields cutting down dying plants to make way for seeds. Death comes before new life; death is part of the rules. The black folks sing the wisdom to themselves as they work:

"You gotta' bend so it don't break ya';
Lay it down now, you can take it up later.
What ain't yours, you gotta' let it go;
Let the sun go down, let the river flow."

He keeps on picking the unripe coffee, and his viewpoint keeps on floating outside his body, riding alongside while something else drives the hands and feet. And this feeling comes from the truth Davy has now accepted: the coffee is not his, his body is not his. In fact, these things belong to the temple.

Distance from their wasted coffee and their aching body is fine. It is numbness. It is a trance, a sleep. He sees two hands out there do some coffee picking, lots of green and yellow cherries that may or may not make okay coffee to drink. There are six baskets to be filled like this, each day to the end of the harvest.

Sometimes during the ride, as the two hands keep right on reaching for whatever fruit the temple wants, Davy's thoughts wander back through the lives he's lived in this camp, life after life, illusion after illusion. How stupid to take pride in what was never his. His newest life would be truthful, accepting all the ugly facts around him as long as his feelings are dead. How long he might continue as a zombie, Davy has no idea. A new life of some other sort could be just around the corner.

Chapter 22
Currents in Camp Ideology

The stripped-naked coffee trees and the ware-bare bean barn lay relieved of the swollen pregnancy.

There followed a day of rest: of eating, napping, playing ball, singing and dancing, shifting about the grassy courtyard mingling, generally rejoicing at the success of the crop and the progress it would bring to the camp. At times the tans and grays joined in the festivities, but mainly kept to lounging near their cabins in a state of semi-inebriation.

All needed the day to simmer down and recharge, for the harvest had taken a toll. The rigor of the task had made the advisers crabby and quick to violence. Several had struck members or other advisers with the stick. Guns had been drawn. The harvest had depleted the energy of the membership, had made them thinner and more prone to sickness, had given them a shuffling gait and void expression. Faithful members had been shocked to find themselves falling asleep during study groups and the Brother K Experience, snapping at friends and family, even acknowledging aloud for the first time some unpleasant feelings about life in Camp Earth.

Throughout the harvest ordeal, a range of more or less plausible interpretations could be heard.

The standard explanation from the advisers was that the extremism of the harvest was necessary in order to maximize productivity, which maximizes camp funds for the completion of the temple. The concentrated work was also bringing about a cleansing effect, a spiritual realignment, a purging of the Evil Mind-Control that had surged into the camp through the abomination of Len. This official view and its variations could be heard by any member at least a dozen times each day of the harvest. It roused positive emotions toward the prospect of a completed temple, while venting an increasing superabundance of negativity upon a black boy and all he represented.

It was of course Evil Mind-Control that Len represented. But Evil Mind-Control was conceptualized in a variety of ways, even among the reliably faithful. The less educated of the faithful had come to speak of it in terms of a supernatural disease which might possess the unwary at any time and cause insanity, the insanity of opposing the temple, the seat of all provision and protection out here in the midst of a brutal wilderness. Many of these people had come from that wilderness, and no amount of hard work was going to drive them back to it. A strenuous coffee harvest was an inconvenience, an acceptable price to pay for nutritious food and clean water, medicine, safety, and all the perks of being alive. As for the more educated of the faithful, the Evil Mind-Control that they were on sharp alert against was a stubborn neurological pattern that had been formed in their brains by the capitalist conditions they had been exposed to outside of the camp, conditions that included a skillfully trumpeted ideology that cast severe doubt upon alternatives like the camp. Though viewing themselves as thoughtful, these people consciously refused to seriously consider the merits of any notion that could possibly undermine their attachment to their beloved socioeconomic experiment. The heavy workload of the coffee harvest was to them a sensible and temporary sacrifice to build up capital that would be applied to advancing the camp's standard of living and Christian socialist aims.

The observer of the harvest during its full intensity couldn't fail to notice that an unprecedented portion of the membership, perhaps half, displayed no firm sense of how conditions might best be interpreted. A prolific example of this was the confession phenomenon, in which a harvester assumed a very solemn air and insisted to members nearby that his faith in Brother K and in the mission of Camp Earth remained intact … *but* … and now came genuine tears … he had to admit to feeling disoriented and broken down by stress, and to feeling confused and anxious about the apparent gap between camp ideals and realities. The therapeutic value of the practice was obvious. Occasionally it met a harsh response from members who could admit no such gap, the ideals and realities of camp appearing to them perfectly joined (though were there in fact such a gap, the fault lay naturally with the congregation, the part of camp farthest from infallible Joshua).

Some of the more interesting interpretations came from the fringes of camp.

Certain members, well known for having their troubles with the Evil Mind-Control, had for years been disseminating a view which tolerant members dismissed as malicious or oversimplified, and which intolerant members cut down with shouts and threats. This controversial proposition was that Camp Earth stood upon a wholly corrupt foundation which all the charming narrative about Joshua and the apocalypse merely served to cover—that yes, the congregation was in fact being used and lied to, systematically and shamelessly, in a coldhearted scheme set up for the financial and egotistical benefit of camp leaders. Was the coffee harvest not good enough evidence of perverse greed and power? The vast majority of members could only find it very hard to think of their house as being so basically vile, and could only find it very easy to think of reporters of terrible news as being driven by terrible personal problems that warped their take on camp reality, a reality which, as any undisturbed member could see, naturally reverted to the moderate and reasonable, with nothing able to stray too much out of its just and proper place.

A peculiarly profound assessment of the camp experience had been gaining adherents among the more extreme Evil Mind-Control cases, radicals who'd long made a fetish of scrutinizing authority and consensus. These members had somehow formed the idea that the really substantial meanings of Camp Earth were obscured beneath layers of meanings more superficial and obvious. Inhabiting the outermost and largest layer were the most popular and illusory meanings, what the camp was basically about to the outside world and to most of the congregation: Joshua the living person, an impending nuclear strike or asteroid, and a holy shining city—a genuine attempt at Christian socialism—preserved for a new world.

Beneath the outermost layer crawled a clay monster called Evil Mind-Control, perpetually sculpted into the image of the temple's latest challenger. Under this lay solid Evil Mind-Control, the capitalist pathology that was quite as present in camp as in the world, with the temple treating the congregation as an economic resource whose hearts and minds were merely targets for ploy and strategy, and the temple fine-tuning the camp arrangement to be the most convenient for advanced persons to receive the money, power, status, and choice women they deserved.

For many members the exploitation in camp life would probably always remain hidden in plain sight. Meanwhile, the radicals comprehended its full extension, seeing the temple and indeed every member use the camp to prop themselves up in a variety of ways, everyone eating and being eaten, the whole thing merging rather seamlessly into the banal savagery of animal life in the jungle surrounding.

Yet something else finally made up the core of the camp: a lurking, permeating essence that no one perceived except the radicals and a few select persons of the temple. The deepest purpose of the camp was the unfolding of a play.

Through endless discussion, points of agreement had emerged among the radical theorists about this play. The authors of the play were held to be certain temple inhabitants connected to certain American organizations. The chief character was Camp Earth itself (though all camp inhabitants had some role to play, whether scripted or not, and everyone should attempt to realize his greatest possible role and become, as it were, author of it). The scripted plot covered the lifespan of Camp Earth, from Colorado estate to African settlement to completion of the temple to the camp's demise, the latter to occur in an unforgettable manner. The oppressive coffee harvest was scripted, and its effects would lead to the next scene of the scripted plot. The most appreciative spectators of the play were of course its authors—though only somewhat less important was its general audience, which was worldwide. The play would teach its authors something about human potential and the management of it; the world would learn something rather less empowering, another memorable lesson in the natural fate of Christian socialism.

This theory of a secret play offered little to the mass of members maintaining a dear expectation of Joshua's arrival. The standard camp narrative from the book and temple already provided great theatre, with a clear plot, divine protagonist, and happy ending. The radical theory threatened to reduce a noble saga to absurd comedy or awful tragedy.

No matter where one stood in the convoluted spectrum of camp outlook, one was at least glad to be done with the coffee harvest and to have a fine day to savor the relief with everyone else. As much as there was talk today about looking forward to camp improvements resulting from coffee revenues, there was talk of wanting to die in today's splendid state of rest, to somehow stay in it forever.

Meanwhile, way out in the jungle, lower-ranking members in a pack of chimpanzees were planning a coup with looks and gestures they hoped would escape the notice of the alpha male and his allies. This very thorny enterprise among chimps was even thornier among the residents of the camp, as a number of the faithful had been secretly commissioned by the temple to display sympathy for reform and to report anyone revealing a similar attitude. These informants varied in quality, some so lacking as actors and so transparent as to their true aims that they became walking jokes, their phony displays of rebellion drawing little response except phony displays of love for the temple. On the other hand, the most skilled informants had eyes and ears and neck hairs detecting any disturbance or commotion in the human environs, and it was not beyond their capability to spy on the tans and grays, and to discreetly enjoy temple rewards. But even with the possibility of these jackals in the midst, discussions about change had certainly taken place throughout the camp. All concerned parties had thoroughly considered the feasibility of requests for reform, of demands for reform, and of outright revolt.

Obviously, the primary obstacle facing any serious insurrection would be the guns the tans and grays carried: sixteen handguns and thirty-two semiautomatic rifles in all. Although these weapons belonged officially to the temple, and in theory to the membership of Camp Earth, practice held that each tan and gray considered a particular firearm to be his own, to be slid under his belt or slung over his shoulder when on duty in the fields, to be set by his bed or under his pillow when off duty in the cabins. It was sometimes the case that a tan might exchange his rifle for the pistol of a fellow tan for a while, or an ill gray might stay in bed for the day and allow a fellow gray to prance about camp with a rifle and a pistol.

Several tans and grays also carried radios to circulate intelligence among themselves and the temple.

A revolt might well begin with a few dedicated, Len-like comrades getting the guns off some careless advisers, the comrades proceeding thus armed to get more guns from more advisers. At some point gunfire or radio message would alert the temple and dissolve the element of surprise. The outcome would hinge upon what support a likely wavering and possibly clueless congregation would throw behind the besieged comrades.

Members viewing themselves as comrades of this nature, as the militant vanguard of an oppressed congregation, therefore schemed about stoking the general discontent. They enshrined for themselves an admittedly unrealistic scenario in which every camp member felt a berserk hatred that made everything, including survival, seem less important than fighting the intolerable enemy, the temple. A successful revolt would then surely unfold from the slightest catalyst, a simple act of defiance by a single person. Currently, however, the hatred existed only in scattered pockets, and the mass of members stood in need of some assistance to share in it. The mass would be helped to share in the hatred of their true enemy, or else they'd just keep to the prudent path of least resistance, sitting inert on the fence, leaning toward whichever side seemed the likely victor, gawking feebly at the bravery and despair of those blasted down by advisers' guns.

Chapter 23
The Price of Progress is Sacrifice

It was a gray morning, and breakfast was had under a drizzle. Members and advisers helped themselves to thick porridge and fruit, with coffee, tea, or juice. Presently the horns blew, calling Camp Earth to work, and dishes were licked, abandoned, and began to be collected.

After supper last night Brother K had gotten on the speakers: congratulating everyone for a job well done reaping coffee, praising the harvest as a huge step forward for the camp, and concluding with a cold instruction that the bulk of the membership would be going back over to cotton. Brother K had been quick to add that nobody should feel it was now okay to slack off and lower their guard against the Evil Mind-Control and loosen the high moral tone currently prevailing in camp. No, quite the contrary, the tightness of the tone must be preserved so that an excellent harvest can also be achieved with the cotton, the lately neglected cotton which now required extra attention, likely as much attention as had just been paid to the coffee. Thus, Brother K had sent the camp to bed on a sour note that left many wincing in disappointment.

The congregation, though fueled by a fine breakfast, proceeded to meander very sluggishly toward the fields, no doubt lugging hefty memories of yesterday's sabbath with them. Soon they took notice of something amiss behind them, something simple, yet extraordinary. Several members—maybe a hundred members—remained seated, firmly fixed to the benches at several tables, and spread unevenly, with some tables hosting three or four sitters and others ten or a dozen. These sitters beckoned to the mass of members, and a hundred more seats were occupied in seconds.

Tans and grays sniffed blood in the air and began to respond, rapping their sticks on the tables impatiently, shaking their heads and smirking at the pettiness of the childish stunt materializing before them. The members that remained standing were cheerfully instructed by advisers to continue toward the cotton where they should expect to be joined by their momentarily seated fellows. The very faithful among the standing members parroted this command, helping a number of visibly conflicted members standing nearer the tables to remove themselves from the disturbance, even as the odd member here and there was still dashing to take a seat.

The upright members had mostly gotten out of sight and earshot when a tan stepped up to address the seated. These past weeks had of course been misery for most of the camp, but this man had been enjoying himself like never before, strong and satisfied and at the top of his game, glowing from the temple's recognition and rewards. It was he who'd given the congregation such a definitive interpretation of the Len incident.

"So? What *is* this?" he began, his voice without its usual support from temple electronics, but still powerful.

The seated exchanged glances with one another.

"Well? Come on! Anybody know what's going on here?!" the tan demanded.

Time passed as the tan stroked the rain off his slicked-back hair, and at last he chuckled and turned away to wipe his sunglasses, just when a voice, direct and simple and honest as a child, got right to the point with, "We've had it!"

The tan spun around in surprise, muttering something that was roared down by fists and mugs hammering onto tables, the rumbling growl rolling across camp to prick the conscience of those laboring in the cotton patches. A few advisers retreated some distance from the clamor and became active on their radios, furrowing their brows, squinting their eyes and nodding or shaking their heads as they conferred with the temple. The pounding continued as advisers paced along the heads of the tables, pointing their sticks at certain members menacingly, slamming their sticks onto the tables with great fury again and again, proclaiming the persistence of their authority by out-noising the sitters.

Advisers grew visibly anxious as the seated kept pounding with wilder force, each sitter drawing strength from the common outpour, while the near edges of the cotton fields were crowding with curious onlookers despite frantic efforts by advisers and ultra-faithful to keep them at labor.

Gradually advisers stood back from the tables, appearing somewhat resigned with their hands on their hips or their arms folded. The sitters had gotten the camp's full attention. A well-built younger member now stepped up onto his table, waved his hands, and thereby effected a sharp quiet, except for the continued pounding of a few youngsters and the light patter of raindrops.

"By clear word of Joshua, this assembly deserves a full accounting! Everyone can read in the book how Joshua invites the assembly to check his figuring. *His* figuring! This flesh and blood assembly here must have ten times the right to check the figuring of Joshua's so-called representatives!" declared this towering member, thrusting a finger with the tidal wave of jubilant pounding from the seated. After several seconds of this noise the special tan stepped forward again, bearing a cool and serious demeanor, and he raised an open hand, waiting for the rumble to subside, which it did upon a gesture from the elevated member.

"You *haven't* thought this through," the tan explained in a fatherly air. "You *don't* know what you're doing."

"Oh, like hell we don't know! We've had about ten years—long years to think it through! This is no mistake!" roared the member, stomping his table to a chorus of fists and mugs, then waving his hands for silence.

"No," insisted the tan earnestly. "You can't imagine what you're doing, if you're trying to shut down this camp or steer it off course all on your own accord. You can't be allowed to just take it into your hands like this—no, oh no, there's so much more involved with this than you realize."

"Just what in the *hell* are you talking about?!" demanded the exasperated member. "Tell us, finally, *will* you?!"

"I'll tell you loud and clear!" announced the tan, wiping rain from his face in a single violent stroke. "What you're doing is foolish, at the very least, you know, because how do you intend to survive without the pathways that Brother K and the watchers have set up and maintain for us here? But that's beside the point, because really what you're doing is blasphemy. It's outright blasphemy to think you can take control of this camp, when it's always been the Lord's, when Joshua has always overseen it through *his* minister, *his* prophet. The Lord's is a house of order, not the chaos that you propose, and so he gives us direction through a high priest, that we may be one in preparing the way for the arrival that's at our very doorstep. What unbelievable pride, to think that you somehow have the authority to derail this sacred project merely because one fine morning you thought you'd try it! How can you suppose that God and Joshua will be forgiving of the sin of Lucifer? They can't possibly allow their plans for the future of the world to be scuttled by some pathetic … tree-house club of pirates. They'll cast you out of camp. Joshua's plans for this camp won't be foiled by you or anyone else, and even if a third of the camp must be cast out into the dying world in order to preserve the project, then so be it, because Joshua will replace you with the faithful he's gathering out from the world, even as we speak. It's just obvious the Evil Mind-Control has taken possession of you. Can't you see that?"

The advisers who'd clustered about this tan were nodding and smiling in assent. Their man was good. Let's see you top that, said their faces to the opposing member, who looked rather unimpressed as he raised his eyebrows, drew in a long breath, and exhaled wearily.

"You *won't* confuse us anymore. You *can't* shame and frighten us like we're little children."

"But you *are* confused. And you *should* be ashamed and frightened," the tan assured the sitters, pocketing his sunglasses so his audience could appreciate his considerate gaze. "Can't you see that all of us have been feeling the pressure here, trembling under the weight of the mission, straining to stand the power of the Evil Mind-Control against us? We all want the camp to succeed. The camp must succeed, and this … little scheme of yours … simply cannot proceed. How can the advisers let it proceed, when we've been entrusted to protect the camp, and we've sworn to uphold what is ordained by Joshua through his minister here.

"Oh, brothers and sisters, we must not falter! If you think your calling to be too heavy for you, please remember what you'll be facing back in the world. It is a professionally spun web of illusions designed to trap you, and the spider's fangs drip sparkling gold venom.

"But what blessings the Lord has given us here!" proclaimed the tan, holding out an open, reasonable hand. "Who here is ever in need of a doctor? Who can't depend on healthy, nourishing food every day? Wonderful food. Who here is in need of friends and family? Who doesn't have at least a hundred brothers and sisters right here? And we're really *doing* something here, working *toward* something that we've *all* got a stake in. Who can say that about life out there in the world? Have you forgotten what it's like out there? We have a purpose here, and it gives us a focus. It centers us every day. Out there in the world there's nothing solid for you to stand on, no footing for you to go forward and upward. You're there to be pulled this way and pushed that way by those who count. You're there to waste an entire lifetime running on a treadmill with a carrot dangling just beyond your grasp, reassured that you're free and prosperous as you sink ever deeper, selling yourself to a profit machine that sucks and drains you.

"Here in camp we have dependable work building up something we all share in. Our work has been hard, yes, and it's been so worthwhile. Camp Earth is moving forward and upward for all of us. It doesn't belong to Brother K and some little group of guys like things do in America and the rest of the world, you know, massive corporations controlled by thirteen guys sitting around a big table scratching each other's backs, the richest one percent of global population owning almost *half* the global pie, leaving the rest of humanity, nearly all of humanity, with half. Obscene! God damn it! And the half portion left to ninety-nine percent of humanity is itself divided so satanically that billions of people get a bare existence hunting for crumbs beneath the tables of those skilled in the world's ways of getting a slice of pie. Real obscenity!

"I remember what it was like being a dog out there. Hell, I damn near *died* because I didn't have the money to get a tooth removed. Do you believe that? Yeah! I see heads nodding yes, you bet I do! That's what my life was worth back there in the richest country in the history of the world, a great country to be rich in, since there's not much responsibility toward the people who work in the businesses and fight in the wars that make other people rich. The unfortunates that fortunes require are tossed around like spare parts, and some handy excuse will always be around to put 'em behind bars, while gates go up to protect the palaces.

"I did finally get the tooth pulled, but they only did it when I was about to die from an infection the tooth was spreading to my brain. Before this it wasn't necessarily life threatening, no, it was only horribly painful. All the blood, sweat, and tears I'd given my employers and my country over the years wasn't enough to buy me ten minutes in a dentist's chair. I had to be near death, seeing stars and rainbows and hearing voices, in order to be bothered with. They probably calculated the cost of burying me and figured it would be less expensive for them to just pull the tooth. It's typical of what happens all the time out there where those who own the fortunes that you and I help to build are free to sit back and let us suffer."

A few scattered sitters had their faces covered with their hands, and light sobbing could be heard above the gentle rain.

"Join with me now in mighty prayer," suggested the tan, his arms spread wide in invitation to advisers and sitters alike. "We're all under pressure here, we're battling the Evil Mind-Control, and we need help. We need grace. We need providence. We need Good Mind-Control. Let's all put our hands up and pray for it."

The sitters looked on each other. Most were shaking their heads with a stern expression, hands on table. Here and there a member raised hands to the sky. Others put hands up grudgingly, keeping elbows on table. Now others began yelling or pushing. The young spokesman for the sitters, still perched atop his table, waved his arms wildly and hollered over the assembly, "Are we supposed to forget Isaiah, Jeremiah, Jesus, Joshua?! They stand with *us*! They stand against those who grind the poor into dirt! Joshua belongs to *us*!"

Suddenly a voice entered the fray through the camp loudspeakers, a voice reverberating with gravity and authority: "*And then shall a time of tri-bu-la-tion rage upon the faithful, even as a storm rageth upon the waters. Doubts shall enter their hearts, and torments grievous to bear. The hearts of many shall fail them, and their love wax cold.*"

The voice continued in a mild, informal tone more clearly that of Brother K: "Brothers and sisters, our adversary rages upon the community of believers, and we shall be tried for the kingdom's sake. And the faithful shall emerge from the crucible refined to shine in the kingdom. Let us not lose hope. The Evil Mind-Control rages out of desperation, for the days of the Beast are numbered, and in its last throes it heaps curses upon those who shall overcome it. Nothing good and glorious was ever had without trial. We battle here in a test of wills decisive for all humanity. The Evil Mind-Control only gains strength if we falter in our resolve, and then it only gets harder for us. The work needed on Joshua's cotton will not be heavy if Joshua is kept in heart and mind. Attend ye to the fields, and let your labor be your prayer. And I will join you in mighty prayer from the temple, that this crisis may pass, that we may speed the day of our Lord's arrival.

"For behold, saith the Lord, I will send my messenger, and he shall prepare the way before me. And the Lord, whom ye seek, shall suddenly come to his temple. But who shall abide the day of his coming, and who shall stand when he appeareth? For he is like a refiner's fire."

The sitters helped each other digest all this for a minute. A hard-headed cynicism tried loudly to beat back the seductive optimism of the temple. "When your drunk husband hits you," shouted one sitter, "should you stick around 'cause he says it won't happen again?! You think when he does hit you again you'll be any stronger, and leavin' 'im will be any easier?!"

Sitters here and there were slipping away and setting off for the fields with hanging heads. The special tan was quick to lead the advisers in a round of applause and praise for these prodigal children returned to the fold. "You have overcome your trial! Your test is passed! Your faith is the stronger for it!" proclaimed the tan. The powerful young member standing on his table conveyed a profoundly pained wonderment as he wailed out to the deserters, "How can their words still have such power over you?! How can you not see your true test?! How can you not see the true Evil Mind-Control?!"

Ignoring his opponent, the tan strutted along the ends of the tables, looking deeply on the seated members and calling out, "Who else can step out of the Evil Mind-Control? Who can do it?!" Others of the tans and grays joined in the coaxing, strolling from table to table, seeming to aim special attention at the young, the old and the women. As minutes passed like this the advisers did succeed in peeling away for the fields some of the elderly, who were offered time to rest from their ordeal, and a few youngsters, who were bribed with candy. But the great majority of sitters held firm to their stations, showing little ill will to the few who left their side, in fact directing the infirm to depart without shame.

With the lighter elements shaken off and the heavier settled into place, a stalemate ensued. Through six hours the sitters occupied the tables, reading scriptures to each other, praying together with strong voices, inviting advisers to come sit down and discuss the merits of a more transparent temple, challenging advisers to imagine a camp whose true temple is the congregation, demanding that advisers explain why Joshua would keep himself to an exalted few whose power over the congregation is kept so guarded against the congregation.

No adviser could accept invitations to negotiate on an equal level with common members who took child's play to be something that actually had any real right or power to transform this camp. To indulge the children in their little game would only give it legitimacy, would only stimulate them to persist on their naïve path.

At midday the thin, warm rain withdrew, and an especially generous lunch break proceeded with a squad of advisers marching out from behind the temple to parade cold water and juices and even sodas past the tables to the laborers in the cotton fields. The sitters looked on as the faithful couldn't help but relish their treats, which soon included gumbo. How severe a blow this was to the morale of the sitters could be judged by the collective slouch that came over them at the smell of the gumbo's spicy chicken, shrimp, and more than just the occasional crayfish.

Various sitters had answered nature's call by simply stepping a few paces into some tall grass, to the highly embellished revulsion of the pacing advisers. When one sitter rose and set off with a bold stride for the latrines, a pair of grays converged upon the man, jabbed him with their sticks, and informed him that toilets were a luxury reserved to the faithful. The rebuffed member relented with a shrug, dropped his pants to his ankles and squatted, his nether region in perfect view of the two grays, who couldn't restrain their grins of amusement as the member obtained relief. The function performed, and his pants still down, the man looked about for what must have been a leaf, but finding none he merely applied a wad of grass with evident success, pulled up his pants and returned to his table. Applause broke out among the sitters, followed by thudding of fists and mugs. The two grays, still wearing their grins, received a nod from a gray consulting a radio, and the pair strode past the fuming pile to its depositor.

The hero was launched away from his bench, clubbed casually for a half minute, then shocked with a Taser into submission—and all the while he attempted to hold a smile. It was quite a performance, enough to send some of the sitters springing forward, apparently of a mind to give their comrade aid, but these were instantly intercepted by about forty advisers with sticks and Tasers and guns at the ready, who formed into a ring around the league of tables and ensured the hero's easy pacification.

Members witnessing the affair from the fields were escorted out of sight by a few conscientious advisers, but word soon came from the temple that the faithful were not to be kept ignorant of the punishments now to be unleashed upon the sitters, and should in fact be led nearer the tables for a good view.

Some advisers had long objected to any large-scale employment of violence, except as a last resort, and even then it was a course to be taken with utmost caution, they maintained, since it could turn the membership radically against the temple as likely as it might compel obedience. The news from the temple of "punishments now to be unleashed" met with small enthusiasm among the advisers, with even the idealist study-group matriarchs showing misgivings about automatically defending the temple on this one. The feeling among the advisers was that it were better to simply allow the sitters time to realize the error of opposing the temple that provides water, food, and shelter. Missing out on gumbo had brought sitters to tears, and several advisers were looking forward to seeing sitters pathetically losing their willpower and damning their principles as their animal needs grew more urgent.

The temple's response to this counsel was to praise it as reasonable and worthy, then to state that it was nevertheless overruled by a temple consensus based on considerations which couldn't be divulged. The order was that there should now occur a public display of authority, and this simply had to be trusted as being in the best interest of the camp.

It was more a crude demonstration of raw power that followed, senseless to many. At least something would be accomplished by it, namely the evaporation of most of the goodwill and authentic allegiance hitherto enjoyed by the temple, reducing temple authority to a basis of brute force.

The exhibit commenced with the advisers seizing the most notorious troublemaker from each table, standing him at the head of his table, stripping him naked before the sustaining eyes of his comrades, and binding him to his table facing skyward. All members were obliged to witness the tans and grays deliver humility to the proud.

That the batons were padded, and the electricity moderate, was less relevant than might be supposed. Many of the tans and grays had passed through institutions where useful violence was padded for the sake of certain delicate sentiments, even as the violence retained potency. Many of the tans and grays had undergone violence at the hands of well-scrubbed people who regarded slapping a man as the height of barbarism while regarding condemning a man to incarceration, and all the life-shattering it entails, as the height of civilization. How the feeblest little things become intolerable as they continually rub against the grain of one's being, pressing, invading, overwhelming, without leaving bruise or scratch. To have one's feet honeyed and then licked by goats begins with laughs and proceeds to tears. And a drop of water on the forehead, followed by random others, is actually far worse than getting caught in the rain without umbrella. A skilled adviser had only to engage in not many minutes of strategic pecking and jolting to render a typical member whimpering in helpless sickness. Creeping things from the forest were applied to those susceptible to this remarkably effective form of padded violence, silly little tickles, pricks, and pinches from humble creatures of six or eight or sixty little limbs.

Sitters proceeded to lunge out and strike advisers, the disgust and outrage exploding them forth as from a cannon. They were then bound and systematically reduced to convulsive sobbing at the head of their table. The day wore on with sitters leaping across tables to land a foot or fist into deserving advisers, while others merely rose up and strode to the head of their table to present themselves as ready for their turn.

A kid at one of the tables is very thirsty. His body is stuck to the bench. He feels so weighed down by the yelping of these members who had seemed so strong until the advisers found where the weakness was.

Long ago he had looked down from an airplane onto a huge black ocean at night and had wondered what he'd do if the plane went down on that water that just went deeper and deeper into colder, blacker darkness.

Somewhere out there in the ocean of space, someone is getting pulled toward a planet that has a giant storm on it, a speeding swirl of thick clouds flashing with lightning. My God! It's so huge … and so fast … and so deep. Where does it end? He's falling with nothing to catch him, falling toward unimaginable force.

He looks at Bill who's sitting just a few tables away, scratching his beard and sweating. Bill glances right at Davy now, and nods his head with a smile.

Bill's getting up, and Davy feels his own legs spring. Bill raises his open hands to just above his shoulders and he walks to the head of his table. The advisers let him stand there by the guy they've got tied up, who's got big red marks on his ribs. "Take me off, oooh, I'm gunna' get a clot," the guy says, and the advisers loosen the ropes and carry him away and put him on the grass. Bill says something to some grays, and he takes his clothes off. Davy sees the scars that

Bill must have got when he was a soldier. Bill gets onto the table and they tie him tight.

They whack Bill on his stomach, but he just flexes his muscles and doesn't say anything. They put the lightning into his armpits and his groin, and Bill's face crunches up and all his muscles strain, and he grunts and hollers. Then a gray flecks his middle finger into Bill's balls and also the head of his penis, and this is what gets Bill to yelp out in the strange and sick sort of shriek the advisers are looking for, so they concentrate on flecking Bill on the balls and penis head again and again and again, shocking him at random times with electricity.

Of course it was gunna' hurt, and he'd been hurt before, but the outrageous explosions of shaking pain still took Bill unawares. His willpower couldn't much stand up to it. He'd stood up and walked toward it and tried to meet it unafraid, knowing his fear would only empower it to hurt him the more. But in the thick of it, in the fog of war, battle plans evaporate, and you just hope that what's in you is able to take whatever what's out there is able to inflict.

"Not too much," an older gray cautioned a younger who was electrocuting Bill at the genitals. "We can't have 'im goin' into cardiac arrest. All he needs is a little humility, some perspective."

"Yeah, I guess he's prob'ly got it now," the younger gray assessed. They untied Bill and helped him over to the edge of the grassy courtyard where the others had been laid out to take stock of their experience.

Constant sobbing and groaning haunted the camp as evening fell. Several of the faithful members had been calling for the violence to stop, had refused to view it anymore, and had stationed themselves on the grass to help the punished recover. The tables still had sitters attached to them though, and seeming to linger was the perception that this historic confrontation hadn't yet been consummated, that there were still people on both sides of it who felt that more could be accomplished. The advisers casually made their way around the tables and inspected the remaining sitters, pressing a few to finally quit their table and straggle away, others to finally rise in acceptance of what must be done at the head of their table.

A couple of the grays found cause to hover over a boy who was hunching stiffly, his heavy stare fixed upon his table, his frame appearing to crumple under the intensified scrutiny. At last the younger gray tapped his stick on the boy's shoulder.

Of course. Here it is. It's always been coming.

"Hey there, son. Tough kid to stay sittin' here all day. Bet just now you wish you'd gone to the fields though, eh?"

Davy can't speak. His tongue is cotton. His mind is blank.

The wood planks of the table have cuts and gouges from someone's fork. Someone must've been bored with their study group, and cutting the table was what they did about it, small and stupid. This camp is supposed to be about big and important things, but so much of it has been small and stupid … day after day of small and stupid, waiting for big and important. What Len did was big and important. And what Davy has to do now.

"How 'bout havin' a good try of it with us? It's good medicine. It'll clear things right up for ya'."

Breathless, dizzy, sick, Davy is shaking. In the boxing match they put him in when he first came here, all he could do was try his best, which wasn't very good, and get beaten down and throw up. It was supposed to happen like that.

Bill's over there on the grass, looking right at Davy.

I am the wood of this table. Cut into me and it just makes a mark, no feelings.

I'll be sitting there by Bill and the others on the grass after I do what they did.

I'm moving, somehow, I'm walking … I'm naked … On the hard wood of my table, ropes holding me down, I look into clouds high above me … Help … God help … I am part of God's creation—I can take part in what can happen in God's creation … Help.

Chapter 24
The Gathering Storm

The tans and grays had done their duty very professionally. Brother K swiftly organized a substantial crate for each group, full of edible, drinkable, smokable, and otherwise ingestible goodies, and he dispensed this bonus in person on temple grounds, commending the grays and separately the tans for their skill and restraint during the recent crisis. These men had administered correction without creating any martyrs, with the sitters suffering only a couple of mild heart attacks and a handful of broken ribs easily attended to by the watchers, none of the injured being disabled for more than a few days. Quite remarkable, given the generally weak physical condition of the congregation following the coffee harvest.

Daily life proceeded onward with the members nearly as active and productive as before, though in a lifeless and mechanical fashion, their bodies compliantly performing the routines demanded of them, even as their steely eyes glared vacantly off toward some faraway place. It became fairly obvious that only on the thinnest possible layer of outermost surface did the members remain faithful to the temple and its camp. Gone was the spirit that put warmth and feeling into reciting a passage from the book, or that packed an extra wad of cotton into a sack that might already pass as full.

Davy is still dizzy from what happened to him. There's still ringing in his ears. Thinking for even two seconds about what happened makes him sick with a throbbing that tears all through him. But he has to think about what happened, because he has to figure out why it went so wrong.

He let them do it to him because he started with a feeling that he just might come out from it okay, probably even come out wiser and stronger. He went into it the best he knew how. And still it defeated him totally. How *could* he have been ready for it? Everyone saw him there on that table, naked, crying out, shriveling up, failing. It was too much pain—end of story. There's no getting around it. Davy had to leave the table. They all tried to make him feel better, even the tans and grays did … but he was burning in weakness and shame. "It's a good lad," the advisers said, "who finds himself to be on the right side after all."

Davy gets so low thinking of that pain they put in him, how easily it crushed him, how small and brittle Davy is compared to what can be against him.

He can pick cotton fine, his hands work fine, but something inside him is crippled. The sight of a flower is enough to shake him to tears. The flower reminds him of the life and beauty and goodness that somehow exist in a cold and dark universe, and it makes something inside him leap and soar for a second, like a sky-sailing neon bird, only a second before lightning strikes it down and sickness rages through him.

As the lightning sickness slowly leaves, it looks back to make sure that Davy isn't forgetting. When the sickness has gotten far enough away, Davy is able to hate for a while. The hate he feels against the temple is like a live bed of coals deep beneath a doused firepit. He hates God, for being so strong in the wrong parts of his creation, and for being so weak and hard to find in Davy. Davy hates himself, for not being strong enough to beat what he hates. All this hating is dangerous though, because it leads to feeling that you have to hit something, and then the sickness comes on like the shadow or echo of that throbbing electricity Davy took on the table, and this makes him remember how awfully powerful that pain really is and how afraid of it he is. He sinks down to the floor of an ocean, where he's powerless to hit, like a snake whose blood has lost its heat.

When Davy sits for meals and study groups at the tables, it's hard to forget what happened at these tables, and his heart gets to pounding so hard that his shirt bounces and his chest hurts. Davy isn't wood.

On the days when the lightning sickness reminds him of where he stands, Davy is able to stay away from anything risky. He's able to obey. He can't love the temple, but being able to obey it is good enough. Life isn't so bad as a tame animal, keeping your head down, getting your pleasure from the simple things like eating, drinking, and sleeping. Davy can always pick as much cotton as they tell him when the echo of electricity is with him, whipping him right along.

Work gets harder if the bright birds call to Davy from their soaring heights. Work gets harder when still more temple is added on to invade the sky, and Davy knows who's paying to feed this monster that forces smallness and stupidity on this camp. A feeling leaps up in him, telling Davy that he must have some say about his life, about how things are done here in camp. Then the lightning sickness has got to surge up and redirect him or he won't be able to work. He'll just pick a bit of cotton here and there, and stretch, and crack his back, and rub himself, until a tan comes over with his lightning to remind Davy what can happen. Just the nearness of the Taser, which doesn't have to leave the adviser's belt, is enough to put Davy in the right mind for hours of work.

The tans stroll through their cotton patches, and the grays join in too, a bunch of toy soldiers living in their fairytale called Camp Earth, a life of stick-swinging and gun-stroking and magical advising. "Put spirit to it!" That's right, just reach out and grab spirit from the air and feel wonderful about bleeding for the temple, about adding to your enemy. Whatever spirit Davy has is pushing him out of the place they have for him in their fairytale, and this spirit has its own magic, resisting the cotton-picking with a physical power he can feel building up in his fingers as they come near the puffs of fiber, so when his fingers clamp down to pick he feels the bones vibrate and repel each other. More and more Davy imagines wrapping his aching and shredded fingers around the cold, smooth, solid metal of a pistol … a pistol he plucks from the belt of a tan, a pistol secure in Davy's grip as he puts it to the tan's head and squeezes … with a huge, soothing release of energy surging through Davy's hand and exploding the tan's brain straight out of the back of his head.

Heads have been exploding in Davy's mind for a while when a tan yells directly at him for his lagging, and a giant wave of lightning sickness rushes in until the throbbing fills him to the tips of his fingers and toes. "Oh, thank you," Davy says, "I'll get to it now." His shaking fingers fly to a cotton puff, snap together like magnets, then speed the goods directly to the sack. Again and again the shaking fingers do this, and Davy can do nothing to interfere with their obedience to the lightning's commandment. He truly doesn't want to interfere. He's grateful that the lightning's irresistible authority clears away all confusion and drives his fingers along a straight and narrow path.

Only a couple of days have passed when Davy's fingers go back to repelling each other, and a tan's head forces its way back into Davy's view, blowing apart like a watermelon over and over again by a gun that feels so wonderful in Davy's cotton-blistered hand.

A huge dose of the lightning sickness explodes through Davy one evening when he sees the advisers shock a member and drag him away to the box. Davy sees it all up close, sitting for study group only a table away from this man who Davy recognizes as one of the members who'd been tied to a table, where something had tried to burrow into him because its glass cage got heated by an adviser. The man seemed to be studying his book and Bible and listening to the lady advisers like everyone else was, when he just launches himself up onto his table and roars like five men. He throws his book down onto the table with a big smack, and then his Bible with another big smack, and his face is glowing red. He clenches his fists and pounds them against his head, then he throws his fists up against the sky. "We are in *hell*!" he howls. "Joshua is *not real*! Jesus is *never* coming back! Pleeeease push the button already!" This hits Davy with a blast of hot force, like the man threw open the door to a furnace. Right away the tans and grays tackle him and grind their knees into him so he's bolted to the table, and the lady advisers ask him how he could ever think such things, let alone yell them in front of children. His hands and feet get tied tight together, and a lot of electricity goes into him, and he growls and snarls and thrashes like a wild animal, and says things like, "hrrrgmafaka zanbas yohoehe," which makes white members look to black ones, who shake their heads and say, "No idea." The electricity makes Davy clasp his hands together and squeeze his legs against them. Some members look disgusted at the man's growling and twisting and foaming at the mouth, but to Davy it seems to show that the man has power to fight the electricity. The throaty snarling injects Davy with some of its power, which acts like medicine against the sickness. Finally the advisers quit shocking the man, and they drag him out to the jungle, and everybody settles back down to their books. Davy tries to pick up any hint that the man impressed anyone, but members mostly say things like, "Sheesh, if someone could use a little time in the box, that's the guy. Hoooleee hell, poor bastard."

Three days later, Davy sees the man sitting quietly for study group, turning pages in the book and reading aloud and even smiling, with his face a nice, normal color. There is something miraculous and wonderful about this to Davy; and something wrong.

Aching and hunching and picking and aching, Davy begins to imagine dying. What is death, compared to going on like this? What is death, but an escape from this hell? Davy can't stop coming back to that man's wild, red face. It's like the man had to be burning in hell already, with nothing to lose, to be able to tell us those terrifying things, and to be able to believe them.

"Davy, you are dead already! You are a slave, the walking dead!" roars the wild, red face, louder than the tans and grays. "Feel the sweet life of a whole lifetime in the time it takes to grab a pistol and blast an adviser's head away!"

But Davy would probably be shot dead five seconds later.

"Shot good by twenty bullets, after tasting life beyond anything you'll ever taste as the walking dead," sings the wild, red face with animal eyes. "Take a sweet taste with you into eternity."

Davy lies on his cheap mat at night, sharing a room with a bunch of little kids and a few older ladies, in a cheap shed that probably took two weeks to slap together. And building the temple has taken how many hundreds of weeks now?

The temple looks done to Davy. Maybe it'll never be done, they'll just keep adding to it. As long as it still needs work, the members have to keep on sacrificing, keep on looking forward, keep on giving their best. Davy tries to imagine camp with a finished temple. No more monster to feed, no more bottomless pit sucking and swallowing every possible dollar. There would be better clothes, and houses, and new crops to farm … We'd still be waiting for Joshua, which might be enough to hold the camp together.

Davy stares through mosquito nets and examines the thin metal roof that's getting hammered by rain. The fear has been retreating, and the hate is bubbling to a dangerous level. Back and forth these have been swinging him. The will to do something is painfully strong—to do anything that could decide this battle. Let the temple burn and crumble, or let it rule with whip and muzzle. One way or another, let there be peace. It's hard to rest when he has to vomit. The temple should do its damn duty and crack down on him, hard enough to crush his spirit, or he can't survive in this place. The box could do Davy some real good.

Minutes creep by, no sleep, just pressing a pillow against his ears, and sweating. The kids are whispering to each other, caught up in some very serious make-believe, trading their own inspiring versions of what's special about the camp. Adults in the next room are mumbling some noise, too, going on and on until it's almost as loud as the rain. Davy grinds his pillow into his ears and imagines punching his fist through the shabby wall, shattering it to pieces. A crack of thunder suddenly strikes, rattling the shed and killing off all the voices. Davy loosens the pillow from his head and takes in the lovely silence, as refreshing as a draft of cool, rain-cleaned air into a room of hot stink. He sits up when he notices the door is open a bit, and a wet man is staring at him.

"Can we count on you, Dave?" whispers the man.

"Yes," whispers Davy. "For what?"

The man silently puts a finger to his smiling lips. His wide eyes shift to Davy's roommates for a second, then come back to Davy. The man makes a fist, and brings it down onto his other hand, which he's holding out flat.

A flash goes through Davy, bouncing him straight up.

The man takes Davy out into the rain, and as they slide the door shut they see one of the older ladies rise up with a scowl. The man rams shut the metal door like a thunderclap, grabs a rope tied to a lamp on the wall, knots the loose end to the door handle, and when the lady yanks the door she can't get it to slide. All she can do is yell something about Joshua seeing us, which is mostly drowned out by the rain.

The man takes Davy into the other room, and in here are lots of husbands and wives with serious looks on their faces, and there's lots of hugging and crying. Davy is the youngest, and the wet man puts his hands on Davy's shoulders and kind of presents the boy like he's a prize or mascot. The man announces, "We've got around three hundred from all the sheds now, ready to go, all right? We've got the weapons out, the weather is perfect. Tonight is the night."

It's hard for Davy to believe what seems to be happening. It's too big and important to be real. The big and important things in this camp are lies and fairytales. Big and important belongs in imagination, in expectation. Joshua might as well show up in camp tonight, now that things have gotten to this level.

Some of the husbands and wives are asking if tonight should really be the night. Davy realizes that they don't want to lose the comforts they enjoy in each other's arms, and he can't help being annoyed by this, since these comforts for him have been gone for a long time. It's thrilling all through Davy's bones to hear the wet man answer these people the exact way Davy would love to. "Yes, tonight *is* the night, because enough of us can't live like the living dead even one more day. And we've gotta' go now before word can travel. Brothers and sisters, we march."

The rebels emerged from their sheds and assembled in a nearby grove. Two companies swiftly formed, then set out in opposite directions: one commencing a creep of more than a thousand yards through lightly forested terrain to the hill of the tans, the other launching into a trek of similar distance but through heavier foliage to the hill of the grays. A motley arsenal of crude and vicious weapons accompanied them, pikes and axes and everything in between, comprised of wood that some of these militants must have ripped from the jungle and endowed with metal shards before stashing the things away in some cache to be safe-kept for an opportunity such as this. A few marchers were even carrying little bombs they'd managed to fashion from chemicals smuggled away from legitimate agricultural use. Close behind the hungry vanguard of flesh-seeking points and edges, a host of grunts wielded fists and determination.

The two companies advanced such that their stealthy approaches reached the base of their respective hills at the same moment. The two assaults could then coincide and expect to enjoy the advantage of surprise, of bursting in on unsuspecting tans and grays lying snug in their cabins in avoidance of the heavy rain.

The craziest rebels began the upward charge, already bloodied, apparently having wounded themselves in psychological preparation for what might befall them on the hilltops.

Neither the tans nor the grays appeared to have any awareness of the onslaught of desperate humanity that was fixed on flinging itself through cabin windows and doors.

Many casualties could be expected on both sides at both sites. The advisers were better armed, and would be defending their homes, while the rebels, cranked up to a high state of offensive morale, could tolerate some early losses to firepower, and enjoyed a six to one numerical superiority. It seemed within the realm of feasibility that the rebels would overcome the tans and grays, and proceed with firearms against the temple.

Chapter 25
The Age of Aquarius

Dawn arrives with the boy straightening and rising. In one smooth motion he goes from lying down to standing up, his body springing forward and upright on planted feet.

His mind is clear and calm. The fever has broken.

The others too are awake and standing.

Around him is the camp everyone went to bed in last night, ages ago. This is the first time he's been in this camp.

The air is alive with something he can almost see, and he feels himself soaking it up so gratefully, rejoicing, tears streaming down without any shame.

The sky flows above him like a brilliant ocean, its shimmering waves of yellow, green, and blue rippling from the gleaming temple to the opposite horizon.

The rain has stopped. The storm has passed. Sunlight has broken through the dark clouds. The cliffs are polished, the trees are shining, the dirt is sparkling. The sweet golden tone of a child's voice fills the camp. It's all so peaceful. Everything has stopped moving. Earth has reached its resting place at the center of the universe.

The boy wonders if he and the others are dead, and have passed into the perfect camp, as Osiris dwells in perfect Egypt. What took us away to this garden?

Everyone walks around, young dogs let out into the yard for the first time. The boy tries to remember what it was like back when, ages ago, he was looking out through a window onto a yard, wondering if that yard was really there or just painted on the glass. Now the door has been opened, and the boy finally knows the yard is truly real. He explores the yard and talks with others about how real the kingdom is now that it can be seen and felt like this. He stares at old faces that are new and fascinating. He touches his power-conducting hands to other hands. Everywhere people are stretching, swaying, hopping, dancing, trying out the kingdom.

The guys with tan or gray pants are walking around like young dogs, too. Some in the gray pants are doing push-ups, and some kids grab the feet of the push-uppers who then walk forward with their hands. The boy tries to remember what the tan or gray pants meant, ages ago, when they must have meant something.

Maybe tan or gray had meant something. But now there is only now, this warm and calm *now,* forever.

The sun is moving across the sky, and the boy feels that eating would do him good, would push him forward to action and goodness in the kingdom. Food can wait, though. Let us march, brothers and sisters, let us gather to the beautiful temple and sing praise. The boy beholds importance as he nears the temple, the tree of life, whose fruit is radiant.

The temple doors open wide, and out steps Elder Brother, with long, curly, silver hair and a golden robe. He's so beautiful. He's waving and smiling at us. He's bringing light to us. Our voices ring with each other, making each voice stronger, the whole camp ringing in song, in one song. The boy's tears gush all they can, because now, at last, the song is his too.

"Come unto me, all ye who are weary and heavy laden, and I shall refresh you," Elder Brother sings through the speakers. "The year is one!"

The boy cries out, "Oh holy God!" People fall to their knees, beat their chests, and weep, calling out, "We shall be faithful! We shall obey!"

"I know, I understand," Elder Brother says with his arms stretched wide open. "I forgive you. I forgive you. It was hard for us all. Those were the conditions we were under. But we have proven our worthiness of this blessing. This is the golden age."

The words don't sound silly to the boy; they sound sacred. The words actually mean something. They refer to something real, something nobody has to invent for him, something he doesn't have to try inventing for himself.

"In our days of iron, gold was too good to be true," Elder Brother says. "For we were made of iron, and we sought greatly for gold, but even gold did become iron to us. Now we are made of gold, and all things are gold to us. God hath done a new thing, and former ways shall be forgotten, as God declared unto Joshua upon the holy mountain. Rejoice ye therefore, day after day for a thousand years! Congratulations on your rebirth."

Elder Brother steps down from the stage into the middle of all his people, and everyone puts their hands on him.

People drift toward the cotton and coffee fields, the ginning house and the bean barn, and get to know these old friends they spent so much time with ages ago. The boy strolls a while in a cotton patch, pressing his hands into spongy red soil, rubbing his fingertips into bursting white bulbs of fiber, delicious smells swirling all around him. The cotton field experience delivers its own rewards. The boy picks … and fills a sack to fullness of fine cotton. He picks with many satisfactions, and fills another sack.

A bowl of stew and a mug of coffee set off a million tiny pops and buzzes all through the boy's brain and body, a million tiny explosions of energy and flavor, overflowing into deep, sweeping sounds and shifting mixtures of color oozing from mountains, trees, and soil.

By evening, the boy just knows that God has always existed and has always been holding this perfect world in store. It makes perfect sense. He reclines on the courtyard grass and looks on the heaven-touching temple, so solid and clean and complete, glowing and humming to him in its holy light, blue and gold and white. The temple stands there at the center of all things forever. Nothing can move it.

How can things be different? It's unthinkable. Everything is proper. Right feels right. Doing good feels good. The law is written upon our hearts.

The day calls us to enjoyments and satisfactions in the kingdom; the night calls us to rest. We love Joshua's cotton and coffee, love to pick and clean and load the best we can, the best the watchers have ever seen. The trucks take the white and red worth to the town way down the road, and we're so grateful we have Elder Brother and the watchers to deal with what's left of the world out there. In the jungle there's a strange artifact with vines growing over it. It must have served some purpose to people who lived in this area ages ago.

Every day Elder Brother comes out of the temple to walk among his people, speaking good words to us, eating with us, playing games with us. He always joins us in the fields and picks as much as he can before the watchers come looking, and then he hides in the cotton plants or coffee bushes while we just keep on picking like we don't know where he is, and Elder Brother picks some final handfuls and rubs it to his face and smells it. "Aaaaaaahhh," he says, "smells like a laughing baby … our baby … so easy to love." When the watchers find him, he puts his hands up, and they say, "Come here you bad boy, playtime is over, you've got chores at the house," and we wave to Elder Brother as he goes back to his temple duties.

The boy's body doesn't use pain to force information on him. His body trusts him to pay attention to sensations that are like colors and sounds. One day the boy chops his pinky toe off while hoeing in the cotton fields, and he feels a tingling where the cut is, and the watchers sew the toe back on with a needle that feels smooth as it goes through his flesh. The boy tries to remember something about pain, but it's so far behind him.

The boy ought to be about one thousand and twelve years old when he's awakened by a terrible clap of thunder that leaves him a sobbing wreck, paralyzed and stinging.

"No," Davy objects, "no, no, not again."

Chapter 26
Handling the Truth

Nighttime was overtaking Washington, D.C., where Brandy Miller stepped out onto the balcony of her hotel room to take in some air until Ed and Carol were ready. She pushed her blond hair back behind her ears and straightened her black dress. Under the starry sky, the illuminated monuments of her nation's capital appeared so holy. She pictured Joshua preaching at the gates of these temples, railing out against their high priests and disturbing the reverence.

She guzzled a few swigs from a little bottle of vodka from her room's well supplied minibar. It made her insides feel warm and clean. She realized and accepted that she felt a definite satisfaction in the complete and terrible collapse of Camp Earth. She wasn't happy that Louis was dead, that his followers were dead; but the camp's demise did have for her a glorious quality to it, like a long-festering boil finally exploding all its bloody pus. She had always wished the thing to fail, to disappear.

That it had failed, and so spectacularly, had helped her to reconcile with her father. For a long while she couldn't forgive him for what he and Louis and the Institute and their circus had done to her, for how she'd been shoved aside so coldly by the onward rush of that train of the insane. But the camp had obviously failed, and therefore so had her father.

She stood vindicated and could now reclaim the old man in his waning years.

She held a similar complex of feelings toward Louis. She'd hated him, hated his scheme to get even with the world and prove himself superior to the simple and believing. She could imagine him going down wretchedly at the hands of his followers, those betrayed lovers wild for vengeance. He got the apocalypse he wanted. But old feelings of compassion for him had lately been stirring in her, feelings of pity for the desperate and twisted stepbrother she'd grown up with and tried to help.

She reflected on the irony of having spent about the last fourteen years denying him to others, denying she knew him at all, and earlier today she accepted an offer of half a million dollars to write a book telling the entire world about him.

Carol Koenig Miller relaxed in the shower, heavily medicated by the heat—and a variety of drugs. No, not *that kind* of drugs. Hers were all right. They were designed and prescribed by professionals. She hadn't been feeling well lately. She'd been experiencing … sort of a non-stop barrage of … disruptive feelings. Ed took her to some doctors. They diagnosed her condition, and they applied medications that had been developed and approved for that very condition. And the medicine has helped her, unquestionably. She can live life again. Under the downward rush of opposing showerheads, her mind wandered in green pastures … though she mustn't lose track of time and be late for dinner. Ed was turning seventy-five, he was retiring from the Institute and it was giving a dinner here in this wonderful hotel in his honor. She felt so blessed to be married to Ed, such a solid and reliable anchor.

She emerged from her sauna and was pleased to see she still had plenty of time. She wiped a mirror with a towel and noticed she had not many wrinkles, and did appear to be ageing rather well. Ed frequently told her this, as did friends at church.

She was glad Ed sold the house, though she'd always thought it a grand house, and the landscape so beautiful. It was just that so much had happened there with the Enlightenment Center. And Carol had always wanted to live in New England, a plan that easily won the approval of Ed, who loved the colored forests and colonial history of the place. The estate in the Rockies was going to a blooming young family full of happiness, a happiness bright enough to banish any lingering shadows of the past, a forward-looking family too busy with life to dredge down into the dead layers beneath their marvelous new possession. A fresh chapter would open for the estate, and a crowded chapter would close for Carol and Ed.

Carol remembered the final conversation she had with her son before he left for Africa. She had always tried to give him the best influences she could, Carol told him, but it hadn't been easy, a single mother trying to scrape together a living and be the best possible mother at the same time. She told Louis she was sorry that he might have gone through things when she or a dad wasn't there to help him through and help him figure things out. Louis told her that those things were in the past, and that the future would be plenty good enough to make up for all that had gone before.

What Carol was most sorry for, as she watched her son depart, was what Louis had become, what he had come to think of himself and the world.

She had always felt he would make a special mark on the world. But she never had—and probably never would—come to grips with the whole Brother K thing.

As the Enlightenment Center was starting to get regular visitors, Carol's feet turned ice-cold with anticipation. She had read her son's book and understood that these people were attracted by its justification of their feelings about their condition. To some of them it was great literature and important social criticism. To others it was some kind of prophecy, a revelation even. What or where exactly did they hope this Enlightenment Center would get them? Ed was frequently counseling her not to worry. She should be proud that her son's book was serving to inspire and organize the marginalized and dispossessed—in fact the very sort of people the Institute was founded for—and she should take comfort that Ed's firm was in fact interested in the situation to such a degree that Institute funds and expertise would assist these people around her son to make something of their enthusiasm.

As Carol watched the Enlightenment Center slowly gathering form like something in a petri dish, her husband's consistently positive take on the weird project actually did lead her to feel some enthusiasm for it herself. Enthusiasm took some effort in the face of a hundred reasons to worry. She often caught blatantly messianic tones in the preaching of her son, and more than anything it was this that disturbed her, sensing that bitter wages were the likely result of such blasphemy. She noticed that many of these poor souls were developing certain expectations of her son, yearnings which he seemed only too happy to stoke, but which could never be ultimately satisfied by anything less than the real thing. The Brother K thing simply didn't possess the authenticity required to make it safe or worthwhile.

For two years she was fearing the worst, getting reassurance from Ed, watching the thing get bigger, hoping it could be kept in bounds, hoping it didn't degenerate into a perverse abomination … realizing there was really no way she could stop her son, short of killing him.

She breathed easier when the thing was transplanted, and she could drive straight up her driveway and into her garage without running over Daniel Boone or John the Baptist or someone who'd escaped from a cage at the county fair. For several years the news she got from Africa was surprisingly good, with Ed making many visits to the camp, always coming back with reports of progress and wellness, frequently noting to Carol how pleased the Institute was with the camp, even mentioning that several of his colleagues shared his view that the project was developing into perhaps the most rewarding ever taken on by the firm. Louis sent her pictures of a community of smiling faces and sweaty bodies busy at work and play among orderly rows of tents, fields blossoming with fertility, warehouses taking in successful harvests. How very strange to her, that this was actually her son out there. What was he truly thinking about this whole thing? Had she ever really known this person?

How relieving though, that the camp was amounting to a quaint farming town nestled deep within the bosom of a country on good terms with the USA. These were happy years for Carol and Ed, enjoying many afternoons together in the sharp mountain air, salvaging their battered estate.

Then struck the sudden, evil wind. How very startling to see the camp splashed across the internet, the TV, the magazines at the supermarket, revealing a camp so violent and out of control, a situation so degraded, Ugandan soldiers moving in to restore order … How completely overpowering to realize that the whole Camp Earth project had culminated in a horrid bloodbath.

A clearer picture soon took shape for Carol and the media at large when Institute personnel gave their eye-witness accounts of the camp's collapse. They told of a *malaise* gradually forming in camp, first revealing itself in a sagging work-ethic, with camp members just not as productive, not as willing to work as they had been. A perception grew among members that they weren't seeing the rewards of their labors, that these rewards were being appropriated by others, that the camp arrangement was providing benefits to certain undeserving parties. Members increasingly voiced a desire for greater control over their work and greater ownership of its fruit. Arguments arose over whether these new feelings had any valid basis. Blame was thrown in this direction and that. Threats were made. Institute personnel of course did all they could, short of violence, to keep the peace and to rekindle some motivation. Members in leadership positions, however, became so anxious to hold things together that they did in fact resort to violence, though without much effect, since no violence seemed worse to discontented members than merely applying themselves to labors they could no longer stomach. Brother K for his part was getting on the speakers every day, asking everyone to pray, reminding them of the power of faith to overcome the power of the world, all of which had come to sound fairly ridiculous to his audience. The Institute was contacting the embassy, trying to get some police out to the camp … but meanwhile the guns carried by certain members to protect the camp began to be used against other members. When Ugandan forces finally did arrive they found the survivors around the temple area, and these greeted the soldiers with a hail of bullets that called forth a devastating response. Institute personnel witnessed Brother K being removed from the temple by a few members and being shot in the head.

Carol was appreciative of the remorse and care that Ed's colleagues demonstrated as they recounted the travesty. A little later she noticed that confusion remained in the media on a number of points, including whether Ugandan forces had for years held a position near the camp, whether any camp inhabitants escaped the slaughter, and what was removed from the camp by Ugandan forces.

The storm of sensationalism slathered the public plate with a memorably sour serving of Camp Earth. Meanwhile, an abundance of expert commentary proceeded to steer the public mind to a sensible understanding of what had happened. Camp Earth was simply the latest in an endless line of similar disasters known as socialist experiments, often of a religious flavor. The Camp Earth experiment followed an utterly predictable course, beginning with a honeymoon and nice fuzzy feelings, which soon enough faded away. The people found themselves no longer able to share or cooperate, but plenty able to see the flaws in their half-baked operation. They preferred to call it quits, but their leader wouldn't give up (his power) so easily. The solution had to be violence, which had the added appeal of satisfying their deep longing for doomsday. It's really no wonder the camp's destiny should be crazed collapse, because after all, these were folks who thought it wise to journey thousands of miles to build a temple and grow coffee somewhere beyond the reach of the mind-control powers that enslave us.

Carol slid into a radiant, gold evening-dress and fastened her diamond earrings. Ed walked by and kissed her on the cheek while tightening his scarlet bowtie. His tuxedo fully in place, he looked himself over in the mirror.

"Handsome devil, you could have gone into politics," observed Carol. Her husband chuckled at this.

"You'll do fine," she said, "you always do fine."

They met Brandy at her door.

"You look … wow," said Brandy to her elders.

"You look wow, too," said Carol warmly.

The three took the elevator down to the ballroom, where they were greeted by pleasant faces and the sweet tones of Debussy gently flowing from a grand piano, drifting through the atmosphere to merge with the gentle flickering of crystal chandeliers. Voices hummed and cooed. Glass, silverware, and china clinked and chimed. Ed led his two ladies through a fleet of tables whose smiling occupants raised their jeweled paws in salutation and whetted their palettes with crisp, white wine. At a table below the podium where Ed was to speak, he seated his wife and daughter, then himself.

Lobster bisque arrived, and Carol marveled aloud that it could be possible for something to taste so good. Ed agreed, and observed that the rich, creamy bisque was well-complemented by the ethereal texture of the Rhineland Riesling. Soon came spinach salad and bread toasted with asiago cheese. For the main course, the three were presented with broiled scallops and seared steak, which moved Ed and Brandy to request a bottle of Pinot Noir. A generous portion of raspberry cheesecake rounded out the meal, along with coffee—of a smoother and mellower flavor than the camp's product, which had carried more of a robust edge, Ed informed the ladies.

Not quite satisfied, Brandy ordered a glass of her namesake, and to the table it descended, blazing with alcoholic aroma and the amber of a sunset. Ed was shortly required on stage, and this he saw as good cause to be allowed some of his daughter's "medicine," but his daughter and wife united to refuse him any access to the powerful drink. Ed protested, and the ladies became serious, conjuring for him images of an old man stumbling and slurring away in front of all these important people. Brandy veiled the vapors with a napkin and suggested that the question be decided by a single brave gulp on her part. Her father waved her off such foolishness, and quickly realigned himself to the bearings of his ever-sound internal compass.

A merry gentleman of seemingly unprecedented obesity was soon standing at the polished mahogany podium above Ed, tapping the microphone and calling the revelers to attention.

"To business then, ladies and gentlemen, to business."

Through dainty spectacles on rosy cheeks the man reverently read out the life of Edward Miller, speaking first of a lowly farm boy's dedication to bettering himself and raising his station, then of a young man's success in the army, at university, and in private enterprise, then of a graying man's years of devoted service to the needy. Ed sat back, his expression steeled to the flattery, his eyes fixed humbly on the speaker. At last the enormous man finished his praise and reached into a case, pulling out a miniature grandfather clock whose edges were gilded in precious metals. He identified the item as Ed's retirement gift, and beckoned him to come up and receive it. Ed ascended to center stage, took the clock into his hands, looked it over with obvious satisfaction, then hoisted it up before a glittering sea of applause. The flesh continent walked off with surprising vigor in his colossal stride, hinting that decades of rich living had yet to weigh him down to utter decadence. Meanwhile, Ed announced that his acceptance of the lustrous gift must be "on behalf of my beautiful wife and daughter here with me tonight, as well as other loved ones across the Earth—and beyond."

Ed cleared his throat.

"The Institute for the Progress of Human Wellness," he said, lightly grasping the sides of the podium, on which he had set a small notebook, "was established in the wake of two of the greatest challenges in human history. I refer to the First and Second World Wars, though they can be designated together as the Second Thirty-Years War, covering the period of 1914 to 1945, with a lag occurring through the middle, a lag in which the, ah, unsound results of the initial phase would fester, and then unleash the furious conclusion. The First Thirty-Years War occurred almost exactly three centuries before, and over much of the same territory. Both wars of thirty years overstayed their welcome, spilling over proper boundaries and inflicting the most unacceptable collateral damage.

"Just prior to the Second Thirty-Years War you had a civilization that had reason to believe in the progress of human wellness: Europe had just seen a century without unmanageable war, and the general standard of living had been on the rise, with vast advances in science and economic productivity. Then the drop of an archduke's hat sent everyone eagerly jumping into the deep end of the pool, where emperors would drown, and far uglier powers would emerge in their place. What can you really say of the ugliness of Communism and Nazism and World War II? You might say that any and all evils took place as easily as a leaf falls from a tree, and that it doesn't bear thinking about for too long. It's a picture of immense darkness that people react to in different ways. Many keep it out of their consciousness and go forth in good cheer to live in the sun-drenched land of the living, and I can't say I blame them. Others peer too deeply into the abyss and come away with a sick feeling that God must be dead, and I can't say I blame them, either. Some though, and this is really the point I'd like to make here, some people react to the picture with missionary resolve that humankind must gain control of itself, must somehow grow out of being an untended toddler who's got hold of a butcher knife. The six men who founded the Institute in 1953 had all seen the Second Thirty-Years War up close, and had come away from it convinced that humankind needed serious help to face a future that could very well roll out wars and 'isms' ever more terrible.

"Through the decades, the Institute has received funding from a variety of organizations and individuals who share its humanitarian vision. My colleagues and I have always exercised prudent stewardship of these funds in pursuing studies that bring the insights of our several disciplines to bear upon problems of human wellness. Part of our work deals with social movements, religious groups, and other current programs for human wellness that constitute living laboratories that demonstrate what works and what doesn't. Some of the ones that seem promising, we help them along.

"One of these, ah, programs that we assisted … was the Camp Earth community. This was a study that I was especially close to, as it happened to involve a member of my own family." Ed looked down at his wife and daughter, drew a white handkerchief from his pocket and kept it in his hand, grasping it frequently.

"This movement grew up from a sort of fan club which surrounded the young author of a certain book, a novel that's based on an interesting premise. It imagines the Second Coming of Christ to be the reincarnation of the soul of the man who taught in Palestine two thousand years ago. In depicting the kind of life this second Christ might live, the book tends to emphasize a particular aspect of Christ: his preaching of good news to the poor, his healing of the brokenhearted, his proclaiming of liberty to captives. It tends to present Christ as a redeemer of those sunk by the world, those unable to swim a world of necessary evils. The people enthused by the book felt used up and cast off by society. I saw firsthand the power this book had for gathering these people and directing their enthusiasm toward a definite course of action. I saw that the author of this book possessed the qualities necessary for leading these people along that course. And the Institute was well-disposed to offer them charity and guidance.

"The group quickly became something more than a fan club, and plans developed for relocating to establish the ideal society sketched out in the book's latter chapters. Many of those who loved the book may have taken it to be prophecy of actual events, and may have seen its author as someone vitally connected to the actual return of Christ. The book's author may have tolerated, perhaps at times even encouraged, such beliefs, for the benefit of those who drew inspiration from them. On the other hand, probably just as many folks drew their inspiration from the book's ideological marriage of Christ and Marx, and were eager to participate in a community that would try out such a program.

"For many years the group made a valiant attempt to realize some of the promise they saw in that program. The effort required enormous faith and a certain amount of blindness to harsh reality. Fortunately, the watchful assistance of Institute personnel was ever present. And ah, when the Camp took its turn for the worst, nobody was more stricken with grief than we Institute folks were. How could we have studied so many societies like these and still not foresee what would happen?

"I must now confess. I confess that in dealing with the Camp Earth community, I myself became one of the many who let hopes get the better of reason. We who wanted so much for the thing to succeed were blinded to its dangers. I can see now in retrospect, all too clearly, that its doctrines and practices were fundamentally flawed. The members of Camp Earth and I were so eager and impatient to treat the social ills of the world, we opted for a medicine we hoped would be faster and surer than the established prescription. In other words, we simply fell under the spell of that age-old mirage known as the shortcut to paradise. We saw the marriage of Christ and Marx glimmering out there on the horizon, we set off for it, and got something much worse than what we turned our backs on. The medicine proved far more harmful than the ailment.

"I acknowledge the difficult fact that the book and the Camp Earth movement will forever live under the dark shadow of failure and catastrophe. Forgive me for tolerating the movement's extremism. I always regretted that much of the attraction the movement held for the discontented lay in the far too critical attitude the book takes toward the society it alleges to be the source of discontent. Such a critical attitude toward the American way did prove effective at gathering the discontented, but proved quite hollow when the movement's own planned society poured out discontents and then some.

"The experience of the Camp Earth community adds another tarnished page to humankind's mounting historical record of egalitarian utopias. When productive resources are arranged to be the property of everyone, I'm sorry to say that instead of freedom, justice, and equality, the typical results are totalitarianism, stagnation, and convulsion. The property of everyone is really the property of no one, leading to the poverty of everyone. You've got to conclude there are powerful forces set against that type of society.

"Many decades of the most arduous and thorough case-studies establish a rather clear pattern: what really works in human affairs, and what tends to produce the greatest good for the greatest number, with an abundance of goods reaching the hands of the lowest, is in fact a system in which private property is protected, with resources and markets open to private investment. This verdict has gained increasing acceptance worldwide, with little effort required to recognize that peoples lacking prosperity are frequently those refusing to integrate into the global consensus, instead clinging to outdated and extremist ideologies that belong in the dustbin of history. The extremist insists that private enterprise has irrationalities and excesses, that its abundance can be somewhat unevenly spread, its booms can bust, its bubbles can burst, its dynamic engine can melt itself down. We'll concede it's a terrible system—if the extremist concedes it must nevertheless be considered superior to any alternative, and it's thus a system worth promoting and protecting. If mistaken hearts and minds would simply face the facts that bloody history has worked so hard to establish … but this is not the way of the extremist. He would rather see the imperfections of the system lead it toward crisis and render it vulnerable to being imprudently altered or done away with altogether. He hopes to see a stirring among people who consider themselves victims of the system, and he'll do what he can to coax a stirring into a swelling. Lurking beneath our soft beds are real monsters. They grow in swamps of resentment where masses are prone to manipulation by parties of truly sinister aims. In the extraordinary case that some monstrous extremism reaches a stature that threatens the very existence of the system that's in the best interest of everyone, even extraordinary measures may justifiably be taken in defense.

"Thank you all for your understanding and support, and for your furtherance of human wellness. Perhaps through a path we have helped to make straight, the kingdom of God will at last descend upon the Earth. Thank you all very much."

Ed contritely stepped down from the stage as the object of a standing ovation's universal sympathy and acclaim.

Chapter 27
The Secrets of the Temple

The three ate a fine Sunday brunch together in the hotel restaurant, with plenty of coffee for Ed and Brandy. A fresh newspaper was provided at Ed's request, and Brandy watched her father crack a strange little smile as he paused upon a front-page article that carried the headline: Charity Director Confesses Role in Cult Disaster, Denounces Marriage of Christ and Marx as Phony Shortcut to Paradise.

Today Ed would take his wife and daughter on a tour of their nation's capital.

The mood of the three was subdued and reflective, and their pace was pleasantly slow. Brandy continued to feel from yesterday evening that this was a religious setting, that this whole place was a shrine to a beautiful ideal. No matter what president or agency, which war or tragedy that was given memorial here, no matter what the actual history and controversy surrounding each, they were all made to shine from the light of the beautiful ideal, regardless of the actual service they'd given to it.

Brandy believed there were solid grounds for loving her country. There was an ideal of freedom here, and the freedom that really existed here was due to the real service that the ideal had been given. Such were conclusions Brandy had reached for herself through years of study, solid study provoked to some degree, to some large degree, by her stepbrother's challenging rhetoric. Her studies had planted her firmly in the Age of Enlightenment (the real kind), the Declaration of Independence, the Constitution and its Bill of Rights. And onward she had driven, through two centuries of … well, the Louis in her might say two centuries of certainly constant lip service to the ideal, with much of the real service to it coming through struggle against powers who claimed to embody the ideal, powers who staunchly defended their traditional freedom of denying freedom to others. There sat Louis in the back of her head, wagging that finger at her and working that silver tongue, summoning for her consideration a plantation owner from the Old South, mint julep and fine mustache and all, who explained that his was the freedom to possess black persons under a Constitution that respected the right of property and the right of states to determine their own affairs. Louis then invited Brandy to follow this man's cotton north, where it was laid at the polished boot of a man standing beside a cloth factory, his gold buttons straining to hold back a swollen belly as he issued cold blasts about his freedom to buy human labor as simply as a bale of cotton: on terms as maximally advantageous to himself as he could wrest in a system of free enterprise and under a Constitution that respected the right of contract, even a grotesquely lopsided contract with a party under the duress of desperate need and powerlessness.

She had to concede that the ideal was vague enough to be abused by those committed to some narrow version of it. But it was also expansive enough to accommodate broader versions, and to inspire them. She suspected that Louis, all his role-playing aside, would have to admit a real difference between freedom in the United States and freedom in Uzbekistan, and admit a certain amount of American freedom to struggle for freedom.

Such striking imagery surrounded her in this mystifying city of temples. The colors of the flag carried a special potency, as though capable by themselves of delivering half the nation to whatever faction that simply waved them most. She felt herself slipping into a dream, into a clear, warm lake where primal feelings of patriotism bubbled up to the surface. She thought of childhood, of sunny blue skies, emerald grass, golden skin, and cool breeze. It was a little like being drunk. Or being seduced. That was it: seduction. Brandy loved her country, but would do so only on solid grounds, on grounds more solid than these warm feelings. She had, after all, gained some sense of the dangers of mindless seduction.

In the evening, Ed suggested the three eat supper at an enchanted, little-known place he knew called Kingdom of Jordan. Over lamb kebab, unleavened bread, eggplant, rice rolled in grape leaves, and hot tea, they discussed whether they had kept the sabbath today, with Carol expressing some regret that they hadn't attended church, while Brandy and her father maintained that it was lawful to do good on the Sabbath, and therefore to make use of all the opportunities for worship and gratitude and uplift and instruction that a tour of this city provides. Carol yielded, and said it was nice that Ed and his favorite daughter were once again close, as they should be.

After supper the ladies returned to the hotel, and Ed went to meet some colleagues in another part of the city.

Ed's aim was a brown brick building, easy to miss as it stood among many others of its kind, except for the slightly orange tinge of the bricks, and the green gargoyles glaring down from the corners of the roof to forbid the half-hearted. Shortly after World War II it became government property, but before then it was for many decades the meeting place of the Frontier Club, a society of newspaper men, bankers, magnates of mining, oil, timber, and fruit, retired military brass, professors, and of course politicians, with the full roster of these gentlemen meeting here for four days each spring and autumn equinox to hear reports and studies presented by fellow members, to commission the studies and reports they'd hear the next time, to less formally discuss world affairs with one another, make connections, plan joint ventures, and certainly to enjoy the best liquor and cigars and women that money could buy, with the place serving for the remainder of the year as hotel, library, social hall, really whatever any member should require of it.

Ed now presented himself to the gatekeepers. They accepted his credentials and granted him clearance. He proceeded forward and upward to the porch attendant, who spoke into a shoulder radio and received confirmation that Ed should gain entrance. Promptly the bolt across two vast iron doors was released, and Ed passed through into a hallway that still sported fiery brown wood paneling from the Frontier Club era, along with the hallowed portraits of many notables who'd sometime walked here. There also remained from that bygone age a parlor in which one could still enjoy the comforts of a bar, billiard tables, and a wall full of books. The rest of the building had, however, suffered considerable loss of decoration in being outfitted to host some of the many agencies that would fight the Cold War.

Alone in a lengthy restroom of spotless white tiles and gleaming chrome faucets, Ed let hot water gush down upon his reddening hands. His head spun and his heart pounded at the reality of what he was involved with. He mustn't shrink from what history is full of. The way of the great ones had always been to take the pain of life—and to inflict it—in hardy acceptance of what the gods have obviously ordained as the price of all living. The greatest general sucked the blood of his horse and kept riding, slaughtering millions.

Just keep my hands here, until … "Aahhaggaahd … sssssssssssss … oooohahgahd … damn it! I'm sorry son, damn it I am. Oooh, damn it. But you did have help. We gave all of you help. Aaah."

Of course too much could beat him like anyone else, beat him easily, Ed had always realized. But the bright burn gathered his demons and boiled them away. Ed pressed his wet, scalded hands against his face and neck.

"Well Doc … and uh, Louis … it may just come down to this," Ed noted aloud. "I'll give it my best."

Ed entered the Star Room, a gray rectangular chamber, its long walls and sloping floor lit orange every twelve feet by a lamp, each of these wall-mounted lamps having a fixture on top that projected a fiery constellation upon the dark blue ceiling. Actually the oldest part of the building, this room was built in the 1870's as a private theater for séances and burlesque shows, and it would go on to host every proceeding imaginable. Though refurbished, it continued to exude a magical, even sacred, atmosphere. Several rooms in the building were fit to hold a presentation. Ed had considered using the slick and glossy Silver Room, popular with business people. He'd also considered the Steel Room, full of squeaking-tight leather fastened by iron, popular with military people. He'd decided on the Star Room because it most suited Doctor Crowley, a man involved in matters of silver and steel while his gaze roamed a little higher, upon something closer to the gods.

Everything looked as it should in the Star Room as Ed began greeting the many key people who would be in attendance tonight. He showed them to their tables and their drinks and their copies of the project outline, and some of them strolled down the aisles to scan the carved, painted creatures jutting out from the ceiling. Ed grinned with joy and sweated with terror as the room filled with the ladies and gentlemen of the Global Asset Security Consortium, who sipped their scotch and skimmed their papers with furrowed faces and more than a few raised eyebrows. When Ed sensed they were nearly ready to hear him out, he walked down to the stage, stepped up to the podium there, and checked his notes before clamping a little microphone to his jacket.

"Good evening," Ed began. "I am very grateful so many of you are interested enough to be here. I certainly believe the subject of this presentation reaches a level of importance that justifies your attention.

"Let me start by dedicating what follows to the late Dr. Solomon Crowley. I regret it must be I, rather than he, who conducts this briefing on Project AQUARIUS. It was always the Doctor's brainchild, and I always played junior partner in it. That the project was entirely successful in every phase came as no surprise to the Doctor, for he'd committed himself to battle only after he'd seen, before any fighting, that victory was his. At any rate, I'll try to deliver something tonight that might give the Doctor some degree of the honor he deserves.

"In his last days, the Doctor grew concerned that posterity might misunderstand his motives, might envision him as some kind of villain who lurked behind the scenes, pulling strings to manipulate people. And I had to remind him: people are manipulated. We just want them to be manipulated more effectively.

"Many people of goodwill prefer to view the centralized manipulation of human awareness as imaginary or unnecessary. They acknowledge its presence and perhaps even its usefulness only in regard to some distant time and place they'd rather not dwell upon. That it could long abide among themselves is simply out of the question.

"Even the reluctant, though, can observe the thriving presence of such manipulation at the dawn of civilization, in the river valleys where priests tied the natural fears and hopes of the people to graven images in temples. Where, six thousand years ago, could a simple farmer look for assurance that the land yield up its fruit and his household see increase and security? Deities had to be abroad in the land, wielding such powers of fortune, and had to be susceptible to influence; this has always been basic to the popular imagination. The key development occurs when the people become convinced, perhaps by some leading family, that this indispensable influence with the gods is accomplished by way of a certain expertise, one which, of course, is possessed only by this leading family. This professed expertise was crucial leverage for the rise of a priesthood that could collect tithes from believers, tithes that priests applied to achieving the favor of the gods through maintenance of temples and sacrifices, and tithes that priests applied to irrigation and flood-control projects, to armies, art, and technological innovations like writing, the plow, and the wheel.

"I think these priests may or may not have believed their own hype: they may or may not have believed that their expertly performed rituals truly secured the productivity of the soil by truly activating the mystical forces of fertility and virility, frequently pictured as full-breasted Mother Earth and her companion the Sun Bull. What the priests did believe was that their performances truly secured popular support for the priesthood. The effective tithe-collecting priest had to at least appear to believe his own hype, and should he ever have second thoughts about the deception and manipulation he was engaged in, he had only to look around him and count off its numerous benefits—benefits to himself, yes, but even more the benefits to the economic and psychological condition of his entire society.

"By two thousand years ago, the generous mother and her accomplice, radiant from his triumphal rebirth after his descent into darkness, were easily assuming the names Mary and Christ. The desired resurrection had become more personal than agricultural, though all regeneration remained to the archaic mind a single mystical principle administered by the Fertility Mother and her Virile Companion. Thus Constantine standardized worship in the Roman Empire upon what had already been for thousands of years the typical objects of worship in the civilizations of the area.

"Even more plainly than at the dawn of civilization, we may in recent centuries observe the manipulation I have dared to posit, the fashioning of graven images for the popular imagination by priesthoods wishing to capture mass support and mobilize people to achievements not otherwise possible. The common person in the Age of Revolution and Great War has been presented with a series of inspiring, expertly promoted images that amount to modern deities: Liberty, Equality, Democracy, the Nation, Civilization, the Workers' Paradise, the Master Race, the Free World, and so on. These have proven quite as capable as the ancient divinities in drawing tithes, raising temples, advancing technologies, and certainly in carrying out sacrifices.

"Psychological manipulation is more vital in an era of mass-produced guns, militias, and mass citizen armies than in an era of elite-controlled bronze weapons; the ancient priest could resort to his arms monopoly should his propaganda fail to convince, whereas the modern priest has often had to face relatively armed and free peoples who may well resist his policy unless it's presented to them with special flair. American entry into World War I immediately comes to mind, popular support being achieved by the Committee on Public Information, which employed mass media to overcome the unhelpful attitude held by many workers that they had no interest in shipping off to kill other workers.

"The realist accepts that government consists of making people well-disposed toward doing great and necessary things that people by themselves would regard as distasteful and contrary to their narrow personal interests. Mass desires must constantly be shaped to dimensions agreeable to the well-being of society, and priesthoods have the difficult task of making people hate things seemingly inoffensive or even enticing, and of making people love things that hold them in place. The person in society cannot be expected to see things the proper way without constant reinforcement. A citizen can easily come to a belief that his best interests are not served as an upright member of society. He may feel that his sacrifice of freedom is not worth the benefits he receives from the social order. He may long for some theoretical state of nature, for that always elusive mode of human experience fancied to be the essential one.

"The Doctor sympathized with the struggle of the citizen. He recognized that much of modern civilized life goes against the grain of the citizen's Stone Age DNA. Humankind's biological recipe, like that of every other creature, has constantly had to keep up with a changing environment as well as it could, and where genetic changes haven't been providential enough we've had to adapt through our tools, our culture. It's been chiefly through technological development that humankind has met the demands of an uncaring environment, but this very process of cultural acquisition has drastically altered our social environment and heaped new pressures upon us. Civilization brings its own set of demands and discontents. The Doctor feared that the demands and pressures of mass regimentation, mass dependency, class inequality, economic depression, and total war approach a weight that citizens and societies simply cannot bear without new help from the toolkit. It was the Doctor's aim to craft a grand tool to be applied in crisis situations by a well-qualified priesthood such as this audience, so that desirable mass-behavior can prevail even in extreme environments.

"One need not be a disciple of Marx to recognize the truth in his observation that capitalism tends to produce crises whose cyclical return puts on trial the entire system, each time more menacingly. This tendency was rather too frankly shrugged at in the recent testimony before Congress of the CEO of a premier investment bank, one of a handful of such banks for which the recent bubble and crash proved a great opportunity, booking profits on the way up and buying out bankrupt competitors on the way down. There are incomparable thrills and jackpots to be had in riding capitalism's cyclical crises, and we who know how to ride this dragon want to keep on being able to ride. It's what freedom means. But let's remain aware that the dragon is a fire-breathing colossus and plenty of folks get burned by it. We need to be aware that increasing numbers of not totally impotent people are questioning the need to preserve this system that must, every twenty years or so, condemn part of itself to bankruptcy and idleness; this system that distributes purchasing power not quite broadly enough to purchase what the system is able to produce; this system of credit expansion and constriction in which debts so easily issued on the way up are so hardly paid on the way down.

"In his sixty-year quest to remedy nature's frequent failure to provide a necessary psychological state, the Doctor tested a series of technologies at numerous stations in the field, right on the ground in the midst of convulsive social upheaval. His deployment of a three hundred-foot hologram of Krishna reversed the communist orientation of thousands of villages; the same effect was achieved in Christian areas with his deployment of a hologram appropriate for them. In fieldwork and historical study, he gained an appreciation of the psychological needs of populations shifted from peace to war and then back again. Such shifting can result in catastrophe without sufficient controls on the shifted. Of particular interest to him were World War I for Germany and for Russia. The militarization of these societies released demons that couldn't be bottled up by treaties: militias on the left and right, armed with guns and slogans they weren't just going to drop for a life of good citizenship, particularly not during conditions of mass economic collapse. A much easier century would have unfolded had the militants been pacified, but instead, as we all know, a militia on the left was able to gain power in Russia and a militia on the right was able to gain power in Germany, and out of this came a hell-storm unimagined by the sowers of 1914.

"So just how would the Doctor pacify the militants? How would he militarize the pacifists? I myself am not a neurologist, so I will confine my remarks to the global asset security implications of Project AQUARIUS, and will not attempt any detailed explanation of the marvelous science which underlies the Doctor's technology—though you are free to consult the description offered by the Doctor himself in the final pages of your outline. Ask Professor Ferdmann, over here under Sagittarius, how Dr. Crowley's vein of classified research compares with gene editing—which the Doctor regarded as a fundamental solution in the long term.

"Well, before I fire up the screen and show you our footage of the technology in action, let me address a few possible concerns.

"Some may view the Doctor's technology as a tampering that destroys something natural and proper in human experience. The question I ask is, What necessary development has there ever been which hasn't taken humankind a little further away from some supposedly essential mode of experience that existed before? Since that distant creature who roamed the grassland on two legs first picked up a flake of stone, or, if you prefer, since that son of Adam first smelted bronze, we humans have been altering things to our own purposes, making our experience the product of our artifacts. Something artificial enters human experience with any technology.

"The Doctor always spoke of his work in terms of helping those in need. Now and again he even got carried away, and ah, spoke in terms of ushering in the dispensation or bringing forth the kingdom. The Doctor recognized that a sort of new order for the ages could be the broadest potential of his technology. The fact is, however, that he had no intention of displacing or rendering obsolete the existing social controls provided by the military, law enforcement, religion, medicine, psychiatry, education, the various forms of mass media, and other traditional instruments for which he retained great respect. He intended his technology to be used as a stopgap measure in cases where standard methods prove inadequate to bridle or spur masses as the situation requires. He personally reassured representatives of affected interests that his technology is best considered a nuclear option that leaves ample room for the continued use of conventional weapons.

"Ladies and gentlemen, now that you have the rationale behind the project, let's pull the curtains away and take a look at how this thing actually played out."

Chapter 28
Apocalypse Now

An eye hovering among sunlit clouds peered down into the emerald jungle, tracking a cable of silver water winding through vapor-haunted mountains and scraping against nude clearings of rosy soil. A prominent shaft of black stone, eons ago driven up by enormous geological force, signaled the observer to depart from the river and seek out certain nearby fields flecked with white, orchards speckled with pink, clusters of modest habitations, and the commanding spectacle of a pyramid temple standing as a testament to human force—the beautiful, frightening magic that converts vision and will into reality.

The workday hadn't yet moved over the afternoon hump, the time of day when the camp normally fought universal sluggishness. Events began with Bill simply taking firm hold of his pruning shears and driving them several inches into the back of a large adviser, who barely managed a sharp yelp that blended into the constant cry of the forest. Bill deposited the man under an umbrella of broad leaves, and now he had a rifle with a score of rounds at his disposal.

Bill had recently become convinced that his true path lay in taking down as many advisers as he could before going down himself, crowned with the glory due a good soldier. He felt a glow resting upon him, sort of a spiritual armor, something he hadn't felt since his days of triumph as a boy soldier striking down the Godless by the power of soaring faith. There was no need to coordinate this action with other members, who would probably just foul it up, maybe on purpose. Bill wanted a wide berth for himself to do this thing of his. For so many years he'd been regretting that he hadn't met a good soldier's end in that other jungle. How much disappointment it would have spared him. Now, in this moment, all his wastage could be redeemed. Bill was right where he needed to be to make his final, honorable mark upon the world. It was easy for him to imagine the camp as already reeling under the force of his intention.

He slipped the gun under his shirt and trousers, fixed an arm on it, and then scurried along the wilderness edge of the coffee patch at the far corner of left field, making his way toward a shed that housed a few old tractors and a jumble of worn out farm implements, along with a bunch of half empty buckets of fertilizer, pesticide and herbicide. It was usually unlocked and disregarded, though occasionally a refuge for indulgent practices known to members and advisers alike. Bill could climb atop the structure from the inside, and once above he could enjoy a decent view of the grays' cabins with some of the orchard terrain the grays roamed, and he could even enjoy some cover behind the crest of the roof.

Two grays propped themselves against a shaded side of the shed, on their feet, though somewhat unsteady from the bottle they were engaging. Bill paused near the scene in a good position to size it up, then took his rifle into hand and crept along a wide arc behind obscuring foliage, poking out to glide up to the shed, where he stood for a moment just around the corner from his oblivious prey. Bill listened to some heated talk about how the camp should never have planted cotton, since it had to compete against government-subsidized American cotton. If the temple had much sense it would till the cotton under this very afternoon, and sow in its place a certain other plant that grows like a weed and has a catalog of uses. Bill boldly turned the corner and fired into two chests before any defense could be given. The advisers sprayed red onto the shed and fell to the dirt, dying very quickly, leaving Bill to collect a pistol from one and a full magazine from the rifle of the other.

Bill slipped inside the shed, scrambled up a rusty tractor and monkeyed his way onto some scaffolding, where he kicked through a ventilation screen and squirmed out onto the roof. He spotted a couple of grays at two hundred and fifty yards, already advancing on him with great speed but little subtlety on the plain that rolled between the grays' cabins and the shed. Bill swiftly sent two more chests bleeding into earth. Naturally he could expect the camp to shortly be put under some kind of security lockdown, which still left some chance that these tremors of his would aggravate the camp's fault lines and jar some people into adding their part to what might become a transfiguring quake.

A few grays were running from cabin to cabin, banging on doors and windows and shouting the news. One gray in particular spent too much time rapping on a window and railing at someone inside. Bill shot, and in one terrific instant the barking gray collapsed with a blast of red as the glass shattered and the gray in the cabin staggered wounded and fell out the window. Bill scanned the forested barrier of the orchards on his left for the emergence of any grays there, and shots from the cabins were soon singing around the shed as the grays got wise to Bill's position, the occasional shot biting into the shed and devouring clear through its flimsy metal flesh and lanky wooden bones.

This time of day is usually very heavy for Davy, very hard to keep pulling the weight through the gluey thickness pressing him on all sides. They have him out hoeing in cotton patch two, even though there's hardly any weeds, and he could much better be doing some tilling, or chopping down old plants with a machete. But no, they still think he's a child, and he has to wander through the cotton with a hoe and look like he's doing something valuable. Of course they see it's obviously not valuable, and of course this is Davy's fault—come on kid, haven't you struck oil or gold yet with that hoe? Damn this waste. I'm being wasted.

Something like a wave hits Davy, rippling through him like the darkest coffee, lifting forty or fifty pounds right off him, taking the pressure right off his heart and feet. He tastes something salty and sweet, something very much like blood. It feels like it's not allowed. They can't allow this feeling that Davy *must* allow. The law will now be written by his heart. What will now be allowed is Davy. He wonders why he didn't do better in that boxing match, when vomit had risen like lava in the same way that this thrill is rising in him now, forcing his focus up from the dirt. He stands tall, wipes the sweat from his face, leans back and stretches, casually looks about and takes the measure of his surroundings. He notices the bright birds sailing wherever they want in the giant trees that are there for them.

Crackling noises are coming in from the distance. Davy's neighbors are looking around and saying all sorts of "yep" and "uh huh" and "das' right" everywhere. The tans are drifting toward each other while advising members, "You actin' a real fool," and, "Bad time to test me." It takes only seconds for the tans to get to higher ground along one side of the field, their guns cocked and pointed at the fool-actin' members. Davy realizes what the crackling over by the coffee is. It's gotta' be more than drunken grays trying to shoot monkeys stealing bananas. The members are grinning and dancing, the tans are yapping at each other in some kind of code talk, the jungle birds are putting up a good squawk— and suddenly there's *really loud* shooting.

An old black guy is hunched over on the ground, and he's splattered with blood. He starts hollering, but not much like he's hurt, more like he's angry. "Oh no, sheeet no, come on!" he says, poking at the hole in his side. He lies down in the dirt with bright blood flashing on his black skin and white shirt. A tan nearby has his rifle fixed on the sorry little scene, and he keeps looking around at the six tans who've begun circling cotton patch two like sheep dogs. One steps into the trees to talk to the voices erupting from his radio. Davy joins the members as they gather to help the bleeding man. The nearby tan says it's probably not a deadly wound, and the old man had it coming a good while anyway for making the evil eye every chance he got, and just a moment ago he was pointing his machete where he ought not. "There's plenty more left in Old Bessy!" says the tan, and he fires a shot that buzzes just above everybody's head. This makes Davy's heart really start to pump. It also makes the tan with the radio jump out from the forest and yell, "No more shooting, damn it! All this shooting is just an accident! Everyone calm down, okay?! Son of a bitch!"

The wounded guy is shouting out powerful curses between his moans. "I send back de' evil you put in me, I send it back double!" he says to the tan who shot him, and he aims a long bloody finger. Then the man curses all the advisers for being such cowards, siding with Brother K so they could fight with all the advantages. He curses Brother K for "luring us out here jus' so we build a big house for him." He asks God, "Why you don' seem to care your children eating each other?" He curses the members for being weak, for making guys like Brother K possible. Then he grabs his machete and tries to get to his feet and charge at the tan, but he's only able to stumble a few steps and fall into some cotton plants, snapping and crunching them. Propping himself up onto one arm, he flings the machete at the tan. The gleaming blade soars elegantly through a long bow, and plows up the soil just beside the tan's boots. It is a breathless, excellent moment. More gunshots come calling out from the coffee.

Well, this guy has left nothing more to be said, and only one thing to be done.

The members have a good look at each other and take a hard look at the advisers and their guns.

Davy's hoe seems fresh to him in the new light of this strange afternoon. Here's this sort of snake that's been hiding in the weeds here, a wood body and a metal head that curves to a poisonous point. The snake suddenly comes to life in Davy's hand. He feels a pulse beating through its body, and its head begins to rise. He must be channeling to the snake some of the river of life-force that Davy is sponging up, soaking in, dripping full of, flowing with, gushing. He is the center point of all life. He has the only life of his. What lies about all around him is still and silent as clay—a lifeless, powerless lump ready for sculpting. He runs straight at the nearest adviser.

Blood paints the scene, as expected. Davy is aware of pangs racing through his shoulder, which changes nothing. He cannot be stopped from sinking the pointed metal into the target neck. The world is warm wax to the cold iron stamp of his vision. His spirit wills, his flesh carries out, and the world receives. There is no argument at any stage along the way, just a total unity. The tan drops with hot, red wax spurting out from the deep gash, and he wiggles a bit under some finishing gouges from Davy's snake-wand. All the while, a giant wave is building up behind Davy … surging up beside him … and Davy witnesses all the wrecking of its crash into a wall of bullets. Oh … oh glory … what a testament! Every member doing whatever they can with whatever they have! No wall can stand it! The old, bleeding, black guy is crawling into the fight and cheering the smashes and slashes coming down on the advisers. It all goes by like a cartoon Davy used to watch on TV, where clay figures move around at a weird speed that's outside of real time, and the set is made of plastic and looks like the landscape of the Moon or Mars.

Davy leaps about for more action, but the work here is already done. The tans who ruled cotton patch two are lying deformed and motionless … beside maybe five times as many dead or wounded members. These bloodied and crippled members aren't asking for help—they're commanding the rest of us to take the fight to the rest of the camp right away. Quit arguing over the rifles and the machetes and the handgun, they say, and let the rifles go to members who were in the military, and the machetes go to the fittest, and let a teenage member who has the handgun keep it only if he'll save the shots for close range. They order us to move against cotton patch one, which is the smallest of the patches, and the nearest to the coffee. They say the orchards should then fall easy to us, what with the grays busy with all that shooting over there. The last cotton patch can then be easily dealt with. Nobody has to say what the ultimate move will be, because there it towers in the distance, a three-layer cake.

Some members are staying to care for the wounded, and Davy moves out from cotton patch two with more than a hundred in his band of hunters. The temple is as good as conquered. Davy is already running naked through halls of gold and purple, with parts and pieces of advisers and watchers put up everywhere like Halloween decorations, headless bodies sitting comfortably on the finest furniture. Davy sees it, he wills it, and it must be so. The magic of this place is no longer a mystery to him.

Davy and his gang make their approach through the rim of the forest. The one hundred and thirty or so members on cotton patch one are kneeling all together in one bunch at the center of the field. Their tools are all in a pile off to the side. Seven tans with guns drawn are spread out, pacing back and forth, turning this way and that, rattling off code words and numbers at each other.

It seems too difficult and slow for Davy's gunners to take good shots on moving targets from a position in the forest. What we all agree on is to spread out and just swarm the tans like a mass of hornets, with our gunners getting off some good shots before hackers like Davy get close to the enemy. Hackers must keep an eye open to pick up what a fallen gunner drops. We note that our targets carry extra clips of ammo. We get our weapons ready. Every step toward those tans will just happen. Every step is a step closer to the temple.

As soon as that horde of bloodthirsty wretches sprang out from the shade of the trees, the tans knew it, and sprang to meet the onslaught, delivering very respectable fire before going down every one.

Skirmishing was meanwhile afoot in the coffee orchards, with grays running to and fro along neatly trimmed rows of bushy trees, firing at the ragged blurs streaking past with pruning-hook spears and plowshare swords.

Opportunities were presenting themselves all through the camp for members to settle old scores, to lance temple informants like abscesses in front of choruses crying out in satisfaction.

A near platoon of casualties lay strewn across the grounds Bill commanded from his perch. He spent his last rifle cartridge, and therefore got moving to make some use of the pistol. He scanned his perimeter, slithered back through the vent, dropped onto a tractor, then onto the dirt. Crouching, he gently pressed the door open a bit and peeped out onto the grassy clearing. Then he darted for the shelter of vines drooping from branches that beckoned him to come hither. Voices entered the scene, the all-too-familiar blend of bossing and cussing, pushing Bill back a few steps into heavier shadows, where he sat poised on the knuckle of a surging root.

Three grays hustled around and through the shed like hummingbirds, crashing through stacks of buckets and tools, only crudely acknowledging the two corpses of their drunken comrades, all while hurling blame and feverish obscenity in every direction. The temple was run by a fraternity of unabashed pedophiles, who had the camp surveillance cameras monitoring not the camp's trouble spots and troublemakers, but the next crop of young teens to be harvested for temple pleasures. The cotton and coffee was worked by not quite people, who'd been very soundly rejected out in the world. "Brother Dumbass gathered up every kind a' mental defective, every held back product a' incest he could find out there, jus' herded 'em all together into this here."

If the three grays hunted snipers even half as well as they sassed, Bill was in trouble. But the poor fellows began arguing about whether to fly off into the coffee orchards and release their frustrations upon easier prey, or to attack the temple in hopes of finally getting a good look inside and maybe victimizing some very deserving people there. The three grays appeared to have opted for counter-insurgency in the coffee when Bill lunged out from his curtain and had one of them assassinated.

Bill raced into the jungle with bullet on bullet whining after him, two grays chasing with the fire of mad bulls, not at all deterred by a startling slaying that would have sent others scrambling for safety. Seconds later, Bill was squatting behind a leafy veil, in full possession of, or fully possessed by, abilities bordering on feline. His adversaries blew right past him. A little farther into the woods the grays halted. Panting heavily they pivoted about and scanned a shadowy forest crawling with covert life.

Sweat steaming on smoldering faces, the two turned back for the camp. Passing their prey again, the grays each received a pair of bullets before meeting the forest floor in stillness.

Bill bounded off toward the coffee trees with a fresh supply of firepower, the whole camp a harmony of delirious upheaval.

Chapter 29
Regime Change

This was a land without natural seasons, always warm and more or less rainy. Other seasons, however, did make their presence known in Camp Earth, and they shifted harshly. The passing of a glorious summer of wine and song felt like a plunge into bracing and sobering winter, softened somewhat by the residue that lingers upon one's abrupt awakening from a sweet dream. Even Brother K had felt the cold and sorrow of the recent year and had asked why the dream hadn't been allowed to stay longer. He had actually shed real tears over it with the congregation. But the watchers had their own grand purposes for this camp, and the good of the camp was to come not from understanding the purposes but participating in them.

So of course this last year had not been the camp's best—though the congregation had actually taken it fairly well. What had sustained them was a widespread belief that another enchanted summer had to be coming closer. Perhaps it was just around the corner. Perhaps Joshua would accompany it. Time had thus trudged onward not unlike the gloomy hours of a Monday following an extremely pleasant weekend.

Brother K recovered by busying himself toward the capture of a certain bee that had long been buzzing under his skull. He wanted to stage "something approaching an opera," in which a watcher not known to the congregation would be equipped with false beard, wig, white robe, and wine-red vest to present himself as Joshua appearing in camp at long last. Brother K composed and recorded a score of music, basically an ascending series of power chords on electric guitar, with streams of glittering sixteenth notes culminating in resounding splashes of cymbal. He drew up a storyboard choreographing the Lord's every location and word and gesture. Joshua would make his entrance at the edge of the jungle, visible from the tables, with the camp in evening study. The humble man would walk among the membership, lay his hands on them in implied healing, and teach them some new parables, such as, the kingdom of God is like unto the coin that the traveler finds on the beaten path. Joshua would personally encounter the coffee beans and cotton fibers, nodding and smiling in approval of this business that was proper for his disciples. Then he would come up to his temple, the gates and doors would open for him, and he'd walk inside, music at its triumphant zenith. Several minutes later, after deep conference with Brother K, Joshua would relieve the suspense by leading his high priest onto the stage in heavenly tones of blue and gold and white, there solemnly declaring Brother K worthy of his special calling.

To close the production, the Lord would depart into the forest, promising to wrap up his ministry in the wicked world and speedily return with a bountiful harvest of faith-fired new members. Presumably he would have to dissuade a number of unhappy campers, as well as several super-disciples, from following him straight into the jungle.

Well, that's … quite an interesting idea … quite a daring one in fact, the watchers told Brother K, their tone even more inscrutable than usual. But would the members really settle for it, really swallow what amounted to a tease, a cheap knock-off of the truly outstanding event so very long in expectation? There were also concerns that the new parables had Joshua sounding more like Confucius than Christ, and that the congregation might react rather negatively should the false beard be pulled away by an unruly child if the adhesive gave out in the humid heat.

A wounded Brother K retorted that more Confucius and less Christ would be to the advantage of temple authority. And the man playing Joshua could grow only a flimsy and un-Semitic beard and so had to employ a false one. "A bomb that levels an entire city … a man on the moon … but you shudder at the logistics of a fake beard," observed Brother K. After a few chuckles from the watchers, they took him to task for a thoughtless omission in his shortlist of technological wonders, and they mentioned a few other omissions that came as breaking news to him. Put in his place, Brother K lamely maintained that the members would benefit from a ritual enactment of their faith. Why didn't the watchers put forth some ideas of their own about what to do with the opportunity they enjoyed here of having a captive audience of a thousand?

Brother K's partners calmly responded that they did in fact realize what enormous opportunities this camp presented for persons of imagination. They'd certainly give his plan due consideration, they said, but whenever he pressed them to approve it they had too much on their hands just then, bandits or bureaucrats halting a shipment of supplies, etc., and they'd send him away with a memo regarding what he should say over the loudspeakers. It annoyed Brother K that these men lacked his vision and lacked an appreciation of his importance to the organization here. He put aside the Joshua play and comforted himself with the cornucopia of temple pleasures.

Sometimes in the dark hours of night, with the camp in blessed slumber and a pacified concubine breathing softly at his side, Brother K would stare with his mind's eye until clouds swirled and lava pits simmered before his inner sight.

There he saw snakes devouring their own tails. There he saw an endless line of children slogging forward to fall off the edge of a cliff.

He might see a wild boy, sinewy and slippery and black as a panther, sprinting and piercing through barricades of sacred, foolish majesty. Brother K hadn't counted on such craze for life in that crowd, such need for prime experience, such zeal for revelation at any cost.

For some time the friendless African child refused to utter a word to his inquisitors, and enhanced methods had to be called upon to sap his mysteriously fervent militancy. Inevitably he did open up and explain that he'd taken matters into his own hands because it would have been more painful not to. He had always suspected that the temple wasn't worth all the work and all the talk of all the years, and now that he knew it for a fact, he felt okay about leaving this relentlessly hard and empty camp, even dying. All present stood back amused and amazed at this living Joshua leapt straight from their book to face them in fitting form.

Look, Len, the temple isn't finished yet, and life in Camp Earth offers plenty, they reminded the boy. Had he forgotten the starving and the sickness and the burning villages? Shouldn't he be glad to get his daily bread, and not be so eager to bury his face in the cake? How did he become so spoiled and demanding? The time would come for all to eat cake, if only the Lens of the camp could be kept from interrupting the steady march of progress.

The only member to have violated the sanctity of Brother K's home was the only member to have earned his deep sympathy and respect. Brother K hoped Len was out there continuing to be his own Joshua.

As for the other members, well, Brother K felt toward them roughly the same as he felt toward any of the factors required to keep this great enterprise of his afloat. Naturally he was concerned for the health and maintenance of his humans, no less than he was for the soundness of his coffee trees and cotton plants.

And if guilt or fear ever met Brother K in the far and out of the way corners of his conscience, if the bleak face of a member ever caught his eye during a show and asked of him, "How can you do this to us? How can you not expect the gods to avenge us?" Then Brother K could always find refuge in the answer given by the Athenians, that imperialist democracy, to those who had asked the question of them. Brother K and the watchers could look down from their palace and answer, "May we not as fairly as yourselves expect favor of the gods? Shall we fear punishment from them for acting in accord with a necessary law of our nature? Men rule wherever they can. Did we make this law? Were we the first to act upon it? We found it to exist long before us, and shall leave it to exist forever after us. All we do is make use of it, knowing that you and everybody else—having the same power as we have—would do the same."

And if Brother K did nevertheless fear the end he knew the Athenians met along with dozens of other empires far grander than a little patch of African jungle, then Brother K could yet simply tell himself that Camp Earth was different, and it would not perish as dictated by the books. The book on *his* empire hadn't been written. He needn't worry about ever having to answer for himself. The little goblins of guilt and fear had a way of receding into the woodwork when Brother K grasped the sweet young flesh of his pleasant companions in his impressive living space.

The watchers had been busy for many hours when Brother K arose with difficulty one particular afternoon. He felt the sickness and confusion of a hangover as he rolled to the side of his bed and attempted to stand up without success. So he merely sat on the edge of the bed, pressed his fingers to his brow and tried to dispel the grogginess that swam through him. The radio console was alive with chatter that Brother K couldn't quite process. Through blurry eyes he saw watchers wheeling boxes to the elevator. He got to his feet, asked what was going on, and promptly reeled back into a chest of drawers.

When he awoke again it was to shattering glass. The shrill noise broke into his spinning head and stayed there mixing with far off voices. He struggled to pull his inert, naked body up from his green carpet, but could only lie on his side as field implements flew in through the broad open space of his devastated window, bringing along ropes which drew the picking hooks and hoes back up the wall until they caught on the window frame. The shouting from outside grew livelier as Brother K saw shards of glass being chipped away … then hands achieving a grip beside the hooks and hoes … then wild-eyed savages thrusting themselves over, landing muddy and bloody on the lush carpet of his sanctuary.

Brother K wasn't fully sensible of his predicament as his ankles became tightly bound, his wrists were tied behind him and a leash was secured to his neck. He began his reception of what would be a long train of members, each having a choice comment for Brother K, often punctuated by a heavy slap. After several such vibrant bashes in the face, and the convulsively good vomiting that followed, Brother K's wits and muscles underwent a blessed process of resurrection, and he soon found himself very able to scold his captors for "trusting the arm of flesh" in forcing their way "unlawfully" into the holy temple and laying hands on their priest. The members answered this with roaring laughter and shaking heads and a round of blows that sent Brother K vomiting onto his carpet again, at which point he caught another splendid wind and reaffirmed his position as their "consecrated guide," cautioning them that "whatsoever ye do unto me, ye do also unto the Lord."

In refusing to recognize the realities of his new situation and by clinging to obsolete supports for himself, Brother K seemed to be preserving some of the strength attached to his former status, and this aggravated the members now towering over him. So while others kept pouring in through the window three by the minute to help themselves to a grand tour of Brother K's home, the ones near him rubbed his face into what he'd thrown up onto the carpet and pressed him to admit his true identity of fraud and con artist. He confessed only that he was a prophet, a "Moses unto you, ye thankless children I led out from the bondage of Egypt," and he declared he would no longer restrain the Lord from taking vengeance upon them, unless they released him at once. All this became really too much for some, who jumped forward to reduce their captive to jelly then and there, but these were blocked by the one holding the leash, who asserted that the fate of Brother K rested in the hands of the surviving membership as a whole.

Music now thundered from the entertainment console, the opening strains of the Macabre Dance, Old Scratch striking up his fiddle to initiate the revelry that he and his ilk were by rights now due, demons enjoying payment in full until the crow of the cock.

As Brother K looked on, girls were ferreted out from various rooms, painted canvases were torn and trampled, computers and notebooks were searched, books, magazines, CDs, and tapes were rifled through, drawers and cabinets were overturned and their contents were scoured by dozens of grubby hands and feet. Grinning members strutted past Brother K with his fine robes draping their scarred and slimy bodies. They hurled billiard balls into his busts of Alexander and Newton and Bach, and even dashed his sculptures *Lion Jesus* and *Lamb Jesus*.

Members fired up the big-screen television and skimmed through footage Brother K himself had filmed over the years. The viewers ignored the sequence of landscapes shot from atop the temple—footage Brother K was rather proud of, since the shots caught the camp under slightly differing conditions of light and atmosphere, so that the sequence made the camp appear to reside on some restless and fitfully forming planet or plane. The critics did offer praise for a series of short films in which Brother K documented his sexual relations with his concubines, each girl choosing her own music, lighting, costume, cinematography, and carnal technique.

In the midst of a barrage of harsh sensations, Brother K puzzled over this situation that somehow failed to strike him as the inevitable outcome of all that had gone before.

Long ago he asked the watchers what backup plans existed in case the camp ever got out of hand, and they informed him of fallback positions they had lurking in the mountains, places to which temple inhabitants could retreat from an overtaken camp, places where other operations had in fact been ongoing for some time.

Such an assurance had been good enough for Brother K. Besides, his excellence in his craft, combined with the technical sorcery of his stage crew, should prevent such ultimate measures from ever becoming necessary.

So this afternoon then, when the camp was actually being overrun, why wasn't Brother K simply roused to pack a suitcase for a stay in the mountains? Apparently, Brother K's partners judged him unfit to be included among the valuables spirited out the back door. They stabbed him right in the ass. Yes, they'd made good use of him, and then, probably regarding him as a loose cannon, they left him to the mercy of this mob.

Maybe Brother K had at times overstepped his boundaries when dealing with the watchers, forgetting his place in the partnership.

He remembered the night he gave Mr. Kidd and Mr. Wint a piece of his mind after coming in from a performance and finding them fooling around with the concubines.

Why did those two have to irk him so? They were constantly taking food and drugs and other items Brother K considered his property. They never showed the slightest respect for what Brother K contributed to the camp. They treated him like he was just part of the help, some hired hand who'd never paid his dues, didn't know the secrets, didn't belong in the brotherhood—as if Brother K wasn't the centerpiece of this whole operation, the very keystone in the camp arch!

Moreover, Brother K had found it nigh impossible to gain any idea of what these two were ever supposed to be doing in camp at all. The Institute people's duties here were regular and mostly evident to him. And the people from the various other agencies, whose duties here were less regular and only somewhat evident to him, could at least be seen on occasion attending to some component of the camp operation. But Kidd and Wint (if those were their real names) spent most of their time back in the mountains, and when they did appear in camp it was only to swagger through the temple, conferring in guarded mumbles with eminent watchers they might encounter—no doubt business of the highest importance, which nonetheless claimed but a fraction of their visit, the remainder being devoted to corrupting Brother K's chambers, amusing themselves with whatever belongings of his that struck their fancy. His art projects constituted exciting towers of blocks for the inner child of these men to kick to the ground with adult sophistication, dismissing Brother K's work as "derivative," indicting it as "plagiarism, and poor at that," and generally groaning and snickering at the many ways Brother K was simply reproducing the work of real artists who his followers were too ignorant to know of.

The night that Brother K caught them contaminating his girls, he instructed the two that since they clearly had nothing worthwhile to do here in camp, it was best they find some cozy spot out in the jungle where they could "go bugger each other out of the way of useful people," and they were welcome to take along some paint and canvas and see if they could produce something that Brother K wouldn't be able to criticize as derivative of Bacon or Mapplethorpe. The two silly twits didn't belong in the temple, which was being built for a grand deity, not "the god of farts and giggles and foreign stains on my bed." If the two couldn't take a hint, Brother K would apply his clout to have them reassigned elsewhere, or even force them from the premises with the strength of his own person.

And to this eruption the two responded merely with odd smirks. They shifted their hollow, hungry eyes from the girls to Brother K, and from him to each other, and then to the whole of his giant room. They finally moved toward the staircase, but before descending it they turned to Brother K.

"What lovely girls, and what a lovely temple, Mr. Kidd," said one.

"Indeed, not bad, not a bad life at all, Mr. Wint," said the other.

"The Lord giveth, Mr. Kidd."

"And he taketh away, Mr. Wint."

The two then waved to the girls and disappeared. Were they what rendered Brother K now vomit-smeared and hogtied? Fate's the harder to stomach, the more trivial its instruments.

All tiers of the temple were bustling with human traffic now that the great doors had opened following the members' discovery of the control panel. Brother K continued to sit stiff on the edge of his bed as anyone so inclined drew near to confront him with looks, words, and smacks, and he continued to shut out shame and terror, clenching to the role of Brother K, exhorting the members to repent of their abomination. The master of his leash managed the flow of class-action plaintiffs, allowing each a satisfactory comment and strike before sending the member off to pillage and consider a fitting end for the tethered vulture.

Brother K hurt in many ways and places, but he didn't feel overpowered by it. A difficult death was beginning to stare him in the face, and he felt vigor in refusing to recognize that stare as long as he could. Time dissolved. He was standing firmly in the bedrock condition of existence, war against the world. A pair of members hoisted him up between them with a cue stick and hauled him down to the stage for judgment.

Now outdoors, Brother K was dropped roughly, and as he struggled to right himself it was truly a sight that met him. Evening approached a camp that blazed with a sinister radiance. Flames devoured the ginning house and the bean barn and several of the advisers' cabins, the smoke of it wafting into a great glowing canopy that lit up the aftermath of a costly battle. Many members were yet chasing through forest and field with gun and machete, yelping to fellow hunters, while here and there members gathered to drive a captive adviser forward with sharp jabs.

The majority of the concubines had not required much coaxing from the intruders to abandon their temple posts. These young ladies were now led before a kneeling, pathetic Brother K, and upon him they unloaded kicks of tremendous force, and upon him they released condemnations of finely honed edge. They then descended the stairs at the side of the stage, slipping away through mangled fence to tearfully reunite with loved ones after long separation.

An audience began forming around the stage, and Brother K felt a need to look for Sarah.

There she stood for him in the front row, his lovely princess, his beloved queen, the precious material he had refined and polished to a sort of brilliance. There in her purple pajamas she gazed up at him in his naked helplessness. Whatever happened, Brother K retained this one ally who thought the world of him, and he just might be able to perform well enough tonight if he kept her in mind.

The temple lights now flared to life, flooding the stage with all hues of the spectrum. The members at the control panel proceeded to showcase a variety of color schemes for the audience, who cheered for the ones they liked. After much trial and error it was orange that lit center stage with red at the sides and purple upon the temple itself.

Members hefted boxes full of food and wine out of the temple to parade and distribute among the gathered. Others did likewise with armloads of goodies plundered from the cabins. Others rounded up copies of the book, every copy they could locate, and a great pile was committed to flames in full view of Brother K. Wandering pigs and chickens were soon skewered and roasting for supper, and a member shouted up at Brother K that humans are supposed to taste like pig. "Not surprising," came the response.

The loudspeakers crackled under the control of a series of delighted members who took turns blasting their enhanced voices over the riot:

"Holy holy holy … comin' to ya' live from the holy temple now … come on up to the temple, where we do not hunger, where we do not thirst, where we do not burn in a fire of discontent, where it is given us to know, and to be filled. Praise! Thank you."

"Here's a little number you might have heard, brothers and sisters: six hundred sixty and six. It is the number of a man, and we got 'im right here on stage for ya'. For the Beast had given him power to oppress the saints … but now we see him aaah-baaannn-donnned."

"We gunna' get loose here tonight, we gotta' get looooooooosssssssse … We got the power now, okay?

We've taken the pow-wah and we gotta' get looooossse heeeaaah toniiiiiight-ah."

"Gather to the temple … get yer' heads together campers … wrangle up what's left a' them evil ones and drag 'em on up here. Don't need another swig, don't need another puff, we got us the temple, that's plenty enough."

"For I the Lord shall come near to you in judgment. And I will be a swift witness against the sorcerers, and the adulterers, and the liars, and against those that oppress the hireling in his wages, oppressing without fear of the Lord. Ye have said it is vain to serve God, for the proud are called happy, and they that work wickedness are established, and they that tempt God are secure. But behold, the day cometh that shall burn as an oven, and all the proud and wicked shall be stubble."

Then there was music upon the camp, a selection from Brother K's vast collection of classic rock.

The music hums through Davy's bones as he lugs a box of medical supplies toward the wounded of the cotton fields. Members are bobbing their heads and swinging their arms and yelling out with the music, just like the Brother K lovers used to do when he played on stage. Davy tries to figure out the words, something about parties in the streets where shotguns sing songs and idols are thrown down.

"I tip my hat to the new constitution, take a bow for the new revolution," Davy hears. "And I get on my knees and pray … we don't get fooled again."

Something touches his blood-caked shoulder, and Davy sees his old friend's leathery hand. Yesterday Davy would have jumped like a little dog to this hand.

"Looks like they gotcha' some there, son, might need a bandage on it," said Bill, keeping pace with the lad.

"It doesn't hurt much, it really doesn't," says Davy. "It was just so easy to go right at 'em. I didn't care."

Bill began sifting through the supplies to make a dressing for the youngster's wound. "I was told you were outstanding, you led men twice your size."

"I did, yes, I did it. I did what I had to and what I wanted to. I felt so much strength. I didn't care about the little things I cared about before. It's like how an eagle must live, or a lion."

"I think I feel the same way, Davy, that it was about doin' what had to be done, and feelin' right about doin' it," said Bill, dabbing the boy's injury with disinfectant.

"What should we do to Brother K?" asks Davy. "I mean, if you add up all the stuff he's done to us over the years … we should do something that'll really balance the scales."

"I guess one or two things come to mind that might approach the weight a' what's been done to all of us. I know some fellas who'd be real happy to peel his skin off and then roast 'im over some coals. Though maybe this'd just be pilin' more weight onto the evil side a' the scales, ya' know, makin' the scales even more out of balance."

Davy frowns. "All I want is for him to feel how he made me feel. I really want 'im to. The evil he put into me … I'm gunna' put it right back."

"I know the feeling," said Bill, juggling gauze and tape while trying to keep up with the boy's determined stride. "It just seems right to make 'im pay. I need something to heal me too. But it's somewhere else, I think. God's harder to find than vengeance."

Davy shakes his head. "God …" he says, squinting. "I don't know how to find God, but God has to be something like I feel today. And if my God is wrong, I don't wanna' be right. I'd rather be strong, rather be happy. I am David Schmidt, and today God loves me."

Bill gave a nod of sympathy. "I don't blame you, son, or ah, brother. I really can't say I know any more about it than you. I'm sorry it's been so hard to live through, and so damn difficult to understand. I know you're not a kid anymore, and I won't think the less of you, whatever you think about all this." Bill hurried the rest of the way to the cotton patches with Davy and helped him distribute his delivery there.

A solid, heavy voice was soon rumbling across the camp. "Good evening, Camp Earth. Today is deliverance and judgment come unto us. Let's begin our business. But let us be watchful of the forest. Keep our weapons in reach. Fine. Now we'll ask our brother here some questions and see if he'll clear a few things up for us."

The shining black member on stage affixed his microphone to the hem of his glinting silver robe, and he turned to Brother K's leash-master, who now hurled up his rope to a member standing on the edge of the roof of the first tier. This man fed the rope through a pulley he'd lashed to the end of a ladder—a gallows arm that was soon jutting out several feet horizontally on the roof of the first tier, secured by the weight of several members seated upon it. The leash-master drew the rope through the squeaking pulley, wound it a few times around his wrist, and stepped back until it was taut. A kneeling Brother K closed his eyes and a girl wailed "No! Why?!" as the hangman drew rope and pulled Brother K up to a standing position, where he was left to wobble for a few charged seconds until another steady pull on the rope had him ascending two feet into the air, dangling without breath amidst calls of "Hang, Judas!" and "We gave you everything!" and "Where's Joshua when you need 'im?!"

Less than a minute had passed when Brother K's twisting feet were returned to the stage, dousing his silent inferno. He was allowed to fall to his knees, and there he gasped freely and pounded his head onto the planks he'd long known from a somewhat different perspective. Soon enough he was pulled back up to his feet, and again a girl with a good view of the proceedings cried out for it to please stop.

"Okay then, brother. Please tell us what it's all been about here," queried the voice over the camp.

A hoarse Brother K spoke into the microphone now held before him. "They wouldn't say … huhgaakha … when I asked, they wouldn't tell me … it wasn't my business … but I do know … ohhgghuh … I know they got places back in the mountains, and uh, soldiers with 'em. They might be comin' any minute."

The member in the silver, flame-gilded robe now returned the microphone to his collar and held out his arms before the crowd. "Satisfied?" he asked.

The resoundingly negative reply had Brother K hoisted up again to dangle and squirm, this time for more than a minute, a very broad and thick minute in which Brother K's bowels evacuated onto the stage with some force, provoking the spirited laughter of a few of the advisers kneeling bound in red light. The members keeping watch over these irreverent captives advised them that they were free to laugh it up all they wanted, but should bear in mind that they were up next, and probably wouldn't do as well as Brother K, and should definitely be amazed to hear any crying on their behalf.

Brother K was dropped into his vile excretion, and prostrate there he hacked, heaved, and moaned. Meanwhile the cries of his young lover grew more frantic, and her former co-workers converged on her.

They had matured into young women, steeled by cold lessons hammered into them on the daily battlefield that had been their life. It was high time for Sarah to learn, to be made to see what she'd never been willing to see in all these years of her blissful immaturity. They had to take hold of her and take her aside, away from the disgusting child-man, and she had to be slapped to get her attention, slapped to attention the way reality had been slapping all the girls but her. "Now you have to face the truth, princess, you have to see past the fairy tale you've been living in. Brother has only been *using* us! Do you understand what it means to be used? It means Brother has never really cared about us, he's only ever cared about the pleasures we give him. That's not love, that's just taking what he wants from people because he has the power. You can't imagine what goes on in people like Brother, what really drives them, unless you can allow some dirty facts of life into your squeaky-clean paradise. Don't you know how many girls he's gotten tired of and thrown to the tans and grays, so they get passed around like a bottle of whiskey, so they get gambled away from one guy to the next like cigarettes?! And no, he didn't do it for their own good or for the good of the temple, he did it because he had no use for them after all the nasty things he'd got them to do for him. He just got bored with 'em and gave 'em to his friends to play with, because he could. He's not some great man. He's not even a man. He's a little boy with no rules. You know who he is, Sarah? He's that monster in the Twilight Zone, that little boy who has the whole town terrified of what he's gunna' do next, and everyone secretly wants to kill him for the hell he's created."

Sarah stared at the dirt, red-cheeked and teary-eyed, and claimed none of this made sense to her, no, not at all—but completely obvious to her was that "Brother provides so much for us" and "his ways will always bless us if we let them." It just made you really wanna' beat this garbage out of her, the simple stupid loyalty of this puppy. She did have to be slapped again, hard enough to knock her wiring back into proper place, to reboot her programming to where it could make some very basic and necessary computations.

"No more tears now, okay Sarah, no more walls, just take this in. Brother has taught you what to think and feel. Just let Sarah's brain take that in and work on it. We know what you're thinking and feeling, because we've all been through it, and we've all come out of it into the truth. The truth is plain as day, if you would just take a step into it. What you've been thinking and feeling is nothing but Brother's thinking and feeling in you. You are ready for the key, Sarah, the key that will open the door for you. Here is the key. Brother teaches only thoughts and feelings that give him power, power to use us, power to use the camp. *This* is the Evil Mind-Control. He's pumped you full of it. Is there anything in you that's free of him, that doesn't serve him in some way? Does this even register as a problem to you, or are you perfectly content to be the perfect slave?"

For a flash of a second, Sarah looked like she might actually be thinking it all through.

But quickly and fiercely she tore herself away, yelling with pouring tears that she always knew a time would come when she would be tested to see if she would stand beside Brother. The poor little princess was leashed as tightly as her poor little prince up there.

The noose was pulled taut on the filthy man in the lava glow, pulling him up so he stood before his interrogator. "Can we get a decent answer from ya' this time?" asked the master of ceremonies through booming speakers.

"They ... uh ... jus' usin' me too," said Brother K into the microphone held out to him. "Ah ... I tried to help you— haahgghah ... hooahgghhah ... I couldn't ... they had plans I couldn't change. This was never supposed to work the way you ... the way you an' I wanted it to. Mmmmhah ... they didn't tell me much, but ah, I'll tell ya' what I know."

The robed member turned to the audience. "Well, that really is good news, brother, I hope you *are* finally going to tell. So level with us then. Why *did* you gather us up and bring us out here? And mind you, answer well. We don't wanna' hear any more about Joshua or Evil Mind-Control. We'd simply like to know what you and your friends hoped to accomplish here. And I really do hope it's about more than just the bricks of cash y'all must've stacked through the years. Tell."

Brother K nodded conspicuously. "Yes, money, right. That's part of it. I think they got accounts … haahgghah … ohh. But I believe there's something else. Huhggrrmm. Because there were scientists, ah, engineers, all kinds a' doctors a' this an' that, soldiers too, officers … all comin' in an' outta' here. They seemed to care most about XXX XXXXXXX, which I think has gotta' be some kind a' XXXXXXXXXXX. I think they were XXXXXX XX and watching XXXX XXXXXXXX. I don' know who they all belonged to, but I'm sure most of 'em had to be XX XXXXXXXX and XXX."

Hundreds of gasps broke forth from the assembly, with many shouts of disbelief, of outrage, of agony, and a few of immensely joyous vindication.

"I think the camp is a model," continued Brother K. "I think they made a model of the type of world they expect to deal with. I think they wanted to work with a model, ahh, before dealing with the real thing out there."

"Okay," said the interrogator, bringing his gaze back down onto Brother K and then the congregation. "This was a laboratory experiment. Damn. Damn it all, brothers and sisters, I've gotta' say … after all the crazy talk we've heard in this place over the years, what our brother just told us doesn't sound too crazy to me. Damn."

"Yes. I'm sorry," said Brother K. "I'm sorry. I know how strange and wrong it must seem, in view of … what we've believed together here."

"Sure, brother, it does seem strange and wrong, you delivering us straight into the mouth of the very beast we were trying to escape," said the robed man, his tone increasingly menacing. "What irony … wow!"

The robed man paced some as he returned the microphone to his collar, then he stopped in his tracks and began clapping his hands together slowly. "How clever," he announced. "The systematic destruction of an ideal, by way of this camp that supposedly stands for the ideal. Thank you, brother, for playing such an important part in this whole show, for helping to teach us all such a worthless lesson."

The congregation had fallen silent. Brother K appeared willing to say more, but his interrogator would no longer provide him a microphone.

"Now you know what I know, what I've had to try and figure out all through our years together!" offered Brother K to his audience as forcefully as he could without something to aid his crippled voice. "Now I hide nothing! I am the lowest among you!"

The robed member grinned wide and again clapped his loud mocking applause. "Oh, that's fine, brother. Our years together! I remember it more like we members had our years out here with the mosquitoes while you had yours in there with the steak and lobsters, hiding behind the Lord like he was just your own personal bodyguard. Well, I have a hunch you'll be seeing the real Lord soon enough, and you'll have to look him in the face and tell him how you used him for a bag of silver. Your heart will be weighed before him, weighed against the feather of truth, and your heart will be heavy with your silver and your lies, and you will be given to the crocodiles. So, just to make it easier for you, just to lessen the Lord's wrath a little, we'll put you through some hell before we send you off to meet him."

The legion of Brother K's scorned lovers roared their overwhelming approval of the suggestion, and the naked king began to pray. He prayed the only prayers he knew. He called for something deep inside to come out and help him. He called for the strength of that black boy. He called for the spirit of the dog he'd buried nearby in better times. He thought of Sarah. He felt a power flowing in him, pushing back against panic and the nearing walls of his tomb.

Chapter 30
The End

The master of ceremonies gave his opinion of how the proceedings should be carried out. Brother K could be taken down to the front row and placed in a proper chair for an excellent view of the stage. Each surviving adviser could be marched up under the infernal spotlight for a chance to plead his or her case. The members could conceive fitting punishments and administer them, and Brother K could witness it all as he contemplated his own imminent ordeal, which would arrive as the climax of justice. Asked if this suited them, the congregation consented with hoots and hollers in an outpouring so savage it shook the stage planks.

A silent Brother K was carried down to his seat of honor, a plush, high backed, purple suede chair taken from the third tier, and from his throne he saw a procession of thirteen trials, lasting deep into the night. Only one adviser was found worthy of pardon, and this was due to a surviving member recalling that this tan had given him water and a good word as he lay despairing in the box. The remaining dozen were each sentenced to death.

Two of the condemned were female. It was alleged by many in the audience that these two rulers of study groups had engaged hardheartedly in willful blindness toward any facts departing from temple propaganda, blissful dismissal of the hard facts that constituted the very lives of the members, real lives which just didn't matter compared to a fantasy. On stage with the microphone, neither of the ladies issued a denial or a defense for themselves, despite long and successful careers in conjuring up denials and defenses for the temple, tirelessly offering even the most absurd justifications without so much as a smirk. Looking down on a scene probably too disgusting to allow their full apprehension of it, each of the ladies delivered one last scolding, extended variations on the theme: "Look at this mess you devils have made out of what was such a blessing for all of us!" Each of the ladies testified that the book was still true even if Brother K was now removed from his holy calling, and each concluded with a firm declaration that she wouldn't taste the pains of death, no matter what was done to her. Faithful to the end, they were simply stood up against the temple and shot in the forehead.

It was hoped that the hearings of the tans and grays would have them tearfully confessing their many abuses of the congregation, requesting the mercy they'd never shown, perhaps shifting blame onto Brother K, the watchers, other advisers, America, God, or bad upbringing. The tans and grays had already been wounded in battle, had afterward been roughed up for good measure, and had been told to expect the kind of treatment they'd seen Brother K get. Thus it was interesting that they proved as unrepentant as the two ladies. To be given a microphone to command this crowd's attention in what amounted to a personal grand finale put a sparkle into the faces and words of these men. Presented with all the charges befitting a street thug in an organized crime racket, and asked to assess his degree of guilt, it was common for the tan or gray to deny the very concept of guilt and to claim that every person acts according to a set of conditions under which any other person would act the very same. Several admitted that the years they'd spent as advisers were undoubtedly the best of their lives, and they'd do it again without question, their only real remorse being that they hadn't tried to take over the temple themselves. They salted their language with some of the crudest curses imaginable, and generally expressed the free and honest spirit of wild animals, guilty only as much as wolves who kill with God-given fangs. They would each receive a bullet to the head, eventually, after being forced to undergo a variety of tribulations which couldn't fail to make subordinates of even these men. By dawn's approach, the stage was a slimy, sticky, stinking mess of broken human matter.

Brother K's pains had been growing. He needed water very badly. Insects were exploring and biting all over his body, dripping as it was with blood, sweat, and excrement. His head was pounding with ache. He witnessed advisers perish in ways that flashed his mind's eye with old German depictions of the deeds of a fifteenth century Transylvanian prince. But throughout, there remained a floor, a weird and wonderful cushion, below which his spirits did not sink. Of all he was experiencing, it was this that most amazed him.

And then, as though by act of a hostile God, a bolt of lightning surged out of the dawn sky into the temple's grand steeple, sending a rain of sparks upon an assembly that began to look about with unease.

"What the hell was *that* all about?!" asked a member.

"I don't know, but … I don't feel so well," said another.

Suddenly and simply, Brother K found himself no longer adequate to face his colossal reality. He was completely lost, alone, helpless, groundless in the middle of a vast, cold ocean, head barely above water, staring out at massive oncoming waves of black. Seized by terror, he began to tremble and cry.

Members were rubbing their heads, moaning, muttering in bewilderment over the meaning of what had just happened. A few, however, adopted a stout bearing and moved about the congregation to argue against pessimistic interpretations of the lightning. They cheerfully reminded members of the justice of their revolutionary actions, and convincingly demonstrated that sufficient power could still be drawn from the good old well of intentional attitude. This ministering, combined with the spectacle of the former king's psychological disintegration, enabled the crowd to recover a mood to take care of its business.

Concubines were anxious to have damage done to Brother K's genitals, the real god that the girls of this temple had been forced to serve all these years, they testified in detail without embarrassment. Several members put forth their own unique requests, with a line forming at the side of the stage so each had a chance to come up to the microphone and talk down to a destitute Brother K and see if he cringed at their suggestion for him. The turning point in this process came when a member identified Brother K as "a real Anti-Christ, who assumes Christ's image in order to oppose Christ's cause, proclaiming liberation in order to conquer people and become God to them." The man accused Brother K of being a "Christ merchant" who "claimed ownership of Christ" and "sold Christ in the marketplace." The true work of Brother K was "to nail us into place." All this being the case, a fitting punishment for him might well be crucifixion.

The very word cut red hot through the congregation. Many thought the idea superb for its poetic justice and horrific severity. Many others objected, not to any undeserved cruelty, but rather to the undeserved dignity bestowed on Brother K by the obvious connotations of that form of execution. It was argued that Brother K was of all persons the least fit to be associated with the one figure still highly revered by most of the congregation. Far better to associate Brother K with his true parallel, Judas Iscariot: deceiver and betrayer, servant of greed and tyranny. But then it was objected that merely having Brother K hanged and disemboweled as Judas would be insufficiently harsh, and besides, they'd already seen him hanging and gushing out his bowels, and many were now interested in seeing what he looked like nailed onto the temple with his genitals annihilated.

A general shouting match ensued around the naked, thirsty, aching king, who thought about his fate.

Of course. Of course. His whole life has been leading to it. This cross has always stood planted out there for him, pulling him forward by the steel strings of his God-given nature.

To live has only been to seek and savor a little warmth while ever inside the heavy shadow cast back by this … while ever inside a funnel swirling to this abysmal sinkhole long held in store, and now staring him in the face.

Oh God! Oh Lord! Oh Power greater than I!

Oh Power greater than my weakness!

You who descend into hell to blaze the saving path out:

Tammuz, Osiris, Attis, Adonis, Dionysus, Mithras, Jesus.

Oh Lord Jesus! But can *I* call on thee?

Brother K could see temple girls demanding his genitals be removed before anything else was done. The young ladies savored every moment of the carving and cauterizing, every shrill vocalization from this vampire who had used them so casually.

Brother K could see his quaking body transferred onto the stage, where members formed a line and took turns driving rusty iron into him, fastening him in a figure X to the wood beside the temple's gaping mouth. A welding torch was kept busy about his wounds, lest he lose his blood and leave before his rightful time. And in all this, in reducing him to such a state that even the beasts in the surrounding forest were compelled to pause and shift their ears—the members felt the pain of this horrible creature as little as Brother K had felt theirs.

He wondered about the balance between life and its world. He wondered about the providence that gives life the strength to live against all the weight surrounding. He wondered what could be available to the living thing who faces extraordinary weight, who faces trauma well beyond the pressures of the creature's typical environment, trauma of little precedent, perhaps, in the whole history of the species. The blessed bulk of wondering creation need only ever wonder at such things, indeed *can only* wonder at it, comprehending it only through hints and echoes. The riddle's solution is known only to those few chosen for the furthest frontiers of possible experience.

It was a goddess of providence and mercy who came for him, removing his cup from him, the cup of the chosen, the cup overflowing with the utmost weight of the world, dashing it upon the ground before it could be given him. The goddess emerged through the thick, twisting heat and noise to stand beside Brother as he wept in his stained and soaked chair of anticipation. She smiled into his infinitely grateful eyes, and fired a pistol into his fever-swollen head.

The explosion startled the mass, bringing them out of the quarreling that they now beheld had been in vain, for there was Brother K leaning over the side of his throne with his punctured skull draining onto the grass. Before collective confusion and disbelief became wild fury, the princess fired into her own head, and joined her king in eternity.